First Published in Australia in 2016
by HelassInk
ABN 92 025 730 860
P O Box 117
Sandgate Queensland 4017
www.commontheology.com

Typeset in Bembo

ISBN 978–0–646–95786–9
Logos – Fiction

Logos

λόγος

In the beginning was the Word… John 1.1

a novel

In memoriam

Brother Jeremy Platt

Prologue

For more than thirty years I have tried to tell this story. In the beginning it was harder than it is now. I am a better writer now, but more to the point, in those days spiritual odysseys were not in fashion – certainly not if they had anything to do with the church. It was the 'seventies and the church was history. Back then I had to invent a whole new language to write about my adventures inward; or else wrap them up in a story teeming with make believe characters. Nowadays everyone is talking about the inner journey.

The first time my manuscript came back from the publisher, together with its slim rejection slip, I was literally struck dumb with grief. I hid the egregious brown paper parcel under the bed and did not speak a word for ten days. Indeed I couldn't speak, as if the power to make words had been taken away from me.

My mother, with whom I was sharing a flat at the time, surmised that depression had rendered me into this slough of despond, an illness which by then had a proper name. Depression was no longer just teenage sulks. She took me out to cheer me up. Not that depression is amenable to being cheered up. It just sits there like an old-fashioned London smog, impervious to daylight, to chatter, suffocating all attempts at cheer.

She took me downtown, where she was helping out backstage at the Old Vic. I adored the Old Vic. As a teenager I joined a students' club attached to this venerable theatre company, which granted us cheap seats for dress rehearsals, usually in the gods but sometimes we got lucky and sat in the stalls. The two-hundred-year-old auditorium had gold paint on the curlicues, crimson velvet curtains on stage. Names such as Richard Burton and Paul Schofield were written into its cast of alumni. I was in love with Richard Burton from hearing his voice on the wireless. Paul Schofield I saw in the flesh when he played Macbeth at Stratford-on-Avon on the night we went there for a school drama outing. "Is this a bloody dagger I see before my eyes," cried Schofield from the vast darkened stage, pawing the air, grasping at his nightmare. Some wag in the audience waved back and it brought the house down.

Those teenage theatre outings seem to float in an alternative universe, soaring above the drudgery of school days, bearing the stamp of intellectual endeavour but without the graft. We went by coach to see a student production of The Tempest in Oxford. When the curtain went up on the ship foundering at sea, seamen on the port side swayed to starboard, sailors on the right swayed to port, as if the ship were yawing in two directions at once. A bad start to my favourite Shakespeare play. It made me feel superior to be critical.

In sixth form we went to see Dr Faustus, once more at Stratford on Avon. All I can remember of that occasion is the embarrassing spectacle of our English teacher ogling Helen through binoculars. It was the first time we had seen a naked person on stage. I didn't look, even though we were up in the gods and you couldn't see much with the naked eye. I watched my English teacher instead, who gawked at her open-mouthed through his opera glasses, and I blushed for him.

Theatre gave me respite. Everything on stage was larger than life – the lights, the clothes, the voices – a potent echo of the quality of life I yearned for, had embraced once upon a time, and lost. I could fall in love with an actor with no fear that the object of my desire would turn out to have feet of clay. There was no chance of 'getting real', as young people say these days, as if such a thing is desirable. I wasn't keen on reality. It was too much like hard work. Much better to get lost in a book, or fall in love with an actor coming and going with perfect timing, speaking lines according to his script.

Backstage with my mother I watched her apply pan stick to the chorus of the Pirates of Penzance. It was hot behind the scenes, humid with sweat and nerves, as an amateur cast geared up for its annual concert. The excitement was infectious. I felt a frisson of life, and the fog of misery lifted a fraction.

Depression has a life of its own, quite apart from a person's will. It comes and goes according to its own rules and that is the horror of it. You find yourself with a lodger who turns up uninvited, intending to stay for an indeterminate period, who commandeers your time and energy until nothing is left, even for daily chores. This unwelcome house guest supplies an endless monologue of critique and threat – 'stinking thinking' as the therapists call it. The only escape is in sleep, or getting drunk – which is what I did for more years than I care to remember.

Going out, if one can find the energy, sometimes provides a slim fissure through which one can wriggle – an escape from the negative prattle in one's head. Mum's energy had got me dressed and onto the bus into town, away from that brown paper parcel under my bed. The heat of pent-up excitement backstage aroused me, the smell of greasepaint oiled my starved synapses, anticipation watered the arid soil of my heart and I actually felt something for the first time in ten days.

At first I was not sure what I felt, and sniffed around the emotion like a dog around a bone. Feelings of anticipation and hopefulness are what betrayed you in the first place, so you don't welcome them holus-bolus back into your life.

I can't remember if we stayed to watch The Pirates of Penzance. It must have been a matinée, because I do remember that it was still daylight on the way home. Drizzle rendered the passing streetscapes into monochrome grey. On the bus I spoke for the first time since my manuscript had come back. I said, "Mum, what would you do if God turned out to be evil?"

She was appalled – good Roman Catholic that she had become of late. She blustered a bit, then relapsed into silence, frowning out of the window at rain veiling high street shops.

I was angry and it felt good. It cleansed me. It mopped up the smog of depression. An updraught of energy shifted the inchoate grief of the past ten days. A truth was laid bare which would stand guard over me through what was to come. "Well," I said. "If I found out that God was evil, I would have to revise my idea of what is good."

At the time I had no idea that I was echoing Job.

Faith, hope and love survived;
indeed, only these three were saved.
And I will testify that the way is strait;
it is a steep way down into the womb of the universe.

For there one is born anew,
recreated in the white fire of the nebulae,
breathed from the nostrils of the beginning.

Gathered one is from the fingers of eternity
into a place.
Or rather, a place is made by the gathering
and this is pain.

Remorse;
the blacksmith with the terrible brow,
blow after blow to the writhing iron;
myself in the making
the breaking under his paw.

Still I am not yet what I shall be.
Born in pain, delivered into despair,
where white light rends the night into day;
the cry of anguish alone
was the faith and hope I lost
in love.

1

It wasn't the book that did it to Amy. She read it again many years later, and it was just a book. But the fact that Alfred gave it to her made the first reading like a sacramental act. She opened her mind and heart in a most imprudent fashion and simply swallowed the contents of *The Spiritual Man* whole.

Secreted between several hundred pages, which take her only ten days to absorb, are the hieroglyphs of a Confucian mystic, a passionate young man from an ancient civilisation whose every word is forged on the escarpments of a higher consciousness, a place infinitely far removed from Amy's untidy nest of life experience.

She sits down with a sense of purpose, desiring to essay the mountainous path towards that place where Alfred dwells in blessed, all-knowing, blue-eyed splendour. She wants to please him by her willingness to read his book. Reading is something that Amy does well.

The house is quiet this weekend, except for the creaking of the corrugated iron roof in the afternoon sun. A light breeze stirs the fronds of the pepper tree, which drop a shower of pink berries onto dusty earth, swirl shadows on the polished boards of the verandah. Down in the old tennis court chickens murmur and peck at the dirt.

Wolf is out doing overtime, stirring up sparks and steam in his forge at the theatre workshops. An opera is in production; operas need chandeliers and wrought-iron balconies by the hundredweight. Wolf, a master blacksmith, cheerfully works a fault into each intricate piece of wrought iron he makes as a signature, because his work will be stolen after the show. His chandeliers will end up in the mansions of wealthy Pretoria suburbs; his gates will guard forests of cycads purloined from the veld to grace their well-watered lawns.

The Highveld is as dry as a broom at this time of year. Blond grass, dazzling in the midday sun, undulates as far as the eye can see, patched with outcrops of red earth, dotted with clumps of thorny acacia. From below the horizon skeins of brown smoke rise from cooking fires, wafting lazily along the skyline, marking non-white townships hidden from white folks' view.

§

Amy opens the book and begins to read. At first she feels a mild euphoria as the first chapter introduces the spiritual man. She is accustomed to gender specific language which gives men right of way on consecrated ground. She has been reared on such language. She has no argument with the spiritual man, *qua* man. Men still rule the world in 1977 – particularly in South Africa. Although it does pierce her to the quick when she ventures onto the monastery lawn with her painted toenails and notices a lull in the monks' conversation. Disapproval of her gender is normal, indeed she disapproves of it herself. Since childhood she has learned that being female is a handicap, particularly in the realm of spiritual matters. She bears it manfully.

This is a book in three volumes. During the days it takes her to read it she goes about her normal business; weekdays at her desk in the office; cooks the evening meal for Wolf; goes to church on Sunday. She remembers buying the daily carafe of wine on her way home from work, but she does not remember drinking it.

At first the book is a place she retreats to, a way of pledging her fealty to Alfred, of slaking her thirst for understanding of the spiritual realm. But after three days she finds she cannot leave the pages of these volumes. Some part of herself sits in the office, cooks bratwurst and sauerkraut, watches people conversing with her. But she, Amy, is somewhere else.

The writer of this book is a magus, a man from the orient bearing forbidden knowledge. At first his language is clinical, impartially describing the constituent parts of the spiritual man, soberly considering their various functions. Here is the soul with its vaulting ambition to dwell in the realm of the spirit. But the soul would perish in an instant should the fire of the spirit touch it. No, the soul is merely mind and heart, tragically without access to that for which it yearns. Neither heart nor mind would survive that fire.

What then is the solution to this existential dilemma? How can a human being aspire to that which is beyond its capacity to endure? Give oneself up, the magus advises. Surrender. It is the only path, the only gateway into the realm of the spirit. Amy ponders this stumbling block for several days. Give herself up! Such a prospect is more awesome than the triple rails in a steeplechase, more dreadful than giving up Aslan. Why, without her hardwon selfhood she might end up just like everyone else on the conveyor belt of life. But it appears she cannot continue on this adventure without taking such a reckless leap of faith.

By this time it is evening and already dark on the Highveld. The old farmhouse is cold, poorly equipped for winter because these few weeks of bitter nights are scarcely worth the trouble of proper heating. There is a single-bar electric fire in Amy's study. She huddles at her desk, rugged up in several layers of woollens, gnawing at her dilemma.

2

The Soweto uprising of last winter is just an unpleasant memory for Amy. Not that such a seismic howl of indignation from the townships had entirely passed her by. It had alarmed and puzzled her. She had been in South Africa for only three years and still believed what she was told by her new friends and associates, that South Africa's black people were the happiest on that benighted continent, that tales of racism and mistreatment were just mischief spread by Communists.

She sees neat smiling maids in *doekies* and lanky, jovial 'boys' going about their work in white people's houses and gardens. In the city, black messengers flit through lifts and corridors, polite, deferential, incapable of not responding to her smile. She smiles a lot, out of a vague sense of guilt inherent in one who has never before encountered a servant class.

The black townships are out of sight, and out of bounds for white people. Millions of 'non-whites' are embedded as servants in white households throughout the land. They are part of their employers' domestic landscape, but the townships where they live are another country, an alien place, to one fifth of South Africa's population who are classified as white.

Amy's office in the city is overlooked by the elegant sandstone edifice of the Union Buildings, where parliament sits during the winter months. One early morning last year in June, the first reports of trouble in the south-western townships of Johannesburg (known by the now famous acronym SOWETO) filtered into the capital. A helicopter hovered overhead, sentinel over the parliament buildings. Someone in the office turned up the radio to listen to news bulletins from the South African Broadcasting Corporation. But it all seemed to be over pretty quickly, or perhaps she lost interest? Only later, after the news of Soweto had ricocheted around the globe, searing the psyche of millions; only as foreign outrage filtered sporadically through the South African censors, did she uneasily recall the incident.

In June 1976 television had only just arrived in South Africa and for a brief moment censorship faltered, for no-one was au fait with this new medium. Meanwhile the news got out. Wires hummed around the globe, live newscasts stormed the English-speaking world. Helicopters buzzed over Soweto, hired by the world's media to record those historic days, as a generation of young people drew a line in the dust and bawled "No more!"

No more kowtowing to the white oppressor, no more obedience to his laws, away with his *verdoem taal*. While mothers wrung their hands and wept; for these children were also casting off an ancient tradition of respect for their elders.

"No more!" they cried against their parents. We reject your vile inheritance. We have watched your humiliation day after day; your compliance to this oppression; this boot upon our neck.

Most of this passed Amy by as the rumours whispered through the isolated pockets of white populations, protected by state censorship, safe within a pipe dream. But in townships across the land, broadcast on the fine web of word of mouth to the smallest rural hamlet, news spread that things would never be the same again.

Quietly, under cover of darkness, from all over South Africa, desperate young people, passionate, fearful, angry young men and women in their thousands, seeped across the borders to join the struggle in exile. Throughout the western world – that is, the world of television and the mass media – Soweto became a byword for the struggle against apartheid.

A year on, international censure has made itself felt. Australia will not play cricket with the Springboks. The lash of public opinion from home, from Britain, raises painful welts on the hide of the republic.

Rhetoric from Pretoria is ramped up. Proudly the nation stands alone on the southern shores of Africa, a bulwark against the Communist threat from Angola in the north and Mozambique in the east. Voortrekkers are invoked, those heroes of Afrikaner legend and nationhood, whose mythology is sniggered at by English-speakers. They do not, however, snigger at the rumblings in the townships.

Here in Albion where Amy sits and reads Alfred's book all seems peaceful. The whitewashed farmhouse where she lives once stood amongst smallholdings, but is now part of a suburb of red brick, crenellated sandstone, and mock Tudor dwellings – a dormitory for city workers. A stone dam, a remnant of the farm, stands empty in the yard, its pump house now a garden shed. Not that any gardening has been done for a while. The property is on a slope of shale and barely sustains the coarse kikuyu grass overrunning it. The ground is bare beneath the old pepper tree, beneath the soaring jacaranda which shades the house, dropping detritus upon its corrugated iron roof. Kikuyu will not grow in the shade.

Amy has never met her neighbours. She has an idle dream of filling the dam with water to make a swimming pool. This should be a simple matter for Wolf, who is a ship's engineer as well as being a blacksmith, but he has not done anything about it. Merely peered down the borehole and declared it blocked. They do not communicate well any more. Since Amy met Alfred at the priory last year Wolf and Amy have not been communicating well at all.

~3~

Wolf was born a refugee. His mother gave birth to him during the bombing of Leipzig. He was found as a baby, with his name tucked into his hat, by a gentle couple who took him with them on their haphazard journey north west, fleeing from the advancing Russians.

Like many Germans after the war, Wolf's adoptive family subsisted on potato peelings and bone broth, living in makeshift accommodation. It wasn't a good start for the boy, but worse was to come. By some miracle, amongst the millions of displaced persons, Wolf's father found him and took him home to Hamburg.

There the former Panzerführer had a new woman with two other children nesting in the rubble of the ruined city. But Wolf could not settle, hated his stepmother, quarrelled with his stepbrother and sister, ran away constantly. Until, one evening in the dark of the cellar, raising his shovel to hack into the precious cache of coal, Wolf's father on impulse stayed his arm and peering into the bunker saw his truant boy asleep there. Shocked at the harm he could have done, the consequences should he have injured, or even killed this delinquent child, his father decided to send Wolf to the orphanage. First to the Catholics, and then, when he ran away from them, to the Lutherans. Wolf's experiences in these institutions, which he was never averse to talking about, inculcated in him a deep aversion to churches of any ilk.

Until Alfred came along Amy and Wolf shared this abhorrence of church. Although, if truth be told they were averse to authority of any kind. They met in that mythical haven of runaways — at sea, and there they formed an alliance of revolt against the world at large. Aboard ship was a safe place to indulge in such collusion.

Before container shipping, when merchant vessels tramped coastlines for months on end, painstakingly collecting piece goods, crewed by thirty men or more, shipboard provided a close knit community for runaways. Senior officers dealt with life's practical difficulties. Should you accidentally sail out aft[1] the company would make arrangements to fly you home, whether from Mombasa or

---

1. Vernacular for getting left behind when your ship sailed.

11

Rotterdam. The first mate was always on hand to get you out of jail, or with a syringe of penicillin should you pick up a problem in the brothels. Pay was always on tap to buy grog and cigarettes. There was even a Chinese laundryman to take care of a seaman's prize possessions – his clothes, his plumage for trips ashore.

Leaving the sea had been hard for Wolf, who had worked on ships since he graduated at sixteen from a blacksmith's apprenticeship. Even getting around ashore without a taxi proved to be problematic for this seafarer. He was accustomed to setting out from point A in the direction of point B in full expectation of getting there in due course. Roads on land do not behave like that, a fact which greatly enraged him at times.

Amy cajoled him ashore with an invitation to visit relatives in Pretoria. These cousins had been tracked down by her father, whom she telephoned from shipboard with the news that she was going to sea. The conversation went like this:

"Hallo Dad. It's Amy."

"Hallo love. Where are you?"

"I'm in the English Channel."

"I hope you've got a boat?"

"Yes Dad. I'm working on a ship."

"Ah, I thought the line was a bit wonky. Where are you going?"

"Oh, just coastal shipping."

"Which coast?"

Silence. "Um. Africa actually!"

Silence. "Well, be sure to be back in time for university."

Which she wasn't. But her father wrote to his South African cousins who drove all the way to Port Elizabeth to meet her ship, and invited her to stay with them next time she was in Africa. By then Amy and Wolf were inseparable so she took him with her. The cousins were generous to a fault. Retired and living comfortably in Pretoria, with five dogs and a growing clan of grandchildren populating the rambling house, gardens and swimming pool, they welcomed the seafarers and pressed them to stay.

§

The weather was beautiful during that southern hemisphere autumn when Amy and Wolf came to Pretoria. Highveld skies were always blue, lawns soft and lush, flower beds – tended by Sam – always immaculate. Television had not yet arrived so instead, every evening, visitors came to drape themselves on the *stoep*, to gossip, and drink sundowners before dinner. On these evenings Wolf sat beneath his long blond fringe, nursing his Bacardi and coke, smiling his crooked smile, grunting amicably when addressed. His English was rudimentary. Even now his accent remains strong.

Somehow they drifted into a tacit agreement that they would stay. Wolf readily found employment with an elderly Swiss blacksmith who had been commissioned to construct wrought iron gates for the botanical gardens. Amy found work copywriting for the state tourist board. They rented a studio apartment and moved in together, to the wonderment of workmates and acquaintances.

Marriage had never been on the agenda for Wolf and Amy. This understanding was part of their pact against social mores. They had already discussed the matter while they were at sea. Wolf's father, like many Germans after the war, did not marry his woman because she would have lost her war widow's pension. Amy had no discernible maternal instincts. No, they would not marry. That pedestrian, middle-class life with its pedestrian middle-class commitments was meant for ordinary people. Not for gladiators who had survived arctic gales of existential angst, such as Wolf and Amy. They had earned the right to make their own rules for living. People such as the war baby Wolf and Amy who had run away to sea simply did not fit into other people's expectations. So they lived together, which was not done in Pretoria in 1974. She had a vague idea that she would help Wolf settle down with a job and a home, before continuing on her life's course – wherever that may lead her.

But Amy had not taken into account the work of assimilating into a foreign culture. For it was foreign, in spite of the English speaking community's attempts to mirror life in the home country. Wolf was helpless on land, which undid all her plans. She had to fill in forms for him, explain daft table manners, teach him to drive a car. She became capable. He became childlike. This was not like their mateship aboard ship – their adventurous, fearless companionship against the odds.

At Christmas, after the office party, on her way home in the back of a taxi, Amy found herself entangled with a wealthy businessman, who fiddled with her breasts and made alluring propositions. Filled with good wine and deeply compromised she nonetheless remembered where her loyalty lay and rebuffed him. No! She had Wolf. Wolf was her mate. "Ah Wolf," chaffed the businessman, who was also German. "What is Wolf? He is nothing!"

Amy was outraged. She swatted at his fat fingers and sat in frigid silence while he continued to tease and cajole her. He let her out of the taxi with a light-hearted farewell which made her feel like an abandoned toy. Her anger burned slowly. By New Year it was apocalyptic. Then she decided to marry Wolf.

It was not an instant decision. Not one to rush into commitments Amy understood that this one must be for life. But, she mused to herself, she had already done more-or-less everything she wanted to do. She had travelled the world and seen the sea. This place seemed as good as anywhere else to stop, and was certainly better than England. For one thing, the sun shone all the time. And wine was plentiful. A certain moral tenor entered this inner dialogue. Perhaps it was time she did something for others now she had everything she wanted. And who better to spend her life helping than her old shipmate, Wolf?

§

Wolf changed. Overnight. As if the bond of marriage had suddenly domesticated him. He stopped drinking after dinner although he usually downed a couple of Becks when he got home from work. He frowned at Amy's undiminished consumption of a bottle of red a night. Although he stopped short of voicing this disapproval it was manifest in his body language, his sighs of resignation.

Amy, attempting to be a good wife, bought a German recipe book and cooked *Erbsensuppe*, with mixed results. The first time she served this classic German soup it seemed to be full of buckshot – she had omitted to soak the dried peas overnight. After a couple more hours on the stove the soup was more or less edible. Seven years later, after she left him, Wolf cited dinners not served on time as grounds for divorce.

Weekends were still like old times. They caught up with friends. Gaunt, free-wheeling artists and craftsmen from Wolf's theatre workshops gathered at weekends on each other's rural properties, braaiing boerwoers, baking duck in an earth oven, drinking from late morning until evening. Afterwards they drove erratically home along corrugated dirt roads.

Amy loved these sociable moots of men, pissing on each other, gathered around a forty gallon drum glowing with charcoal, Wolf roaring his fantastical stories – about the giant manta ray which leapt from the ocean off Bermuda and sank a lifeboat full of men; the sailor who fell overboard and was scalped by scavenging seagulls; the castaway off Mozambique who was rescued from sharks by dolphins. Affable, gregarious, he was quite his old self, his eye no longer critical when she poured herself another glass of wine.

Amy set about improving her new husband. She introduced him to a Bridge circle which met every Tuesday night over gins and tonic. Soon he invited the circle to their house, where Amy served snacks and drinks before retiring to her study for the evening. He learned to play tennis; a triumph not least because he had suffered polio during his childhood and was painfully shy of his emaciated legs, which were however quite handsome once tanned and clad in white. She taught him to drive their car.

And then she met Alfred.

~4~

Jacaranda time in Pretoria and Amy's mother Anna has come to visit the newly-weds. They got married in the city registry office on the first available date, giving friends and family a fortnight's notice. No-one from overseas had been present at the brief ceremony. Now Anna is relaxing in a deckchair in the garden, unfurling in the warmth of a Highveld spring, replacing the pallor of England with a biscuit-coloured tan. She has painted her toenails red.

She declares that she must visit her old friend Alfred in Johannesburg. She pronounces every syllable "Jo-han-ess-burg". Her friend has just come back to South Africa after a twenty-year sojourn in England, and she would like to visit him. She is sun-bathing near the birdbath, which is the household's latest nod to domesticity. She is regarding Amy speculatively, twirling her sunglasses in her fingers, waiting, cat-like, for her daughter's response to this proposition.

Amy has never heard of this Alfred, but is unwilling to play into her mother's hands and ask how she comes to know a man from Johannesburg. So she smoothly agrees that it would be a good idea to visit Jo'burg. We could take a look at a gold mine while we are there, suggests Amy. Would her mother telephone this friend and arrange a suitable time?

After the appointment has been made Amy finds out that they are to visit a monastery – that her mother's mysterious friend is in fact a monk. Amy baulks at this. Wolf baulks terminally – he is definitely not visiting any monastery. But Anna simply can't cancel the date now – it would be so humiliating.

Taxis are discussed, but are clearly too expensive, it would cost hundreds of rand. Short of casting her mother adrift on the ponderous and unreliable rail network, Amy has no choice but to chauffeur her to this odd assignation. But she is adamant that that is all she will be – a chauffeur. In fact she will stay in the car while her mother goes in and has tea. Alright darling, says Anna, and smiles sweetly.

§

On the day of their meeting with Alfred a veteran anti-apartheid campaigner is also visiting the priory, and delivering a feisty rebuke. The fathers are too timid in their opposition to the apartheid government, she declares, and she is making her protest clear by resigning from the fraternity. She is surrounded by a bevy of monks of varying hues, wearing an array of white and black cassocks and grey scapulars. The scene is a tableau of English teatime. Fine china cups are sipped from, laughter is modulated, voices are rich and dulcet. The lawn is very green in the quadrangle where the tea party is set. Amy is fascinated by the quarrel which appears to be going on here in such a courteous fashion, for of course she cannot wait in the car. For one thing it is too hot.

She is introduced to the Prior who displays a remarkable talent for drawing out this sullen, suspicious, under-dressed young woman. Somehow she finds herself discussing Medieval Europe and, like Tom Thumb, pulling out opinions on everything from feudal governance (a self-regulating system based on trust) to Charlemagne's inspired use of monasteries to preserve the culture of the old world. "Without which, of course, we would not have the bible today!" proclaims the Prior, as if the bible was just an ordinary book. These amiable, courteous people, this arboured quad, remind Amy fleetingly of another place long ago and far away.

Her mother is deep in conversation with Alfred, a tall, slender, grey-bearded monk who appears to have been poured into the deckchair where he lounges. His knees are crossed. One of his sandals drops off and he fishes about for it with a suntanned foot, modestly folding his cassock over bare brown shins, like a girl. Amy wonders how he got so tanned dressed like that? He could be half-asleep but for the intensity of those blue eyes fixed upon Anna, who blossoms under their gaze – waves her arms in animated fashion and laughs a lot. A tinkling laugh which she employs when she is being flirty.

When tea has been drunk and cake consumed, and after the venerable anti-apartheid activist has been affectionately farewelled, monks fuss about mopping up crumbs and clearing away china, while the remaining visitors embark on a tour of the priory. Alfred shambles ahead, loose-limbed, sleepy-eyed, followed by Anna and Amy. Fr Cuthbert brings up the rear, talking incessantly. First they venture into the library which is through the cloister and down a couple of stone steps. As the latch on the wooden door clacks Amy enters another world.

The place smells of books. Old books, church books, redolent of incense and candle wax. Daylight shafts through motes of dust, puddles on mahogany desks in nooks; ivy sways through mullioned windows. The floor absorbs their footfalls as if the bare boards were carpeted. Book-lined walls accept their presence with a sigh. In shadowed corners cassocked ghosts stir. Even Cuthbert has stopped talking.

Amy scarcely breathes for fear of disturbing this place. It is as if the library were set in amber, with its dog-eared texts and antique lead lights. Shades of monks who once studied here press on her consciousness, like developing images on a photographic plate. She remembers just such a breathtaking space; but the memory is fickle and vanishes when she tries to focus on it. Odours in this library plunge her into remembrance, bypassing any rational faculty. Books and dust and furniture polish, faintly lavender-scented, transport her to a dear familiar place which is however as distant as the stars, and equally enigmatic. She cannot remember that place, but feels, somehow, that she is remembered.

They follow Alfred in Indian file through walled gardens steeped in herbaceous borders. Next stop on their tour is the parish church. The private boys' school, which is attached to the priory, assembles here daily for services. Sundry items of clothing and gobs of chewing gum are strewn about the pews, together with tumbled hassocks and prayer books. A dishevelment unbecoming to a church, notes Amy censoriously. Alfred strides down the north aisle with a sudden air of purpose. He halts, spreading his arms before a monolithic sculpture, which immediately reminds Amy of work she has seen in East Africa. Family trees carved out of ebony, closely plaited figures embodying the ancestors, were on sale to tourists everywhere on the east coast. She still has several exemplars of makonde work at home.

This piece is also made of ebony but is one massive figure. A sinuous brass inlay traces the mother and child against the black wood. It is the African Madonna. Today she lives in St George's Cathedral in Cape Town, but when Amy first sees her the sculpture is presiding over the homely rumpus of schoolboy devotions. She reaches out to touch the polished wood, runs her finger along the narrow brass inlay. The madonna is massively hewn, her contours voluptuously spun with this thin golden thread. She is gorgeously black. Amy's hand recoils. She glances uncertainly at Alfred. He is watching her and does not look away when their eyes meet.

She cannot remember ever being looked at like this, although she has dreamed of such intimacy – written about it in secret. On board ship surrounded by men Amy learned how to veil herself, to protect herself from intrusion, from trespassers, for men often looked at her as they might regard a lamb chop at dinner time. She accepts this as one of the tiresome handicaps of being a girl – although it does have certain benefits. Amy is not averse to making use of a man's lust at times, but in the end, being desired for her body was never enough.

Amy feels, has always felt, since she was fifteen years old, when she transformed almost overnight from an ugly duckling into a beautiful swan, that she is captive in her body, a prisoner lurking behind lucid eyes. She looks out upon a world where normal people walk about and talk, eat and sleep, make love, go to work, and never really notice the creature hidden away in here, behind her eyes.

Alfred looks at her mildly with sky blue eyes like those worn by old sailors. The thousand-mile gaze she calls it – eyes accustomed to scanning far horizons. Now she is caught up in that gaze, somehow made visible, pinioned momentarily, held up to the light and examined, laid bare to the marrow, then gently set down in the here-and-now upon the cool flagstones of this church. But she knows she is irrevocably changed. She feels naked. It is as if she has been rinsed with icy water from a mountain stream. Painfully self-conscious, Amy is now ashamed that she has touched the African Madonna. Perhaps she has polluted her? She mutters that the sculpture reminds her of Henry Moore. This remark serves to restore common sense to the tableau. Cuthbert claps, cries with delight that the sculptor was indeed a teacher of Moore, and how clever of Amy to notice the propinquity.

Sunlight pours from the west end, casts pools of mercurial light upon the ebony form of womanhood in pain, on rotund arms and cheeks, the shuttered eyes of madonna and child embracing perpetually, their ovoid forms exposed in light and shadow. "You can see he knows about spaces in people," murmurs Amy. "There are spaces in people you know?" She gives Alfred a quick, defiant glance. "Of course there are," replies the monk. "I'm glad you know about that. Not many people do."

When the shadows have lengthened and they make their farewells, Alfred smiles kindly at Amy and says she should come and visit the priory again.

~5~

Wolf and Amy decide to take Anna to the mountains for the summer holiday. No lion or elephant up there, but it is far too hot in summer to go to the Kruger Park in search of the big five.

Anyway, Anna has already encountered lion, during her first visit to Pretoria before Amy and Wolf got married. She landed at Jan Smuts airport wearing a pure wool safari suit, tailor-made for her first trip to Africa, for it was winter in the southern hemisphere. She had not expected the balmy 25^C degree daytime temperatures of the Highveld. Anna's wool suit and boots were quickly divested in favour of an airy cotton maxi dress and sandals, the outfit she wears, topped by a large shady hat, on their safari to Thornybush Game Reserve.

Thornybush is five hours drive from Pretoria, on the western border of the Kruger National Park. Evening is nigh as they turn into the gate of this private game reserve, rattle over the broad cattle grid, bump along the dirt road towards the lodge. Unseasonable rain in the Eastern Transvaal has washed away parts of the road and Amy swerves to avoid potholes, struggling to stay on the track where it is churned deep in mud. Wolf has not yet learned to drive and Anna has never tried, so Amy is on her own. Finally the sedan bogs in a dip where water pools up to the axles.

Night is encroaching. The three tired travellers survey the muddy track ahead which is hemmed in by acacia bushes armed with long white thorns gleaming like razor wire in the twilight.

"What now?" trills Anna, nervously.

"We will walk," declares Wolf, taking charge.

Amy hesitates to mention that leopard, lion and cheetah are among the wild animals proudly listed in the reserve's publicity brochure.

"It's probably only another mile or so," she says, hopefully.

They set out, after Wolf absurdly insists on locking up the car. The going is rough. Anna's sandals are soon impregnated with mud, the hem of her dress flaps wetly around her ankles. She has her handbag clutched under her right arm, the left is securing her hat against an imaginary breeze. The air is perfectly still.

20

"What's that funny smell," asks Anna after a while, sniffing the air.

"What smell. I don't smell no smell," barks Wolf irritably.

They reach the lodge as night falls, as it does in these climes, suddenly, implacably, like a trap door closing. Their hosts gather them into the aromatic shelter of the lodge, exchanging worried glances, settling them beside the pool with drinks and macadamia nuts. The ranger sets off with a couple of men in a Land Rover to collect their sedan and their luggage. Comfortable thatched huts await them after a lavish dinner of braaivleis and salads washed down with plenty of wine.

Next day they are on safari in the back of the Land Rover, bumping over rough ground between clumps of acacia, when Anna exclaims, "There's that funny smell again!"

"You're in luck," replies the ranger, who drives with a loaded rifle on the passenger seat beside him. "That is the smell of hunting lion." Presently they spot a lioness beside a waterhole, tearing at the remains of a warthog. Her size, even at this distance, causes Amy to shudder.

§

That summer when Amy first met Alfred, her brother Jonathan flies out to join them in time for their trip to the mountains. He is making the most of a break before going to Sandhurst. He mutters darkly about not being able to visit Amy once he is absorbed into Her Majesty's service. For South Africa is rather on the nose in Britain, together with Rhodesia, although sanctions have not yet been declared against the republic. There is a bruised disappointment amongst the anglo-saxon community. People are beginning to sense a loosening of bonds with the country many still call home. On the landward borders an iron curtain, patrolled by the South African Defence Force, holds back the tide from disintegrating colonies. Isolation has left white South Africans feeling as if they are an island civilisation in a shark-infested ocean.

But Amy does not yet know these things that summer. People say it is impossible that ordinary Germans did not know about the concentration camps during the Second World War. How can a nation of such efficiency not know what is happening on its own railways? Today in South Africa it is hard to find anybody who supported apartheid, few even remember. Time has a habit of erasing bad memories. In the summer of 1976 white people lived in comfortable ghettos, oblivious to the black townships seething behind hillsides, beyond city limits, wreathed in smoke – apart. It served whites well to be ignorant. It would not be comfortable in the white ghetto with its verdant lawns and spacious mansions if one knew how most people were forced to live.

§

But now it is holiday time and after driving three hours south, Amy, Wolf, Anna and Jonathan leave the Highveld behind and make the long descent into Natal, before striking westward towards the Drakensberg. That rearing spine of mountains is named in Zulu *uKhahlamba* – barrier of spears. Anna exclaims in wonder as each new vista is revealed by twists and turns in the road.

It is late when they approach Cathedral Peak Hotel. Evening has veiled the full majesty of the peaks beyond, which loom as shadows in a velvet sky. That view must wait until tomorrow. Now they settle into comfortable rooms, before meeting for dinner in the dining room where a log fire burns in a stone alcove high enough to walk into, for it is still chilly after dark up here.

§

How they came to get lost in the mountains is something Amy cannot properly explain to this day. Dew still carpets the valley as they begin their walk, although the high flanks of the mountains are already basked in sunlight – bronze buttresses rearing into an azure sky. To the west looms the purple dome of Cathedral Peak. They follow a path across damp meadows where wild orchids bloom and larks rise from the turf, cascading praise.

Jonathan carries a canvas rucksack from the hotel, equipped with sandwiches, oranges, and a mud map of walking trails. He is a veteran of the dour Pennines. He grumbles about the lack of warm clothes, first aid and emergency rations. "Shut up," says Amy at intervals, until the path sucks them into rainforest, hushing their quarrels.

Damp, cavernous shade swallows them up. They pad along peaty slopes, clambering over the mossy trunks of fallen trees. Antediluvian tree ferns canopy the track, their roots in a rocky stream which accompanies the path with water music. The din of cicadas falls silent as they pass by, as if they travel in a space capsule, aliens in the emerald forest. Hidden eyes behind jewelled green curtains silently watch them go by, then the see-sawing, chirruping, deafening gossip of the trees resumes. A baboon coughs from bluffs rising out of the rainforest further upstream. Another answers. Now it is the visitors' turn to falter. Jonathan declares that they should have brought a knife. Wolf barks defiantly back, beating his breast and grinning madly as his voice echoes amongst the bluffs.

They eat their sandwiches where the stream has sculpted a broad basin of calm water, terraced with sun-warmed rocks. They rest their steaming feet in the shallows and give themselves up to the sunshine for an hour. They reckon they are about half-way along the trail they have chosen, according to the map. They must just go a little further into the gorge and a path to the right will take them back to the hotel.

The gorge narrows into a ravine. Sheer cliffs rise ever higher and squeeze the stream into a torrent, which swirls around gigantic boulders. One rock of several hundred tons has been arrested in its fall between the walls of this ravine. It looms like a meteor thirty feet above them. They wade silently beneath it, up to their knees in the rushing stream, clasping each others hands. They yell now and again to comfort themselves. The baboons bark back.

Finally they confront a waterfall; a slender white serpent gliding from an impregnable precipice.

"What now?" asks Anna, with a vague sense of déjà vu.

Jonathan looks pained, silently declaring that he told them so. It was bound to end in tears.

They forage back downstream until they find a path leading upwards to the left. They sniff at it doubtfully but Wolf leaps onto the precipitous trail like an impala, returning a few moments later to yodel, "Come! This is the way!"

Higher and higher they clamber, steeper and steeper, until they can focus only on the next handhold. Then Amy makes the mistake of looking down. The narrow path seems to plunge away vertically into the green slot of the ravine far below. They are clinging like flies on the bare flank of the mountain. She knows with a terrible certainty that nothing on earth could persuade her to crawl back down there. The only way now is up. They are following Wolf who has the agility of a mountain goat; but then of course he is an Aries.

§

She remembers the first time she suggested that they should go walking in the mountains. Wolf looked at her with blank astonishment. He asked why should he walk in the mountains when he has a car? The car is still a novelty. He loves the ease with which it transports him wherever he wants to go.

Somehow he is persuaded to make the trip to Mount Anderson in the Transvaal. After three days climbing through mist and rain, resting up for the night in well-provisioned huts, Wolf loses his heart to the mountain. Up here he is as happy as he was at sea, he is his own master, far from the madding crowd. In time, he becomes the nearest thing to a professional mountain walker that his radical code will allow. Of course, he never follows the rules.

§

At the top of the path they are confronted by a sheer cliff about twelve feet high. By the time Amy scrambles up, Wolf is lying on top of this cliff, reaching down with a stick for Jonathan to grasp onto so that he can shin up the rock face. Amy peers back down the vanishing thread of the antelope trail which they have mistaken for a walking track. She regards the sheer cliff above her. She lies face down on the rocky slope and bursts into whooping, hysterical tears. Anna tries to comfort her, but cannot prevail against her daughter's panic.

"Just leave me here to die," bawls Amy.

"Look darling. Look!" cries her mother, running up the rock face like a *klipspringer*, as Jonathan lifts her flyweight on the end of his walking stick. Now all three are up there, peering down at Amy from the brink of the known world. She howls harder. Anna slithers back down the cliff and shins up it again. "Look darling, it's easy." Such is the maternal instinct.

Pride eventually overcomes terror. Amy sheepishly allows herself to be shoved and hitched up the sheer rock face with Wolf pushing from behind and Jonathan hauling from above, while Anna prances and yells encouragement.

Once there they appear to be on the roof of Africa. Far below, wooded slopes penetrate into the terra cotta folds of the mountainside, but here, high above the tree line, only grasses and heath flourish. A pair of blue cranes fly aloft from a neighbouring spur with great slow wing beats, their melancholy cries echoing back and forth in the empty fastnesses.

They have a choice of walking to the right or left along the ridge on which they now find themselves and Wolf wastes no time in setting off to the right. They follow hopefully for a mile or so until they reach the edge of a precipice.

"This is the way," declares Wolf. "Hotel's down there."

And indeed, red tiled roofs are clearly visible about a thousand feet down amidst the forest. Wolf clambers over the edge of the cliff and, with a rattle of falling scree, disappears from view.

They wait, sitting on the tufty grass. A sudden breeze licks their eyrie. "I expect he is looking for a path," remarks Amy plaintively, although all has fallen quiet below. They wait for ten more minutes.

"I'll go and look for him," says Jonathan, setting his jaw like flint, cautiously lowering himself over the edge.

Now two of them wait. Amy extracts an orange from the rucksack, peels it carefully. She gives her mother a segment, and puts one in her own mouth. They chew. They recall in silence Jonathan's horror stories of retrieving the bodies of amateur mountaineers – ordinary people like themselves who died from hypothermia, from sheer carelessness, curled up in a foetal position in the snow. How stiff and awkward they were; what a bother it was to get the silly sods down.

"Oh darling I'm scared!" sobs Anna, her mouth full of orange.

"So'm I!" whimpers Amy. They fall into each other's arms, into the warmth and comfort of grief.

§

Presently Jonathan returns in a shower of small stones, white-faced and shaken. "Rotten basalt," he growls. "Crumbles if you touch it. No way of getting down that way without breaking every bone in your body."

"So where's Wolf?" Amy whispers. Jonathan avoids her eyes, surveys the horizon, mutters that his brother-in-law is probably all right, in a nonchalant tone of voice so maladroit in this sticky situation that Amy immediately sits down and disposes herself to widowhood.

"There's a contour path over there," exclaims Jonathan, shading his eyes and pointing to a narrow thread of red earth winding below distant bluffs at a regular height as far as the eye can see. Heartened by the sight they decide to head back along the ridge to find a way down to this path. But first Amy lies down and peers over the precipice, searching for any sign of Wolf. There is no sign of life at all, just a dizzying perpendicular drop vanishing into thin air. It is hopeful, she tells herself. She can't see a body.

§

At one point during their hike they spot two tribesmen armed with rifles, riding ponies, shadowing them at about half a mile distant. They wave and shout, but the horsemen do not respond, moving like artefacts of the landscape, keeping pace with the intruders' erratic progress over the tussocky upland.

When it is all over they learn that these are BaSotho tribesmen policing the frontier between South Africa and Lesotho – the neighbouring Kingdom in the Sky, a landlocked country of mountains and few roads where people must travel on foot or on horseback. Once upon a time an Englishman strayed over the unmarked mountain border and was taken prisoner by frontiersmen, spending months in a Maseru gaol before anyone noticed he was missing. They are lucky not to have met a similar fate, they are told, chided gently by their hosts for taking such risks.

By mid-afternoon cloud is building up from the south. So far it has been a clear day, sunny and cool. Alarmed, they eye the roiling thunderheads creeping north along the spine of the Drakensberg.

Soon, coming over a rise, they see the path they had spied from a distance, wide and safe, sculpted into the mountainside by hefty caterpillar tracks. "Well, if they can get a bulldozer up here, we can certainly get down," crows Jonathan. Later they learn that six helicopters flew the bulldozer up in bits, assembling it on site in order to carve out the contour path. But now, in their ignorance, they are happy, relieved, and prepared to soldier on to their journey's end.

Except it doesn't end. Anna is wearing a white t-shirt with a design of newspaper clippings. A bold 40^{pt} font on her back declares *Je suis une tigresse*. They are walking in single file with Jonathan in front. Amy follows her mother's trim little back for mile after mile, *Je suis une tigresse, Je suis une tigresse, Je suis une tigresse*, jogging up and down before her eyes. They transverse the mountains in wide arcs, the path never rising and, more important, never descending.

Amy reflects on her life with Wolf. She is distressed that she feels no pain. Surely she ought to feel something over his loss – anguish, or fear perhaps? Given to too much introspection, she worries about herself. Has she become somehow immune from normal human emotions?

But look! Here is a spring trickling across the path. They stoop and catch the cold droplets in their palms, sipping thirstily. A large boulder swathed in orange and yellow lichens swallows the spring on its downward course. Amy scrambles around the boulder, and lo, there is a small track leading down through the heath towards the treeline.

It feels like Christmas. All the pent up anxiety of the afternoon evaporates, like mists rising from the valley whence they cheerfully set out that morning. Down and down, heathland giving way to protea and tree ferns, primeval denizens of the subcontinent, crowding around them now in the gathering twilight.

At last they spot the lights of the hotel glimmering between the trees. A sudden turmoil on the path below reveals Wolf, shouting lustily from amongst a posse of tribesmen on horseback, preparing to ride up the mountain in search of them.

The hotelier's wife fusses over Anna, wraps her in blankets, carries her off for a hot bath in epsom salts, the perfect antidote for muscular aches and pains. Anna enjoys the attention; she flaps gracefully and demurs without conviction, saying it was really nothing, nothing at all.

Later, as thunder rolls around the mountains, she wafts into the dining room where the three young people are taking brandy for their nerves, allowing firelight to lick their weary limbs, enjoying the companionable silence of a shared odyssey. She is radiant, pink from the bath, flushed from the attention, and the prospect of reliving the adventure over dinner.

~6~

Wolf and Jonathan have set off for Cape Town in a camper van. They plan to spend three weeks on the road, driving back up the east coast to Durban, where Amy will meet them on Christmas Eve. They set off early one morning in their hired combi, which is packed to the gunwales with provisions and equipment for a month away. They will pick up Amy at Louis Botha airport, after driving up the Garden Route and through the Transkei. They will all three then travel north into Zululand, where Jonathan has his eye on the rich repository of historic military sites from the British wars with the Zulus.

Amy is more interested in the beaches. She is homesick for the sea, after living here on the Highveld, four thousand feet above sea level and hundreds of miles from the ocean. She is after all an islander; nowhere in England is more than seventy miles from the sea. She misses it sometimes with a physical ache, longing for immaculate horizons where sky and water meet. But that is for later. Now Wolf and Jonathan have gone she has three weeks to herself; blessed solitude for the first time since she can remember. Every night and at weekends she can eat what she pleases, drink as much as she wants, do whatever she likes.

For the first week this is paradise. She feels as light as a feather, no need to plan dinners, and who cares if the washing up is not done? Johanna will do it when she comes to clean the house on Friday. She plays her favourite LPs – once finding herself listening to Vaughan Williams singing In a Monastery Garden. A wisp of nostalgia attaches itself to this song, but vanishes as soon as she pays attention to it.

After several glasses of wine one evening, she wonders idly if she should phone Alfred. But the distance between here and now and that sunlit afternoon at the priory seems too great to bridge via the telephone. Besides, she is afraid that he will turn out to be just another ordinary person after all. That would be too much to bear. She remembers a poem she wrote as a teenager to her secret friend, whom she called the Judge.

§

The Judge had authority over the waves of exaltation and despair which rocked her days – a mighty man whom she loved. She chose him for his mental fortitude and self-sufficiency. This man could not be moved by fear or passion. He had need of no living soul – her adoration could not harm him.

This personage is more than an imaginary friend. He lives on in her memory. There he walks, shoulders bent, hands clasped behind his back, perusing the deck, not far from where Amy reclines on the sofa with her glass of wine. As she watches sea-spray blows around him, his gait easily accommodating the steep roll of the shining deck, a bearish figure with pleated brow, capped by a fleece of white hair. Perhaps he is thinking of her? It is possible to call out to him, and she does so, watching him pause, the easy shift of his body poised on the swell. It could be possible to touch him, but she shudders at that. It is expedient that they should not meet again because he once said that he loved her. These words revealed a fault in the colossal perfection of a man otherwise untouched by life and storm and death.

Amy scorns romantic love. The happy-ever-after Hollywood scenario is not for her. Hers is an altogether more exalted calling. Goodness, beauty and wisdom are not, in the end, to be found in eros. Hers is a tragic quest, to pursue her heart's yearning for a greater love than mere romance.

There she is, in her reverie, walking quietly in the dusk of the departing day. Not herself, but some truer self whom he remembers, and turns to greet with an eternal smile, and waits for, and walks beside. Amy keeps herself veiled, crouched over her wine glass, while her other, better self paces the windswept deck in his fellowship.

She does not have to reread the years of correspondence with the Judge to remember every word as if it were yesterday. Her own persona, the Madam, appeared late on the scene as a foil for the white-haired Judge who himself had originated up a tree in a children's story. Amy cannot remember what he was doing up the tree, but recalls her admiration for his radical position as he defied the scandalised community below, and made courteous love to an elderly spinster whom he had had the foresight to take up the tree with him.

Amy lost her heart to the Judge. He had wit. She is captivated by his dignified presence. His elevated position, both socially and geographically, precluded him from deceitful behaviour. He was a public man. Amy wrote his letters for him, mapping out his authoritative intellect, handing down judgements on the world at large.

For eons she tried to capture his eye and make her adoration known, but he ignored her, as if she were not there. At last Amy invented the Madam, a being so unnervingly frigid, whilst suffused with the heat of passion, that the untouchable Judge became at last her conquest.

The Madam kept a high-class brothel and had a spirit as elevated as the Judge. She made no excuse for her profession and liked to invite any gentleman who caught her eye into her private parlour for a tipple. These were men who descended sadly from the upstairs rooms, hesitating under her sleepy eye, as if they had forgotten something.

"Is there company in the limbs of beautiful women?" she would ask in her soft contralto. The discontented one would find himself guided by a plump bejewelled arm into a deep armchair, warmed before the fire. There, for an hour or so, he would find his mind and heart as exquisitely seduced as his body had been in the upstairs rooms. Depending on his resilience he would return repeatedly to feed on her company, until she cast him aside.

The Madam could not have climbed the tree. She was too fat. Anyway, her flowing kaftan and bangles were unsuitable garb for tree-climbing. But the land of make-believe allows for carrier pigeons to fly letters to and fro. So it was that the Judge and Madam crossed rapiers for years, discussing in their epistles the deep things of the human spirit. Unspoken in all this lofty correspondence was their need for love.

The Madam gave herself freely, declaring her admiration for his splendid isolation, revealing her own desire for a strong heart to rest in. He responded with dignified contempt, until he became very old and knew that death lay before him.

Dewlapped eyes, faded from piercing some shadow hovering in the sun of countless lonely years, turned at last to hers. There was a question reflected there which she could not answer; so she destroyed him by turning away.

§

Now, well primed with wine, Amy looks up the telephone number for the priory. She is astonished when she hears a normal ring tone, as if the place ought to be in another dimension.

An irritable voice barks, "Priory". Could she speak to Brother Alfred? Silence. She wonders if the gentleman has hung up, but then hears the echo of distant voices in stone corridors. There is a crash and a thump, as if the phone handset has been dropped.

"Hallo," says Alfred abruptly.

She is at a loss how to reply, and hums and hahs a bit, before announcing herself as Anna's daughter.

"Well, hallo!" cries Alfred, as if she is the person he has been waiting all day to speak to.

"I, um, I wonder if it would be all right if I wrote to you?" she bleats, blushing furiously, hoping her words are not slurring. "Only, you see I am a writer, and I am much better at writing than talking. What I mean is, I am going to write a book, but I need someone to write it to, a real person or else it could become obscure."

"Yes," replies Alfred thoughtfully, and there is another long pause. She wishes she could reach her glass of wine.

"We're praying all night for South Africa. D'you want to come over?" he suddenly enquires. She struggles with an inchoate sense of anxiety.

"I'm not very good at praying."

"Nor am I," laughs Alfred, and says she can write as often as she wants, blithely unaware of what he is letting himself in for.

So begins a pen friendship which will eventually fill two box files. Years later Alfred returns her letters. They are stashed away in her archives – grey cardboard boxes filled with dangerous memories of her violent passsage over the threshold of the spirit. These letters describe her naive hopes, her ignorant probings, her pomposity, her vanity and pride. This correspondence is written on pages torn from notepads, the backs of envelopes, some on pretty stationery. The letters are mostly handwritten, some are almost illegible. Many are watermarked with tears, or with wine. All are yellowing with age.

Alfred doesn't write back. Fortunate really. Later in life he confides that he never had a clue what she was on about, just went on hoping that the writing of these letters helped her somehow. In fact, early in the piece she entreated him not to reply; that she just needed him as a blank wall to write upon. How pompous, how vain is that!

The truth is that Amy is terrified of being misunderstood, betrayed by an all too human being. What she desires is an angelic presence to accept her soul-baring without causing a ripple in her self-reflection. She wants to pour out her heart without restraint then gaze into its mirror until she understands what she is made of. This was to be an entirely self-centred enterprise, this pen-friendship. But Amy does not know this yet.

Until now, at home alone, she has not realised how perilously lonely she has become. For years the detritus of disappointment has banked up in her soul, clogging its arteries. Her life has become a quagmire in which she is sinking without trace. Is this all there is? This endless round of waking, working, eating, sleeping? She had been willing to give up all hope, but at the last moment this ardent existentialist has been betrayed by a spark of desire. A spark was struck on the stone altar of Amy's heart that afternoon in Spring at the priory when she met Alfred.

Amy's first letter to Alfred resembles the contents of a garbage truck; one of those compacter jobs which travel along kerbsides swallowing the refuse of daily life, crushing it into neat cubes.

She was certainly drinking while she wrote; she can tell by the lachrymose self-satisfaction with which she heaps censure on the world at large. After all, she is superior to ordinary people; this is why Alfred should take notice of her. She alone pursues the good, the true and the wise in a world of mediocrity; only Amy is left of those who sought the meaning of life. The rest have gone to the East. Or retreated to suburbia with a couple of kids.

In this first letter she mentions that she studied the problem of suicide according to Durkheim, whilst reading sociology at university, which means it can't happen to her. She pours scorn on alcoholics by suggesting such people just need a kick in the arse to sort out their lives — the latter remark punctuated with a wine stain in the margin

Next she embarks on her favourite subjects, an obsession with the deceitful motives of the human heart, and the quest for perfection.

Amy's genes have bestowed on her an over-active imagination, and a spooky intuition — probably through the matrilinear Romany connection. Her mother has this sixth sense in spades. Once at the vicarage, as the family sat down to lunch the phone rang — as it usually did at mealtimes, that being the best time to find the vicar at home, which caused endless domestic conflict. But on this occasion Anna announced, "Oh, that's Gwen," and answered the phone herself. It was indeed her sister. So far so normal. But the sisters hadn't spoken to one another for years, and Anna did not, by the flicker of an eyelid, find her precognition of this out-of-the-blue phone call at all odd.

So Amy grew up finding it normal that one could hear the subtext in people's conversation. Most intelligent children can, especially when adults address them as if they are simpletons. But for Amy the gift, or curse, however one perceives this confusing double vision, continued into adult life.

It became particularly awkward when she began dating men, whose testosterone messages out-shouted their soft words, and left her hopelessly bifurcated between the person she jealously guarded as her self, and the sexualised one they were making eyes at – one that made her feel like a rack of lamb.

This confusion, this lack of integration, between what she perceived as her real self, and her sexual being, was not unusual amongst English girls growing up in the 'sixties. Sexual mores had leapt out of the Victorian lacquered box which had contained them for so long. Sex was potentially free for all, if you liked that sort of thing. Trouble was, if you didn't, you were not with it; worse, you were probably a prude.

Amy's formal sex education began with a book about the mating of whales, which her father pressed upon her when she was eleven years old. This coy gesture embarrassed Amy. She had already found out how babies were made from gossip in the playground at school. She didn't like thinking about it, it was so disgusting. Apparently conception occurred when the father spat in the mother's mouth.

A more comprehensive lesson occurred at age thirteen. During an uproarious biology class, a discombobulated teacher outlined the Facts of Life, with the help of an overhead projector. The screaming! The hysteria! The giggling! It was woeful, but then it was a girls' school. By then Amy had the gist of it.

She did like sex. A lot. She experimented extensively with her first boyfriend under the billiard table in his parents' drawing room. Between games of snooker, which became less and less the focus of their interest, she enjoyed the feelings orchestrated by their questing fingers, but most of all she liked the power.

Now, embarking on a new relationship with the holy Alfred, she is fearful that any taint of sex could damage this tenuous, crucial, life-giving liaison.

There are two of Amy. One is a thoughtful poet, embalmed in solitude, clinging to a faint memory of the sound of a golden horn which still echoes from the distant woodlands of childhood. The other is a lioness who likes red meat for breakfast, who enjoys exercising her sexual power – and who secretly despises men who fall under her spell. Naturally, the dungeon of her mind is like a zoo, roaring and mewing, a miry pit. A chaos of predatory and captive creatures.

Next, in this first letter to Alfred, she boasts about her understanding of medieval history, comments shot through with allusions to monasticism. The Prior had been impressed by her erudition during that first, portentous visit to the priory. In fact Amy would have had no history at all, except that she was tossed out of art class at school and took up history at the last minute – to fill the gap, so to speak.

The history teacher, the illustrious Billy Bantam had a classroom lined with leather-bound editions of *Punch*, dating back to its first edition – a library which seemed out of place in the formica-clad, neon lit classrooms of the first comprehensive school in England. Amy had by now been removed from the girls' grammar school, which felt she was unlikely to amount to much.

Billy's classroom was situated as far as possible from the headmaster's office, because the history teacher was hopeless at keeping order amongst his pupils. Whenever the ruckus reached a peak, without fail, Billy would jump up on a chair, tear his thinning hair and yell, "Knickers!" Which was naughty enough in 1969 to bring about an instant, if temporary, hush.

To cut a long story short Billy told Amy it was too late to study the history curriculum for A Level. "But read these," he said, stacking up a pile of biographies of the period, gleaned from his copious library.

She read, she learned, she passed, and was bequeathed an enduring fascination with the sedimentary layers of human experience which constitute history, and upon which her own generation is now depositing its contribution, like grains of sand upon a beach.

So Alfred gets a blast about the Dark Ages, the Reformation and the Thirty Years War, alongside muddled ramblings about the evils of materialism, and the higher realms of philosophy which, of course, Amy purports to inhabit. All this is rounded off with a bleat about her current inclination towards nonbeing, a residual attraction from her reading of Jean Paul Sartre.

So much is compressed into a few pages in that first letter. A whole grab bag of allusions, wild references, anxieties; such a plethora of repressed life exploding between the handwritten lines. Amy is simply ravenous for conversation. To a sober mind it reads like a suicide note. No wonder Alfred phones her.

§

It is a cautious phone call, coming just after dinner when she has eaten a solid repast of fish and chips to soak up the wine, and has not yet got stuck into the whisky. She is, after all, more-or-less on holiday.

"Hello, is that the divine Amy?" enquires the divine Alfred in a dark brown voice which turns her legs to jelly. "Um, oh, er, yes! How absolutely marvellous to hear from you," she gushes.

There is a silence which, had it occurred in his presence would have been bliss, but silences on the phone are just awkward.

"I got your letter," says Alfred, gingerly.

How thrilled she is that he has received it, she cries, as if he lives at the North Pole and it is utterly astonishing that her letter has made it all the way to Johannesburg.

She gabbles on about how much she enjoys writing, she does it because she loves it, she really does, writing letters that is. But he mustn't under any circumstances feel any obligation to reply. A voice in her head remarks that she sounds just like her mother.

Alfred invites her to visit him at Nazareth House. There is a little more chit chat, and they ring off. Then she gets very drunk, out of sheer happiness.

8

Nazareth House is a cottage sandwiched between skyscrapers on the crest of the inner-city district of Hillbrow – Johannesburg's red light district. This insalubrious dwelling is destined to become a drop-in centre for the city's poor and homeless, to be financed by local churches. Alfred will be in charge and will commute there daily from the priory.

Amy visits Nazareth House promptly on Saturday afternoon. She wants to reassure herself that she has not just imagined the precious intimacy with which Alfred regarded her that time she met him at the priory, the warmth of his voice on the telephone. The house is mostly unfurnished, echoing with footfalls and voices. Traffic noise filters through dusty windows. Several people are shuffling around – street people by the looks of them – to whom she is introduced, but she doesn't remember their names. Alfred saunters about in his white cassock with a black scapular instead of the grey one he was wearing at their first meeting. She notices he is wearing jeans under his cassock, and sandals.

"Let's pray!" cries Alfred, as if he is offering them all something nice to drink, and subsides onto his knees on the bare floor boards. It looks like folding laundry, a graceful concertina of those long limbs into repose, like a camel resting. She later learns that he has thick callouses under his knees from spending so much time praying.

The little band of castaways obediently joins him, settling in a semi-circle on the floor. Amy self-consciously kneels down too, thanking God she didn't wear stockings.

Now she has her first experience of Alfred praying. He exhibits an excruciatingly familiar tone with the Almighty, asking for all sorts of things to happen – for blessings to fall upon them, for the future prosperity of this house – as if they were in church. It goes on for a long time, and then there is silence. She dares not open her eyes.

Soon she is aware that things are running amok in her head. She very much wants to look at Alfred. She steals a glance. He is just as gloriously technicolored as she remembers him; lissom and kind, and wearing *jeans*. Quite why this should make him as ravishingly attractive as he now appears to her chaotic brain she does not know. Jeans are everywhere – she even has some herself. Wolf got married to her in jeans. Perhaps it was the combination of the jeans and the cassock? She was always attracted to wacky partnerships.

Unexpectedly the word 'partnerships' morphs into a lewd image and copulates behind her eyes. Shocked, she tries to curb the thought, but it has a life of its own and flies about in her head, giggling, throwing up a myriad lascivious images behind her retina.

She draws a veil around herself, as she used to do on board ship when she wanted to be invisible; this time to protect Alfred from her promiscuous thoughts. She is terrified that he can see into her mind, and knows what is going on there. Shame, and a genuine fear that he could be somehow tainted by the escalating pandemonium inside her head cranks her anxiety up to an unbearable pitch, and she cannot suppress a moan.

"Time for tea!" declares Alfred, as if in response to her distress, clambering to his feet, leading the way, like the Pied Piper, to the kitchen.

§

Later she gets a chance to talk to Alfred alone. He has furnished an office for himself in the front of the house, with a broad oak desk and two threadbare armchairs, where they now sit. She is tongue-tied by the experience of being alone with him. She cannot think of anything sensible to say, except that there isn't anyone like him in Pretoria.

"I am in no-man's-land there," she says mournfully.

She is painfully aware that something very important is going on, only she doesn't know what it is, and she has only this brief moment with Alfred to get a grip on it.

Perhaps she is haunted by the memory of her father's study; his *sanctum sanctorum*, no trespassing, on pain of death, or worse. If you got in there it was usually for matters so grave they were beyond the usual punishment – a spanking with Anna's slipper. This room smelt like her father's study, the odour of shabby upholstery, garnished with a wisp of cigarette smoke.

Alfred discerns a world of meaning in her stuttering attempts at conversation, and suggests that there is always 'Tim'.

"Tim?" she parrots.

Timothy is the Bishop of Pretoria, he explains, and a top bloke. Alfred first met Tim in England, when he, Alfred, was a novice and showed Tim around the 'pad'.

Alfred's conversation is littered with colloquialisms, which she finds almost as unnerving as the jeans. She somehow can't get her head around this monk who now takes a pack of ten Gold Dollar from under his scapular and offers her one. Then he does a one-handed conjuring trick with a box of matches, lights both cigarettes and leans back inhaling with sensual pleasure.

Amy is used to shocking people. She and Wolf have made a profession of it. She is not used to having her own prejudices randomly overturned.

She should go and see Tim, Alfred now opines. Why on earth she should go and see the bishop is beyond her, even if she had the courage to do so. But Alfred says without a flicker of humour that he believes in starting at the top and working down. His eyes rest upon her with that long-distance gaze and she nods like a robot. A visit to Tim is the next clue in this paper chase, for clearly she is not to have her curiosity satisfied today about what is going on. The interview is over. As she rises from the armchair she hears Alfred catch his breath.

"Are you a dancer?" he asks mildly.

"No, why?"

She rose so gracefully from that deep armchair, he explains, that he thought she must be a dancer. She tells him she goes to the gym at lunchtime and is quite fit. Somehow she doesn't feel so terribly out of her depth any more.

Amy hasn't a clue that she is about to lose all sense of direction, all sense of up or down, or right or wrong, all points of her personal compass. That her feet will not touch terra firma again for a very long time.

9

On Christmas Eve Amy flies to Durban as arranged. The humid air of Natal engulfs her as she disembarks onto the tarmac. A light sweat touches her lip and she breathes in the fecund warmth of the sub-tropics, laced with a hint of the nearby ocean. Wolf emerges from a crowd at the arrivals gate, looking somehow different after two weeks' separation. He takes her hand luggage and the bag of Christmas gifts, beaming, all teeth and eyes amidst a thatch of sun-bleached hair and shaggy beard. "Come!" he cries. "We must find Jonathan. He has lost me!" He strides off and she trots behind his broad shoulders parting the press of humanity. Wolf parks Amy and her luggage close to the main exit, plunging once more into the crowd in search of his brother-in-law.

Amy gazes through glass doors to the glare of taxi ranks baking in the heat. Whiffs of aromatic oils and sweat reach her nostrils as Indian women in bright saris press close around her. Then Jonathan arrives, tanned, smiling, kissing her cheek.

"Hallo Sis. Where's Wolf?"

"He says you've lost him."

"We said we'd meet in the bar then we could explain what's happened. I've ordered beers." He smiles comfortably as Amy perks up at the mention of a drink.

They quaff ice-cold beer at a table overlooking the runway, where planes ferry people home from Cape Town, Bloemfontein, Port Elizabeth, Jo'burg, for the Christmas holiday. Jonathan refuses to break the news of what has happened before Wolf arrives. Eventually he goes off and finds him in a downstairs bar waiting with three beers. They bring the drinks upstairs with them, haranguing each other genially, an anxious Indian waiter dancing alongside, appealing for the safe return of the glasses.

"What has happened?" asks Amy, caring less and less as the alcohol quells her anxiety.

"Well," said Jonathan, with a steely glance at Wolf. "It rained in the Transkei and there aren't any roads. At least there are, but the tar ends 'chop', just like that at the border, and we came over the mountain passes... mostly sideways."

"Well?"

"Well. By the time we got here the combi didn't have any tyres to speak of. So it's in the garage."

"But it's Christmas Eve. Are we going to celebrate Christmas in a garage?" Amy is appalled. Wolf and Jonathan exchange glances.

"We hope not. We can go and see now. We made them give us a car to come and fetch you. Wolf said you were the Prime Minister's daughter."

§

The new tyres are on and most of the mud is off the battered red combi when they pick it up at the garage.

"*Eule's* here now. Everything will be alright," mutters Wolf, as he takes the wheel, using her German nickname 'Owl'.

But it wasn't. They head north towards Umhlanga in the late afternoon sunshine. The little camper van purrs up the highway between plantations of sugar cane. Jonathan is cheerfully recounting their adventures, although she has a feeling some episodes are left out. They have definitely had a wonderful time on their trip around the country. Jonathan managed to stay astride an ostrich at Oudtshoorn for nearly two minutes before being thrown off. He bought a kilo of ostrich biltong to pay it back. She listens with one ear. She is looking forward to beaches and good food.

But there isn't any. Food, that is. She only finds this out when they stop for the night at a small beachside resort. Boxes of provisions she has noticed in the back of the van turn out to be cases of wine from Cape vineyards.

"Where's the food?" she bleats, fearing the worst.

They thought they could buy some on the way north.

"But it's Christmas Eve, everything's shut for the holiday!"

Jonathan explains that they couldn't shop before because they had to fetch her, Amy. And anyway, it is Wolf's turn to shop today. Wolf is trapped and has to think carefully about restoring the pecking order.

"Didn't you bring any with you?" he says at last, plaintively. "Turkey and plum pudding, and *Christole*?"

"What! on the plane? I didn't think of it." Amy feels unaccountably guilty. Wolf follows up this victory with the remark that there is lots of wine.

They crack a couple of bottles right away, which are indeed very good – Spatzendreck, the Delheim late harvest, with the picture of the sparrow shitting on the label.

§

Most of the Cape vineyards were founded by French and German settlers, who brought European wine-making skills to the fertile land around the colony from the seventeenth century onwards. South Africa's best kept secret, Amy thinks to herself. Once on a trip ashore in Cape Town, some of the ship's crew hired a car to visit a gracious old estate in the Cape winelands.

The road delves into vinyards on fire with autumn, into a riverine valley where thoroughbreds graze, and an ancient homestead stands foursquare beneath oak trees. There is a spacious courtyard with well-groomed gravel and a slave bell. The place smells permanent, more solid than anything she has seen in Africa so far – anything man made, that is.

The vintner is loud and blond and hospitable. The wines come in fine hock and moselle glasses, and have German names. They sit in the stone-flagged parlour and quaff for hours – waxing merry and silly, while the vintner pokes fun at them for being German tourists. *Hüte Dich vor Sturm und Wind und Deutschen, die im Ausland sind!*

He gives them a case of his best wine to take back to Europe. Show them, he says, that we are not barbarians in Africa. Let them taste the nectar of the gods. It is indeed wonderful wine. They drink it all before they reach Durban.

§

Darkness falls over the beach where the travellers spend the night. They sit in the van, drinking. Presently two young Indian men come by, asking to borrow a pan to braai their chops. The hungry campers hand over their grill pan, and soon smell meat roasting on a wood fire further down the beach. When the men return the pan they present them with a joint by way of thanks. Jonathan cheers up and shares it with Amy, but her one cautious inhalation does nothing for the hunger pangs. More wine helps however.

Later Wolf and Amy take themselves off to the dunes beyond the beach to reacquaint themselves with each other after three weeks' separation. The sand is silky and the surf surges on the white beach with the indomitable rhythm of the ocean. Stars glitter in the sable vault of the sky, and she is happy to be here, in Africa, by the sea, with Wolf.

§

The sun has risen when they awaken and find Jonathan gone from his swag on the ground outside the van. He had given his bunk to his sister. Fortunately there is filter coffee in the sparse larder, and by the time it is brewed Jonathan is back with a bucket of mussels and some seaweed, crowing that his foraging skills come in handy in a crisis.

As usual he has a good story to go with breakfast. He was chipping mussels from the rocks when a Zulu ranger turned up and with eloquent gestures indicated that this was not the right thing to be doing. So Jonathan drew himself up to his full height of six foot, saluted the ranger and barked, "Remember Isandhlwana!" The ranger saluted back, grinned, and left him to his task. That's Jonathan's story anyway. Mussels fresh from the ocean, swiftly poached in wine, are a divine breakfast for Christmas morning.

§

They eat a lot of fish during their week on the shores of the Indian Ocean. Far up on the St Lucia peninsula they discover a remote colony of fishermen camping with their families. They settle in with them, their van piteously small and mean, surrounded by a tent city equipped with humming generators, shower enclosures, and freezers to store the daily catch. Towards sundown, people stroll from the shade of the forest camp, over the dune, into the glare of the beach to help bring the boats ashore. Game fish are lugged back to be gutted and scaled. The evening air fills with the aroma of grilled mackerel and tuna, the chink of ice in glasses, guffaws over tales of the day at sea – an orca who came alongside to have its back scratched with a boat hook, dolphin sporting with shoals of sardine, and the swordfish that got away.

Sometimes Amy wanders off by herself to sit on the dunes and watch the far off ships sailing north to Mozambique, south to Durban, slim silhouettes slipping silently through the haze of subtropical seas. She imagines herself aboard; dreams herself back into the calm routine of days at sea, anticipating the next harbour, remembering the one left behind, unencumbered by news from distant shores.

Amy was only nineteen when she first came to Africa. She vividly remembers her first dawn over Table Mountain. The ship had dropped anchor outside Table Bay because there was no berth in the harbour until morning. She stayed up all night, afraid to miss the slow unwrapping of the dark continent as the sun rose on Cape Town.

Ten days before, she had had her first glimpse of the purple outline of Africa, where Dakar perches on its western edge. Later they dropped anchor in Walvis Bay, in that deep, dour harbour where festoons of blue jellyfish trailed long tangled tentacles around the hull. But Dakar was far off, just a faint scent of the tropics wafting on the breeze. Walvis Bay was arid and gritty, surrounded by glaring sand dunes. Neither was the Africa Amy had imagined – the one where lions roar at night, where palms sway, where black people in loincloths do whatever you say.

In the breathtaking hush before dawn, she leans against a railing on the boat deck, and waits. She feels the leisurely pulse of the ship at anchor, gazes up at the canopy of stars growing pale above a monolithic presence, which looms larger on the shoreline as dawn approaches. Brooding, sphinx-like, Table Mountain slowly comes to life as daylight fingers its way down bluffs, into ravines and fissures. As the sun rises the surrounding ocean is unveiled as a plate of burnished pewter. Cape Town at the toe of the mountain sparks with small details of colour and movement.

How well she remembers it – the breathless waiting for a dream to come true. Africa at last, and her first real mountain. She holds the anticipation hard against her solar plexus, pressed into the steel of the ship's rail, not wanting the dream to slip away as reality dawns.

Dreaming pink mists drift upward to reveal bronze buttresses rearing to the sky. Table Mountain – aloof and distant as a picture postcard. She feels a fleeting moment of wonder, as her child's heart makes a little 'oh!' of astonishment at something so vast and so solid. Then her mind names the experience and files it away, complete with colour code, for future reference. The moment is past.

Cape Town unfurls below the mountain, creeping into its skirts, spilling down to the shores of the bay. It is a city just like others she has seen in Europe, only brighter and cleaner in the sparkling morning sun.

Later, when she ventures ashore into macadam streets and sleek shopping areas, she feels a furtive sense of shame for her fantasies about Africa. Cape Town really is much the same as cities at home — especially the white people, who are dressed as if for garden parties and speak with BBC accents.

When she goes up Table Mountain, however, gazing towards the Constantiaberg, she feels a tremor of that awe which is her soul's quarry, the quiver of delight in an unseen presence. It is so high here, the air as clean as a whistle from the scouring crosswinds of Indian and Atlantic oceans. She is so high the ocean curves like the rim of a saucer, shimmering in the sun.

To the north east the blue mane of Africa stirs and trembles slightly, as if disturbed by a dream. Surely a mirage? But her child's heart, humiliated by the prosaic streets of Cape Town, now embraces the notion that Africa has marked her arrival, and will remember her.

There is a cable car to carry tourists to the top of the mountain. It makes the way up easy, although some people still prefer to climb to the top. It is not an altogether tame mountain. Every year there are casualties; even wildlife perishes on its escarpments. The cable car descends through a foul miasma from the carcass of a long-haired sheep lying in the bottom of a ravine. Protea bloom on the slopes, that prehistoric species of flora with spiky petals which sustains an entire ecology. But the fabulous botanical wealth of the Cape just looks like desiccated bushes to Amy's ignorant eyes, the sheep merely stinks. Judgement comes readily to the young. Armed thus with multiple delusions, Amy first sets foot in Africa.

Now, ashore on a sand dune in Zululand, Amy feels a dumb ache where she imagines her solar plexus to be. Melancholy reminds her that she is human, that she can still feel, if only dimly. This burden of humanity is too painful to sustain for more than a few minutes. She slides down the dune, ambles back to camp and pours herself a drink.

§

One sultry afternoon Wolf and Amy venture out for a stroll in the dune forest behind the camp. They take a narrow winding track. Everything is so green, unbearably green to eyes accustomed to the bleached plains of the Highveld. Sunshine filters through foliage, casting iridescent specks on verdant undergrowth, which vanishes right and left into dense shade. Vines swoop, slung like fishing nets, like hammocks, from the canopy. They walk in silence, Amy in front. Barefoot, clothed only in shorts and singlets, they feel suddenly naked.

A footfall ahead of Amy the path suddenly undulates eerily, silkily, in patterned splendour. The glimpse is burned forever on her retina. With one foot still raised to take the next step, understanding impacts upon her like a car crash.

"Snake!" she squawks, leaping backwards into Wolf's startled arms.

And what a snake! She never saw its head nor its tail, just its magnificent girth slithering on and forever on over the path, a sight eternally grafted into that split second of cognition. They are in the presence of a leviathan, with whom their kind have an ancient enmity. They scramble back up the path until pride gets a claw-hold on their panicked senses. They skid to a halt, clutching each other, petrified.

"Did you see that?" gasps Amy peering back down the path towards the now vacant spot.

"Of course I did. I warned you, otherwise you'd have trod on it." He sniffs and adjusts his spectacles, eyes still fixed on the place. "It's gone now. Shall we go on?" His voice quavers.

"No, no let's go back," says Amy.

At first they walk. Then they walk faster. They burst out onto the sunlit dune at a sprint, collapse on the beach, stare gratefully at the sky, the sea – anywhere but at each other.

11

Amy is driving her brother Jonathan to Jan Smuts Airport, cruising along the narrow swathe of tarmac which slices through the everlasting blond grass of the Highveld. Today he is returning to the low, pewter skies of England – and Sandhurst.

Why, asks Amy, would a young man with the world at his feet, want to give his body and soul to the British Army? She is still, at this stage of her life, resolutely opposed to all forms of discipline; ideologically opposed. She did rather enjoy the iron routines and daily chores of life aboard ship, but she only had to sign up for three months at a time – for one voyage. Her brother is signing up for a lifetime.

Jonathan opines that he needs the discipline to keep himself sane. He is one of those astronomically intelligent people who have so much energy fulminating inside them that they could internally combust without some sort of scaffolding to contain them.

There were two career options, he says, the army or the Church of England. And we know why he wouldn't choose the C of E – whilst admitting, of course, that the established church has a lot in common with the army. But the army, Jonathan reckons, is safer than the church. The CO is more straightforward and the uniforms are nicer. God knows his place in the army – which is in church on Sundays.

His seems to be a well thought out position and Amy is a little envious. It occurs to her that she has washed up on these shores more or less by accident. In fact most of what has happened to her since she left home has been accident, serendipity, a passing whim, a sleight of hand by an enigmatic fate. Of course, she is very glad she is not in England, that place of rain-swept afternoons and terminal despair, where one is lost in the crowd, dancing itself to death on weekends, crammed behind the foggy windows of public transport, breathing second-hand air from nine to five in claustrophobic offices. How happy she is that she is here in the sunlight.

She is sorry, nonetheless, that her brother is leaving. It seems to her that, for all his optimism, he is disappearing into a sinister and uncompromising future. She will miss him. Although he was such a disappointment when they were young, he has grown into a handsome, gentle and witty man, taller than she is now; already a stranger.

She is suddenly lonely, and astonished by the sensation. She weeps a little as she waves him goodbye, as he is swallowed up by the machinery of international departures. Staring at the plywood hoarding behind which he slips, grinning back at her, stiff upper lip, saluting like an actor in a play, she dabs the tears on her face and peers at her wet fingers as if at some weird phenomenon. She cannot remember the last time she wept.

12

Amy prepares scrupulously for her appointment with the bishop. She washes her hair. She dresses with care in a sensible linen suit, puts on stockings and dons court shoes.

The bishop's secretary, formidable beneath a lilac-rinsed beehive, regards her gravely over pink-rimmed spectacles, indicates a chair, and continues typing. Amy tries not to fidget or look around, for that would surely be impertinent. Eyes front is the ticket in these cool, whitewashed rooms. Behind an inner door lurks the bishop about his mysterious business. She waits, with mounting anxiety, for her first adult encounter with the purple.

§

When Amy was a child the bishop was a daunting, although invisible, presence at the vicarage. He never appeared in person to exercise his authority, but there was always a spare room ready for him, should he need it – this was church law. He maintained a theatrical persona; he could drop in at any time.

Every year the children went up to London for the bishop's Christmas party, together with dozens of other clergy kids. Once there was an outbreak of diphtheria, unbeknown to the happy company, and a couple of children died. Amy and her brother were quarantined at home until the danger was past, which imbued them with an odd sense of self-importance.

Later, as a teenager, she remembers having Christmas dinner with the bishop's family – just the two families together. After the turkey and before the Christmas pudding an ornate silver goblet filled with red wine was passed from hand to hand around the table, each person bestowing a simple blessing upon their neighbour as they handed the chalice on. As she took the cup Amy's heart was shaken with a powerful emotion. She could barely get the words of benediction over her lips, or pass the chalice without spilling it, she was trembling so much.

That memory revisits her as she awaits her appointment with the bishop. Now here he is, slighter and younger than she had imagined, coming to fetch her into his study, smiling with boyish charm, resplendent in purple stock and silver pectoral cross, amethyst ring glowing on his right hand. The amethyst is a symbol of sobriety, he later tells her gently, a virtue recommended by St Paul to bishops of the church.

There is a book, a bound thesis, on the coffee table in his study where they sit in armchairs, not at the desk. He shows her the folio and tells her that the dean of the cathedral has written a doctoral thesis on Christianity in Shakespeare. She finds this alarming, as if discrete categories have been muddled up – how could literature relate to theology? She feels rather muddled herself. This bishop is not at all what she expected. He is too young, and is altogether too delightful. Nor is he going to tell her what she needs to hear, but is sitting expectantly, although relaxed, inclining his head as if waiting to hear what she has to tell him.

At a bit of a loss, she asks him if it is permissible to write letters to God? To his credit he does not blink, but declares that letter writing to God is perfectly permissible; in fact, historically, has been a well-respected method of going about the business of prayer. She has not thought of writing letters as prayer.

Lately Amy has become painfully aware of the potency of her own thoughts, hyper-aware that the thought is mother of the word. She is fearful of each word's influence upon its neighbour, of their symbiosis, consequences rippling outward in ever-increasing circles, with burgeoning power, to the edge of consciousness, beyond her control. She has not heard of the Butterfly Effect – anyway an absurd epithet for this cosmic dread, exorcising it, stripping it of power. She is paralysed by her secret knowledge. It renders her dumb. She is afraid to give voice to her thoughts because of their portent, their ripples upon the fabric of the universe. She is afraid of consequences. Writing is okay. It is private. Writing does no harm.

Stumblingly she tries to explain this dilemma. It is extremely difficult, because of course she is breaking the taboo on occult knowledge by attempting to speak of it at all. That cosmic dread is upon her again; she is trembling, stammering, sweating. The more tongue-tied she becomes the more she is tormented by the belief that she is drawing back the veil on things which should remain unspoken.

The bishop watches her turmoil with a kindly expression, apparently undisturbed by what is certainly some sort of nervous breakdown. He asks her if she would like a cup of tea? She says she would, and spends a few minutes collecting herself while he goes out to ask the formidable secretary for refreshments. When he returns she calmly asks him which translation of the bible she should purchase.

They decide on the Revised Standard Version, which she buys on the way home at Van Schaik's bookstore, placing it on her desk at home with the feeling that she has crossed a rubicon. That nothing will ever be the same again.

13

Amy sprawls on the cool oak pew, moleskin chaps spread over bony shanks, six-gun safely holstered, and squints towards the silver crucifix above the altar at the far end of the sanctuary.

It is Monday and the church is empty, but the west door was not locked. The click of the latch echoed in the dim interior as she kept her appointment with destiny. Strobes of afternoon sunlight play with stained glass, like a kaleidoscope swirling on the ancient flagstones of the nave. Amy's mission today is deadly earnest and requires solitude. She feels safe here in the family pew, at the front on the right hand side, where she sits with her mother and siblings on Sundays.

She focusses on the silver crucifix and attempts to invest it with Aslan's glory. Tensile nine-year-old ribs flutter, panting with the sheer effort of resurrecting her secret friend in his proper environment – one that is acceptable to grown-ups. But this enormous effort of will does not work. The sterling figurine on the silver cross hangs without blood and breath, shorn of warm golden fur, sterilised of life.

The problem is infinitely serious, a matter for the Lone Ranger, which is why she is wearing her cowboy outfit. Even Tonto could not help here – this is not Red Indian business. Amy is aware that wearing one's six-gun in church is frowned upon, but she hesitated to leave it at the door in case some bad guy pinched it. It fires real gunpowder caps with an impressive bang, leaving a whiff of cordite in the air.

Authenticity is important to Amy. She is not averse to filling the gaps with imagination, but the fundamentals have to be real. Trigger, the milk horse stands in for the Lone Ranger's faithful steed, Silver. After his rounds he is kept in a paddock down the lane from St John's Church. The bay horse ambles to the gate, winking at her when she brings him bread crusts, mumbling them out of her hand with his hairy old lips.

Once she unlatched the gate, better to stroke Trigger's coarse black mane. With astonishing alacrity the welsh cob took the gap and cantered off to Cony Green, there to espy with joy an endless greensward, with white-clad cricketers plying the turf in the distance.

A policeman caught the horse in the end, but not before he had scattered cricketers like sparks and ploughed up the pitch with his plate-sized hooves. For Amy, the incident proved Trigger's secret identity, a spirit belied by the patient, blinkered nag who plodded between the shafts of the neighbourhood milk float.

Animals of any kind found a ready home in her heart. Once, when walking barefoot on the municipal rubbish dump she had startled a field mouse which promptly ran into the flames of one of the spontaneous fires which broke out there from time to time. The dump was her playground, a source of countless treasures simply left lying around. She had burnt her feet seeking to rescue the mouse, but in vain. The barefoot exercise was during a Tonto phase; she was toughening up her feet so that she could track things silently, like a Red Indian. The natural world was her muse. She was often to be observed tenderly rescuing earthworms from damp pavements, and making herself late for school.

Various neighbours' dogs found themselves regularly exercised by Amy, who aspired to train them to sit and walk to heel − amongst other tricks. Elderly mutts would raise patient muzzles and cloudy eyes, comprehending not a word of the girl's repeated commands, but glad to get out of the house, and anxious to please.

But it was horses she worshipped above all − with the noble exception of Aslan. On Saturday mornings she cycled seven miles to the riding stables, over the bridge where steam trains sometimes puffed past below to envelope her in smoke and smuts. In winter, by the time she reached the cobbled yard where children and sundry mounts milled about, all bawled at by bossy Miss Bonas, she was frozen to the bone, barely able to uncurl her fingers from the handlebars of her bicycle. But after a few minutes snug in the saddle, inhaling the scent and heat of pony, she was as warm as toast.

In an ideal world she would have had her own horse, but a clergy stipend was only forty pounds a month, hardly enough to feed and clothe a family of five, so riding lessons would have to do, and a luxury at that. To make up for the deficit she drew horses copiously on textbooks, the margins of homework, story books, on bedroom walls, on her arms − even on drawing paper when some turned up. She also galloped about a lot, striking her flank and yelling 'Giddyup!'

In spite of the absence of her own pony or dog, Amy mustered a considerable menagerie at the vicarage. There was a belgian hare which

Uncle Gerry, their journalist lodger, bought for her in Hounslow. He had taken her with him on his regular round of the pubs, collecting stories for the newspaper. In those days journalists picked up tips in pubs and phoned their stories into the office from public telephones. Amy began her career as a newshound by persuading Uncle Gerry to buy her the hare, which was unadventurously named Bunny.

Uncle Ron, the local plumber, arrived to update their antiquated bathroom, and became another of her adoptees. The house was an old hunting lodge named, with English understatement, St John's Cottage, despite sporting five bedrooms. The claw-foot bath squatted on an acreage of linoleum and was fed by a gas-heated boiler which belched and leaked rust at bath time, which happened twice a week, when the children shared a few inches of lukewarm water. Uncle Ron came to replace the boiler and afterwards took her home with him to show her his tropical fish.

This was the beginning of a chapter of happiness. Besides tropical fish Uncle Ron had a car – a Hillman Minx in which he took her on outings into the countryside. He also had a garden full of ponds and streams with stickleback, newts and frogs in them. He had two grown-up sons whose childhood he had missed while he was away in the war, so there was space in his heart for an eight-year old son – even if she was a girl. Amy filled that space with joy.

The fact that she was a girl irked her terribly. She had her hair cut short, urchin-style, and she affected lace-up shoes and boy's shorts when she was not at school. Nothing pleased her more than being called 'son' by the shopkeeper when Uncle Ron took her to buy an ice-cream.

"What will you do when you grow breasts?" lisped Uncle Ron, coyly. "Cut them off," she replied cheerfully, unconscious of future assets.

Weekends became their time for mucking about in ponds, collecting frog spawn in Spring from the bluebell woods at High Wycombe. They used nets and jam jars to collect daphnia from village duck ponds to feed to the tropical fish, then drove home singing raucously; 'My ole man's a dustman' was a favourite. Uncle Ron was a fan of George Formby and Elvis Presley.

At home in the greenhouse a dozen aquaria housed neon tetras, zebra fish, black mollies, angel fish, blue gouramis, guppies, and the solitary siamese fighting fish. The fish had to be kept at a constant temperature and the tanks had aerators bubbling constantly, heaters warming the greenhouse to sub-tropical temperatures. A pineapple grew there, amongst the delicious monsters and maidenhair ferns. She breathed in the atmosphere of tropical forests, of leech-infested swamps, her heart expanding with joy.

§

Amy first met the Lone Ranger after befriending Auntie Long who lived across the road and had a television. St John's Cottage had no television, and no refrigerator. In summer ice-cream came on Fridays with Trigger the milk horse, wrapped in smoking dry ice to keep it from melting.

After the racing results, which Auntie Long kept a close eye on, Amy was permitted to watch The Lone Ranger. The black-masked hero on his white horse ('gray' actually, to those who know about horses) provoked an ache in her chest, which she nursed jealously. First love leaves a brand on the heart and the William Tell Overture still thrills her even fifty years later.

Her maternal great-great grandmother was a Romany princess, according to her mother, which could account for her affinity with dogs and horses. For the Romany nation was an equestrian tribe from North India, driven out during the holocausts of Genghis Kahn. In exile from their land they learned to live by their wits and horse-sense, which was valued highly in the royal houses of Europe.

Anna often told the story of this great grandmother who eloped with a Cotswold gentleman, pursued by a fratricidal bunch of Romanies, who were horse-traders, not tinkers, she stressed. The Cotswold gentleman was cut off from his inheritance and was forced to take up window-cleaning. Love proved to be the death of him when he fell from a ladder one day and broke his neck.

Anyhow, bloodlines are strong, and there is no doubt that horses bend an ear to Amy with grudging respect, even though she is only little. She feels a visceral kinship with horses, so that her own flanks shiver with delight as the curry comb rakes her pony after riding on Saturdays. Dogs whine and grumble at her, as if she knows what they are on about, which of course she claims she does.

She learned to read whilst very young, having made an early cognitive leap from hearing stories on the wireless to realising that unlimited adventures were hidden between the covers of countless books around the house, if only she had the skill to decipher them.

During her reading one day she came across an account of the wild west – a place she already considered to be her natural home as it was the region patrolled by the Lone Ranger. This historical account told of the tragic demise of great herds of bison which once roamed North America. Tens of thousands of them shot for fun, for their hides, their tongues, for any damned reason. Appalled, she read that whole islands off the coast of the continent were made up of discarded carcasses. The grief she felt for the innocent bison mounted in her breast until she could bear it no more and spewed out her revulsion one lunchtime at the dining table.

Amy's father was a philosopher, as well as being a pilot in the war, and a Church of England priest. He took the matter of the bison in hand, explaining sadly that it didn't really make any difference how many of them died; each one had only died once. She must think of it that way. It might help.

Her father never spoke about the war. Fifty-five thousand men in Bomber Command had been lost in the second world war, but their remains were so spread about that this monumental sacrifice had never entered public consciousness as Paschendale or Mons or the Batttle of the Bulge had done.

One day her father brings home a black polythene bag, a new invention that would revolutionise the world. He explains to the children that things can now be made chemically out of petroleum products, things which are virtually indestructible, and can be used for more-or-less anything. They are impressed. Within their lifetime a garbage dump the size of a continent made up of the detritus from this new wonder product will accumulate in the Pacific gyre. Quietly, without fanfare, the world is changed.

§

Amy yawns. Late afternoon sun is tessellating the nave with primary colours. Drops of crimson stain the silver crucifix. All is still; the battle is over; the cross has won. It is not possible for warm–blooded Aslan to live in this place.

People called her a bookworm, and so she was, absorbing *The Famous Five, My Friend Flicka, White Fang* as ravenously as *Sir Gawain and the Greene Knight, the Illiad, The Third Eye*. But the Narnia stories ravished her imagination more than any other. She hid the books, afraid that someone else might read them and guess the truth, give away the cosmic secret. She idolised C S Lewis for his tales of talking animals and living forests. She planned to paint a picture of Aslan and send it to him in Cambridge where he lived. It would be a secret code between them, for she would paint Aslan in such a way that he, the author, would understand that she knew *who Aslan was*.

The secret of Aslan's identity was revealed to her in *The Lion, the Witch and the Wardrobe*, in the scene where the lion gives up his life to the White Witch in order to save naughty Edmund. Tucked up in a cosy spot near the rayburn she pores over the account of the great lion's sacrifice, and feels her heart bursting within her. Wrenching sorrow, plumbing deeper even than her grief for America's lost herds of bison overwhelms her. But no tears fall. Amy does not cry. Boys don't cry. There is no happy end in prospect to this tragic tale, no glimmer of hope. Aslan is dead, shorn of his magnificent mane, his poor legs roped together, lying lifeless on the cold slab of Narnia's stone altar.

Amy reads painfully on. In the darkness squadrons of mice creep out of hiding to gnaw at the ropes tethering the dead lion. Dew falls. At long last dawn breaks over Narnia. The first rays of the rising sun glance off the stone altar which, astonishingly, appears to be bare. Silence falls for about half an hour. Then something stirs beyond the altar and wonder of wonders, here is Aslan padding towards her, alive! More alive than he ever was, glowing with life, his honeyed breath drying her joyful tears.

Miracles change people. Invalids take up their beds and walk, blind people see, a hospitality crisis becomes a feast when water turns into wine. After Aslan rises from the dead, it feels as if she herself has been delivered from the miasma of death. She is enfolded in a solemn gladness which seeps through her limbs, tingles in her fingers and toes, its energy touching her whole personhood with its benevolence.

She wraps her arms around herself to contain this celestial warmth, tucking her head into her chest to hide the radiance she feels must be streaming from her face, betraying her secret. No-one must see, no-one must ever suspect the tremendous revelation which is bearing her down with joyful paws and ambrosial breath. Aslan is Jesus. Not just an image of Jesus, but the real thing.

Down through the ages a man-made saviour has infiltrated the church. A mistake was made long ago. How far the error has spread she does not know, but it certainly includes London, for she has been there, to the bishop's palace. During the children's Christmas party one year, she took herself off to explore. She peered into the bishop's chapel where a ruby lamp burned to indicate Jesus was there, in a box behind the altar.

Jesus did many things, but they were long ago and far away, in Palestine. These stories are kept in church in an enormous book supported on the wings of a brass eagle in the sanctuary where the choirboys sit. These stories are read aloud on Sundays.

For days Amy is absorbed in the vision splendid of Aslan risen from the dead, padding through the forests of Narnia, hidden from ordinary view, but living within her, closer than breathing, his royal heartbeat warming her breast. She hardly dares breathe for fear of disturbing this diaphanous presence, which swaddles her like a baby, but at the same time clothes her with dignity, calling her by name – a secret name known only to her. So rapt is Amy that she starts violently when her mother taps her shoulder, saying it is dinner time and she should go and wash her hands.

§

For many weeks the lovely presence is waiting for her whenever she finds time alone, at the bottom of the garden, in Bunny's hutch if it is raining. The hare sits companionably beside her in the straw, his quick breath warming her shin while she surrenders herself to the blissful company of her secret friend. Time seems to fade during these sessions and she returns with a jolt to ordinary hours when Bunny, bored, stretches and lollops off to feed.

One summer's evening, in the dimness of her bedroom, Amy feels herself raised bodily, borne upwards, complete with sheet and blanket, towards the ceiling of her room. She is swooning with the ecstasy of being lifted so tenderly, until confronted by the uncompromising slope of the ceiling she cringes, fearing to be crushed. At once the enveloping arms let her go, and she lands with a light bounce back upon the mattress.

Often she sings in bed before she goes to sleep, beginning with hymns remembered from church, which fragment into another, foreign language when the English words run out. She is quite carried away by the beauty of this hymnody and cannot understand why the rest of the family do not come running to share in the joy of it. Her song seems to resonate beyond her room into the twilit garden, up into the starlit sky, onward, forever on.

These wondrous experiences tear at Amy's loyalties. Although it is powerful enough to absorb her entirely while it is there, when it leaves her it seems as if the shy, diaphanous presence is easily frightened. She feels a fierce protectiveness towards it. Something tells her that speaking of it will cause her secret friend to go away. That, she cannot bear to think of. But the sweetness and lingering joy of each assignation lays a fresh burden on her conscience.

§

Amy's parents were not a happy couple. She knew this with a searing sense of personal responsibility. Once, when they displayed unusual affection, hugging one another with painful desperation in the kitchen, she rushed to join them, begging to be included in this rare embrace. Hermetically sealed in her secret friendship, she became certain that Aslan had the power to make her parents happy. She spent long hours at night imagining the perfect house for them to dwell in, with a crazy paving front path, mahogany furniture, flocked wallpaper. She even itemised utensils in the kitchen drawers. Each detail was carefully committed to memory in the hope that this paradise might one day spring to life and provide all the comfort and security her parents could desire. She spared no effort in this enterprise, keeping for herself only a small paddock at the bottom of the garden with a pony in it.

It was inevitable that in due course the realisation had dawned upon her that her mother and father were going to die. Not tomorrow, or even next week, but sometime. Everybody died. Funerals cropped up regularly in the routine of the household. This appalling realisation, once owned, began to haunt her. The two most beautiful people in her world were going to die. There was nothing she could do about it. Inconsolable, she sobbed herself to sleep at night. But now there was hope. Aslan had the power of life over death, if only there was a way to confide this secret knowledge to her parents, without betraying its source.

§

Her mother was doing the ironing on the afternoon Amy chose to tell her secret. The ironing board was about head height to the girl, the smell of freshly ironed linen permeated the kitchen. Clinker shifted in the rayburn, on which two tins of bread dough rested with a chequered cloth over them. Her mother said "Mmm" a lot, as Amy embarked on a shambolic account of her inner adventures. Linen rose in neat stacks on the kitchen table.

After a while Amy had the feeling that her mother was not paying proper heed. She began again, more fluently this time, confident that the sheer glory of her narrative must capture her mother's attention. After a while she noticed that the maternal brow was creased, with concentration perhaps, even admiration?

Amy redoubled her efforts, speaking with eloquence, flushed with love and pride. But her evangelical fervour was brought to a sudden end. "You must stop these silly 'maginings," said her mother mildly but firmly. "For goodness sake, be yourself." Her mother often said this: 'Be yourself,' although what it could possibly mean had so far eluded Amy. What self might she be, other than the one she already was?

Amy begins a third incarnation of her narrative. Worried now, her mother squats down, takes the girl by the shoulders and shakes her lightly, once more insisting that her daughter should give up such silly 'maginings. Amy notes the rising anxiety in her mother's voice and backs off. An upset Mummy was not a pleasant prospect.

She would have to wait for another opportunity to bring the good news of salvation from unhappiness and death.

But now her mother kneels on the linoleum and looks deep into her daughter's eyes. Eye to eye, she asks the girl to forget about the world she has so newly discovered. Make believe is not real life.

§

Amy leaves the church and retraces her steps through the cemetery towards Cony Green, where cricket is packing up for the afternoon. She feels worn out by the desperate quest to smuggle Aslan into church. He simply would not fit. There was no room for the noble king of the Narnian forest amongst the neat pews, and certainly no place for him next to the silver mannikin reigning over the sanctuary. It was all too tidy, too domesticated, too small to accommodate Aslan.

At the lychgate she pauses, thinking to hear a leonine footfall behind her amongst the graves, but looking back there is nobody.

Near this gate to the churchyard a man in a raincoat once approached her. She greeted him politely, as she had been brought up to address strangers. The man surveyed the urchin and bent to whisper in her ear, "Would you like to see a cock?" Thinking he meant a cockerel she said yes, she would very much like to see a cock.

He led her back along the cemetery path beneath the drooping yews to a secluded spot, unbuttoned his fly and produced a limp morsel of flesh. Amy, who was surveying the undergrowth in search of the bird, only belatedly noticed what had been produced for her inspection. The man was sweating.

Startled, she felt embarrassment rather than fear at this extraordinary behaviour. Willies were a very private matter. She had only ever seen one, by accident. She excused herself politely and scooted off down the path to Cony Green, quelling her impulse to run, as that would appear rude. Later she told her mother she had met the man and, after some desultory conversation such as one has with a nine-year-old, the situation became starkly clear to her mother, who promptly rang the local police station.

Soon she found herself in the back of a police car, cruising the neighbourhood and looking for the man in the raincoat.

"Did he have black hair, like Constable Perrett here," the policeman in the front passenger seat questioned her, indicating their driver, "Or ginger hair like me?"

"Oh, ginger, like you," she replied, adoringly.

She had been in Uncle Ron's car often, but this one was bigger and had a lot more dials on the dashboard, together with two men in uniform who had nothing better to do all afternoon than to drive her around. She pointed out Trigger in his paddock, told them he was her horse. She pointed out Ian Carmichael's house and prattled on about the time Ian had shot her with her own bow and arrow, right between the eyes. She felt some satisfaction in traducing Ian in this way. Fortunately the bamboo arrow was not sharpened and the bow was loosely strung, but she had a purple bruise exactly where her third eye was. Did the policemen know about the third eye?

"Was he tall, like Constable Perrett, or short, like me?"

"Like you," she trilled.

They never caught sight of the man who had accosted her.

§

She feels a great sadness accumulating like rain clouds as she trudges homeward. She comforts herself with the thought that when she reaches her tenth birthday she will be grown up – a most desirable state. That date is not far off. If she must give up Aslan in order to grow up then she will do so, in spite of the pain.

For seventeen years Amy has searched for another Aslan, who would fit into the grown-up world. Sometimes she catches a hint of those childhood hours when a leonine presence with honeyed breath embraced her, or hears a trace of grave laughter echoing down the years. Her heart never quite gave up the memory – the sound of the golden horn as she named it. But this memory became a curse, for nothing, no-one, was good enough to match the lost childhood friend whom she never quite could give up.

14

Truculent would best describe Amy's mood this morning, as she makes herself a cup of tea and sits down at her desk in the office. It is cool, the central heating has not yet removed the chill of the July night. The sun is rising on the ramparts of the Union Buildings, just visible from where she sits. No-one else will be in the office for another hour. As usual, she has dropped Wolf off at the theatre workshops for a seven o'clock start and come straight into the city to work.

Last night was the penultimate meeting of the Life in the Spirit seminar at her local parish church. This involved the laying on of hands, an event which Alfred trumpeted about, declaring that after this experience she would never be the same again, a prospect which appalled and terrified her in equal measure. It was indeed a ghastly experience, which came at the end of the meeting when she was obliged to surrender to the Holy Spirit. A dozen eager, sweaty hands descended upon her person, messing up her hair, massaging her shoulders, whilst a babble of voices held forth about driving out evil spirits, and, even more embarrassing, begging for the gift of tongues to fall upon her. She gritted her teeth and prayed fervently that no such mortification would ensue.

Alfred had prescribed the Life in the Spirit seminars for her spiritual well-being – attendance was not optional. Said that she would enjoy it. Well, he was dead wrong there. She baulked at the notion of going back to church at all – the very thought was excruciating, for she felt only contempt for an institution which had delivered so much pain and loss to her family. When she eventually sidled into the local church one Sunday morning her initial feeling was one of humiliation to be returning as an ordinary person, instead of the vicar's daughter. But she swallowed her pride and asked humbly if she might join the Life in the Spirit seminar. They were delighted, thrilled! They were all over her like a rash, as if she had wandered in from heathen lands afar, begging her to feel welcome to join their cosy little huddle.

The people at the Wednesday night Life in the Spirit meetings lived up to all her prejudices. They were shallow, offensively middle-class, and relentlessly nice. The Anglican Church in South Africa at this time was in the grip of the charismatic movement, which was shaking its respectable foundations. This pentecostal revolution had come from the very top after the Archbishop of Cape Town had been overwhelmed by the Holy Spirit one Sunday morning, "between The Sunday Times and the pink gin," as he put it.

The archbishop's baptism in the Holy Spirit happened in his own chapel at Bishopscourt. He felt an inner urge to visit the chapel while he was reading the newspaper, after celebrating in the cathedral that morning. "But I have nothing more to say to you, Lord!" he protested, regaling his audience with the story. However, he was obedient to the call, and lo, in his own chapel was laid prostrate by a life-changing experience. He had been spreading the good news of life in the Holy Spirit ever since. Other South African bishops were infected by the joy and had taken the message to the world-wide Lambeth Conference, where it was received with scepticism. The renegade bishops were reputed to have been seen one night dancing around the high altar in Canterbury Cathedral, but Anglicans would not believe such rumours.

Amy had seen the archbishop in person – a lugubrious man, immensely tall – addressing a packed cathedral in the city. Alfred had signalled that he was coming to Pretoria, in a tone of voice which suggested Amy may like to be there. She arrived late, barefoot, and walked the length of the packed nave to sit in the front row, so truculent was she, and, it has to be said, a little drunk.

Sunday services were also part of the package, in the gospel according to Alfred. For several months she rocked up faithfully, if sullenly, to St Wilfrid's Sunday morning eucharist. The new church was still under construction so services took place in the parish hall. It was all rather makeshift to someone brought up in the venerable sanctuaries of the Church of England.

Then there were the hymns – ghastly cocktails of jollity and sentimentality, during which people waved their arms and affected rapt expressions – even at times, God help us, weeping. A few of the lyrics got her goat so badly she could not refrain from scowling, and refused even to pretend to sing along. 'Take my silver and my gold, not a mite would I withhold' was cringeworthy hypocrisy, with the impoverished black township of Mamelodi a stone's throw away. 'We'll protect each man's dignity and guard each man's pride' was equally offensive, sung heartily by a wealthy white congregation. Was the irony only apparent to her?

Parishioners were kind to Amy, but gingerly, treating her as if she were an unexploded bomb. She would not let down her guard. At times it seemed as if she watched these people through the wrong end of binoculars, as if they were distant, toy town figures, mouthing words she could not hear. She found this faintly amusing, watching their words rise like bubbles from their lips, whilst sneering at them from behind her eyes. How foolish they were, believing they could rope her into their comfy little circle.

During the Life in the Spirit seminars held in the sitting room at the rectory, they would encourage her to share her thoughts with the group. "What do you think, Amy?" the leader would say, ingratiatingly. She found it difficult to say anything at all. She felt scruffy at these meetings, no matter how well she washed herself beforehand. Increasingly she felt like a rare specimen, goggled at by these people, who were so nervous of anything out of the ordinary. Their tentative kindness was like a red rag to a bull. She said shocking things to frighten them, and soon it became obligatory for her to come up with some outrageous remark for them to titter over.

For one thing she simply couldn't stand the Jesus cult. She had nothing against him personally, but what she could not hack was the way people, especially the women, swooned over him and spoke his name in silly, simpering voices. On one occasion Amy remarked that Jesus was just a goody gumdrops and she would much rather follow someone with a bit of character, which caused something of a stir.

Jesus was clearly the Father's favourite and she felt locked out of this cosy arrangement. Not only because she was a miserable sinner, which she was prepared to admit, conditionally, on Alfred's orders, but because she was a girl. There was clearly no future for girls in the all-male sanctuary with an all-male God. There was something unholy about women. Women were only allowed behind the altar rail to arrange flowers and polish the brass, and had to be well out of the way before the real action began.

This unhappy situation might have galvanised Amy to take up the cudgels for women's rights, but such an idea just didn't occur to her. She simply accepted the consensus of opinion handed down for millennia. And decided she wanted to be a monk. After all, she had held down a man's job in a man's world on board ship, and the possibility of somehow joining a monastery did not seem too far-fetched in her imagination. She was also used to getting her own way.

§

One evening in April Amy phones the priory and declares that she wants to join the Community. Fr Frank takes the call, and sounds appalled. "But this is a men's community!" he cries, with an undertone of horror that raises her hackles.

"I know," she says, as kindly and gently as she can. "I want to join the tertiaries." Alfred has told her about the tertiaries, people who are indentured to the life of the Community but live in the ordinary world.

Fr Frank's relief at this clarification is palpable. He goes to fetch Fr Cuthbert, who thinks it is a great joke, a jolly good show, and says she must come and see him next time she is in town. But currently there is a log jam in this line of investigation. Alfred says that she will be obliged to make her confession regularly if she joins the tertiaries. And no, he cannot hear her confession because he is not an ordained priest. He is merely a lay brother. Amy is stumped by this. The notion of discussing her faults with anyone else is out of the question.

Her future as a tertiary is still blowing in the wind on the morning after the Life in the Spirit seminar, when Amy settles down at her desk with a cup of coffee and watches the sun rise on the Union Buildings.

She is so grateful that she did not dissolve into tears, or worse, into gibberish, at the Life in the Spirit seminar last night. Such tactile encounter with people for whom she feels such aversion had been a shock. It felt like being mauled. Their hands on her head and arms felt clammy, some were trembling, all were invasive. Their prayers called for some kind of exhibition, as if she were a seal expected to jump through hoops, or to give birth to something – to pray in tongues. Praying in tongues had become the cachet of the charismatic movement. People said it doesn't matter one way or the other, whether one does or one doesn't – but it does matter! People pray in tongues at the drop of a hat in church to prove they can, although it is supposed to be something one does in private. Anyone who is known to pray in tongues has definitely got the Holy Spirit, and is rated as a gold standard Christian.

Does Alfred pray in tongues, she wonders, rolling a few syllables experimentally around her mouth, smacking her lips the way he does when he's thinking of something nice to eat? It's easy, pleasant almost, to whisper sounds like little puffs of air. Soon whole words come unbidden to her lips with a strangely familiar sweetness, although she can make no sense of them. Slowly, reverently, she spills these words into the cool, quiet morning air.

It is utterly absorbing, this conversation which she is having with herself, although she cannot understand a word of it. After a while she thinks she ought to tell someone – not that she really wants to. This seems to be a deeply private conversation, intimate, something one does not tell other people about – or only someone entirely trustworthy, like Alfred. She would prefer to keep this precious secret to herself, safe from prying eyes.

For three days this intimate monologue continues, *sotto voce*, in Amy's interior world. From time to time her tongue gently touches her teeth, her upper palate, sensuously tasting the unknown words as they float into the ether. It annoys her when mundane tasks demand her attention, separating her for a while from the amniotic fluid in which this new language bathes her. She feels safe here. As if nothing on earth can ever harm her again.

15

On Saturday Amy drives over to Nazareth House to tell Alfred face to face about what has happened to her. It seems sacrilegious to talk about such things on the telephone. She feels bashfully proud, as if she were pregnant – a little afraid of talking about it in case it's not true, or that something might take it away. What exactly 'it' is, she does not know, but confidently expects that Alfred will tell her.

The big community room, which she remembers from six months before as such a hollow space, is now carpeted with golden haircord. Sunlight spills through the bay window. Traffic sounds are muted now. The house is light and airy, warmth and quietude reign in this room which had trembled with the roar of Hillbrow's streets such a short time ago – although it feels like a lifetime to Amy.

Sundry bodies are disposed about the carpet in an untidy crescent. Alfred is there – praying as usual. Some of the men are snoozing, one snores gently. Womenfolk sprawl, some smoking. Alfred has a bible open on the floor in front of him, but he is away in another dimension. No-one seems to mind; in fact the company seems to be happily soaking up the peace and quiet. Those who are not already sleeping appear to drop off at intervals, cigarettes drooping perilously from slack fingers.

Later on Alfred makes time for her in a proper interview in his untidy study, across the hall from the community room. But she does not know what to say, how to broach the perilous subject of what has happened to her. He sits patiently, waiting. That is one thing about Alfred – there is always time. Time seems to bend around him. With Alfred one gets to places on time although one started out already late.

At last she spills it out in a rush; embarrassed, blushing, garbling the account, running out of words… wringing her hands. He smiles, calls her Ames, which becomes his pet name for her (although sometimes he forgets her name altogether). Something wonderful has happened, he tells her. She has been given a great gift and he is proud of her. She feels an immense sense of relief. She is proud of her, although she is none the wiser as to what it all means.

Painfully conscious that she is taking up a busy man's time – book-lined studies have that effect upon her – she demands to know what she should do next? What is required of her in response to this mysterious gift? Alfred suggests that she should just enjoy her new relationship; get to know her Lord a bit better. But this seems to her to be inadequate. She does not want to be dilly dallying, when one should be putting one's nose to the grindstone, getting on with the job. She is anxious to embark, to be on the road, picking up the traces. She wants to be useful.

Alfred wanders over to a bookcase and takes down three slim volumes entitled *The Spiritual Man*, by Watchman Nee. He says that sometime, in the next few months, he would like her to read them. She receives the three purple volumes as if they were the holy grail. She promises to read, learn and inwardly digest. And to faithfully return the books to him soon... very soon. "There's no hurry," says Alfred mildly.

~16~

Amy has read *The Spiritual Man* again since that time. On the second reading it seemed just like a normal book. She found it interesting, but not in any way remarkable. It did not turn her world upside down. During the second reading she will be irritated by the gender specific title, although now she does not notice it. Later, when she learns that the author is a Confucian scholar who is also a Christian, she will wonder if it was the oriental culture from which he came that equipped him to annihilate everything she had ever believed in, when she first read his book.

The three volumes are stacked in front of her. She hefts the first one in her hand. It is a paperback, cool and slim. She sits at her desk at home, a carafe of wine beside her. Rough red Tassenheimer is sold in two litre bottles; dark viscous liquid contained in green glass. She opens volume one of *The Spiritual Man*. She would rather put off her first glass of wine, so that she can do a good swag of reading before losing the thread. But the wine has a magnetic attraction. She stares at the carafe, which seems to stretch sinuously, as if she views it through a fish eye lens. She shudders, and pours a glass.

Amy's mind retains the shape of Watchman Nee's thesis to this day. The human being is made up of three essential natures – the material body, the soul, and the spirit. She brings to this encounter the usual carpet bag of prejudices from her anglo saxon protestant upbringing. That the body is bad – especially women's bodies – mostly because of sex, but also because of drink and greed. The soul by contrast is good – the bit God likes, although one would be reticent in public about actually having one. Spirit is something of an intrusion in the civilised human being, something not quite nice, pagan, diaphanous – analogous to 'soul' in church parlance. She has mental reservations about Nee's anthropology – but if this is what it takes, what Alfred requires of her, she's game.

She reads for ten days, to all intents and purposes going about her normal business. No-one notices that after a few days she is as present to her outward circumstances as a zombie; a nominal being with vestigial sensory attachments to the outside world. Her exterior life is operating on automatic pilot.

She reads whenever and wherever there is a space in the diurnal round, pulling the progressively dog-eared volumes from her handbag, from her desk drawer, from under her pillow. She reads voraciously. But the truth is, she is being read. The text has her entirely in its thrall. It possesses her like a vortex, a one-way rite of passage. There will be no way back to her former life.

Afterwards, for years, she cannot remember what occurred in there — in the vortex. If she tried to force her mind to recall that passage a dolorous headache wells in her skull, like a warning, like a foghorn bawling *Danger!* The skin of her scalp creeps, as if recoiling from the memory.

One thing is certain. There is no relationship between the person who went into that vortex, and the being who eventually came out. That person, the one before, was a different creature altogether from the life-form which emerges, fragile, blinking, from the silken cocoon spun around her old self during those ten days of devotional reading.

The ordeal begins relatively harmlessly, with Nee plucking out her little prejudices and illusions one by one. Having been formed in the school of hard knocks — in her own opinion, that is — she greets these little deaths of lifelong attachments with a curl of the lip: "Didn't hurt!"

Loyalty, for instance, that treasured virtue for which she would lay down her life. Loyalty, she reads, merits naught in the ethereal world of the spirit. Loyalty is merely a symptom of the soul's attachment. For, contrary to her former beliefs, the soul — repository of that intense and private life she entertains in her poetry, whence comes, occasionally, the sound of the golden horn — her soul is merely a servant of the spirit. Her great loves and yearnings, her dreams, achievements and high aspirations are mere manifestations of life below stairs, in the world of the spirit. Heroism, adventure and self-sacrifice in the service of high ideals are all, in short, self-indulgence.

Up there, in the spiritual realm where Alfred dwells, that enigmatic cloudscape whose chilly fingers claim everything they touch, up there — it slowly becomes clear to Amy — everything that is dear to her will simply vanish.

There is a critical mass of loss after which the human being cannot survive. From this point on a mind cannot lose any more of its landscape without disintegrating. This hiatus is what awaits Amy after a week of reading *The Spiritual Man*.

She waits, passive on the executioner's block, waiting for the coup de grâce. She understands finally that all she held dear is a delusion. No vestige of her former self will survive. But worse than any other dreadful thing she has encountered on this journey is the nightmare that Alfred is really the high priest of some fiendish cult that now has her in its grasp. She has become a living sacrifice to her own sinful attraction to him. She should never have dared to approach him. She ventured where angels fear to tread, and now she must bear the consequences. Which she cannot bear; for nothing is left of her.

Nothing relates to anything else any more. Her life is stripped down like the parts of a car laid out randomly on an oily tarpaulin. She feels she is looking down on this chaos of spare parts without the faintest notion of how to put herself back together again.

Wedded by upbringing to the notion of sacrifice, she feels obliged to do the commitment thing again – the handing over of her life to God, like at the Life in the Spirit seminar, only properly this time. That had been a bit of a joke, that time she gave her life to Jesus at the rectory, all the while snarling silently at the trite phrases she was obliged to repeat, but doing it anyway, for Alfred. Now, like an exhausted animal gathering itself for one last shot at life, or death, or whatever crouches on the other side of this final act, she gives herself up.

She seems to be on the brink of a high cliff, so high its base has vanished in darkness. Here, she understands, she must throw herself off, in faith that she will sprout wings, or plunge to perdition. She is aware of herself as tiny, like an ant, lost in an inner vastness. It takes a long time to gather strength, recoiling again and again from that nauseating abyss, before she finally musters enough courage to make the leap of faith.

As from a catapult her body – or the body in her inward eye – springs. But in the instant before her feet actually leave terra firma an invisible force snatches her back. It feels like an angelic arm clad in chain mail, its torque is palpable, strong as Thor, more adamant than the doors of Hades. It knocks her to her knees.

She is devastated – she is gutted, bruised, by this interdict. For it seems as if powers beyond her imagining have deemed her unfit to make this sacrifice, this ultimate gift of herself.

Following this humiliating event which occurs after seven days of travelling inward, and for the remainder of her journey through this purgatory, a gong reverberates at irregular intervals in her skull.

$§$

Once again she is alone in her city office. Her colleagues are out for the afternoon. A storm, unusual in the Highveld winter, bruises the sky deep purple over the Union Buildings. The gong in her head pounds the far frontiers of her consciousness, as if it stretches across the void of the universe. Sonorous, deep, far-reaching, this sound absorbs all being into itself; all memory, all thought, all senses are drowned in its reverberations.

The genesis of the sound may have been in little pluckings of feathers of illusion; *pluck, pluck*, each little loss a pain, aggregating over time to larger pain, until nothing is left but this starveling creature which is herself, featherless, suspended here in outer space, bruised by the pulse of the cosmos.

For she is alone. She has ventured where no human being has ever gone before. She gazes at the endless night lit by stars – one pale blue distant planet her own, and knows for certain that no-one on earth can know what has happened to her.

In time the interval between pulses becomes more painful than the impact itself. Waiting for the satanic blow is worse than its arrival.

She knows, as if in some distant memory, that she is in her office in the city. It is afternoon and a storm is thrashing the Union Buildings. No-one else is here. Probably she is in great pain, but she is not really sure if she feels anything at all. Normal parameters have vanished and she has no means of discerning whether she is dead or alive. Why, only this morning she looked in the full length mirror on the verandah at home, and there was nobody there! That was when she knew for certain that no human being could survive the maelstrom she was in. *Ergo* – she is dead.

The end comes quietly; almost stealthily. In deep space, in the womb of the universe, a sable form emerges from eternal darkness. Immutable, moving with indomitable power, this inky mass glides towards her, absorbing everything in its path, swallowing all things into its own amorphous being. Nothing can escape.

It would be untrue to say that Amy is frightened by this presence, which seems intensely personal, organic, omnivorous. Amy is beyond fear. She is beyond dread. There is nothing more to fear when there is nothing left. Awe would be a good word; but awe means some body is there to respond to that which is awful. She is no where. She is no thing. Even moving a finger, or a thought, is beyond her power.

What does shock her senses into a quiver of life is the realisation that the thing has *no gender.* Why this should be so shocking is a mystery. Then it passes her by.

A long time after that the universe lifts its skirt a little to reveal – human feet. A wisp of humour in the air, a wink almost, restores Amy instantly to common sense.

She feels newly minted. She senses no trace of the torment and chaos of past days. Light-headed she regards thunder clouds over the Union Buildings, her heart quickening with joy, and slowly she smiles.

Mount Anderson is three hours drive from Pretoria; a featureless journey east across the plains of the Highveld before turning northwards. Amy drives while Wolf and Roger quaff beer, regaling each other with hackneyed stories of mountain escapades. Wolf gives his throaty guffaw at intervals, slapping his thigh, roaring, *"Ach was haben wir gelacht!"*

Beer in the early morning hours tastes like forbidden fruit, supped before dawn as the darkened landscape speeds by. As day comes the veld gives up its contours, bursting into bronze vistas as the sun god strides aloft for another day's reign in his cobalt heaven.

Once, on their way to the Lowveld, they stopped to visit God's Window on the Eastern escarpment, where the land falls away for more than two thousand feet. The place is an outlook, an eyrie with a view bestriding the Kruger National Park to the Lebombo Mountains in Mozambique, and a hint of the distant Indian Ocean.

Wolf and Amy tread tentatively on the fragile platform named God's Window, gazing at the vast canvas of pastel hues painted over the subcontinent. The panorama is warmed by the winter sun, although up here the air is chill. Far below them an eagle circles, a Lammergeier, scanning the ravines for breakfast. Wisps of cloud thread through the sheer precipices of the escarpment, which tumbles down and down into pre-dawn darkness.

Wolf moots the possibility of climbing over the safety fence, better to see down into the dizzying abyss. Amy shudders, turns away and strides back to the car. She is not in the mood for horseplay. The sheer grandeur of the view catches her throat and makes her want to weep. It is an old wound. Helplessness in the face of such beauty, an aching desire to somehow share it, overshadowed by a nameless fear.

Two more cars belonging to their party are on the road. They are scheduled to meet for brunch at the foot of Mount Anderson, before beginning the climb. They will carry food supplies in their rucksacks for the two-day hike on the mountain, but no tents or fuel as the trail is furnished with mountain huts.

By the time they reach the base camp the others have already lit a braai with wood provided at the spot, and boerwors is sizzling, alongside billies of mealiepap and rich onion and tomato sauce.

From now on rations will be limited to rice and dried vegetables boiled up with dehydrated egg and meat. Brandy will take the place of beer because it is lighter to carry.

§

Clouds cloak the seven and a half thousand foot peak, rolling steadily down the mountainside. Wraiths of condensation begin to finger the walkers, who are strung out along the narrow track. Amy has chosen to be last in line, relishing the solitude, the quietness broken only by the sound of her boot dislodging a stone, by the mournful *hoop-hoop* of a coucal announcing rain. Silence thickens as cloud envelopes the walkers who climb steadily into its foggy embrace. Each one becomes hermetically sealed, warmed only by their own breath and blood, hearing nothing but the muffled sound of boots padding on dirt. There is no fear of getting lost. The path is well-worn. The first walkers will reach the rest hut well before dark.

Visibility is down to a few yards; there will be no views today. But this suits Amy's purpose. She feels as fragile as a bird's egg. Her mind flinches from the memory of the past few weeks, the odyssey which swallowed her up as she read Alfred's books. She tests her legs, the supple flex of ankles and knees; she swings her arms, curls her fingers – all seems to be in good fettle. She is mildly surprised, as if her body ought to be in some way crippled by the galactic journey from which she has so recently, remarkably, returned.

Amy does not yet know about psychoses. Her mind, the neurons, the filaments through which she ordinarily views the world, has passed through the eye of a needle. There is a primary disconnect between her life before that rite of passage, and the person who is now climbing up Mount Anderson. If she is indeed still a person? Even that seems in doubt. But here she is, walking, thinking, hoping against all odds that life may go on. Amy has determined to clean house. She cannot let the grass grow under her feet. Her days of rebellion are over.

Confession was never part of her religious upbringing but Alfred has suggested she might give it a whirl. Said it made one feel newborn, like cleaning house. Said that he cannot hear her confession himself as he is not a priest. But she cannot imagine baring her soul to anyone else, particularly a stranger. Perhaps if she does it on her own first, by way of practice, it will not be too ghastly when she has to do it in the flesh in front of a priest?

She remembers her father once telling her how an untruth creates the first crack in one's personal universe. How one lie builds upon another, gradually; one deceit, another white lie, until one loses sight of the truth altogether. She does not want any cracks in her life, which has suddenly become immeasurably precious to her. Cloaked now in cloud, plodding up the narrow mountain path, Amy begins a review of the life of that person who lived in her skin until a couple of weeks ago.

She intends to lay bare all her imperfections, the things she has done wrong, her lies, deceits, all her omissions, and her downright wickedness. A frightening prospect, even in this clammy solitude, far from prying eyes. She fears punishment, but mortal dread of divine wrath has retreated apace. After all, the worst has already happened. No human being could have endured the ordeal she has recently passed through. Death has claimed her. Her life seems ephemeral now, she may not even be able to feel pain. But still, she fears remembering the past.

§

When Amy was three years old she assaulted a baby at the post-natal clinic. Amy's mother had left her to play in the toddlers' pen while she took baby Jonathan to be weighed. Amy was on top of the slide, which seemed to be very high off the floor, when she spied an unattended babe in its pram nearby. Swiftly she slid down, crept to where the baby slept peacefully, coddled in its white wool, pinched the infant's cheek – hard, with her nails – until it bled and the child bawled its shock and indignation. Whereupon Amy scooted back up the slide to await developments. Glee, like a warm bath, washed over her as the baby's mother came running, yelped with horror, cupped the tiny wounded face in her hands. Wept.

This was not the only occasion that Amy assaulted other children. Once whilst idly dangling her legs over the garden wall, she cajoled a little boy who was loitering below into showing her his bottle. He was taking it back to the shop to redeem it for a penny. "Gis a look," she wheedled, smiling wolfishly, promising to give it back at once – she only wanted a squiz. The lad explained that he would be in trouble if he lost the bottle, but, intimidated by the great height from which she addressed him, reached up to show it to her. She snatched her prize from his grasp, jumped down behind the wall and ran off, relishing the sound of wails and vain entreaties from the distraught lad.

Then she was caught red-handed. The next door baby was sometimes left out in the sunshine on the lawn in his pram. The garden was shared by the vicarage and the curate's house, whose windows overlooked the back lawn. Amy was spotted poking a twig down the baby's little red throat, while it roared with rage. She was confined to her room, after a thorough spanking, and spent the afternoon gloomily watching her brother play in the sunshine in the garden below, plotting revenge in her heart.

Violence has a strange attraction for Amy. She remembers with pain one afternoon at Uncle Ron's house when she was occupied, as usual, in the pond. She fished a newt from the water, inspected it closely, threw it in the air, and gave it a serve with her hand as if it were a tennis ball. She will never forget Uncle Ron's shocked face. Or the sight of the tiny reptile which landed on a rock and pulsed blood from its mouth, before slipping back into the water. The really bizarre aspect of this crime was that she loved newts. She didn't love babies. The sound of a baby crying made her angry. She could not understand all the fuss over such annoying little bundles of pooh and piss.

And then there was that day when she was nine, watching her father build a hutch for Bunny. It was a masterpiece of carpentry, with a steeply sloped roof clad in shingles, offering the hare wide views through chicken wire frontage. It had a snug, adjoining bedroom with its own door for mucking out the straw.

Amy stares at the back of her father's neck, for he is kneeling at his task. It occurs to her how easy it would be to kill him with a single blow to the neck, the place where his curly hair meets the soft flesh. This thought frightened her so much, so shocked her, so flooded her with guilt, that she gave up carrying her six-guns. In fact, on reflection, Amy cannot remember ever going about as a cowboy again.

Her best friend Ted, who was born on the same day as she was, but twenty minutes earlier which gave him seniority, played cowboys and Indians with her after school. She was always the

Indian, always tied to a tree, whooped round about and beaten with a stick, and eventually shot. It seemed unfair that she should never be the cowboy, but she accepted the argument that Ted was older so got to choose, and even after a while began to enjoy the role of victim.

Childhood dealt with, causing nothing more gruelling than flushes of embarrassment, Amy now turns to the monster lurking in the primeval swamp – sex. She heard about sex first at primary school and the rumours caused Amy to announce that she would never marry. "Ho ho ho," chuckled the parents at the dinner table, the usual venue for her public declarations. "You will grow up and marry and have babies like everybody else." This of course only strengthened Amy's resolve not to.

§

She investigated the various orifices of her body which were hidden in the thick darkness of a region which was taboo in normal conversation. Whilst playing doctors and nurses between the bedsheets with her school friend Pamela, she was surprised to find not two but three apertures in the tender groin of her friend. She felt a tide of fear and pleasure flush through her body, together with the tamperings and penetrations of childish fingers.

Later, after the family had moved to the west country, she learned the power of shame. One evening lying in her bath – a few inches of lukewarm water – gazing dreamily at the ceiling, she noticed a trapdoor giving access to the attic. It suddenly occurred to her, out of nowhere, that the angels could see her. Perhaps even God could see her! She covered her newly budding breasts, the blond fluff between her legs, and shrank with embarrassment.

By then it was the early 'sixties. A great gulf had opened up between the older generation and the newly-invented species of teenager. Outright alienation between the generations came with the advent of the long-haired Liverpool pop group The Beatles, and the even more depraved Rolling Stones. Sex and culture had married – or skipped marriage as the case turned out to be. One could not talk about one without involving the other. In adults' conversation the Beatles and the Rolling Stones usually got the blame for the moral breakdown of one's generation. Which wasn't helpful when trying to fossick through the thickets of adolescent emotions.

Amy chose to explore the business of sex with the boy next door, under the billiard table in his parents' front room, where they were left alone in the afternoons to do their homework. Which they did, with increasing pleasure and skill, although always stopping short of going all the way. Amy had her first orgasm under the billiard table, and wondered what on earth it could be. She described the overwhelming rush of heat, the ecstatic light-headedness to Simon, but he didn't know what it was either.

She was sixteen, and much better informed, when she formally lost her virginity. Amy stops and sits down on a boulder patched with orange lichen. She takes a drink of mountain stream water laced with brandy from the canteen clipped to her rucksack.

She is suddenly suffused with shame by these recollections of her youthful lasciviousness – a word she has recently learned. She jibs at this exposure of past sins, matters which have been as good as forgotten, until now. But she nerves herself, knowing that this must be done, now, on this climb. She hopes that by some sleight of hand this ritual act of purification on the hike will excuse her from mentioning the worst bits when she makes her confession; matters she will now suffer the remembrance of, and leave here, on the mountain.

§

The painted narrow boat lifts gently on the swell from a passing barge. The young couple in the rear cabin lie entwined on a blue eiderdown, sprawled on the double bunk, gazing into each others' eyes, breathless, open-mouthed. He whispers, "Can I?" She nods, almost imperceptibly.

They have been together for more than a year and spend most Saturday nights petting in the back of his car, after drinks at the pub. Sometimes a policeman stops at the lay-by where they are parked and shines his torch through the window into her face to enquire, "Alright, Miss?"

He is much older than she is. Gently, slowly, he does it, but holds himself back for fear of making her pregnant. Afterwards she is engulfed by sadness and turns away from him to watch a pair of white swans glide past the cabin window.

Everyone thought she would marry him. Indeed, she thought so herself. Perversely, she sent him away on an adventure to broaden his horizons, weeping copiously for days after his plane flew overhead, away to the other side of the world.

Later she found that having a lover abroad, who wrote beautiful letters every week, suited her almost better than seeing him each weekend. The romantic conceit of keeping a lover on the other side of the world, the longing, the absence, had a seductive melancholy about it.

§

Amy stirs from her rock, shoulders her pack and heads on up into the mist. There is no wind, the cloud squats sullenly around the mountain. She must catch up with the others before nightfall.

Ahead of her like a road block, like a giant pothole in the path, like a rockfall, the next chapter of her confession awaits.

It was the night the men landed on the moon. Amy was just out of high school, working as a barmaid for the summer holidays in a swanky city hotel. The awkward tomboy had by now grown into a leggy young woman. One of the hotel managers, a pretty lad who claimed he was of royal blood – Russian, in exile – had asked her out clubbing with him after her shift ended at 10.30pm.

She waited for him in the foyer; was still waiting when the cocktail barman came off duty. He reported that the manager had left already, but he would take her out instead. Mortified at being jilted by the Russian count she accepted the Irish barman's invitation without a second thought. They must just go back to his flat so he could change, he said. Which they did. He did change his clothes there; but in the course of doing it he raped her.

She resisted and things became moderately violent, before she gave in. Afterwards he was polite, as if nothing serious had happened. Being a well-brought up young woman she responded to his politeness in kind. By then there did not seem to be much point in making a fuss. Docile, she went with him to the night club for drinks before he drove her home. She had gin and tonic. Amy cannot stand the stuff to this day.

When she arrived home her father and brother were watching the moon landing on television. She has a vague recollection of fuzzy figures in white pneumatic suits cavorting about. She went to bed and stayed there for three days, complaining of a bad cold.

She told no-one; had never told anyone what happened to her the night the men landed on the moon. The barman called at the house and left flowers – pink carnations. She loathes pink carnations. When she finally returned to the hotel he appeared once in the pub where she worked, but she snatched up a paring knife from behind the bar, its blade winking malevolently at him, and he did not come back.

Rage, guilt and grief are a potent cocktail. Amy pants, but not from the climb. She squeezes her eyes shut, and shakes the condensation (warm and salty) from her lashes. She feels uncomfortably hot and stops to tear off her jacket; then she feels ice in her veins and puts it back on again.

"I'm sorry; I'm sorry," she murmurs, slogging onward, grateful for the enveloping mist. God can see her now, she knows it. She squirms under that searing gaze, trying fruitlessly to calm her mind; that menagerie with its caged animals shrieking, bawling, and, God help her, fornicating behind her eyes.

After the moon landing Amy changed. Until that night she had felt special; chosen almost. She had a vague but persistent notion that she was keeping herself for something; someone. That she mustn't put herself about. Had in fact suffered at the hands of her peers for being standoffish, for being a prude.

During the next three years Amy put herself about with gusto; but she cannot bear to think about that now. She hears muffled sounds up ahead where the gang are making themselves at home for the night, up at the rest hut.

§

The log cabin is set in a verdant gully, just below the tree line. The air is chilly at this time of year, the grass wet, but there is a newly-lit fire, over which a cast iron pot hangs from a tripod of stakes. Amy breathes in the scent of wood smoke, which wreathes a scene of quiet industry. The walkers are hushed from the day's exertion, unhurriedly going about the business of making camp for the night, which is now almost upon them.

There are plenty of bunks for the ten of them to choose from. No other hikers are out on the trail today. Amy bags a spot against the far wall of the cabin, although it will be colder there than with the others grouped in the centre. She craves solitude after the excoriating inner exercise of the day. She is exhausted, although the few hours easy hike would not normally tax her. Bone-weariness bids her lie down and sleep, but she would lose face if she flaked out at five o'clock. She pours three fingers of brandy into her tin mug and makes her way outside to join the others around the camp fire.

Several billy cans now steam in the ash rim of the fire, which has settled, its core a furnace beneath a carapace of charred wood. Feathers of smoke rise languidly. Firewood is brought to the hut by rangers who also maintain the water tank and the latrines – long-drop pit affairs set away from the cabin. No-one is talking, all are sitting quiet-eyed, regarding the theatre of fire and steam.

It occurs to Amy that people change as they walk up mountains. In the foothills there is little badinage between strangers, who keep themselves to themselves. Further up there are genial exchanges amongst walkers already en route. By nightfall, up here, conversation acquires a certain gravitas, as if the task of taking on the mountain has sobered even the silliest individual. For Amy has decided that these people she is with are rather silly. Superficial. A small demon nags in her ear. These people don't care about the deep things of life. Just the price of eggs, and how to manage the servants… and the kids. But up here even they are impressed by the impassive mountain, the deep silence as night cloaks their circle of fellowship.

Higher up, in the real mountains, hikers meeting along the track will pause to swap weather forecasts and local wisdom. Higher still, strangers will make camp together, and even share food which has been laboriously lugged so very far. On the summit there are no strangers, just human beings pitted against the mountain; where people have been known to lay down their lives for each other.

Amy feels the brandy dulling her remorse. Soon she will be swaddled comfortably in her sleeping bag, all pain asleep until the morning. How wonderful, she muses, that her ubiquitous angst vanishes, even from memory, with the balm of alcohol. She can't recall the shame of the day. It is like trying to remember how it feels to be cold when basking in the heat of summer. One knows cold exists; but one has no means of actually feeling it.

Dinner is rice with a stew of rehydrated vegetables and beef, doled steaming onto enamel plates. Instant coffee laced with spirits lulls the company further into sleepy silence, broken by an occasional reflection on the day: the weather – miserable; the track – easy but set to improve tomorrow; a snake sighting – impossible at this time of year. By seven o'clock everyone is ready to turn in. A much heavier hike awaits them next day, along an undulating ridge unprotected from winds which are forecast for the morning.

Amy kicks open her sleeping bag; it is padded with duck-down, too hot while she is still flushed from the fire and the brandy, but she will be grateful for it when the cold seeps in later. Safe in the sanctuary of this opiate glow she wants to review that other journey, the inner pilgrimage she has made. That person, whose life she has reviewed today seems like a stranger; someone she met in a book. But she feels less revulsion for that stranger now; a lurking empathy causes her to murmur, before falling asleep, "I am sorry; I am so sorry."

~18~

3rd August 1977

Dear Alfred,

Today I went to church for the first time 'enlightened', with your books lying finished on my desk. I wasn't fighting tooth and nail as usual, kicking against the goads, about having to go to church. Now and then I had to sit down because my legs wouldn't hold me up. I remembered a warning in your book: "Borne down by custom... the disobedient should not be obeyed even by himself." Perhaps I have been humbled at last? I was afraid that if I passed out, or trembled like an animal, people in church would be frightened. I can't seem to blend in like a normal person.

I will never forget how I phoned you at the priory on Ash Wednesday, in some sort of a pickle, pleading with you to help me get away for a few days somewhere – a retreat or something. It was night-time and you said, as gently as possible with your teeth gritted, "It is Ash Wednesday you know?" I did know, but I had no idea of how much I was trespassing on your sacred space. You welcomed me anyway and that is why I am now able to welcome every invasion (almost) of my privacy, as if from an angel of God. You see how you teach me by example?

My inner ear hears two distinct voices of Alfred. One of them makes me feel like cuddling up and purring; the other I trip over myself to obey. The first time I heard the voice of authority from you was when I was generating all sorts of excuses why I should not attend the Life in the Spirit seminar. I was sure you were my way to the life of the Spirit, and if anyone were to lay hands on me it would be you. "Cleave to your Lord and him alone," thundered my Lord in Alfred's voice. How kind he is – and me going astray with his servant!

There was the same ring of authority in your words about those books: "I would like you to read..." you said. During the torment of those days reading *The Spiritual Man* I kept your words in my head as a talisman, to keep me safe through it all. Then came real despair, the night when I really needed to speak to you on the phone and I could not reach you. Then you became in my fevered imagination the high priest of some cult disposed to filling lunatic asylums with idiots like me, for I was surely out of my mind. Tongues seemed to be just another manifestation of insanity – which I employed anyway because I felt so utterly lost to the world and to myself.

These words always remained, after every trial, "I would like you to read…" And I did. And now my life is no longer my own.

6th August 1977

It is so wonderful, Alfred, to watch God's plan unfolding in me. Not looking back or forward, or wondering, or worrying or anything. Just constantly recapturing my errant mind; and letting truth unfold in its own time. Fifteen minutes ago I was resisting drinking a glass of wine – now, after a glass of wine I am less fearful of sharing these things with you.

9th August 1977

What a beautiful day it is. When will all telephones and letters cease to be necessary, when will sleep and darkness fade away forever? When will my sister here in the office stop worrying about the length of her eyelashes? How much longer must the mountains yearn? When will the plan be perfect?

I remember one early morning long ago at sea, where Portugal is just a purple smudge in the east, the last trace of the freezing smoke of Europe. The sky is a cupola rising from the disc of the sea, opaque like the inside of an egg, rising into azure, deeper and deeper blue until you are giddy from gazing. The ocean is calm and as deep as the sky. Far away for'ard the prow of our cradle rises and falls – maybe fifty feet with each long breath. Flying fish scatter like a welder makes sparks.

The young sun is already hot and you can't look at it, even this early in the day. You could fry eggs on the deck by noon. But the eye of the sun cannot fathom the depths of the sea. The sound of a rust hammer far away on deck is carried lazily upward on the morning air. The cook is frying bacon in the galley and you can smell coffee. Up here, above the bridge, near the funnel, you can feel the ship's heart beating beneath your feet. Below are a crew of thirty-five men of whom I am fond, afraid of, love, dislike – who are boring, fascinating – unknown. My arms lift themselves, my eyes weep, I sing silently to… I know not what.

16th August 1977

Slogging through sleet and cloud up Mount Anderson I was happy that I couldn't see the view. I thought it was probably good for me that I should battle up umpteen thousand feet to conquer a mountain, but be beaten by a cloud.

Doing nothing is very difficult, I find. After that time with your books – when I could feel my brain moving in my head, when I was aware of a deadly, persistent headache, although it did not hurt me physically – I found Wolf perusing thin air in the sitting room.

"What are you thinking of?" said I.

"Nothing," said Wolf, and raised those lucid sky-blue eyes of his. "Not so easy thinking of nothing you know."

Wolf still surprises me sometimes.

It's late and the old familiar ache returns. It is no longer something I want to drown in a bottle of whisky, or commit mental, emotional or any kind of suicide for. It is more real and solid than I am, this inchoate sorrow – and I must wait, maybe even longer than you have, for rest.

18th August 1977

There is always one who talks and one who listens. And the one who talks is not necessarily imparting information, or even asking the other anything. This one is holding a rambling but necessary conversation with herself to arrive at the ultimate hush.

Perhaps it is more lonely to have to listen, especially when the other actually believes she is conversing with her companion. It would be so simple to take the one who struggles to be understood, and shake her gently, and say, "Hush. Listen. I am here. I love you. That is enough." But there would be a swift glance of incomprehension, a "Yes, but..." and she'd be off again – in misery because she would believe the ear of her companion had not heard her complaint.

I want to wish you, "Top of the morning," but your phone is out of order. I checked with the exchange:

"Yes, it is definitely out of order."

"Do you know when it will be fixed?"

"Oh, it will be fixed if someone complains."

"I see. Well, I'm complaining."

"Have you complained?"

"Er, only to you."

"*Ja*, you must phone…"

It's still out of order.

I wish I was trotting around after you – carrying those things you keep in your pouch under your scapular, which makes you look like a kangaroo. But I'm not.

Top of the morning, Alfred. I wish you a listening ear, and an "I love you," and a hush, and a "well done".

20th August 1977

Today was a beautiful day and I wish I could have shared it with you, in real time rather than letters. What drives me to write to you? It is my favourite time of day when I write. I feel guilty because I so love it, but maybe I should be using this time for something else? After all sorts of weighings up and scruples, I proceed to write – if not with a blessing then at least with no outright guilt.

We ended up today at Wolf's friend Marius' flat. I made him play his guitar which he leaves lying around under his bed collecting dust. He sings with his beloved Judy, for only we are there and she's shy if there's a crowd. He hangs his harmonica around his neck and they sing songs he composed himself, harmonising perfectly, shyly looking into each other's eyes.

Marius said to me, "When you sing you sing from your stomach (I think he means 'heart'). You must be able to hold a candle in front of your mouth and it won't flicker when you sing". And what they sing! Words of eternal longing. When we leave he'll pack his guitar away again under the bed. But when we do go he says hopefully, "If you ever hear of anywhere I could play…?"

Yesterday we visited friends who live on a saddle between the hills high above Pretoria. The house has belonged to the family for generations. It is landscaped into the hill on both sides, not a house just plonked down where there is nothing, like so many properties. They farm, and tend their inheritance in every sense.

The old man next door is German and, like so many Germans, terribly shy. Our friends wanted to get to know this chap but they don't speak German. Wolf and I brought the old man over to say hallo. Then he said to me, "Go and fetch my wife" – not "please" or "will you?" – it was lovely, so typical. So I fetched her and the daughter came too – and the old man pottered in the garden with our friends, understanding each other very well in spite of the language difficulties.

Later we discussed language and found that words do not have meanings – they are given meanings to bridge the gap of understanding between speaker and hearer. Our friends understood German quite well after that.

St Francis called his body 'Brother Ass'. I find it an admirable description. Vulnerable and humble, but most of all slow, is Brother Ass. In comparison the mind moves like lightning. I have twenty-six years of memory to draw upon – and you have much more than that. It takes me five minutes to walk to the dairy to fetch the milk – but in my mind I can travel twenty years in a flash.

The spirit I cannot, and may not try, to look at. But there is a certain quality in sunlight, best expressed in a song I first heard seven years ago, "the shimmer of light as the seagull flies"; or in a shaft of sunlight swimming with golden motes of dust in an old library. Above the atmosphere the light is unseen, but it emanates from the sun and is reflected back by all it meets. Such is the spirit.

When I compare slow Brother Ass with the lightning of my mind, and then reflect on my true master I am… well, amazed. Here the poverty of words becomes evident. Better change the subject! It is very good to know that you would never call me a fool – even if I am foolish.

I feel it is a bit of a cheek to send you this pencil-written letter. A while ago I would have torn it up because it wasn't good enough. But I remember one of the first things you taught me – if I do things wrong even that will be used for a purpose.

P.S. You will be pleased to know that owing to a certain difficulty in breathing I have been forced to give up smoking.

P.P.S. Our postmistress lent me a stamp for this missive. Then she gave me this smart envelope, so you won't be presented with the usual tatty one. Say, "Bless her". She is sick and thinking about leaving the country to escape her children.

St Bede's retreat house is across the road from the priory where Alfred lives. The house is surrounded by a stone wall, over which the priory roof and bell tower are just visible through a lacework of trees burgeoning with spring leaves. Five nuns, clad in grey habits, live in the convent which is attached to the retreat house.

On the verandah at St Bede's, a dozen retreatants gather one late Friday afternoon, agog with the prospect of spending a weekend together. Amy is by far the youngest of this company, and feels sheepish about it, but an hospitable Sister makes a fuss of her, as if she were accustomed to welcoming young creatures in short skirts; shows her to a small room; begs her to make herself entirely at home.

The room contains a single bed, a washbasin, a small armchair, a bedside table which doubles as a desk, equipped with a reading lamp and an upright chair. In the corner behind a floral curtain there is a rail and several hangers for articles of clothing. A worn rug on the green linoleum completes the furnishings.

Her room is upstairs, with a view onto a courtyard with a lawn. Her window faces the chapel. Amy has a frisson of déjà vu, but the feeling is elusive. Cool linoleum, an embroidered cloth on the bedside table, glimpses of stained glass comfort her.

The garden is large for a suburban site, and surprisingly quiet, although the traffic of the southern suburbs weaves around it. A path leads through borders of perennials, shrubs and trees to a circular lily pond. Up against the rear wall a young lemon tree bears sweet smelling flowers.

"Lemon tree very pretty, and de lemon flower is sweet; but the fruit of de poor lemon is impossible to eat," hums Amy, balanced on the rim of the pond, walking around it clockwise, then turning to retrace her steps anti-clockwise. Half a dozen goldfish flicker lazily in the water.

Over the wall she can see the tiled roof of the priory chapel. She will sleep next door to Alfred tonight. He has been so kind, so concerned about what happened to her when she read his books. Not that she was particularly coherent when she told him about that. She tried to describe an essentially out of this world experience for which there were no words in her vocabulary. He responded with the strange remark that God often gives us a honeymoon period after baptism in the Spirit. Amy, appalled, asked herself what on earth would married life be like if such an unspeakably terrible experience had been the honeymoon? Alfred's prescription for her was a weekend retreat. So here she is, now, at St Bede's.

The chapel bell rings a summons to the evening office, gathering retreatants and Sisters for prayer before nightfall. Incense still perfumes the chapel from the morning eucharist. They find their places, some retreatants huddling together, others preferring to sit apart, the Sisters in the front row in their accustomed places. Someone has marked Amy's book for her and she follows the service without too much trouble. Familiar words and phrases fall upon the quiet air, coming to her as if from a great distance – from far away and long ago. Sisters chant the psalm, back and forth across the aisle; the antiphon soothing, healing, as the dusk gathers outside and the candlelight bathes bent heads and grey robes with silver and with gold.

Meals are taken in silence, which provides unsurpassed theatre for Amy. She is beset by a critical spirit which pounces upon small embarrassments, peccadillos – her own and other people's – and gnaws incessantly at scruples. She is feeling thoroughly exasperated with her fellow retreatants – nice elderly women who are attempting to exercise normal etiquette at table whilst maintaining the obligatory silence. This involves much pointing and smiling, gesticulating and nodding. Amy can't help feeling that such behaviour misses the point of silent meals, which are surely supposed to be calm and reflective. In addition they are, perforce, listening to the Brandenburg concerto on the Sisters' gramophone. Which makes Amy wince because there is a scratch on the vinyl.

In the midst of all this demure turbulence Alfred floats through the refectory, bowing silently, smiling at the smiling Sisters. He smiles at Amy and she grins back, like a dog being offered a bone. She can't stop grinning although she is wildly irritated by the scratchy record and the bizarre table manners. She notices Sister Elizabeth looking at her speculatively. The toothy grin is instantly wiped from her face. She feels guilty, as if caught out in a school yard misdemeanour, and concentrates on her steamed pudding and custard. When she looks up Alfred is gone, but he has left a wisp of graciousness behind him, reminding her to be kind towards these women with whom she is spending the weekend.

In the library cum sitting room at St Bede's Amy comes across a book by her childhood hero, CS Lewis. *Surprised by Joy* turns out to be an autobiography, describing a child not unlike herself in some respects. Certainly this memoir of the author's solitary, introspective childhood speaks to her heart. Curled up in the bay window, while outside the sundial marks the passing hours, she feels as if an intimate friend has come to visit her – she who has no flesh-and-blood soul mate, only imaginary ones.

Presently she falls asleep and dreams that she is wrapped in a fur cape which falls in soft folds to the floor around her. A mouse is pulling at the hem, dragging the cape away from her sleeping self. She gropes unwillingly towards wakefulness, desiring to snuggle back into her dream. But now the tea bell is ringing, and there will be cake.

This benign routine, ambling twixt bed and board and chapel, begins to unknot Amy's ubiquitous anxiety. It seems it is never long before the prospect of something comforting to eat, or the chapel bell ringing them to prayer, or the yawning anticipation of an early night in her little cot. She has a bottle of whisky hidden in her suitcase, but scarcely has time to sample it, such is the stately progress of the day from morning until night; from waking, to praying, to breakfasting, to instruction on matters spiritual, then morning tea, midday office, lunch, an afternoon nap, and tea again.

On Sunday morning Amy sets off down the garden to paint a picture of the lemon tree. She has brought with her a small tin of water colours, and she completes the painting in an hour. It has been an entirely absorbing exercise and she is childishly delighted with her first artwork since she left school. She has it still, framed, on her bedroom wall. The colours have faded, but the young lemon tree stands spruce before the garden wall, with a background of suburban roofs and a church spire.

A Sister by the name of Angela gives the retreatants instruction on prayer. She is visiting from the mother house in England. She has the most remarkable feet. They are large but finely boned, tanned, shod in leather sandals, and stand extraordinarily four-square upon the stone flags of the chapel. As if she owns the spot upon which she stands, inhabits it entirely – as if she were a tree.

Angela is exceedingly wholesome. Without a stitch of make-up, of course, and her hair invisible under her veil, her face is handsome rather than pretty, her smile very white, her eyes very blue against the tanned skin. She is tall, lanky almost, but moves with grace. Her robes rustle lightly and smell of soap.

Amy is not used to noticing women *qua* woman. She doesn't really have a great deal of time for them. Men are much more serious, have more interesting things to say. Women are always talking about children and servants – gossiping about superficial stuff. But Angela is almost another species; androgynous. She speaks to them in her sonorous voice about what she calls the spiritual life.

It is necessary to pray, Angela says, in order to progress in the spiritual life – about half-an-hour a week if you can. There's not much point in doing it for less than half-an-hour, she says. The sheer matter-of-factness of this information stuns Amy. How does she know? Is there a text book for praying? If so, Amy has never heard about it.

Amy gave up saying prayers – grace before meals – when she left home. Prayers in church were the business of the professionals – the clergy. Extempore petitions by the charismatics in her parish church are in a class of their own; she does not rate these as proper prayer, they are more like advertisements. Of course, Alfred's habit of hunkering down and praying whenever the fancy takes him is something else altogether, something exotic, like transcendental meditation.

Now, this woman, Angela, who is not quite a woman but something more noble, is telling them that they should pray regularly – much as one would suggest a game of tennis. Alas, there is no discussion of how one would actually go about it, how to pray that is, apart from the obvious bit about going down on one's knees, folding one's hands, and closing one's eyes.

They are in silence until afternoon tea on Sunday. At tea, when conversation breaks out, it seems as if the secret business of prayer spoken about in chapel has become a foreign country. It is in a different dimension from the chit chat which erupts like champagne from a bottle when the silence ends. Amy is not game to ask Sister Angela how she should pray. That would be too humiliating for words, to display such ignorance after spending the entire weekend masquerading as a spiritual person. Besides, it seems irreverent to talk about prayer amidst this vociferous chatter. But before they leave she does ask if she may pray every day. Angela looks pleased, says of course she may, but not to overdo it.

$\S$

September 29th 1977

Dear Alfred,
There are two places to sit at the bottom of the garden here at St Bede's. One is a cypress where you can rest with your back on the trunk and you can feel the whole tree moving in the wind against your spine. From there, looking towards the priory you can see many trees, a frosty fir, a mossy coloured one, a copper beech and a sycamore, all waving in the wind, shifting shadows and glints of sunshine, myriad shades of green.

The other comfortable spot is about halfway up the sycamore tree. You can sit on a branch grown 'specially for leprechauns, and blow smoke rings. The compost heap is conveniently below for tossing one's *stompies.*[2] It looks to me like a very good heap for jumping into, full of pine needles and sycamore wings – but I haven't tried it yet. Looking up you can see weavers' nests hanging like little shopping baskets, and if you sit still enough you can watch the yellow weaver birds tidying up their handiwork. Below are white daisies turned up like stars – and the occasional lady retreatant, wandering wraith-like, communing with nature. You sit very still and hope she won't raise her eyes and be shocked by the impious leprechaun in the sycamore tree.

I don't think I have ever eaten so many mulberries in my life. I wanted to pick some for jam but Sister Elizabeth didn't seem very enthusiastic, so I ate 'em. I've just scooped up some extra tea and cake which someone unwisely left lying around – it's five o'clock. I am beginning to feel very much at home.

2. Cigarette butts.

~20~

Would anyone like to come to a gig this arvo?" asks Alfred. He is in the habit of using this hybrid argot when he is at Nazareth House. He acquired his lexicon of slang in the RAF during the Second World War when he was a Spitfire pilot, augmenting it during his days on tramp steamers and when he was a lumberjack in Canada. This mongrel vernacular was vamped up during a stint on the Isle of Wight at the 1969 Rock Festival.

Inhabitants of the little island had been so appalled at the prospect of tens of thousands of hippies arriving to camp and party on their green and pleasant land, doing the heinous things that hippies were reputed to do, that they appealed to the monastery to send some monks to deal with it.

The Community set up a Jesus tent in case anybody wanted sanctuary from Bob Dylan, The Who, Joe Cocker and The Moody Blues.

In the event, Alfred, who had been chosen to go on this mission, had his first encounter with 'dope' (as he calls marijuana – smacking his lips and adopting a leering grin). Assimilation had followed rapidly, as years of monastic formation yielded to the ecstasy and companionship of a new generation doing its thing, unmolested by rules and commitments.

Alfred has a gift for friendship, which is why he was chosen to go on this dangerous mission. He did not once consider leaving the monastic life during those few days of dancing and din, but he took a distinct whiff of anarchic joy and insubordination from the Isle of Wight Rock Festival back home to the monastery

§

Now Alfred surveys his flock lounging like broken dolls on the lawn in front of Nazareth House. It is a warm Spring day and he has persuaded these denizens of the night to come outdoors and enjoy the sunshine. No-one responds to his invitation to go to the gig this arvo.

Alfred removes the sticky remains of a roll-up from his lower lip and parks it carefully upon a nearby pebble. He rouses himself from his elegant sprawl upon the grass, curls up into a ball, and with breathtaking mastery raises all six foot plus of his body into a headstand. No-one can ignore the bizarre spectacle of bare feet, stone-washed jeans, and white cassock tumbling to the ground like a skirt around his shoulders.

Someone snorts, someone giggles, then all give way to helpless laughter. Serene in his pose, Alfred's muffled voice emerges: "Who's coming to the gig?"

Nine, including Amy, follow him, like the Pied Piper down to the Central Methodist Church in the city. It is a modern building with glass doors, through which they view an auditorium packed to capacity with a congregation of blacks, whites and coloureds, all jostled together in the pews.

Amy has never seen anything like it. Nor have her companions judging by the shocked looks on their faces. But Alfred, insouciant, leads them onward, down the central aisle to the front of the auditorium where there is still space to sit on the floor. He nods his head, bowing, shaking hands with a myriad of acquaintances as he wends his way through the mixed race gathering.

As if attached to him by an invisible thread the little band from Nazareth House follow, shell-shocked. Of course, they have seen black and coloured people before – non-whites, as they are designated by the apartheid government. But not all sitting down together like this. Next to each other.

Proceedings are already under way. A black man is speaking from the podium and takes absolutely no notice of the strange little band of castaways finding a spot to sit on the floor at his feet. Indeed, there seems to be a constant flow of comings and goings. Babies cry. At times there is a palpable stillness in the whole auditorium as a door slams, or some small commotion erupts. Then the congregation shivers as one, like the pelt of dog, before settling back into its sociable murmurings.

People are afraid. What they are doing, being here together, is illegal. They are in unknown territory. They are vulnerable in this place with its many doors. At any moment the security police could arrive; tear gas will be thrown; people will be bludgeoned, arrested.

But the memorial service continues peacefully, celebrating the life of a young man called Steve Biko, who has died in police custody.

In later years Amy will remember this afternoon as her initiation into South African politics. But for now she is content to sit close to Alfred; observing him lovingly, covertly, as he listens to the speakers, eyes shut, kneeling back on his heels, hands clasped in his lap, head bowed. The auditorium lights play on his silver hair, so that it appears to her like a halo. She too is afraid, but her fear is more like awe, because she knows who he is.

It is a realisation that she keeps quarantined in the back of her mind; she cannot name it, even to herself. While she is with him like this, in his company, not needing to say anything at all, just resting in the sunshine of his presence, she is perfectly at peace.

21

Late in the afternoon the party returns to Nazareth House, after what seems like hours of watching Alfred greet people of all colours and ages and estates, throwing up his arms as if each one were an angel in disguise, whom he instantly recognises and hails as a messenger from God. Back home the house is in shambles. One of the church volunteers has ventured into Auberon's room (strictly out-of-bounds) and discovered with horror that the walls are plastered with pornographic images.

Auberon is one of Alfred's protégés. He came off the streets a couple of months back when it was really cold, suffering delirium tremens, incontinent, and without a cent in his pocket.

Alfred spent a lot of time with Auberon, who at first viewed this white-robed monk with wall-eyed pessimism. Over time, however, he unravelled from his semi-foetal posture to reveal a lanky man as tall as Alfred, with a mien as aristocratic. In fact their lean features are very alike – in Alfred's case chiselled by ascetic life, in Auberon's by destitution; both silver-haired and blue-eyed. But beneath the skin they are as different as Gabriel and Lucifer.

On the evidence of two months sobriety, Alfred made Auberon the warden at Nazareth House, giving him a room of his own. More and more people are dropping in – some having nowhere to go for the night. Strictly against the rules Alfred allows a few dossers to sleep over. He himself is obliged to return to the priory in time to say evening office with his brethren – although this actually happens less and less. However, for Alfred to sleep out of bounds was another matter; that the Prior would *not* countenance. Auberon presents a solution. He is the very man to keep watch at Nazareth House overnight.

Except that now Auberon has been 'sprung', as Alfred sorrowfully puts it. It is no use protesting that the church worker has ignored the big sign on Auberon's door – *Noli me tangere!* It is too late. Everybody now knows what is posted on the walls in there. Sustained hysteria has broken out amongst the volunteers, who have telephoned the church authorities for help. A trustee, a bishop, is expected to arrive at any moment to calm the scandalised women and deal with the offender.

Amy perceives that Alfred is at his wits end. Two worlds have collided here, and Alfred is in the middle of the crash scene, trying in vain to staunch the bleeding. Auberon stands in a corner with his head down, looking mulish.

"I could take 'Bron home," says Amy.

A glimmer of hope crosses Alfred's face, which makes her go weak at the knees.

"Could you?"

"Of course! We have a spare room." She does not consider the logistics of getting Auberon home, or what Wolf may think of the arrangement. Wolf bears a growing resentment towards Amy's frequent trips to Nazareth House, and has forbidden her to take the car to Jo'burg, so she now travels by train. The return journey from door to door takes several hours.

§

So it is that they find themselves, Amy and Auberon, in a 'whites only' carriage on the long trip back to Pretoria via Germiston. She has yielded to 'Bron's argument that he needs a drink to prevent an alcoholic seizure, following this afternoon's bender. They have a bottle of Johnnie Walker in a brown paper bag between them on the seat, and a couple of paper cups. Amy views her companion – saturnine, swarthy, gloomy – with satisfaction. He belongs to Alfred and is therefore infinitely precious. She will make him well, and earn Alfred's undying gratitude.

This object of Alfred's affection looks a little dog-eared in the stark neon light of the carriage; his bewhiskered face has a blueish tinge, and he stinks of alcohol and urine. Amy is not perturbed by the charges against him. She had been exposed to pornography on board ship, and can't understand what all the fuss is about.

The images she saw had been disturbing; but she would rather have died than show a flicker of distaste in front of the crew, as they tested her stamina for the obscene. Just as she drank with them, measure for measure, so she stared, unblinking, at the screen together with the crew, until the bestiality came to an end. Once she caught sight of a comic book with a picture of Popeye the Sailor Man equipped with a gigantic penis which, she was shocked to find, aroused her. The ship's cook was rumoured to have a blow-up rubber doll in his cabin, with which he did unspeakable things. All 'Bron had were pictures out of magazines! Mind you, Playboy is a banned publication in South Africa.

It is late when they finally get back to Albion. Wolf is still up, listening to music. He wanted to have a television, now the technology has finally arrived in South Africa, but Amy in her new-found asceticism vetoed that idea. Wolf complains that it isn't the same listening to soccer on the radio (he had played for Hamburg Junior League) but Amy would not relent.

So here he is, listening to Jonathan Livingstone Seagull. He remains seated when she comes into the sitting room, trailing her companion. Wolf is clearly not amused at the sight of Auberon, who rocks back on his heels, hands in his jeans pockets, something close to a sneer on his harrowed features.

"Wolf, this is Auberon. 'Bron, Wolf," she introduces them curtly in English. Wolf grunts, Auberon remains silent.

"He's staying the night," she says, somewhat defiantly.

"Well, I'm going to bed," replies Wolf in German, heaving himself up and brushing rudely past Auberon on his way out.

"Sorry about the pissing exercise," apologises Amy when her husband is out of earshot. "Have a seat. I'll make us something to eat."

But Auberon isn't really interested in food. Later they crack another bottle of whisky, which Wolf has helpfully laid by in the drinks cabinet. Amy generally sticks to carafe wine these days – the cheap and cheerful Tassenheimer – but she is happy to drink whisky on special occasions. Auberon settles comfortably into his armchair, nursing a goblet of the amber liquid, and prepares to be expansive.

They talk all night. Auberon comes from a wealthy family and is very well-read, has dabbled in philosophy and is always willing to take up the rapier of word play in the interests of his own esoteric world view. He calls himself a humanist with a penchant for nihilism. 'Penchant' is a word Alfred has adopted lately, rolling it around his mouth with gusto. Amy ponders the word as if it is a coded clue to the relationship between these two men. She feels deliciously voyeuristic, and encourages Auberon to talk more. He is a messenger from Alfred as well as a gift; and a grave responsibility. She wonders how she should go about converting him. How happy Alfred would be if she were to send his friend back clean and whole and Christian.

§

Word play is Amy's native environment. The family table at the vicarage was the venue for learning the thrust and parry of conversation. 'Argument', their mother called it; their father mildly defending the frequent fraças as 'debate'. So they argued endlessly about whether it was argument or debate. Words flew back and forth; back and forth, mutating, unfurling abstruse meanings, revealing strange roots, whenever the father chose to apply himself to the furore. The relative merits of the words 'reconnaissance' and 'reconnoitre' had once occupied the conversation for an entire summer holiday, and became a family joke.

The home Amy grew up in was a hothouse of conversation about everything, from politics – she remembers the exile of the Dalai Lama upset her father very much – to the labyrinth of psychology, still a new science at street level. The pater familias majored in the subject at Cambridge and shared the view from those ivory towers with his young family. A magic mirror called 'projection', a concept which was certainly not yet in the vernacular, played a crucial role in family life. "That's a simple case of projection," declared with a smirk, was a perfect checkmate to unwelcome criticism.

St John's Cottage was a cosmopolitan household. In 1958 it sheltered refugees from the Hungarian revolution. Their journalist lodger was first on the scene at the Great Train Robbery. On Fridays Lady Craig's gardener delivered home-grown vegetables to the back door. Late at night policemen brought victims of domestic violence to the front door to be cared for by the priest.

It was not much fun at the time, growing up amidst so many goings-on. Attention always seemed to be elsewhere, instead of on one's person. After such a bohemian childhood it was inevitable that ordinary life would seem a bit boring by comparison; and normal conversation rather paltry.

Amy speaks German with Wolf at home in Pretoria. Enough had been going on in their life at sea to maintain the endorphins (to say nothing of the pheromones), but the dreaded nine-to-five routine of earning a living, of married life, which they had somehow fallen into against their own inclinations, had crushed any feeling of expectation about life. Any feelings at all really.

Meeting Alfred has quickened a lost world for Amy. Alfred is real, or more correctly, super-real. There is a solidity to him as if he is more intensely flesh and blood than other people. Quite the opposite of holy, which one imagines is a bit floaty and other-worldly. Amy has the feeling she could lean her whole weight upon him, figuratively speaking of course, and he would not fall over. Amy cannot bear weakness.

She is surprised at how easy it is to take up the sword of wordplay with Auberon. As if mounting a horse after a long furlough she rapidly gains confidence and nerve. He begins with a declaration that his atheism is an impregnable position in view of the lack of evidence of a god. Amy parries with the commonplace that faith is invalid in the presence of proof. Auberon counters that faith is the hiding place of cowards who cannot face the reality of an arbitrary universe. Here Amy steals the march on him because she has had a brush with the new physics.

Her brother, Jonathan, had been a scientist almost from birth. As a toddler he was often to be found face down alongside a rotting log in the garden observing the behaviour of wood lice, and sampling them for flavour. After he learned to read he collected a formidable encyclopaedia in weekly instalments, called The Book of Life, which he studied diligently.

"Why d'you put all that stuff on yourself?" he enquired of his older sister one morning as she anointed her skin with lotion.

"It's to keep my skin smooth and supple."

"Don't you worry about what's in that stuff?"

"I don't eat it, I just put it on me."

"But it goes through your skin into your bloodstream."

"Don't be ridiculous."

But of course, as we now know, all those perfumed petro-products were insinuating themselves through our apparently impermeable skin into our bodies.

Meanwhile Jonathan had graduated to The New Scientist. During their holiday together last summer he had attempted to explain to her the mystical dynamics of quantum physics, which has put paid to the mechanical universe forever.

§

Quantum physics shows that the universe is not arbitrary, declares Amy with more confidence than she feels. To her relief Auberon seems at a loss to counter this riposte and changes the subject.

"What kind of an omnipotent god would allow people to suffer wars and famine and floods?" he enquires, loftily.

Amy secretly admits that this is a problem, but leaps into the breach with a rather oblique apologetic which she has recently read in a book borrowed from the priory.

"It's a mystery," she finishes up. "And that's the point of having faith. You don't understand at first, but if you are *brave* enough," she smirks, "you trust in God's promise of abundant life. Even if you don't know what that will mean."

"You mean you sign the contract without reading it?" snorts Auberon.

"Exactly!" she cries, as if she has won the argument.

The warmth of the electric heater and the whisky have mellowed Auberon. His fighting spirit is laid to rest and he begins a long soliloquy, which fades eventually into a murmur. Sometime before dawn she tries to get him to his room, but he is too sleepy and too comfortable to move. So she leaves him where he is and goes to bed.

§

When Amy wakes up the sun is high and the morning almost gone. She feels euphoric from the night's adventures. Now to get Auberon bathed and breakfasted, before another session talking about faith. She is sure they made progress last night. She is newly astonished at her own eloquence. It seemed as if she effortlessly knew what to say to 'Bron, regardless of what moves he employed against her. Her head aches, but her spirits are high when she finds Wolf in the kitchen getting a beer out of the fridge.

"Where's 'Bron?" she asks.

"I took him home," says Wolf.

"What do you mean?" exclaims Amy, terror gripping her heart.

"I took him back to Jo'burg."

"Why the fuck d'you do that?" she yells.

"He wanted to go back to that Nazzy-what-d'you-call-it House."

105

Amy sinks to the floor, arms clasped around her knees, engulfed in horror at what this might mean.

What this means, as she finds out when she telephones Nazareth House, is that her hopes of pleasing Alfred are utterly crushed.

"One of the volunteers looked out the window and saw him early this morning," Alfred informs her quietly. "He was crapping on the front lawn."

She tries to explain. She tries to blame Wolf. She tries to describe the wonderful conversation she had had with Auberon the night before. Alfred listens politely, but his tone is weary. Then he wishes her goodbye and hangs up.

22

For two weeks Amy grieves the loss of her friendship with Alfred. She does not dare to write to him. Her soul is frozen, petrified in the moment she heard his voice carrying its burden of disappointment down the phone line on the morning of the catastrophe. This memory winds her up to a pitch of grief which causes her to long for death.

Her mind chases itself round and around the night she spent with 'Bron — what could she have done differently; what might have happened otherwise; what stroke of grace could have brought about a different conclusion? But mostly her mind gnaws at what she did wrong. All she did was to go to sleep. She went to bed trusting that all would be well. And it wasn't.

In truth — at the final frontier of her conscience — she cannot attribute blame to Wolf for the disastrous denouement of this, her first missionary endeavour. That would be cowardly. She alone is responsible.

Eventually her heart, leached of sensory pain, feels like a black hole out of which a continuous static of humiliation and horror is broadcast throughout her waking hours.

There is a Roman Catholic church down the road from their house in Albion. Tentatively trying the door Amy finds to her surprise that it is not locked. She slips inside, notices the sanctuary lamp, bends her knee and crosses herself awkwardly, as she has seen Alfred do in the presence of the Blessed Sacrament.

She slides into a pew near where the red light burns over an ornate little gold box which houses the communion bread for sick people. After a while the buzzing in her head subsides. She has become so accustomed to this hostile static, like short-wave interference in her mind, that the peace seems palpable. She draws a deep breath.

It is like being on holiday. Fears which loomed over her just a few moments ago suddenly fade away into sunlight, vanish into the sand. For an hour she sits, sighing from time to time, resting in the balm of the Presence. When she leaves the church building the torment in her head begins all over again.

§

Amy is in what passes for a garden behind her house; a shallow incline matted with kikuyu grass and weeds, bounded by sweet smelling syringa newly in bloom. A broad bough of the jacaranda tree swoops over what used to be a lawn. The grass beneath the jacaranda will die back after the tree dons its purple blooms in October, when its new leaves thickly clothe the branches. The spot has an air of desuetude, a memory of a garden long neglected and infested with khakibos.

Amy pulls some of the sticky black seeds of the weed from her socks. It doesn't come from here — the khakibos. Named after soldiers' camouflage, it came from Britain in horse feed during the Boer war — or the Wars of Independence as the Afrikaners call that bloody guerilla conflict. Amy notices the seeds are infesting her trouser legs, almost up to the knee. She can't get them off. She picks at them, twisting around to find more and more attached to her like leeches. As she twists and turns the khakibos brushes against her clothing, depositing more of its burden of black seed.

All at once her heart is pounding as if it will bash itself clean out of the cage of her ribs. She gasps for breath. It hurts. Her vision blurs and she feels herself losing consciousness; her limbs are folding into the undergrowth. Panic drives her heart ever more urgently, drumming it towards destruction; she is dying; the world is fading; not a shred of her being seems able to resist. As the ground comes up to meet her, unconsciousness takes her sweetly in its arms.

It must have been a heart attack, Amy decides after she comes round some time later. Dappled sunlight plays upon her skin through the bare branches of the jacaranda. A broken heart, in fact. Her heart, under such duress for so long, had simply conked out.

This explanation proves to be such a relief that her imagination is suddenly set free from the debacle with Auberon. She imagines herself at the foot of a cross on which hangs Alfred; no, she is actually on a cross beside him, their eyes locked, although that requires cricking one's neck. She moves her cross opposite his and resumes her gaze, offers up her own blood and bone, her own substance, to support him in his final ordeal. She is prepared to die for him. Greater love hath no man than this, that he should lay down his life for his friends (man being understood as inclusive of woman).

§

On the Sunday evening following Amy's panic attack, the bishop visits St Wilfs to anoint a young man who has offered himself for the ministry, as the pew leaflet puts it. This ceremony takes place in the parish hall, because the church is still not finished. Amy sits amongst the crowd which has turned out to see the bishop and feels a sense of importance, because she has already met him, as a man, in his own office. This helps her cope with the claustrophobia.

Bishop Timothy is in the makeshift pulpit, talking about the young parishioner who wants to be a priest. Amy finds it hard to concentrate; she is very tired. The bishop goes on to talk about the readings for the day, which includes Paul's letter to the Romans, chapter six verse eight: *But if we have died with Christ, we believe that we shall also live with him.*

The bishop surveys the crowded hall kindly, but with earnestness in his eyes behind the horn-rimmed spectacles.

"Now, I don't suppose any of us here have died," he says with a smile. The congregation chuckles.

Amy is turned to stone. She cannot breathe. Hemmed in on one side by a large man smelling of cologne, and on the other by a woman wrestling with two small children, she suddenly feels intense heat coursing through her veins, followed by a clammy chill.

She knows she has to get out; out into the air; out of the sweating crowd; her life depends upon it. If she has a life, which now seems to be in doubt. What kind of being is she?

She thought the bishop would know; would recognise someone who had made the ultimate sacrifice, who had in fact laid down her life. Was she insane after all? Were those lost days back in winter, during her encounter with Alfred's books, merely symptoms of madness? Was today's rite of passage, the laying down of her life for Alfred, merely a cancer of the mind?

Amy climbs over the woman beside her, kicking a child on the way and setting it off bawling, stumbles up the narrow aisle gasping for air, out into the cold night.

Out here, silhouetted against the stars, a skeletal metal frame rises from the concrete foundations of the new church. She totters towards this place of concrete, leans against a steel girder, gazes up at the stars, and in despair prays to her God to let her die.

Presently she notices one of the stars is brighter than the others. She trawls her memory for its name. As a child she memorised the names of creatures who inhabited the night sky; Pegasus brought her joy when she discerned his outline in the heavens. But here, in the southern hemisphere, the sky is different. She focuses on the brightest star.

She is chilled to the marrow. That terrible claustrophobia, that heat has evaporated now. It occurs to her in a homely sort of way that it would be quite rude to rush off into eternity, to leave her body lying on this place of concrete, just when things were beginning to make sense.

Not that things are making much sense at the moment, but she has a vague feeling that more is on view now than has been before. More of life, more than she can cope with actually, is happening. Common sense enlivens her like a brisk shower. She decides to stay.

Amy never has any doubt that she had a choice that night. Out of her own free will she chose to stay in this world, rather than leaving her young life lying on the concrete foundation of St Wilfrid's church, just on that spot where, a few months later, the new church's altar was built.

23

Amy's letters to Alfred have been her lifeline for nine months. Whilst writing to him she sometimes catches glimpses of Aslan, her childhood companion, who, it seems to her, prowls silently in the dark and perilous wilderness of her interior life, although his job as her guardian has now been passed on to Alfred.

Now and then the curious fluttering of her tongue against her palate, the sensual rolling in her mouth of syllables whose meaning is hidden from her, reminds her of those soaring songs which burst from her lips on summer evenings when she was a child; when she was first in love, as she now is with Alfred.

So strange is this journey into her soul's interior, into the uncharted finsterness of her psyche, that the words which leak from her pen day by day, essaying to describe on the page what is happening inside her, make little sense to Alfred. Nor even to herself, years later after he returns these letters to her safe-keeping.

But these epistles, these marks on a page, were at the time her only anchorhold. They represented a hope that the world goes on, somewhere beyond the night she travels in. Somewhere beyond this inner wasteland, peopled by strange and frightening apparitions, so dark she cannot see her hand in front of her face, Alfred inhabits a place as ordinary as her childhood home. That bohemian, cluttered, untidy existence seems to her now like a blessed dream — her native land which she left behind so long ago. Alfred keeps those home fires burning. Her letters to him are a tenuous connection with normal life.

But the disaster with Auberon has cut Amy off from this life source — her daily ruminations upon the pages of her correspondence with Alfred. The pain of this loss is intolerable, the grief insupportable. She feels scourged, cast out, derelict, homeless, beyond comfort of any kind.

So, following her encounter with the place of concrete Amy rouses herself to write once again to her mentor. It is hard to know how to begin. The affair with Auberon has badly wounded her pride. She has been broken in, like a defiant colt, by the harsh disciplines of this year and she is surprised to find even a trace of pride left in her. A mature analysis of this muddled sense of woundedness might have comforted her with the fact that her annihilated self was still very much alive.

§

8th October 1977

Dear Alfred,

I've just read in the bible that I am 'fully understood', even if not by you. Oh dear, what a burden – to expect you to understand me fully! You do of course understand the scraps of myself which I give to you on paper. But Auberon, the gooseberry, messed everything up in his crooked wisdom. Never mind. I am sure that this too will pass. I had better explain a few things or I might lose the best friend I ever had.

I have never loved anyone whom I have not had to care for in one way or another, including my parents, Wolf, everybody. 'Bron's plea for help looked like an opportunity to care for you. I know you are fond of him – contemporaries, different enough to complement each other. He has a sharp intellect as well as sensitivity. Set all that free and Alfred would have a matchless companion. I also know what happens when a woman comes between brothers, so I was a bit scared.

However, you put him in my care that fateful evening. He could not have been in a worse state. He'd left a trail of chaos behind him at Nazareth House and, by the way, was desolate because he had betrayed you.

That night I did verbal battle with him on whatever ground he chose. When I left him to go to bed in the early hours of Sunday morning, he was definitely thinking about the Gospel, although of course, rather drunk.

Whatever happened after that was not my responsibility. But knowing him as I do, and his pride; and losing your trust, as I have, and two and two making four, I will make what you airily call a leap of faith and suggest that Auberon should not be allowed to get away with wicked gossip. I did not just have a drunken orgy with him.

There now! Another hurdle overcome. It is amazing how dreadful experiences seem almost comical on looking back. Purposely cutting myself off from you for a fortnight was worse than a thousand hells. Of course when one is all alone the horror of it mushrooms out of all proportion. It's what they do in dungeons. Chain a prisoner in solitary confinement, with only the measured sound of water dripping. Under those conditions just a few pints of water can drive a person insane.

What kept me alive during these weeks were small things. I was standing in a queue at the bank, and the woman in front of me had a beautiful little boy, about three years old, beside her. I was looking down on him thinking something like, "Little son of God. Has anyone told you that you are deeply loved and infinitely precious…?" He turned and looked up at me, and an expression of intense wonder dawned on his face. The bank and the chatter faded away, and there were just the two of us in the whole world, gazing at each other. And then he offered up his teddy.

24

Once more in correspondence with Alfred, Amy recovers quickly. She has remarkable powers of recuperation. She is blessed with an unquenchable optimism which has accompanied her through dark nights for as long as she can remember. Like being on the road with an angel, optimism remains invisible for long stretches of the journey, but emerges in the morning. Or perhaps the angel is the morning?

Enough that the world is once again suffused with meaning. That dark power which sucks the life out of her 'til she is but a husk, has roiled its way back into the place whence it came. Instead little miracles visit her daily, which she both desires and fears to believe in. Fortunately she has Alfred to share them with. He will tell her what to think.

§

11th October 1977

Dear Alfred,
It seems it is time to stop beating around the bush. Here are a few of the things which I have noticed happening around me, that I can see but other people can't.

Last night we visited the couple who first hosted us in Pretoria. You may even have met him in PoW in Germany. He was a navigator in the RAF and one of the famous tunnelers in the Great Escape. I first met him when Wolf and I flew up from our ship in Durban to visit them. What drew me here to this country was a conversation I had with him then.

He talked about how South Africa would witness to the whole world about the values of the human family, animal conservation, and true quality of life. I had never heard anyone so passionate about their country before, except in sentimental movies about the Second World War. I saw in him a living, breathing symbol of hope. He deeply believed in his way of life. He had succeeded in business. Now retired he had time and leisure to enjoy his prosperity and practice lavish hospitality. His servants were grateful for his open handed generosity; and he put his dogs to bed himself. What more could a man want?

I told him about how depressed everybody was in England; how it didn't seem to matter any more that being British was best; and at last I shared with him my own hope that somewhere in the world I would find a new way of living.

"I believe," he said with profound gravity, "that there will be a new kind of solution here in South Africa to the dilemma of modern man." That conversation determined me to to live in this country.

Previously our social get-togethers with this couple have been pleasant – but under the surface this man (a cousin, but I call him 'uncle') and Wolf have been fencing bitterly, and neither seems to know why. My dear 'aunt' is usually on the qui vive – thinking of what to say next to keep the peace, and chatting on, mostly about the family.

But last night each one of us spoke in turn – and the others listened respectfully. There was a gracefulness in our conversation which I don't remember before. Wolf didn't interrupt or raise his voice once. Our host did not make one facetious remark. My aunt didn't bother to make pancakes, which she often does to keep everyone happy.

My neighbour, Marie, has been confined to the house with leg ulcers for many years. But now the ulcers are healing. All I do is go and talk to her (a bit brokenly because she doesn't speak much English and I don't speak Afrikaans), and have a cup of tea. And then we pray together. She likes that. I'm a bit scared, but I'm getting better at it. Is it not a mark of a normal Christian life that, not by touch nor by sign, but by a little care, an invalid can be healed, and walk, and praise God?

If anyone knows that they have been helped through me in anything I have tried to do, I am not aware of it. I am very afraid of presuming too much. I see powerful things happening around me and they fill me with awe, and fear that I am not quite sane.

My parish priest wants me to be more assertive. He says that womanhood has changed since St Paul decreed that a woman should not speak in church. But nothing else has changed – why should that be any different? I will not become a female zealot. I learned on board ship that a woman should be veiled at all times, or there's trouble. I mean, one should not flaunt oneself.

That's all for now. You will be away on leave next week. I hope I will see you again before too long.

§

Gender is a vexed question for Amy. Being born a girl was a misfortune she dealt with during her childhood by insisting that people call her Jim. She left England before feminism really hit the streets, to do a man's job in the all-male world of the German merchant marine. Feminism is not much in evidence in white South Africa, where women know their place – in the drawing room – while men yarn over the braai. So far, women's liberation has passed Amy by.

Her parish priest, Fr Albert, finally persuades her to take on the leadership of a house group in the Albion chapelry of St Mark's, an adjunct to the main parish church. Fr Albert is a small man, also born in England, with a fierce little white goatee and flashing eyes.

"You can do it, Amy!" he guffaws at her after church one Sunday. Flattered, in spite of her doubts, she says she will give it a go.

§

14th October 1977

Dear Alfred,

Must get to see you as soon as you get home. You've got to answer a few questions for me. I've just come back from our newly-inaugurated Albion house group – I don't know whether to describe it as 'prayer', 'praise', 'bible study', 'fraternity' – all these terms muddle one so.

I am incredibly happy, and it worries me stiff! I don't want to feel anything – I am not interested in me. I feel like a baobab – planted upside down with a very confusing relationship between earth and heaven. It was much easier not caring where I am or who I am. It is

116

more difficult to care. Living things are swarming around me, and I can see meaning in them, and I can see them answering me – as if I really exist for them.

For example: I go away into myself, to that secret place I have so recently discovered, to reflect on what someone has said in the group.

A girl beside me whispers: "You went far away. Where did you go?"

"Oh sorry, did I? (Sigh) Yes, beyond the farthest hills."

"I saw. What is there?"

(Oh beloved!) "There is my home."

Robert, who is going to London next week overhears us: "Oh, you mean London?"

"Yes!" I say.

But the little sister gives me a secret smile. She knows where I went, although I am not even sure myself.

I went to an evening eucharist in the city this afternoon, on the way home from the office. I wish I could get random thoughts out of my mind when I'm trying to pray. I find it really difficult to pray in church when other people are around. I'm trying to do what it says in your book, *The Cloud of Unknowing*, and just think about nothing. I have been to this church a few times now. The priest walzed out after the service and introduced me to everybody, telling them I was "smashing" – which didn't thrill them at all, and left me feeling very unsettled.

I don't know where I am. I thought it didn't matter. I can be turned into a slug – or disappear altogether for all I care. But people are requiring things of me and I must know if I am alright – sane, blessed even – before I can speak. I mean, open my mouth at all.

16th October 1977

I hope you will open a new file for my letters. The rag doll who first wrote to you is dead. I am now in my right mind.

I've just returned from a lecture with the house group, at the Methodist church, which was salty enough to make a lot of wounds smart. "Thought you were cracking the profound secrets of life, which have evaded great men and women for centuries, did you? Huh!"

My great and glorious evangelical mission of the newly inaugurated Albion house-group dwindled to two – and I got lost looking for Mr Tub's house (whom I can't help calling Mr Plod) – so we were late.

People at the church bustled to get him a chair and a song sheet. He can't see properly, and he is bad at stairs since his wife died.

After the lecture I asked him if he would like to go up for healing – there was an invitation to anyone who wanted to receive the laying on of hands. He whispered, "I'm the sort of a chap who likes to be fair. I've put my case in the hands of a doctor at the hospital. I'll give him a chance before I go to anyone else".

I said: "Some of the group who couldn't be here are coming round to our house tomorrow to hear about it. I don't suppose you want to come?"

"Oh, lovely," said Mr Plod, "It'll be like a second chapter for this evening, won't it!"

17th October 1977

So 'newly inaugurated' got together to hear the words of the sage at the Methodist church, second-hand from the lips of Mr Plod and myself. No tape recordings, no anointed leader plucked from the talent of the mother church – just us from Albion. We told them what the preacher said about God's healing. Our lot, aged between twenty-something to late seventies, listened for hours, and still they wouldn't go home. So we had coffee.

"Let's pray for Gail," said Nora (70, who pitches our songs). "She's going away on holiday." We hold hands and pray.

"Let's say the grace," says Gail (30-something, fallen in love with Mr Plod, who ran silent movies in Cape Town in his youth – how *surprising* people are).

"You've made me get my thinking cap on," says Mr Plod. "See you next week."

Marie walked her longest walk for eight years tonight – from next door. June says, "I'll pop down and see her during the day sometimes. I suppose she gets lonely?" Marie never gets visitors.

On the table is vase of sweet peas from June's neighbour.

"Never really got on very well with people in Albion," this neighbour told me, by way of 'doesn't want to come to our house group'. "Never really worked that chap out," remarked June when I told her where the flowers came from. Do I bring them together?

Or is that trespassing? I'm so sorry they changed the words of the Lord's Prayer.[3]

Today I began a diary again. The first words are: "I won't waste any more of Alfred's time by writing him letters, but I will write a diary. Should anyone ever read this they must know that it is dedicated to him." Anything which I know would make you happy I will write directly to you of course – and you are always free to read it (my diary). But as the great Oscar Wilde wrote at last: "Life cannot be written. Life must be lived."

3. 'Forgive us our trespasses' was replaced by 'Forgive us our sins' in the 1975 South African liturgy.

25

Amy now visits Nazareth House regularly at weekends. It is a whole day's trip by train, and not very popular with Wolf, although he often works overtime on Saturdays, or is away playing tennis. He is utterly non-plussed as to why Amy should want to mix with such people. She feels a hunger for the human warmth of Alfred and his family of derelicts in Hillbrow. It puts flesh and blood on the ghostly apparatus of prayer, which she essays every day. But she remains in the dark about what this tremulous hour of wandering thoughts and delinquent images is supposed to achieve; what constitutes success.

At Nazareth House Amy meets Petunia, who has joined the cohort of women who flock around Alfred whenever he is in the city. At first Amy only registers a foggy image of this young woman, drifting down the corridor in a shroud of cigarette smoke. Amy is attracted to her whimsical manner and eccentric clothing. She affects ankle-length skirts of raw linen, and draped tunics made of the same fabric coloured with vegetable dyes, secured with a leather belt. She is very slim and the effect is winsome. She looks as if she has escaped from the painting of a saint.

Petunia's voice is low and she speaks very fast. You have to bend your ear and concentrate hard to catch what she is saying. Most of it is seriously intense discourse on prayer and the state of the world; interspersed with quaint throwaway lines, which are marked by a swift smile revealing crooked teeth, and a glance of faun-like eyes.

"Alfred made us read the psalm, the one about hiding under his wings; I do love the Lord's feathers. Not that he really made us, he was just wanting to get some sort of order in the house after Jacob poured a mug of coffee over Silvia because she was asleep in prayers. Charity begins at home, sort of thing. Anyway, Silvia's cigarette got wet so she went for Jacob and pulled his earring off. Blood everywhere. The volunteer starts screaming, silly wench, and calls the ambulance; but it was only a scratch. So Alfred gets going on the psalm, although he has to yell to be heard above all the screaming and crying: Keep me as the apple of the eye; hide me in the shadow of thy wings. I do love that bit; and the one about the sparrow finding a nesting place beneath thy altars."

Petunia turns up in Albion one Friday afternoon and asks if she can stay. Alfred has said there is room. Amy, astonished, but falling over herself to accommodate Alfred, if only by proxy, welcomes her in.

Wolf is surprisingly amenable to the unexpected visitor; but then she is a lissom young woman with long brown hair and an enchanting way of peering out from under its silken wings as they flop around her face.

Petunia, it turns out, is a landscape gardener in another life; the one she used to have in Bryanston, before she got religion. Along with her devotion to the Lord she acquired a serious addiction to Berocca, which she consumes in huge quantities at all times of day and night. This substance abuse plus the chain-smoking drives her nervous system at a constant gallop, except when she anchors herself to the floor on her knees and prays to the Lord to have mercy on her. Which she does quite often. Wolf is not altogether happy about this, but finds Petunia so enchantingly non-conformist in every other way he is inclined to overlook this perversity on her part.

Petunia, high on nicotine and industrial doses of vitamin C, reckons the ramshackle garden in Albion will be a piece of cake, as Alfred would say. They trawl the neighbourhood collecting sacks full of plant debris, dumped on verges for garbage collectors following the spring clean-up.

Amy doesn't know the difference between a corm and a bulb, and hasn't a clue what to do with either. But from this unlikely looking detritus Petunia extracts sufficient biomass for whole beds of agapanthus, iris, cannas and day lilies; plus jars full of ivy, daisy and pelagonian cuttings which are set out along the verandah windowsills to take root. For a long time she ruminates over the sterile shale of the front yard.

"*Coreopsis*," she declares at last. "A lot of people think it's a weed, but a weed is just a plant in the wrong place. It's yellow, like a buttercup, and it will grow anywhere. Coreopsis will do nicely here. It will look like a meadow. Of course you can't do meadows in Bryanston; they don't like it. The latest thing is garden gnomes, only people keep stealing them. They have to pay the gardener to do night watch."

Petunia fossicks out a bucketful of gazania roots (they will grow on the *beach*) and some pigface from the salvage, to join seed heads of coreopsis daisies destined to be strewn around the front yard.

Amy incautiously mentions roses, and gets a bollocking. Roses belong in English gardens, not on the Highveld. But then Petunia relents and says iceberg roses would do quite nicely under the back verandah, around the birdbath, between the jacaranda and the pepper tree. These however would have to be bought from a nursery.

Amy regards the half-acre of overgrown land and feels weak at the prospect of digging in all these gnarly, stringy bits of vegetation. Wolf is only just recovering from the anomaly of going walking whilst owning a car. Asking a sailor to dig in a garden that isn't even his would be a bridge too far. But Petunia has the labour angle covered.

§

Spring is in the air and a chain gang is digging in the garden at Albion. There are twelve of them; enough to fit comfortably on the tray of a bakkie, the four-wheel-drive truck that brought them from the prison to do a day's work gardening for thirty rand. Not that they will get the money. The government gets that. They are thin, wiry men all dressed in the same sort of donkey grey colour that they are themselves; as if dust has settled on them and become engrained into their skin and clothing.

You have to book them; chain gangs are quite popular at this time of year when people are doing their gardens. Not that they actually have chains on. They are low risk convicts, in gaol for not having a pass, or just being in the wrong place at the wrong time. The serious ones are in different prisons. They hang them seven at a time in Pretoria Central on Fridays. That's a bit icky, isn't it?

Now Petunia is overseeing the gang with unexpected authority. Her voice is quite stentorian as she organises the digging of beds under the tree line; the clearing of roots thick as fishing nets; the planting in military rows of corms and bulbs and cuttings, which she has carefully conjured from the salvage heap and prepared for propagation.

Amy is cooking vast quantities of mealipap for lunchtime – or ten o'clock when the convicts will eat. They started work at 7 am. Johanna, Amy's maid, has shown her how to do this; white maize

meal boiled with a little water to make a porridge, stirred briskly
with a wooden spoon, simmered for forty minutes 'til it goes brown
at the bottom of the pot.

Amy wants to give the men more than this sad repast. She cooks
up a mess of lamb chops with vegetables. There are not enough tin
plates and mugs. Black people always have tin plates and mugs. She
carts china ones down the garden together with the food; feels oddly
embarrassed as the men tentatively take their meal, ducking their
heads at her, bending the knee, crossing one arm over the other.

After they have gone back to wherever it is they came from,
Petunia arms Amy with a garden hose and instructs her to soak the
new beds thoroughly on a daily basis. She must buy sprinklers and
keep everything moist for a week or two until the plantlings have
had a chance to feel at home and put down roots.

The front yard will look after itself; the rains are coming soon.
Then she leaves Amy alone with this vast nursery, dependent upon
her for its well being.

26

Amy's intention to stop wasting Alfred's time with her letters soon falls by the wayside. She has lost her landmarks during the past few months and when transient ebullient moods desert her she still trusts that Alfred, at least, knows what is happening to her.

There seems to be no connection between the person she was before she met Alfred, and the being she is now. That previous life is like the memory of a movie, or a book she once read. She is entirely dependent upon this monk to tell her who she is; if indeed she is anybody at all, so complete is her alienation from her former life. Somewhere along the way she has gone missing.

§

Tuesday 19th October 1977

Dear Alfred,

Do you like Mahler? Somewhere in that tremendous symphony number 8, in Dr Marianus, the choir sings, "All transitory things are parables". I feel transitory like that. When I say 'I', particularly when addressing you, I don't use the word 'I' as meaning ego. These days I feel as if I am a parable of myself.

I felt it was improper, almost indecent, to tell you about the miraculous things I saw happening around me. Now I understand better why you answer my thanks with: "It's nothing to do with me." It is so easy to fall prey to pride in the spiritual life. But how else am I going to share these marvellous, terrifying, possibly delusional events, if not with you? So I want you to understand that if I write 'I', it is just a convenient figure of speech for the Spirit working in me.

I never let my right hand know what my left hand is doing, because we are not supposed to receive the praise of mortals, or take pride in ourselves. But I was seeing such awesome reconciliation and healing which I thought came about through me that I was frightened. I was bombarded with tormenting thoughts: "You are just a woman," "You have no foundation," "You are only a child in the faith," "Even Satan can disguise himself as an angel of light," "False prophets…" and so on.

I think I can glimpse turmoil and loneliness in Jesus' question to Peter: "Who do men say that I am?" I believe Jesus had an inkling of who he was; but was afraid of such awful knowledge.

There was a time, not so long ago, when I felt as if I had been struck by lightning when I dared to even try to look at the Christ. My literary background includes *Paradise Lost* and *Dr Faustus* – terrifying tales of the cost of pride. All this reduces me to nervous wreckage. But then I read in one of your sensible books that this way of the spirit is for me also.

However, I feel shame. Accused so often of an over-active imagination, I have to squint, and look very hard at every answered prayer, to be quite sure it is real. It gets worse and worse – the anxiety. Is it 'aspiring pride' to use the word 'I' when writing about these miracles, these healings and blessings? After all it is God's work. But then I, whoever I am, seem to be an active ingredient in it.

I am confused. I have been obedient, done as I was told even unto death. I negated 'ego' to such an extent I was barely aware of my own existence. I allowed my circumstances to carry me where they would, as if I no longer had a will of my own. If I looked in a mirror I did not see myself, except as some alien creature. The only time I seemed to impinge on the world at large, to penetrate its reality, was when I smoked a cigarette. Your recognition and acceptance of me was my only human link with the material world.

Auberon, poor fellow, broke that link. He did want to come with me to my house. You put him in my care. It was not me who submitted him to that marathon night, but 'Bron who tested my faith with every argument in his power. During that night I showed him a photo of the Turin Shroud and asked him what he thought of it. He said casually: "Well, it's moving". Then he quite lost his temper. "It's a worldly face. It's cynical and superficial. I don't know who it is or who drew it, but it's horrible". I was quite encouraged by that because he cared. It moved him.

I hope, at this stage, that you are not reading this letter with that chilling expression which says, "I don't quite understand". It is Tuesday, I am well and happy. I am not mad. I am merely telling you a story about what I suppose must be my conversion. Inaugurated by you.

Having loved you, become able to love everyone else because of you, and falling in love with God because of it all – I need to go back together with you to find myself again.

Once, kneeling on the carpet in Nazareth House, your eyes screwed up with concentration, you fluently described Francis McNutt's teaching in a few words. You were cross because you couldn't remember the teacher's exact words – but I was pleased, because your own interpretation of him was so succinct: "Healing comes through acceptance".

You don't have to understand everything about me. I would like to know that you have found time to read this, that you believe that what I write is true, and that you love me. Your recognition and acceptance of me is my sea anchor.

The wounding event is now past. I have died in Christ. Being rather prone to taking things literally, during this process I paid all my debts, put everyone I loved into someone else's care, cleaned and tidied my house, and gave away all I could without arousing suspicion. The interior journey filled my entire horizon; just as a child who has lost his mother is so absorbed in his own misery there is nothing left but the angst, which is so all-consuming the whole world cannot contain it. You may laugh at the image – I can, but with that sad sort of laughter which signals an understanding of the frailty and sheer glory of humanity.

Now I know I am not alone. I have the company of Sister Angela, a woman, like me, but with the wisdom to recognise our selfhood as unique people. Bishop Tim is close by in the world I am returning to. I have you as brother, companion and friend. The reality of this family on earth, reflecting the glory of heaven, dawns on me. I who was nothing, am now, whatever the future holds, secure, loved, and somehow home.

It does not surprise me when an acquaintance gives me a passing glance, and then suddenly brings me into focus. "Oh Amy!" mild surprise, an unspoken, "I did not recognise you," or even, "I have never noticed you before." For I know I am changed.

I also now understand your curt tone of voice when prodded to speak of the war years – of flying Spitfires, of PoW. My father never speaks of it either. It is like another life which one cannot, or dare not, visit. One is no longer that person. One finds it very hard to believe that one has actually survived. Life seems so fragile.

I would like the luxury of a few hours spent with you, preferably by a camp fire with an African night chorusing away – and I can tell you about all the places I have been, and you can tell me what a silly child I am – and you will believe my stories, and I will believe yours, and Francis McNutt will chuckle.

27

In January Amy had enrolled for undergraduate studies in history, art and literature with Unisa, the University of South Africa. She dropped out of university in England. At the time the call of adventure on the high seas, of travelling the coasts of Europe and Africa, had seemed far more attractive than studying in the bleak midland town of Leicester. Now she has had enough of adventure for the time being. Her Unisa studies have taken a back seat since she embarked on the interior journey, with Alfred as her companion. Suddenly first year examinations are in the offing, and Amy is scrambling to catch up with her academic commitments.

§

20th October 1977

Dear Alfred,
This evening I cautiously raised my eyes sufficiently to mundane things to review my exam timetable. I have done well enough in the minimum number of assignments to be permitted to write three modules. I hope to pass or fail gracefully, but I think I am required to pass. That means that your book by Emile Mersch will be imbibed in small sips, *mit Genüß*, and may not even be returned to the priory before my next retreat.

What a bizarre mind I have – and I wonder, where are its limits? I am finishing E M Forster's *Passage to India* and am captivated by that author:"Good and evil are different as their names imply. But, in my own humble opinion, they are both aspects of my Lord. He is present in the one absent in the other... absence implies presence, absence is not non-existent." Forster, p 175, Penguin. How can such a concise and discerning theological statement appear in the middle of a novel?

Wednesday

'Doomed', as Auberon would intone, to fail my exams. Four days is simply not enough for swotting up on a year's work. Now, smitten with Smetana, and a couple of glasses of good white wine, European history is about as important to me as a mosquito bite. The light on my desk makes the buttery grain of the yellowwood swirl like a river. I shall write to you instead. You've shared enough of my misery — why not share my joy? I shall tell you stories about Zululand.

Zululand is the closest thing in South Africa, I think, to the essence of Africa. Dust and sweat, and waiting for buses which never come; gossiping in interminable queues; adaptable prices always open to barter; prayer mats at sundown; blood red starfish left by the outgoing tide; veld fires in the sugar cane; road signs saying 'Beware! Hippos crossing'; leopard tracks on bone white sand; nurseries where turtles lay their rubbery eggs under signs saying 'Trespassers will be prosecuted'. If you go barefoot in the dune forest remember, it is the home of the python; do not be rudely alarmed if she crosses your path.

You wait on the beach for the fishermen, when they bring home barracuda and marlin. They will talk about the dolphin, and the orca who rests her beak on the gunwale to have her back scratched, or this or that or the other story, all full of the day on the sea, far from terra firma.

Then you go off alone and peer into a rock pool — at the whole teeming nursery of the sea in its little circumference. You gather oysters and mussels (forbidden fruit, according to the rangers) and return home to simmer them in wine.

Thursday night

Ten minutes rest from swotting — and to prevent my brain sinking into fatal numbness I shall write to you. Have you ever walked in the mountains in the snow hoping that each new crest will reveal the way down? Eventually you are so exhausted, you are so very weary, that you want to lie down. But you don't lie down, for snow is warm and soft — and deadly.

These exams are no longer just exams but a marathon — trying to do a year's work in three weeks. This evening, every evening, presents a fresh obstacle at which I hurl myself. I am encouraged by a memory of other times when — just before the inevitable fall — another, indomitable will does the doing for me, floats me to the other side in a cloud of indescribable bliss (or shock perhaps?) and I forget to say 'thank you'.

All this reading is turning my head. Milton I have the deepest respect for, even reverence. Wordsworth celebrated in the temple of

the natural world, although not submitting himself to its creator –
my studies tell me he was a pantheist. Keats, young and beautiful did
his best to die early, like any self-respecting poet. What I remember
best from my so-far cursory studies of Gerard Manley Hopkins' work
(apart from the fact that he never meant it to be published) were
his dying words, which might, in any other context, be considered
rather girlish: "I'm so happy. So happy."

Reading has always been important to me. I love C S Lewis
because he introduced me to Aslan. And he brought me back from
the wilderness when I found his book *Surprised by Joy* at St Bede's.

In short, if I fail these exams it doesn't matter because I have
learned so much. If I pass, then I am truly blessed – because the
outcome will certainly have had little to do with my own labours.

It is written somewhere in the epistles that one is to continue
in the state in which one is found. Well, I was found entangled in
undergraduate studies. Tomorrow I will sit for three hours doing
battle with the consequences of that – and God help me!

29th October 1977

I have had a terrible day. I bit my husband, beat my dog, and
smashed a coke bottle; all before midday. Under proper scrutiny this
behaviour would reveal that I am in a stable (if immature) state of
mind, responding appropriately to worldly chaos.

I have given up trying to understand other people's minds. Not
because I couldn't, to some degree, thanks to the Romany ancestor,
but because I now understand that it is trespassing to intrude on
another person's mind without an invitation.

Similarly, my own mind is no longer open to inquisitive probings
by others, or even to myself. I apply my mind to situations as they
arise. It seems to be coping with that degree of engagement. If I were
ever intelligent, which many of my teachers would dispute, I was
obviously incapable of managing that gift properly before, and much
given to speculative dilettantism.

I listen to the words from Dr Marianus, "Blinking, new in the
world of spirits, he knows not where he is," sung so tenderly. How is
it possible to live blind for so long – so conscious of the otherworld,
and yet convinced it is an illusion? And then, even when born again
into it, to think oneself to be alone?

Of course the answer is clearly apparent from the other side of the abyss. The mind has been irrevocably changed by the journey. It no longer operates in the old, analytic way. I remember telling you that I now prefer 'perceiving' to 'knowing' — and you kept repeating, like an antiphon, "I think you are onto something very exciting". There is another sort of knowing now, which is less clear but more sure.

Yesterday, at a prayer meeting which our house group went to, we were asked to talk to one another in pairs. "Open up and share!" as Fr Albert would cry, as if it were something to enjoy. I found a couple of women to talk to Marie and Mr Tubb, and allowed myself to be scooped up by a parishioner from the cathedral.

She asked me when did I meet God? You know, I am totally at a loss how to answer such a question! Obviously, I know I cannot meet God except through the Son, but I could hardly point that out without sounding patronising. She was scrutinising me as if I ought to give birth to something. It made me shy, and cross. If there is anything in the universe I am leery of discussing at the moment, it is myself. Except with you, of course.

I have often noticed a sort of truthful untruthfulness in you — a sort of bypassing of yourself — a sleight of hand, as if you are in disguise, a jesuitical wolf in sheep's clothing. You are not exactly lying, but there is a lot you are not saying. Apropos of nothing in particular, except that I find that quality very attractive. I wish I could do it too, so that I could graciously sidestep such intrusive questions.

But I do have to find a place in this new dispensation. God is not raising up apathetic laity like myself for fun. It is a time for martyrs, especially here in South Africa. Even if my work is only intercession, I would appreciate some guidance from you. I am tired of being idle.

What a stormy letter. Written on the crest of a wave of adrenaline, after swotting. But not altogether rubbish, so I will send it. I don't cling to my letters to you the way I used to. I wrote in my diary on 29th September: "I've grown out of my boundaries! Ineffable!" But diary died rather an early death — there has been no entry since.

Instead, something in the murky abyss of my soul bestirs me to write to you about everything — the joys of life, or "wish you were here" sort of thing — not just spiritual stuff. Whatever I write, however, is usually a circumlocution of "Help!" until each nagging fear in my mind is dragged into the light, put down on paper, submitted to you, and thereby exorcised.

28

The charismatic renewal in the mainstream churches had the initial effect of ushering lay folk who aspired to be evangelists, prophets, preachers, teachers, exorcists, and a medley of other ministries, into something of a cultural ghetto. Emotive utterances and extravagant gestures became the lingua franca of charismatics, which upset traditional Anglicans who were more averse to displays of emotion.

The bible, preferably The Good News version, became a text book for zealots. All matters were measured against its canon, and judged according to the letter of its law.

Unfortunately this bible had little to say about writers and artists; and appeared to be openly hostile towards philosophy, according to St Paul's remarks to the Athenians. This leaves Amy in something of a quandary. She wants to share her passion for literature and art with Alfred. He is himself devoted to the French Impressionists, viewed as profane by charismatic hard-liners. But she has the uneasy feeling that she is on ground where angels fear to tread when writing about such matters.

Garth, a deacon, and the new warden of Nazareth House who has replaced the disgraced Auberon, has ordered all paintings and artefacts which are not specifically Christian to be removed from the building. This includes Alfred's favourite Monet print of the woman and child in the poppy field. Such a hostile act persuades Amy to venture into theology.

§

12th November 1977

Dear Alfred,

It seems to me that Garth has a problem vis-à-vis secular art. With his current attitude, doesn't Garth deny God's right to direct all that is good in his creation? I am asked, in my studies of literature and art, to evaluate diverse works by Wordsworth and Gerard Manley

Hopkins; Chaucer and Pope; the ancient Egyptians and the Christian Romans. What is my standard for such critical analysis?

When I read Tintern Abbey I cannot say, "Ugh! Wordsworth's a pantheist; ergo I must reject his poetry." That wonderful moment when Wordsworth almost transcends the works he worships, is proof of God's inspiration beating on a great poet's perceptions. Praise God. Rest Wordsworth's soul. The same applies to Hellenistic Greek art, and so on.

Oh I have been so terribly wrong to doubt God's hand in these so-called secular works! For so long I have felt their divine power, and truth, and beauty. Even written inspired poetry myself occasionally, when I too did not understand what I was writing, or why I wrote.

If Garth is unable to apply aesthetic standards himself, he is perhaps wise to resist being influenced by anything without a Christian stamp of approval. Shortly after what I describe as my conversion, my mind flinched from anything not one hundred per cent recommended by you – almost as if it had touched a hot stove.

During that time I should have been reading *Paradise Lost* for my studies, but could not. I think my recovery began when I decided that my commitment to my studies was still valid. After forcing myself to return to 'secular' art I rediscovered that also in a new light.

Once Garth's commitment to the needs of those in your mutual care becomes greater than his need to shield himself from 'worldly' things, I think maybe he will discover aesthetic standards within himself. He will find the 'cunning of a serpent' in using all things for good.

I will enclose a stamp this time. I think I am right about these matters – and I know from experience that this is very thin ice! Please write back and correct me where I err.

Wednesday

Yesterday evening Wolf and I sat with two of the chaps he goes walking with in the mountains. They have a spaniel, a cupboard full of classical records, and a vast tropical fish tank.

We yarned about the potential size of creatures ten thousand feet under the surface of the oceans. Roger, who is a scientist, scoffed about the impossibility of such creatures, according to his knowledge and understanding.

I got quite cross and argued the contrary. I finished up by saying something to the effect that I wished scientists would begin with the supposition that anything is possible and use their knowledge to answer 'whys?' as well as 'whats?'

Something dawned on Roger's face like the rising sun. He couldn't put it into words, but he was desperate that someone should understand what he had seen. The words he used stumbled, but they were a lovely exercise in wisdom and humility.

After that conversation, by way of restoring the pecking order, Wolf subjected me to a quiz on Greek mythology out of an encyclopaedia. I did fairly well, to my own astonishment.

The chapel at the priory has a life-sized icon on the left hand side of the sanctuary. Amy enjoys staring at it when she is at the priory in time for one of the daily offices. It focusses her attention. Sometimes it seems to come alive and she feels as if she is following the image instead of gazing at it.

The brethren gather four times a day, for morning devotions, the office and the eucharist, for midday office, evening prayer, and compline. It is a lived-in space, as wide as it is deep, like a normal room with stone flagging. Each brother has his own stall, with his books and sturdy, well worn hassock.

During evensong one Sunday Amy is inducted as a tertiary of the Community. Fr Warwick, the Prior, and Fr Cuthbert who is to be her warden, conduct the simple ceremony and pin a bronze brooch on her jumper, which bears an image of the paschal lamb, the insignia of the Community. Warwick gives her a little book of the night office of compline – which Sister Elizabeth naughtily pronounces 'complain'.

Amy now belongs to the fraternity, and she feels warmed by this acknowledgement, as if the sun is shining upon her, although it is already dark outside.

Preparations for the enrolment have been cursory. Fr Cuthbert interviewed her, following her formal application to join. He laughed a lot, and sought to calm her anxieties about the duties of belonging to the tertiaries. In fact it was quite disappointing how little was required of her. A rule of life had to be agreed upon, whereby she promised to make her communion at least once a week on Sundays; pray daily; give alms – which appeared to mean putting something in the collection plate in church; make sacramental confession; consult her spiritual director regularly; and report to her warden, Cuthbert, quarterly.

Confession at least offered some novelty. They agreed she should make her confession once a month – she had suggested once a week, but Cuthbert laughed all the more and said this was far too often, and every three months would do. They bargained and settled on monthly – but Alfred couldn't do it because he was only a lay brother, not a priest. She would have to find a priest confessor. Cuthbert would do for the time being, she decided, although he seemed to find the dreadful prospect of her first confession rather amusing.

Confession was not funny; it was serious business. Her imagination replayed the drama of walking up Mount Anderson remembering the sins of her young life. She played with countless narrative threads, trying to downplay the sex bits so that she did not appear entirely unfit to be a tertiary. But apart from that there didn't seem to be a great deal wrong with her.

In the event, at her first sacramental confession, Amy whispered a garbled account of past sins, apologising for not having much to confess, drawing a veil over youthful promiscuity. Cuthbert, who had become grave and rather frightening in his purple stole, replied crisply that she should give thanks for a clear conscience. On reflection she wondered if his tone had been a little wry. But he gave her absolution, together with the rather limp penance of saying a psalm. She came out of the encounter feeling like a newly hatched chick.

Alfred is now officially her spiritual director, now she has joined the fraternity. Amy's letters take on a more self-conscious tenor. She relishes the obligation to report everything that goes on in her spiritual life. She has read books on the subject of spiritual direction. Nothing may be left out; the baring of her soul must be complete. Her life depends upon Alfred's wisdom and guidance. She is as a newborn child; vulnerable to any passing, mischievous spirit; powerless to nurture herself; exposed like an abandoned infant upon the mountainside of arid modernity.

§

13th November 1977

Dear Alfred,

It is absolutely no use! My diary happily records things which may come in useful for a report to my warden — or unhappily as the case may be. But I do need a daily heart-searching which only comes out satisfactorily in words to you. Maybe you understand, maybe you don't; it doesn't matter.

When I told you that it sometimes took me an hour to read a page of *The Spiritual Man* you thought it was because I could not understand it. It wasn't that. I understood all too well what it was saying to me – but I couldn't make the leaps it was placing in front of me. "This part of you is foul. Discard it!" with me already lying harrowed in the mud, as doubtless many others have been before me. But at that time I thought I was the only one.

It is true that you can lay down a book, but it was more than just reading a book. It was a pilgrimage. You can't lay down a pilgrimage – otherwise you might just as well have not bothered to embark on it in the first place.

Fr Albert was in bad odour in the chapelry of St Marks. At first his alleged sins had been alluded to in a 'nudge nudge wink wink' kind of fashion, and not taken particularly seriously by anyone. But his misdemeanours gathered substance as the congregation found they could manage the chapelry very well without him, and became keen to get rid of him. He was interfering. He poked his nose in where it was not wanted. He was entirely too bossy at council meetings.

Lay ministry was Fr Albert's passion. He encouraged every one of his parishioners to find their own ministry within the church. You are a royal priesthood, he told them. So they stopped being sheep and became something rather more wolverine; turning on their shepherd with relish. But he was blissfully ignorant of the maelstrom of discontent rising against him in the chapelry.

Amy has watched this scapegoating exercise with a sense of déjà vu. She feels protective towards Fr Albert, as she felt protective towards her father while he struggled to care for his parishioners in spite of a multitude of small cruelties – which were probably just down to carelessness.

§

Monday

Dear Alfred,

I went to see Fr Albert in good faith – intending to confess something that is bothering me. I am trying him out as a confessor. But I end up, totally against all my conceptions of proper order, fishing him out of his own misery (or at least trying). It is all very well for my warden to require me to go to sacramental confession – but who on earth do I go to, when they end up telling me about their own problems?

Wolf was watching television at our cousins' house when I called in at St Wilf''s. Fr Albert could have been out, or occupied with his family, or happy to be alone. But he was sitting in his study, and plainly glad to see me!

I discovered why after about quarter of an hour of exchanging pleasantries. One of the women in my group had decided to tell him about the trouble he was getting into in the chapelry. She had phoned him that afternoon. Only told him half the truth of course, silly ass. He was deeply wounded by it.

I wanted to tell you something ages ago – before I believed in God – but I thought it was too foolish. Sometimes I am engulfed by this desire to gather the whole of suffering humanity in my arms. It is such a powerful feeling it brings tears to my eyes. I couldn't begin to describe it to you. Such an event leaves me feeling very alone, and very much in need of direction.

15th November 1977

Dear Alfred,

I was thinking about the rifts in the Albion congregation this morning and felt moved to write a story about it. I was in the office working with these thoughts when in stomps our boss for his usual coffee and cigarette. He is very into Krishnamurti, and has had a go at the truth drug. I asked if I could read to him what I had just written, and did so in rather a shaky voice.

This man, who is meddling with things best left alone, responded by triumphantly regaling me with the three important things Jesus said about reconciliation – before beating a retreat to his own office. Unfortunately he remains convinced that the rest of the bible is for the birds.

Then Mary, from the Albion house group, visited us here in the copywriters' office. She had to take her child to the dentist upstairs. So I tried the draft of my reflection out on her. This helped me take the plunge and phone Fr Albert: "Got a short article here if you can use it for the parish magazine. Very personal".

"Oh good. We're going to the typesetters at five o'clock. I'll pick it up."

"Well, hang on a minute. You'd better read it. I mean sometime, not necessarily now. It's 230 words. There won't be space!"

His wife fetched it and said it would come in useful because the Presbyterians had failed to submit their copy. So it's probably typeset by now and he hasn't even read it! I hope he can exercise his editorial capacity before printing.

I have been listening to prophecies since my childhood:

"You are a child of your generation."

"We sail on the crest of a new renaissance."

"Do not fear the atom bomb. When they come they will come from Africa, and there are so many of them all they will need is their bare hands."

"Great changes are coming to South Africa."

These things I have heard without understanding, but now I remember them in my heart and they take on new meaning. I regard those who have gone before us with reverence, because they have borne our burden for us throughout millennia of prayer.

Quietly, within myself, I also welcome small children, of whom I was once terrified. You will remain beautiful, I think to myself when I look at children now. Where we once stewed in our frustrated search for meaning, you will tread gracefully in the knowledge and love of God. It is all becoming so clear to me.

Our history is not innocent. When I was studying for exams I discovered that the Jews took up usury because Christians were forbidden to practice it on pain of excommunication. When medieval Italian princes found banking loans expedient, they imposed a penalty for converting a Jew for this very reason. Money has run things ever since. "In the common opinion, that the state that abounds in money hath courage, hath men, and all other instruments to defend itself and offend others, if it have wisdom how to make use of it." Rice Vaughan, *A Discourse of Coin and Coinage*, 1675, p 59. "Hence it was that the precious metals came to be identified with power," *Europe from Renaissance to Waterloo*, Ergang.

This letter has been a luxury. I am stretching the muscles of my mind after the Unisa exercises. I want to become very bookish for a few weeks and catch up on the reading you have given me. I have just read this:

> "If to any the tumult of the flesh were hushed; hushed the images of earth, and waters, and air; hushed also the poles of heaven, yea the very soul be hushed to herself, and by not thinking on self surmount self; hushed all dreams and imaginary revelations, every tongue and every sign, and whatsoever exists only in translation, since if any could hear, all these say, We made not ourselves, but He made us that abideth forever." *St Augustine's Confessions* ix.10

I sense that urgency which hounded the early Christians. Every day seems to be the first and the last day. The slightest event acquires vast significance. But in the face of what appears to be universal chaos, I am perfectly calm.

When I consider how dry this sounds in writing, I wonder what overwhelming inspiration the writers of scripture laboured under – for their addressee was the entire world! Although I s'pose they didn't know that at the time.

31

Alfred is away on leave. She feels his absence like an amputation, but her letters supply blood to the missing limb. She has not visited Nazareth House since he left for what he calls furlough, as the journey by bus and train to Hillbrow takes in excess of three hours each way, and Wolf is not happy about foraging for his own dinner.

Perhaps Wolf notices her drooping spirits, for when Alfred returns to the priory, Wolf drives her over there to visit one evening. He is a good driver now, if somewhat racy – but then he had a good teacher, she tells herself complacently.

Alfred is holding court in his room at the priory with Petunia, who is also making a welcome-home visit, together with a friend from Nazareth House, and her cat. Petunia travels with an elegant Burmese in an antique basket weave carry cot. The cat meows in a tenor voice from time to time. Brother Giles joins the company in Alfred's room, by way of chaperone, for a monk should not be left alone with women about.

Alfred's spacious room with its access to the verandah and gardens is always open house, which does not altogether concord with Community rules. Even bees make themselves at home here, using the room as a convenient passageway between the pollen fields of the courtyard and the garden. When the Prior found out about this, by way of an obtrusive bee sting on Alfred's forehead where he had inadvertently rolled on a visitor in his sleep, Warwick had the hive smoked out and removed, to Alfred's great sorrow.

This evening's company seems ill at ease, in spite of Giles' bonhomie, and Alfred's rudimentary hospitality, pouring the wine Amy has brought into a tooth mug to be passed from hand to hand.

Petunia is telling Alfred about changes in the routine of Nazareth House while he has been away on leave. 'Interference' she calls it, by the committee, who have taken to visiting without notice, and feel free to stick their noses into every corner of the premises. An emergency meeting of the committee has been called for three days hence, which the presiding bishop will chair, and to which Brother Alfred has been summoned. Alfred pats Petunia down, and laughs sympathetically with Giles who complains that secular clergy are always running things, but a small frown creases his brow.

Petunia and company leave at last. Wolf also stands up to go. Giles potters off about his own business. Alfred rummages around in his cupboard and solemnly presents Amy with a brown paper parcel.

"A gift from Swaziland," he says.

Inside the wrapping is a pottery wine cup with blue and grey glaze, which she instantly knows is a chalice. She is speechless with gratitude. She nods dumbly, and takes her leave before he can see the tears in her eyes.

When they arrive back at Albion later that night, Wolf parks the car and she gets out of the passenger seat, forgetting the precious parcel on her lap. It falls to the concrete floor of the garage and breaks into seven pieces. Amy is inconsolable, tearily gathering up the shards, cradling them. Wolf irritably tells her not to fuss, he will glue them together in the morning.

32

7th December 1977

Dear Alfred,

I've had some thoughts about the meeting of the Nazareth House committee tomorrow – I know you are not looking forward to it. Maybe they will help, albeit after the event – my thoughts I mean. An outside observer can see the wood while others are still lost in the trees.

Firstly, an ecumenical centre in the middle of Hillbrow is presumably concerned with the problems of the area – alcoholism, suicide, drug addiction, prostitution. If people are drawn to volunteer at Nazareth House it is reasonable to presume that they are interested in helping these 'down and outs'. Any volunteer who is offended by a swear word or an inebriated visitor is probably in the wrong ministry. Barring drunks from Nazareth House defeats the objectives of the place. To bar a person in a drunken state is, I suppose, reasonable. Wives all over the world do it.

Also, I may be wrong, but when healing addictions I think the individual often has to get worse in order to get better. I was talking to Joe before you went away. He confided, "I'm in a dreadful state. I can't stop drinking. How am I going to stop?" That's an alcoholic on the long road to recovery.

It might be a good idea for the committee to clarify exactly what they want done in Hillbrow. After all, it isn't the place for tea parties.

Secondly, concerning your ministry there. It is plain that your spadework has made the house a living organisation – I hear enough to that effect every time I am there. A criticism which has been, or will be levelled at you is that it is your own personality which draws people to Nazareth House, to the detriment of their spiritual development.

You could point out that a ministry to the 'outsiders' depends on just that – personality, the strange attractor. Having once passed through the eye of the needle – the most difficult part – the one who has been saved can find his own way. He should be beginning his own ministry anyway, and thus your personality will not be a 'danger' to him.

However, should the committee decide that Nazareth House is now established and henceforth the people welcomed in shall fit the criteria of the workforce – then your ministry there is probably over.

Evangelists and apostles are not suitable for directing established institutions – they are wasted on them. But the king-makers should never forget that without charisma there would have been no establishment.

You are bound to draw fire at Nazareth House, because the full weight of responsibility rests upon you. Perhaps it is time to demand some practical support from the committee. It is unreasonable to expect one man to do administration, pastoral work, 'bouncing', and supply lunch for such a large and boisterous establishment.

§

Amy had watched her father sink beneath the waves of pastoral responsibility in the years before she left home. It seemed that the vicar was jack of all trades, expected to repair the lights in the parish hall and mow the cemetery lawns, as well as preach the sermon in church on Sunday. Churchwardens used to manage the minutiae of parish business, but by the 'sixties people were too busy about their own lives to spare time for the parish. So Amy watched her father work himself threadbare, holding together an establishment which was slowly becoming a cultural relic, peopled by the elderly and infirm of the English middle class.

It was heartbreaking to watch her father grow weary and hollow-eyed: "Being ground out for a little flour, for people who do not even know they are hungry", as he once described his ministry. Now Alfred is under scrutiny by the committee of Nazareth House. Ministry is flourishing at this church-sponsored establishment, its abundant life spilling over into all-too-frequent fraças. Amy has seen Alfred looking careworn of late and her heart contracts with fear that he too will be worn down like her father.

While Alfred was away on leave plans have been laid by various busy bodies to reorganise Nazareth House. Now he has returned 'to face the music' as he puts it, with a committee meeting looming.

Amy meanwhile has wrapped up her studies for the year and is sensing a growing lethargy. She is familiar with these episodes of inertia, punctuated by periods of frenetic activity. This see-saw between galvanizing energy and paralysing torpor has marked her life since she was twelve. The times of inertia she dubs 'the wolf in winter', for she feels like a wolf imprisoned in its den by the choking roots of a giant tree.

§

8th December 1977

Dear Alfred,

I submitted a report to my warden a couple of days ago. "Don't kill yourself over it. Just a chatty letter," he advised me. If I were honest I would say to him, "But I want to kill myself over it! It's my nature. I want to write an *encyclopaedia!*" But I wrote a short chatty letter and suggested that Brother Alfred would maybe fill in any missing details.

I have been very free with your friendship, and you have borne the strain like Atlas. If I haven't shared much of my internal struggle with you lately it is because I wanted you to be proud of me. I wanted to be brave and show you that I was no longer a child. However, when I left home I did not really leave my father. He gave me life and taught me to think, and showed me how to dance. He is always with me; as you are.

I've had a premonition for a while that something bad will happen. Last night it began — an awful lethargy which I am all too familiar with. Not a mental disease, but a physical inertia, which has bothered me on and off for as long as I can remember. Maybe I noticed it first when you suggested I should try a half hour extra prayer a day. I am so weary the sheer thought of it appals me!

I've let my house group slip. I felt it was the best way for it to find a new leader. Yesterday it did. Mary led a marvelloust prayer meeting and bible study — but it was bitter for me, because it had to come out of my failure. How brief and fruitless my ministry there seems to be. Marie next door asked me to come over and visit her this evening, but I won't go. I would rather unburden myself to you than pretend to be the comfort she is looking for.

An Afrikaner girl, Rykie, of whom I am very fond chatted with me after yesterday's prayer meeting. She comes from the Dutch Reformed Church which, she says, worships the bible. You daren't drop it; "Oh my God, I've dropped your Word!" She too is often plagued with sleepiness. I found myself confiding in her about a problem I have, and explaining that I couldn't ask even you about it. I only realised then that it was very ominous that I was afraid to ask you.

I remember the dreadful effort it took to write those first letters to you. I felt stripped bare. Exposing my inner life was terrifying; it felt like parading naked in front of the Gestapo. So why could I not ask you about such a simple little matter? The problem is this – when I first began to pray it was like the fervent language of a supplicant. Now prayer feels stilted; when I use words it feels more like the formal introductions of a butler than a loving conversation.

Rykie said that this had happened to her, and it meant she was getting lazy – which gave me a shock. I remembered your advice to practice more prayer, and the lack of effect it has had on me – less prayer, more wine. So last night I got stuck into an extra half-an-hour, and again this morning. It was agony just to keep upright. My brain is clear, but I fidget endlessly, my legs don't want to stay tucked under me, my spine just keeps folding.

The weariness is still with me. At eleven o'clock I put my head on my office desk and snoozed, singing under my breath, over and over, "Lamb of God..." the Agnus Dei from the new liturgy, as if the words could keep me breathing. At lunch hour my colleague urged me to take a nap on the office couch.

Alone there, for the first time since I was a child I sang in tongues. Curled up like an invalid, I felt calm and melancholy. I wished that one I loved would come and put his hand on my eyes and let me slip away forever, because no good can come from me. I was so weary I just wanted to sleep for eternity.

10th December 1977

I have been absorbed by extracts from Père Poulain's *The Graces of Interior Prayer*, but now it lies idle on my desk. I have so much to do but it all seems unimportant, and I am so feeble. In a way I am relieved about telling you this. It is the devil's work. How I loathe him – if one can accord a 'him' to an 'it' – for his damn cheek in interfering with me, even if I am the least of God's children. This I suppose is a confession? It has certainly helped throw a little light onto the current miserable condition of Amy.

My massive self-improvement programme while you were away on holiday was doomed from the outset. Watchman Nee warned me about the vanity of such endeavours, but I somehow forgot. This morning I aspire "to live quietly and mind my own affairs".

11th December 1977

I've had an idea. Maybe you would like to file it away for future reference? What do you think of an orientation school for people who want to learn to pray? A course of intensive study of about three days for up to ten people? One could conduct two schools a week. They could board at St Bede's and study at the priory — in the library or the garden. The course should include three hour-long periods of personal prayer a day; normal offices; intelligent bible study (how to study the bible); and films or tapes (like that magnificent Parable, about God's clown) showing people how Christianity fits into the world today.

The reason I suggest this is because I have never come across anything which really teaches ordinary people how to pray. Church is always talking about prayer, but no-one tells you how to do it. Ordained people and religious have proper guidelines, no doubt. Places like Nazareth House introduce people to prayer. Retreats are power houses for recharging spiritual life. But I can't help feeling that a lot of the talent, particularly in the young, gets lost down the cracks. You can't spend hours meditating on God if you don't know anything about him. God doesn't send you book titles and details of church history, except through his seasoned and knowledgeable servants, who mostly seem to keep themselves to themselves.

The field of the inner life is so large and fraught with dangers it might be a good idea to provide a school where Christ, alive, now, with history, personality and purpose is in powerful evidence. I think you would be amazed at the response.

Maybe there are such schools — but the ignorance in the churches, including my own, continues to appal me. I found the study of history deadly, until an enlightened teacher gave me a stack of biographies to read, and said, "Don't worry about memorising the facts. If you know the people you can't help knowing the facts."

I made a stupid remark on the phone yesterday, without qualifying it. I still find it difficult to remember that you cannot read my thoughts. When I said how good it was to have Brother Alfred to run to when things fall apart, you anxiously told me that one is continually being weaned from dependence on outward things. Maybe I should have said 'a Brother Alfred'. Even I am not so foolish as to imagine that you will always be here to support me. But I am sure that the years that I have spent in loneliness will not be repeated.

There is good and pernicious dependence. The lonely place you found me in a year ago was the product of my own ferocious independence. I aspired to need no-one, and that is why I understood a little of Auberon's predicament. *Noli me tangere* – don't touch me. You rescued me from that sterile isolation and, unwittingly perhaps, began the converse process of helping me live by God's grace, as you do.

It is a jealous God! I was left alone with this God during the Auberon affair. That experience may be called some sort of night, or the wound of love, or whatnot in spiritual language, but the term I am familiar with is 'nervous breakdown.'

Whatever the whys and wherefores of that traumatic event, it was like being abandoned by my mother – you. It actually felt like the shock when the umbilical cord is severed. Life and breath are jammed for an instant. There is a terrifying hiatus before the lungs cough into action.

My difficulty from now on will not be inordinate dependency, but how to submit properly to your guidance. I know very well on whom I depend, and that extremely headstrong and independent 'I' will need a lot of whipping in from you, as long as you remain my director. I return to normal life a thousand times more dangerous than I was before, should I stray from the well-trodden path. Well, I hope that solves any qualms you may have had regarding any unhealthy attachment?

Elsa, my colleague at the office, gave me a good talking to this morning. I have been sick and everything seemed to be falling apart. I lay around half-conscious all day Saturday, and only got up to go to church on Sunday. Prayer was garbled and dazed.

Wolf didn't even ask how I was. He got in at 1.15am on Sunday morning. Then went to tennis first thing. By mid-morning I had a cigarette – I've been trying to give up smoking. I broke that resolution because of resentments crowding in on me that I could no longer control.

Anyway, after the smoke, I wept because I am so weak-willed, and wrote Wolf a long letter. Wolf has estranged many of my former friends because of me going back to church. He is telling people that I have gone mad. You remain just about the only one I can talk to. I wrote him that – amongst other things. He is a softer man today.

Elsa however has warned me that when your body conks out it means you have had enough stress. This sounds like a doctor's report, but there is no point in leaving you in the dark about my health.

The letters in Père Poulain's book comfort me a lot. I will, in due course, try to find out where I stand in relation to his advice. I thought it was forbidden to entertain ideas about one's own spiritual status, that being vanity, but a general notion of where one is at might not be a bad thing. It is impossible for me to describe some of the extraordinary experiences of the past year, and probably unnecessary, but my musings to you might help clear up some of the muddle.

It makes me feel sick now, to think about the breakdown I had whilst reading *The Spiritual Man*. My mind falling into a vortex of insanity, enduring shock after shock until there was no more will to cry out against it. Madness doesn't frighten me any more – nothing does – and that is peace. By comparison this current upset is just mild turbulence on the face of the pond.

I know what a broken mind and a broken heart are. You might think such an assertion is impudent for someone of my age, but I say it with assurance.

How strange that I should find fasting so difficult. Indeed I had no idea what fasting meant until I tried it. You said one needed stamina to walk with God. How right you are. When I consider the fires and darkness and violence of the past year I am overcome by a sort of awe. That God should care so much for me! And I remain so stupid!

15th December 1977

One of the best things about your books is finding out how other people write down the things that go on in the bottom of their hearts. I thought one wasn't supposed to talk about such things. It seemed like talking about God behind his back.

I've spent such a long time lost in the interior jungle, without a map. No one seemed to know where I was, least of all me. It is a bejewelled and frightening jungle, full of things nobody has ever seen before – or so I thought. Until along came Père Poulain. Then, out of the undergrowth, out of the pages of his book, came dozens of wise beings in long white dresses, with stern, kind eyes. Me a bit grubby, and sheepish because they had been watching me all the time from the shadows, while I thought I was lost, getting in a panic, and trying to be brave. I feel as if I have been found.

16th December 1977

Do you remember I once wrote to you that I was tired of being idle? That I wanted a ministry, even if it's only intercession. *Only* intercession. Huh! Did you have a quiet smile? "Wait till she tries it properly," you thought to yourself. Having now tried it, in companionship with Père Poulain, cross-eyed with fatigue and feeble as a toad in the heat, I beg your pardon for that 'only'.

You once casually remarked that Petunia had the strange idea that one "suffers with…" during intercession. Now I don't find that strange. I think intercession, a burden of prayer, is as real as St Christopher's was as he unwittingly carried the Christ child on his back. I can't pick it up and put it down when I want to. It gets heavier and heavier until I recognise it. I don't really know what it is. I am worn out by my growing burden. I remember the times when I was strong, and am sorry I despised people who were weak. Finally, convicted of utter helplessness, I give the burden back in prayer. That is like recovering from illness. Everyone fussing around, "There there, everything's alright now."

18th December 1977

My moral disintegration has included telling you that I fasted for two days when it was only 1½ (actually ¼). That untruth has acquired the proportions of the Loch Ness monster in my psyche. I thought maybe I could actually fast for two days, and then it would be true, and I wouldn't have to confess the fib to you – but that didn't seem very truthful either.

This morning – oh bliss – it is pouring with rain. I'm so happy. I've only got another forty-three years and two months to live, barring accidents, to fulfil my three score years and ten.

A stagnant little puddle inside me is bubbling up, inundating with affection everyone within reach – including my mother and father in England. I feel so safe. Well, as safe as any other chrysalis; neither caterpillar nor butterfly.

Now I see why two or three should be gathered together; and why an hour or two in your company props me up for a fortnight. How dynamic, how magnificent – how breathtakingly simple. You give me an hour or so of your time, which generates in me two hours tenderness for so-and-so, an hours writing for whoever, ten hours prayer for the rest – before I run down. Chain reaction – indomitable; and terrifying if one thinks of what could happen when the mistakes one makes are passed down the line.

I hope you will be able to answer gladly for me when the time comes.

~33~

4th January 1978

Dear Alfred,

I've just about finished the Poulain book. It certainly was a vast enlightenment – it leaves me no room for self-deception. Having discovered that I am not on my own with such a peculiar interior life, which I thought I was, I realise I have not been kind to the person I am.

Here is a poem for the Nazareth House notice board, which I wrote a couple of years ago. Some of your customers might recognise themselves.

A touch of gloom
A glass of golden dreams
A cigarette, warm darkness
laced with nicotine
An empty room
Filled with the space you built
in the starkness
Of my life's routine

A frame; my life…
Glazed
Your image occasionally
passing through
Stirring the reflection
of my introspection

A touch of gloom
In this room
Reflected in a golden glass
… or two

Some people express themselves more freely on paper, are prepared to reveal more. Self-help books are booming business, evidence of the comfort people find in discovering themselves upon the written page. Why don't you encourage your folk to write their own testimonies or poetry for the Nazareth House notice board? Enough people sit around there. Set up a post box for contributions and I bet you'll be snowed under with nascent talent.

I feel inclined to indulge myself further and write some more, although I'm actually not very clear about what I should tell you. Life seems to be bland in the extreme at the moment.

Wolf has rushed in and out, leaving himself just enough time to eat, bringing a friend from work with him. I remember times when I hid my bible before he came home. Now I think he is often frightened of being alone with me. It is true that I have become a tyrannical wife because I came to the conclusion that submissiveness – as recommended by the charismatics for wives – turns him into an ogre. So several times lately I have put my foot down, although I don't enjoy doing it. He becomes dewy-eyed and obedient, which I find quite alarming

My neighbour Marie came to visit yesterday. She said it had been a terrible year for her. Her husband is in hospital and her grown son was "up to mischief" on New Year's Day. I didn't ask if he was in prison but I suspect that is the case.

I described to Marie how she looked to me when I first met her, and how much better she looks now. At times I find praying aloud with people a terrible strain, like being a dishcloth wrung out. However, I had to do it. She was weeping as if she would never stop. It turned out to be easy with my arms around her. She claims I saved her from despair, which makes me feel like a hypocrite. Her muscular husband, for whom we also prayed, is beginning to understand what fortitude an invalid needs. Lesson for today: one doesn't have to be in a state of grace to pray with someone.

I have given up the leadership of my house group. The feeling was that I was too influential (bossy) – very rightly. I was also accused of being too emotional. They think I care too much about odd bods! According to general opinion I am inclined to hysteria. "Jolly them along," people say, "and everything will be fine". Trouble is, no-one confronted me face-to-face about these things until it was too late.

There is one woman in our house group who gossips incessantly. She has a genuine spiritual life, but she dislikes me. I have given her the leadership of our meetings (which she clearly wanted). I've confessed my critical spirit to her. I've given her the kiss of peace. What else can I do? None of them understand the work that goes into running a house group like that, and now it is disintegrating. Maybe it will be better after the holidays are over?

My parish priest thinks I'm nuts, but he does try to care for me. I've told him that I am sorry I can't go to confession with him, and why. This was after a couple of my prayer group people asked him to have a word with me about my behaviour. I do have immense respect for him. He perceives a great deal and, I think, preaches more wisdom than he realises – but a prophet isn't necessarily a good confessor.

I remember seeing you once when you looked haggard, terrible. I don't remember exactly when it was, because I lost track of time last year. I've also seen Bishop Timothy and Sister Angela looking crushed on occasion. So I know these sorrows happen to everybody, however holy. And I am not afraid to care about people who are vulnerable enough to show their sorrows to me – even if that does make me "hysterical".

Maybe gentleness comes out of knowing how fragile strength is without love. I am also coming to appreciate how interior life can drain reserves of physical strength.

The lady I visit at Weskoppies seems to be making little progress, except for becoming inappropriately attached to me. This all came about because I told Fr Albert that I wanted to visit someone at the mental hospital, and they gave me Pamela. She has been there for forty years. Her diagnosis is schizophrenia. She looks ugly and obese, but is sweet and trusting. I visit her once a month, and am trying to understand her language.

Last week Elsa described long and earnestly the humility she had noticed in "those" renewed Christians. It hurt very badly that she didn't include me. I couldn't stop crying in church. I didn't have a handkerchief so I had to wipe my nose on my sleeve. No wonder the priest thinks I'm rather *outre*.

That's all for now. I feel a lot better. That tightrope you are always talking about is not easy to walk – between contrition and hope, freedom and discipline, confidence and humility.

5th January 1978

I've almost finished St Teresa's book, *The Interior Castle*. I can quite see why all her daughters thought she was wonderful. Had I read her book before, my letters would not have rambled on so, and been so obscure. Mostly I was trying to make what seemed like my bizarre imaginations credible. I left out the most fantastic bits because I thought you would think I was being stupid or insubordinate.

I have tried to fly before I can walk. I saw God working miracles in the lives of people I cared for, and I got carried away. Before I began to value my own life, I thought I could risk anything, that nothing could harm me except if God allowed it. But lately, from about the time you went away, after my exams, I've become more responsible. It's like when your mother's continually warning you not to touch the rayburn. Eventually she goes away and lets you find out for yourself that it burns.

I care about my life now. There was a particular evening when I chose life – although I was so heartbroken I would rather have died. I felt then that it would be very irresponsible to pop off to the heavenlies without lifting a finger to assist everyone else. Now I realise it is my own life I must care for.

Learning to care again is painful. Many of my 'letters' to the imaginary Judge and Madam, a correspondence which I wrote at a time when I was very lonely, are concerned with the dilemma of caring – of love. But now they have both passed on, they don't concern me any more, the Judge and the Madam, and I must work out this dilemma in real life.

What does concern me is my thoroughly dissolute habits. I would rather be turned to skin and bone, suffer sunstroke, be covered with flies in the desert, than be plagued with such delinquent appetites as I am now. I thought I could walk unharmed by anything, in any company; indeed, when I am with you these things don't trouble me at all.

As it is, alone, or with people who don't care about anything very much, any 'comfort' will do – food, wine, cigarettes. I'm like a child sucking a dummy. It is humiliating for a person who is fit in wind and limb to be about as strong-willed as a sack of potatoes when craving a cigarette or a drink. I am very well punished for the airy advice I've given people on appetite. I wish God would give my addictions a similar thrashing to the one my soul got with *The Spiritual Man.* In retrospect it seems as if reading that was an easier ordeal than trying to lead a virtuous life.

Oh dear. How earnest I sound. I must be turning into a very dull person. A gloomy, puritanical pen with no praise or joy in it. The way forward seems dark and trackless.

"Where are you going?" – I don't know.
"What are you battling with?" – Nothing.
"Why are you battling then?" – I don't know.

~34~

10th February 1978

Dear Alfred,

I've begun to think freely again without headaches, or fear of bad things popping into my mind. But it is not the sort of forensic analytic thinking I was used to before. It is more like a peaceful dawn, more like realising. Listening to Bishop Timothy's Lenten teaching at the cathedral on Wednesday I realised that was what he was doing too. He was explaining what he knew, what he had experienced. Not just assembling the bits of a religious puzzle to make up the picture. I want to be able to do that fluently – but I never will unless I practice on somebody. I know I am safe with you. I cannot do you any harm should my thinking bark up the wrong tree.

Here is my 'dawn,' my realisation from the cathedral, which is very lovely to look upon, to hear it when spoken in a gentle voice. But it doesn't seem to take kindly to paper.

Honour thy father and mother. Stretching out his hand towards his disciples he said, "Here are my mother and my brothers". After this I understood the world anew.

The new creation is whole in him, in the immaculate birth. If I honour my Father in heaven I come to God through himself, whose Body is the Church – and my mother. In her body I am conceived by the Spirit. Honouring her I honour him whom she serves. Thus the three-fold cord is found in this commandment. Honour thy father and mother.

I have approached the throne of God the Father all alone, afraid, cold and miserable, with the odd thin wail that I would like to be like Jesus, whom I know he loves very much, but that unfortunately I am not. I had forgotten about the the Spirit who cares for me day and night – like an infant who has not yet realised that its mother is separate from itself.

12th February 1978

Very late, and not much to tell. Except that I wrote to each of my family today. I haven't written letters much, except to you, for a while. I wrote a few dried up moralistic morsels to my brother last year – and politenesses to others. I spoke to my father on the phone last Friday. There is a way of tapping the office phone to bypass the exchange and get through to overseas for free. The old pain began to gnaw at me when I asked Dad what support he had in all his years in the ministry. "Well, we had the annual retreat," he said in his sad, apologetic way.

I remember how he was victimised – by all of us – for his peculiar ideas: church unity; the clergy/doctor brotherhood; lay ministry; the power of the resurrection in the world. All these things seemed like pie in the sky in those days. I remember how we teased him for his hours in the church saying his offices, "with the Old Man" as he once sheepishly confided in me. I shudder when I remember the tone of his voice farewelling me on Friday: "Well. Hear from you… sometime, maybe?"

There is not enough love to go round, is there? I spent this evening with Wolf and two other married couples – one with a small baby. During the evening I saw each one with that empty look which I know so well myself. We meet to drink together. I cannot escape that web. I suppose it is salutary to feel how helpless I am, if I am to discern the thoughts of others. Otherwise I might take advantage of them. As it is we all limp along together.

15th February 1978

Dear Alfred,
Thank you for your prayers for Wolf. His long silence – probably most of his life – is broken. He has never revealed his own thoughts about life to me before. Or maybe 'feelings' is a better word for what he revealed.

It appears that he suffers from the delusion that spiritual life is in conflict with a practical life. He is a very practical man and was taught from an early age that he would never be anything else, nor should he want to be anything but *Arbeiterklasse*. Working class, in the German context after the war, meant pride. A battered and hungry nation with its head chopped off, working endlessly to repair itself. Culture, philosophy, social mores and government destroyed by Nazism, must be rebuilt, even though the *Vaterland* had been slashed down the middle, parting families forever. It was the sheer slog of the working class that recovered the beloved country from its destruction. The workers know it and are proud of it.

Their youngsters had to face a cruelly critical world. Until recently no kids' magazine or film outside Germany ever portrayed a good German. You know better than I do what it is like to be derided and despised for something you can't help. In short – misunderstood. "Get your head down… forget it… don't think or feel… Work!"

Orphanages, a tough apprenticeship, and twelve years at sea have fairly successfully sheltered Wolf from life outside an institution. I have waited more than five years for something to emerge in him. My intuition assured me that a personality of unique strength and beauty was hidden beneath all that scar tissue.

This and my conscience would not let me leave Wolf alone in the world. I didn't really have any expectations of marriage. But I was mistaken about what I would find in him. Now he has started talking to me, I feel as if there is no-one there, or certainly not what I expected. Oh well! Back to the drawing board. If it takes five years for a man to learn to trust a woman enough to bare his soul, it would be rather silly to expect to learn to communicate with him in one day. But I am actually rather dismayed. Serves me right for my fine ideas about my superior knowledge of character. It is not very funny to wait so long for someone to unmask… and when he takes the mask off there is nothing there.

~35~

23rd February 1978

Dear Alfred,

Winter is in the air. You can tell by the way the dogs snuff at the wind in the morning. The heat is past. Now is the time to be out on the hills on horseback. The 'outward and visible' – one of my father's phrases – is reasserting herself. Nature is about to put on another face.

I visited Pamela at Weskoppies at the weekend. Her childlike description of her inner experience: "There are five figures – the small town, the big people, the professors and the tiny ones".

"And the fifth person?" I ask. She is disconcerted.

"The powerful one," she says.

"What is your next change?" I ask, because this means what will she do next, and the conversation gets somewhat blurry. She want to be free, she doesn't want to be 'big' or 'hideous' any more.

She called me her 'small professor' which, I think, is a compliment. Someone who understands a little without using that knowledge to teach, harangue or otherwise manifest power. I know I need a big lesson in humility. Her words are part of it. Please remember her in your prayers at Nazareth House. She has an amazing intelligence behind that ugly face – and, I hope, a future.

Healthwise I feel almost on the rocks – though that uneasy hour of prayer at night seems to be bearing me up. I feel like a desiccated sea sponge washed up on the beach. As if I am being progressively emptied, as St John of the Cross promised, of all I reckoned as life.

It seems as if all the sensations and emotions which move one to joy, sorrow, enthusiasm, curiosity etc, are constrained in me – like pieces of cork held just below the water level.

I think I have what the psychiatrists call manic depression. Inherited from my father apparently. If I didn't know better from your guidance, if I had not learned to listen through an inner ear, I would assume I was entering a depression and would fight against it, as I have been accustomed to do over the years. To fight tooth and nail, or to surrender to the will of God? I suppose I should be alarmed that I feel nothing in particular? I welcome immolation, like a moth flying into a candle.

161

I saw 'Hamlet' on Saturday – several of the great soliloquies describe the dark and bloody battle in a man torn between the natural world and the spirits. Now I understand better the power of Shakespeare to sway the world.

13th April 1978

Dear Alfred,

Just returned from a history seminar – knocked off early. Am finding seminars from five o'clock to nine after work a bit heavy going. Tomorrow night our lecturer has invited us back to his flat for coffee. That will be nice... almost like a residential university.

God's done funny things to my brain. I suppose anyone who really searches begins to get clues about what God is like. Like coming into a room after someone you revere but don't know has just gone out, and there is a warm cushion, a trace of scent.

I am beginning to see history rather like an astronaut sees the world. History is like waves and fountains of energy. Events are just stuck onto this great flow, as surf is joined to a wave.

At first the lecturer looked at me all perplexed when I was explaining this point of view. But this evening I think he got onto my wavelength. He looked at me all squiff and said, "Yes, that theory has been explored by a Russian historian... what was his name?" Of course, I didn't know. I hope he is erudite and obscure.

14th April 1978

I wrote quite a lot more yesterday but on second thoughts it is not very interesting so it's gone into the w.p.b. I prayed with Pamela at Weskoppies for the second time. I think God wants me to help her. Only I'm scared. She needs someone with very deep discernment and powers of healing and authority. There is a sort of implacable area in Pamela's mind which I feel can only be reached by a word of authority. I certainly don't feel inclined to mess around with exorcism on my own. The first time I prayed with her she got tears in her eyes – those poor, mad eyes actually got tears in them.

Got a letter from my trusty school chum yesterday. We were actually only together at school for two years, until I got chucked out and went to another one. But we stayed friends, and ran away from home together periodically. She writes, "I have retired from my life of crime for well over a year." You see, we weren't exactly model children.

Felt prompted to write to this long-lost friend a couple of weeks ago. Just after she got my letter the man she has been living with for the past four years ran off with another woman. In my letter I had asked her to contact my Dad and let me know how he is. She phoned him immediately. He galloped to her rescue and found himself in a pastoral situation – which did him the world of good. She wrote screeds to me which prove conclusively that prayer is no respecter of distances. Praise the Lord. And bless him in his mighty firmament; everything that has breath praise the Lord. And bless him for friendship – and kind eyes to rest in.

18th April 1978

I am beside myself – a half a dozen interesting jobs to do (if you discount the ironing) and I am absolutely paralysed with the love of God. Can't do a thing.

It would be nice now, to sit down with you, and Petunia, and the others; talk about this and that; loving the same Lord. I am almost at a dead halt with exhaustion trying to write this. So happy I can hardly move. Joshua to Archangel at the battle of Jericho: "Whose side are you on?" Archangel to Joshua: "I haven't come to take sides. I've come to take over!"

20th April 1978

I seem to have left the copy for the parish newsletter at work – mercifully maybe. It was daft to let Fr Albert saddle me with that editing job. Now I have nothing to do this evening. I am getting good at doing nothing during the appointed times – but this interlude is unexpected, like an air bubble in a drinking straw.

Had it not been for *The Spiritual Man*, and to a lesser degree the Auberon affair, I would be very scared at the moment. I'm not scared of anything now because those experiences tested me beyond my endurance and I seem to have survived. When the saints talk about being 'lost in Christ' do they mean this sort of weightlessness – not physical but perceptual? All points of reference in previous experience vanish, or seem to be transitory. I feel like a stranger to myself.

In the bigger picture it may be a purification, another giving up, something like what you described as 'that finer pleasure' in not smoking? I suppose, in heaven we will only need enough self-consciousness to know we are gazing, and enough other-consciousness to know our neighbour is also gazing at our hearts' desire?

Disorientation is the most terrifying thing for an individual – although it's probably a refreshing and exhilarating condition for a mystic. The knowledge of God is the surest thing around at present. I and my life are mere shadows in a dream compared with that reality.

I wish I could tell you that I am evangelising hordes of erring souls – but I'm not. In fact I get fed up with talking about 'religion' as if the inner life is not as plain as the nose on your face. Which is very hard on the uninitiated, considering I have only just been rescued from ignorance myself.

27th April 1978

One reason why I couldn't express myself clearly when I first wrote to you was the pain inside me. It was like a wound that wouldn't heal. I wrote because of that. I was trying to convey an inconsolable secret in words – mounting phrase upon phrase like a Tower of Babel – and inevitably failing. It seemed tragic that such precious experience could not be shared. I learned that lesson when I was nine.

Now my mind has a managing director, now I know about prayer, my writing has ceased to grasp so ineffectually at meaning. However, I feel uncomfortable about writing this letter. It feels like a load of cheap, popular philosophy – sort of emotional flea-picking. It is facile stuff, and will probably make you impatient with me.

There are times when God says "speak" and times when God says "be silent", and I am afraid I am not very good at telling the difference. Things have happened lately which have brought back that old pain of the inconsolable secret. Can I tell? Should I? Will these precious stories spoil in the telling?

I seem to have spent the last three days or so in the eye of a storm – that calm area. You remember I was so disheartened with my house group? The main reason was because they were always moaning that they weren't 'being fed'. I declined to take the leadership back lately for various reasons. Mary has since become a very good leader, but they continue to foment discontent and malicious gossip – all very spiritual and in the best interests of the parish, of course! They punctuate their remarks with "Don't think I'm criticising but..."

At the last house-group meeting Fr Albert happened to be present. He finally came out with the fact that he felt useless and unwanted in the parish, and asked us if he should retire early? Can you imagine the contrite faces?

This morning I spoke to a girl whom I haven't seen for nearly eight months, although I have been praying for her at intervals. It seemed time to make contact with her – I am stronger now. She was too heavy for me before.

She told me she has given up tranquillisers, alcohol, and sleeping pills which she took by the carton. She is calm, controlled and ruefully says that her friends "think she's joined Jehovah's Witnesses". She says she began to regain her grip on life in February. And she's stopped swearing!

I've told you how incoherence hurts me. But there is also something precious about being mute in the face of such fragile beauty. It doesn't really help to burst out with "Praise the Lord," as one is adjured to do when good things happen. Although I do praise God with all my heart.

When I was seven no-one else understood how wonderful Dreamland was, except me. We used to go there on a summer evening while we were on holiday at the seaside. Dreamland was a magic garden with grottos, gnomes, elves and fairy lights. Mysterious shadows, possibly of deer, or even a lion, slipped behind giant trees as one tip-toed through fern gulleys. There was an aerial walkway through the treetops, which swayed and caught your throat with delicious terror if you dared to look down.

The kingdom of heaven is like Dreamland – there are other people in it but they all see different things. I wish you could get a glimpse of the wonderful things I have seen in the past few days. Just when I thought the lights would never go on again!

~36~

8th May 1978, in the wee small hours

Dear Alfred,
I often wake up early in the morning. These early morning hours when everyone sleeps seem sacred. Loneliness has very little to do with the number of people around — it is more the absence of anyone who really knows you. To be surrounded by people constantly addressing their personal concept of who I am is much lonelier than solitude.

I want to tell you about our trip to Golden Gate Highlands National Park in the Orange Free State. Last winter we camped out at Golden Gate, which is named after the sandstone cliffs there, which glow golden in the setting sun. The earth froze at night and the only sound at 3am was an owl hunting. But I was awake. Between my warm sleeping bag and the remains of the camp fire stretched three yards of frozen ground. I could hear the fire breathing its last as I crawled out of our tent.

Everything was awake, except humans. There was a stream nearby, chuntering away to itself. It seemed to me that the mountains were alive, in a massive, teeming sort of way, like the sea. Mountains are indomitable. They have a hidden personality, in the way that black people have a personhood which is invisible to whites. And we treat them in much the same way; tramp all over them without discernment; bellow into their sacred spaces; leave trails of rubbish behind us.

So I sat quiet as a mouse, small and insignificant. Because if the mountains noticed that I was awake and listening they would surely slip back into pretending they are passive hulks; just shapes in the dark.

§

Beneath the sandstone cliff in Golden Gate Highlands National Park, Amy hears a leopard cough. It is still dark and the ground so hard she cannot sleep. She crawls out of the tent to a spot near the fire, where the last embers glow. Tin mugs are strewn around the site with shards of frozen coffee left in them. Quietly she nudges some slivers of wood into the soft ash, feeding molten embers which flare into life. She sits watching the flames, hugging her knees.

The cliffs which bestow on this place its name glow golden, even in the darkness. Diaphanous clouds of stars, a whole galaxy pulses in the cupola of the night sky. The leopard coughs again. Of course, she does not know for sure that it is a leopard, but not all the big cats have been shot in the Orange Free State, and some are said to survive high up in the reserves.

The night is singing with life, as if these buttresses are holding a conversation with the heavens, while wild things go about their nocturnal business, and humans sleep.

She pours a tot of brandy into one of the mugs. Glass clinks against enamel. Instantly the vast singing darkness is galvanised, alert, straining its ears. Then silently goes to ground. As if the wilderness sings only to itself when safe, unobserved by predatory human eyes. She feels strangely chastened.

§

9th May 1978

Dear Alfred,

If I confide in anyone else that I am unhappy, they are sure to ask why? If I tell you, you will either be sad for me, or say how happy you are because that is exactly, *exactly* how I should be feeling. Either way I shall be greatly comforted because you don't ask "why?" – as if I needed a good reason to be unhappy.

Alfred, Alfred I am nowhere. I have been waiting so long to wake up – I'm like a chrysalis with a metabolism that got stuck. It feels like the time when I went to sleep on a train at Ostend and woke up thinking I was almost in Hamburg – but the train was still in a damp, dark siding in Antwerp. That is how I feel now. I am nowhere. There is no fibre in me, no blood, no pith or whatever it is that gives a person life – just a ghastly, aching void. Imagine me trying to explain this to one of those confounded 'born agains' in our parish.

Now, more about our holiday at Golden Gate. We climbed upward from the camp site to a wooded gully, which debouched into a narrow ravine. Within a hundred yards we found ourselves in a cave deep inside the mountain. It was like a colossal nave, lit only by a narrow aperture about two hundred feet up. This 'clerestory' was fringed with ferns and grasses, all moving like seaweed against the sunlight above. Plashy rivulets of water echoed from the walls of this natural cathedral, which were sheathed in ferns and moss. For me the world seemed suddenly turned upside down for I realised I was standing in the bottom of an ancient river.

Close by, down here, were sedimentary layers of red sandstone where torrents of water had shouldered out whole bays, their walls deeply corrugated, like dirt roads. Higher up white sandstone, more resistant, had been sculpted into gargoyles by swirling waters long ago, before Gothic architecture was even dreamt of. I thought the upper buttresses must be volcanic – the mushroom rock which is so characteristic of Golden Gate. Little birds nested up there, beneath the jutting rock, where diamanté streams trickled over the ledges.

It occurred to me that out on the mountainside I would see a fissure, perhaps a couple of yards wide, left by the original upland stream. But two hundred feet down I am looking at the work of a furious torrent, with the power to carve through a mountain.

Then I noticed a fern. It wasn't a very special fern – it would probably have looked rather cheap in a pot. But the delightful innocence, the exuberant health and downright cheek of the thing to be suddenly, flimsily, growing where my mighty torrent had just been forging through rock.

10th May 1978

Dear Alfred,
There is an article in your Community journal, about the necessity for a Christian environment for prayer to flourish. That is, one where Christianity is openly acknowledged, talked about, and lived.

I have felt for some time that prayer is much more difficult when I'm in the office, or at home, than it is when I'm at the priory or St Bede's. Prayer in my parish church or the local chapel is virtually impossible because everyone is so busy nattering and being a happy family. I had been feeling guilty because my prayers were so clearly affected by my environment.

This discovery, in your journal, that my inclination t'ward cloisters is not just escapism nor muddle-headed romanticism, is such a relief, but leaves me with a genuine problem. I simply have not got a suitable place to pray. My prayer time is 'stolen' because of the hostile environment. It is not impossible, but constantly fighting a rear-guard action is not conducive to rapid advancement!

I think God must have noticed that I never listen to what anyone says, and have to find out for myself. I am fundamentally unteachable. Every time I have a revelation there is a divine chuckle — "She's just discovered another doctrine of the catholic faith!"

Since Amy no longer has the free use of the car, Alfred has taken to dropping in to Albion, usually with one or more of the folk from Nazareth House. He enjoys lounging in a deck chair in the garden, or draping himself over the sofa indoors if the weather is inclement, smoking an occasional Gold Dollar whilst regarding his disciples genially through wreaths of pungent smoke.

When Petunia comes with him she customarily sits on the floor at his feet, her linen garments folded around her knees. Petunia is an escapee from Johannesburg's northern suburbs. She heartily loathes the neighbourhood of her privileged upbringing, and is never backward in saying so. She condemns the hypocrisy of the wealthy matrons of Sandton and Bryanston; the interminable golf stories over sundowners; the keening over the home country's treatment of Rhodesia. Phrases such as 'the sins of Sandton' and 'the Bryanston bitches' routinely garner her conversation.

Alfred gazes lovingly upon Petunia as she spits defiance at her native turf. He murmurs softly:

Fat white woman whom nobody loves
Why do you walk through the fields in gloves…
Missing so much, and so much?[4]

Petunia turns her shy smile up at him, pacified, doe-eyed.

Alfred is very good at tuning in to other people's wavelength. Amy has been badgering him to give her work to do. She wants to be useful. What is the point of all this praying if one is of no earthly use? She feels ineffectual. Everyone else seems to be busy about something or other. Only Amy is left fallow. Alfred says she must enjoy this time. Soon she will have no time to call her own because she will be so busy. But now at last Alfred has a job for her, which she falls upon ravenously.

He mentions it by the way, while Petunia crouches beside him with her eyes closed, presumably praying. Alfred and Wolf are supping on cans of Lion beer. Would Amy like to design a brochure to raise funds for Nazareth House, he asks? This is right up her alley. She knows all about this sort of thing. It is her job, after all. She

4. *Frances Cornford*

accepts the task as a dog snatches a bone, and has the first draft drawn up before Alfred drives back to Jo'burg. He leaves Petunia behind, entrusting her to Amy's care for the rest of the weekend. Amy feels a tide of gratitude washing over her as she shows Petunia to the spare room.

15th May 1978

Dear Alfred,
Thank you for visiting us. It was good to spend Sunday with Petunia (the speckled hoopoes are bickering outside my study window). She really is wonderful company when that sunny disposition decides it is safe to come out. I think she was dreadfully sat upon by those brilliant siblings of hers. If someone could convince her of how charming and lovable she is, just being normal, it would be very nice wouldn't it?

My job as editor of the parish magazine is getting more interesting. I've had a couple of friendly articles, rather than harangues. People do so love getting things off their chest! The content is of secondary importance in my opinion; first place goes to the tone of the message which may imply, "Listen, you halfwits…"; "Do so and so, or else…"; "I happen to know…"; "Would you like…?"; "I want to share…" etc.

I am really very chuffed that your committee liked the appeal brochure. Even more chuffed that they agreed that I should produce it in the first place. I'm sure you put in a good word for me?

The thing that hurt me most when I got committed (to the church, not to an asylum), was that I thought I would have to give up my writing. I thought I had to give up everything. Writing had been my source of comfort for so long. Now it seems God is giving it back to me!

16th May 1978

Dear Alfred,
I have got something to say that will probably make you cross. You may think I am poking my nose into matters which are none of my business. I have noticed lately that you are very sad. Being sad is part of life, and I have occasionally seen you that way. But I have never known you to be as grievously sad as now.

I think crises are necessary. They tend, albeit painfully, to adjust one's path in life. It may seem presumptive of me to even notice that you are unhappy, let alone write it down in a letter?

Whilst praying for people in painful situations I perceived how they were hurting not only themselves but also the Body of Christ. So I asked how it was that the Lord saw and suffered all this? I was looking at him as he appeared to me in this situation – crucified. He answered very quietly and simply that he liked someone to notice.

I have tried very hard to think of something comforting to say to you, but it is beyond words. Does it help that someone just notices?

~38~

18th May 1978

Dear Alfred,

I am not sure if you really meant on the phone that I must actually try to describe to you the difference between knowledge and obscure knowledge, in my understanding. If you did, Yippee! I've been dying for you to ask me questions about these things which are happening to me.

The mystics sometimes use images of violence. So does the bible (eg Luke 16:16). Prayer, I suppose, one can describe as conscious entry into the presence of God. And I cannot see how this could be anything else but violent. God (although dwelling in darkness) is also as bright and terrible as sheet lightning.

When I first tried to pray, it felt as if I were a living sacrifice, hypnotised by my own will, suicidally hurling myself out through the air-locks of a space ship. In truth I do find prayer, or the search for God, better illustrated in science fiction than in other genres. But science fiction authors make a false premise when they assume that the unknown is hostile.

When I was a teenager I lapped up science fiction. During my torrid journey back into the arms of mother church, I was engulfed in dramas as vivid and bizarre as anything described by Mr Asimov in his books. When I was past fear, barely conscious, and ready to die, prayer found me. In the end, instead of wrestling with my inward journey, I was suddenly in the grip of it. God was present in the most terrible way. Not visible, but I knew to the marrow of my bones what it is to be helpless.

So the first real prayer of my life happened *in extremis*. I was crouched at the feet of something that had absolute power over me. I could not see it. I felt nothing for it. Yet I found it possible to whisper, silently into the void, "Help me". That was my prayer.

Obscure knowledge of God is just a way of saying that this knowledge is given in a particular place or particular time – which is valid for no other place or time. It just means personal knowledge. Just so, my first prayer, should I pray it again, would not show me the same thing as it did then.

Objectively speaking your eyes are blue, but I happen to know that they are sometimes grey. Objectively speaking they are indistinguishable from thousands of other blue eyes, but I would recognise yours, not because I am looking for a distinguishable quality but because I would know that the others are not yours. It is this 'quality that is not' that makes all definition of God negative, and personal knowledge of God 'obscure'.

Knowing about God is not difficult if one accepts that all things come from God. If one can see reality – as I did that night at Golden Gate – all created things are a reflection of the divine, and say things about God.

You asked me to talk about where knowledge and obscure knowledge meet. Standing in that natural cathedral at Golden Gate, by then a little older and calmer than when I uttered my first prayer, the presence of God drew another sort of response from my heart. But only one word came out, like a whisper, "Jesus". Nothing more. The name hung in the air, and grew, and filled the ravine, and the whole ancient place ached with the knowledge of God. In that way I learn about God from created things, through a word spoken by me in response to them.

Another way that obscure knowledge is welded into created things is in those great Gothic cathedrals. I have always rather admired them. Recently, when I was praying alone in the little city church, I thought to myself, "This prayer feels like the inside of a Gothic cathedral". On reflection, it occurred to me that those cathedrals were built during a great age of faith. They display, in their soaring airy vastness, an obscure knowledge of God. This secret knowledge is hidden from the casual passer-by, but manifested in the handwork of countless craftsmen of that time.

It is a simple fact, not so, that knowledge of God is only possible to the extent that one lets God know oneself? Only things of God can survive in the divine presence. So I can only know God to the extent I grow in godliness. Then, because God is in me, I can't really know God objectively – just as I cannot know myself objectively, except in God.

It is very difficult to stay on track – 'scuse the last couple of sentences – they are a bit of a knitting pattern.

You mentioned *nada* – nothing. I misconstrued that word used by St John of the Cross. My mind was so severely punished for its sins of intellectual pride as I read *The Spiritual Man*, that I could barely use it (my mind) without getting a headache. So I grabbed this *nada* idea and adopted a sort of Greek shepherd pastoral persona, wafting around trying to look holy. And locked my faculties of critical analysis away.

I had not taken account St John of the Cross' economy with words. "In order to have everything, desire to have nothing," *nada*. He did not say "have nothing". If you ignore the word 'desire' you are talking about nirvana. Indeed I have fallen into that sort of state; was rewarded with weird physical sensations like free fall, or G-acceleration.

I think that over the months an obscure knowledge of God has become so much part of the fabric of my life, I can safely let my mind out of prison now. Trouble is, it seems to enjoy loafing! I do not crave knowledge the way I used to. These days I have to boot my mind out of its customary lethargy if the need to think arises.

At this point I must admit that my thinking is about as clear as a foggy day in London town. But compare this writing with the dirty tide-marks I was leaving on my letters a year ago!

At school Amy was routinely tormented by her peers as she shambled, head lowered against the assault, in the lee of clipped privet hedges sheltering neat council houses along the way to school. "The vicar's good night's work," they sang after her, jeering at her frizzy hair and second-hand clothes.

She watched their parents demanding placebos of peace and love from her father in church on Sundays. But he overturned their sleepy nests, asking them not to wallpaper their houses every year, but rather use the money for more charitable work. He pointed, bright like a young prophet, to the injured world, to the wartorn peoples of India and Pakistan, of tormented Biafra. "Do not fear the atom bomb," he adjured them in his Sunday sermon. "For when they come, they will come from Africa, and there are so many of them they will need only their bare hands!"

The vicarage became a place of siege. His children and their mother bitterly resented giving him up to the parish at all hours. They watched him bleed out his days and nights for his congregation, who came to judge him on Sundays, who pestered him to baptise their babies, marry their children, comfort their families, and expected him to gratefully accept a shilling in the plate. Their hearts they would not give him.

At home his family nagged him, dividing his loyalty against people to whom he was pledged. Divided, his house fell. He left the parish, and the church, with his spirit and his health broken. Amy bears deep roots of bitterness from these memories.

§

9th May 1978

Dear Alfred,

There is no Nazareth House for the middle class. At my church I come across lost people, who may have left the fleshpots of Egypt, although they don't know why, but here they wander aimlessly in a desert of sundowners and sleeping pills and empty, empty days. If you come across one of them alone, and prove that you mean no harm – ask them to lower those defences which make them destroy, like cape hunting dogs, other lame or wounded creatures – you will find a forlorn and desiccated being.

These inheritors of self-righteous Victorian morality have never heard of Jesus Christ. Jesus of Nazareth, sure! They had him in Sunday School. But since then no-one has really loved them and no-one is likely to, because they are so thoroughly self-reliant. Only God can love people like that

Horrors! The child has become too big for its boots! I'll be preaching you formal sermons before long. Dear, loving, generous Alfred. I really only have a faint notion of how terribly painful it must be to want to heal and bind up wounds, and love freely, in this broken world.

21st May 1978

Dear Alfred,
It is 6.30am on Trinity Sunday. I've just packed Wolf off fishing, into a fabulous sunrise.

I read the article about you in the diocesan newspaper. I thought the bit on the Nazareth House funding appeal was excellent. The photos showed two of my favourite Alfred expressions. I would have cut them out to keep – but it was a borrowed newspaper from the back of the cathedral.

I quite understand your chagrin about the article – stories about oneself in the public domain generally make one feel very exposed. I imagine the brethren had an absolute ball at your expense? Just think of all your fans carefully cutting out the newsclip and storing your picture safely away to be treasured, and go old and yellow. Oh beloved Alfred, my heartfelt sympathy! But it is a fact of life that one cannot keep beautiful people hushed up forever.

Sister Elizabeth was scandalised that Joe at Nazareth House was quoted as saying that you are beautiful. "Cor', fancy calling a man beautiful!" She is behind the times. But I notice she is catching on pretty quickly to the latest fashion of greeting clergymen with a kiss.

Last night I dreamed about a heavenly moon (I suppose a moon is bound to be heavenly), which turned into a manic fairground big wheel with mechanical shovels instead of chairs, and proceeded to wreck the church up the hill. Thousands of people came running with cameras because it was the end of the world. Wolf was in a terrible sweat preparing himself for anathema, while I was trying to procure indian tonic for a dear guest, who nevertheless left before I could pour him a drink.

I am aware of a morbid fascination with myself, which is probably the source of my current misery. I have to cope with darkness and turmoil all the time. Although perhaps it is not true that I battle all the time; just that when I am in the middle of it I can't remember a time when it wasn't here.

Moaning and whining to you helps me to regain a sense of proportion. You have always been good enough to listen. And you have accepted responsibility for me (which I think is very brave) as my director.

Being lost in what Wolf called (surprisingly, during a two minute discussion on prayer) "the uncharted depths of God," is perhaps the best way of losing one's self-centredness. But I have to beat a retreat back to Alfred at base camp every time I get scared. And I do get scared, though not for my life. I am, praise God, at least at present, in the position of those who do not fear the second death.

From the books you have given me it appears that God has seen fit, for the time being, to place me on the contemplative way. An experience of nothingness, *nada*, is therefore cause for rejoicing. But I haven't the foggiest notion of where I am on this way, and one is so easily deceived! It is very like setting out in a one-man craft with sealed orders to discover the edge of the universe. You will speak to no-one on the way and you will never come back. On the other hand you may never get there. This is the fear which echoes in the vastness of inner space.

Well there you are, Alfred – a report on the status quo. I don't think I will be able to write my report, which is due to my warden in June. The practical details of my rule of life are much the same as always, I think. Church on Sunday; tithe of income; monthly confession; daily prayer. Prayer seems to be the focus.

~40~

7th June 1978

Dear Alfred,

I'm feeling such a profound sense of loss in my relationship with Wolf. He sees me as grey and boring because the new life in me is invisible to him. What you would value as calm, looks like inertia to him.

When he was 'losing me' to God, he suffered agonies of jealousy and despair. Now the umbilical cord is cut I sense in him a growing contempt for me. It is true that I have been extraordinarily insensitive to him. But he forced me to choose between him and the church, and maybe he will never forgive me for not choosing him.

It makes me sad to the bottom of my heart to know that he is right – there is nothing in me to interest him. He just tolerates having me around. Nowadays I dare not show a trace of weakness because he would use it against me. But maybe that's not true; maybe that's just my own paranoia.

I am not praying enough. God has lost all the homely, loving metaphors I gave him. God is ultimate and there is nothing left to say. But I know I should pray more.

Have broached a bottle of wine, which is easing the tension. Nothing will make me a puritan! I tried to persuade my confessor to forbid me wine for a month, but he wisely forbore.

15th June 1978

Dear Alfred,

I have not told you about the narrative heights my Wolf attains at times. He has a dramatic way of telling stories. He described to Petunia and me the way icebergs travel from Newfoundland to latitudes south of New York. Most men would talk about the colour of the icebergs, and the danger; the cold, the *danger!* Wolf just calmly recounts that a man has to be agile to travel on one of these sea-going mountains, because the warm waters of the Gulf Stream melt the foundation as she sails south, and the iceberg turns and turns about. He smiles quietly.

It is the end of six days in purgatory. I have raged against heaven, which I have not dared to do before. All ideas about God shrivelled up in that icy place. Hell is cold, not hot. Now I understand better the steel in the eyes of holy men and women.

17th June 1978

Dear Alfred,
Here is a letter from hell. I don't expect you to enjoy it. In fact if you are not repulsed by it, the point has missed you. I write to convince you that I am telling the truth about spending six days in purgatory. Thank you for calling today after you got my last letter.

You asked me on the phone, "How are you?"

How am I? Now, shall I do my stiff-upper-lip act, or shall I try the 'damsel in distress' scene? The truth would be much too hard to bear.

It has become clear to me that sane people cannot stand truth. Truth is blinding and incise, and they will do anything to avoid it.

Saying, "I love you," takes courage, and preparation for suffering. And what does the average, sane person reply? Something vapid and un-thought-out like, "I love you too". An instant antidote for that vulgar word.

Insane people are good at dissembling – hiding their true condition with brilliant disguises. Even over-acting their insanity at times so that normal people believe they are bluffing.

Mad people are good at detecting deceit in normal people. They take nothing at face value, but ferret out the inner motive of every word and action.

These talents make insane people doubly dangerous. They have enormous manipulative power over people who cannot recognise insanity – even when it stares them in the face.

You are listening to a laboratory-tested specimen of non-combatant depression. The test is simple. The specimen is dropped on its head at intervals. When it doesn't get up again, it is depressed.

You see how unwise is your question – even assuming you have a genuine interest in how I am. Some of the words I might extract from our tragically blunted English language would spoil our social minuet.

"I'm fine thank you".

Dear Alfred,

I don't think I am insane. At least not yet – because I spent the time between midnight and 2.30 this morning throwing in the towel – giving up! A very sane response to the torment of recent days.

The only outward and visible sign of this inner turmoil comes when I thrash around and shake a bit. However, I am not sure if this is just me making a song and dance about what is going on inside me, or if it is genuinely physical. It is like being gnawed by rats – with a crowd looking on, sometimes mocking, sometimes judgemental. There is no top or bottom or outward limit to it.

My inner tormentors told me that I had irreparably damaged my mental and physical health, and thrown away my life for a mirage; that all the purgation I had endured was only me making an hysterical exhibition of myself. I had committed mental and spiritual suicide. I finally believed them and prepared myself for a breakdown.

Then the Lord himself came. In the light of morning I don't believe it was himself. The very beauty of the one who came somehow said: "I am of him but he is ineffably more so". It must have been about 3am when this occurred, and I felt suddenly strong and healed. How does one describe the beauty of every dawn that ever was? I remembered him from the first time the pain of despair overtook me, which was when I was a child. He used to play with me and embrace me all night, but I did not know who he was then, and thought it was just a dream.

I have told you about the torment – it would be unfair to remain silent about the joy, although I fear you may conclude that I am really mad. My angel did not stay long, and he could not embrace me because I knew who he was this time – and anyway I am a grubby, fat slob and mostly sin. But no-one he touched would ever do anything other than spend all the days of their life looking for the way he went.

I am very bruised and a bit rocky this morning, but writing this has helped greatly. This is the sort of thing I really want to talk to you about, even if I am a bore.

21st June 1978

Dear Alfred,

Yesterday evening was lovely, all bathed in the warmth of the Spirit after your phone call. Your prayer on the phone brought me home. A light gleamed (quickly – on and off) on something awful and frightening and rotten in my memory. But it is so lovely to be home, even with a wounded spirit, instead of being tumbled about in cosmic chaos, in fear and all alone. Healing of the memories may be helpful. I will certainly consider it.

I didn't sleep much, but at least I was fighting back. Got up to have a sing in the spirit in the study. I have been very neglectful of that gift, until you mentioned it last night. It is a melancholy, poignant song, slow, on just a few notes, as if my spirit is weeping, longing for home.

Then Mohican spoilt it rather.[5] He sleeps in the study, and he joined in my song with a thunderous purr. When Sam[6] started sucking her toenails and spitting out the grit, I gave up. But the song follows me. One note breathed on the air is more eloquent than a thousand-word eulogy. God digs the lyrics and the tune – they are divine!

I will seriously think about asking that lady you mentioned if she would help me with healing of the memories. But at present I am a bit fragile and the thought of anyone poking around in my innards makes my hair stand on end.

§

Alfred brings Hilda, the lady who has the ministry of healing of memories, to Albion the following weekend. They arrive in the priory's yellow VW which Alfred has the use of. Hilda is a large, blond woman with a lugubrious expression, a double chin, and slack lips. Amy distrusts her on sight. However they have come a long way to visit her, and Alfred is here too, so all will be well.

5. Amy's strawberry blond cat.
6. Mohican's mother.

But it isn't. Hilda parks Amy down on her knees on the study carpet, kneels beside her, and embarks on a forensic examination of her soul. She exhausts that lode very quickly, in the face of Amy's sullen and unresponsive manner. The woman then places clammy hands upon Amy's head, and exhorts her to ask God's forgiveness for marrying a man like her father. Amy rears up, outraged. "Wolf is nothing like my father!" she yells. Hilda looks pained. Amy catches a warning glance from Alfred, and sinks once again to her knees; maintaining a mulish silence. Hilda then proceeds briskly with prayers for the healing of Amy's memories. Alfred joins in at this point, which calms Amy somewhat. But she feels violated.

The two visitors waste no time in departing for the drive back to Johannesburg.

41

11th July 1978

Dear Alfred,
It seems the whole world is battling over something or other. At least Rhodesia is on the way to independence. Two hundred happy campers killed by a truck in Spain! Me, I am worn out and sore and weary and feel as if I have been beaten with sticks. In an hour or so I will be fine again, and will think to myself for the millionth time, "Aha! This time it's over". But it won't be.

Five weeks of this sort of mercurial mood leaves one sure that nothing in heaven and earth is secure. Hilda can call it "the deeper work of the Cross," which is very uplifting as long as one believes it. But when one is in this sort of pickle one simply doesn't care.

It is good to learn to depend only on God, and be obscurely grateful. Come to think of it, there's the joy! I am not exactly ecstatic about life, but I certainly don't want to be anyone else.

Since the work of healing that night with Hilda (although it was very trying, to say the least) I seem to be growing up a bit. I am making the remarkable discovery that God loves me for, and not in spite of, myself. Now the trouble begins. My anaesthetised self will return to its senses – that self which my mother used to describe as "obstinate, wilful and headstrong," to say nothing of 'arrogant' and 'precocious'.

24th July 1978

I was astonished to hear that you are at Thornybush – but on second thoughts that is excellent. They are normal folk there – not high-flown; not broken-down. They will care for you, as will the bushveld and its beautiful creatures.

25th July 1978

How lovely to hear you sounding so well on the phone this morning. We are already looking forward to seeing you at the weekend. It will be the land of milk and honey in our house because Wolf gets paid on Thursday. I have to wait until the following Monday for my pay, but I will tap him for a bottle or so of good wine.

I've got so much to tell you — I do hope I don't dry up in a tongue-tied miserable heap, as I so often do when we meet face to face. I hope you come on Saturday so I've got plenty of time to get into gear. There's a smashing movie on called Wild Geese — or else we could see Strange Encounters of the Third Kind?

Well, whenever we see you it will be lush — I'll put notes on the door saying where I am, should I go out at the weekend — which is improbable — 'cept church 8.15-10am. Continue to have a lovely holiday and let everybody spoil you — as they doubtless will.

§

Alfred's visits to Albion have become more frequent in recent months, but this is the first time he stays the night. The old farmhouse has two spare rooms, one comfortably furnished as a guest room. Hospitality was a main artery in the life of the home where Amy grew up and she cannot conceive of a house without a guest room. She keeps the bed made up and the room aired, in case someone turns up. The advent of Alfred as an overnight guest amply rewards such diligence.

There is another room. A locked cubicle in the interior of the house with a door and window onto the verandah, is chock-a-block with the landlady's storage. She is a septuagenarian Scot who now lives with relatives nearby. Amy has yet to discover that this room stores various occult objects and books belonging to Aunt Kath's late friend and house mate, who was the neighbourhood clairvoyant and medium. Many a séance had called up spirits under these eaves, until the medium herself died here a decade ago.

Two years later, when Aunt Kath comes to live with Amy and Wolf, Amy unpacks the dusty boxes of goods, laying out piles of arcane books together with the ouija board on the verandah table. She gasps with a mixture of horror and delight, believing that these occult artefacts which have been secreted in her home all this time are the cause of her hallucinations, her nightmares, her groanings, her gnashings of teeth.

A vestibule, which was formerly a whitewashed passage between the verandah and the house proper, Amy has turned into a chapel,

185

or an oratory, as Bishop Timothy dubs it. Here she keeps her prayer times, burning incense and lighting a candle beneath the crucifix on the wall.

The oratory is screened off with white kaffir sheeting, a heavy pure cotton fabric which has since changed its name to something more politically correct. Sheepskins cover the floor, for this inner chamber is cool at any season of the year. Amy spends hours here, safe from Wolf, who prowls about crying imprecations against whatever it is that is going on in his house without his permission.

§

When Alfred comes he brings with him a small haversack and his own wholesome scent which swirls into the house on the wings of his white cassock. "Could a chap stay the night?" he asks, without seriously considering a nay-sayer.

Wolf is simultaneously appalled and fascinated by this monk who has hopelessly enchanted his wife. Shaking his head he declares he is off to soccer practice; the monk and his wife can get up to whatever they want without him. In the event they choose to go and see Wild Geese, which is showing in a cinema nearby. Alfred has a taste for westerns. Mercenaries are an up-to-date version of the same genre, he says, smacking his lips at the prospect of an afternoon at the movies.

That evening Amy lights a fire in the sitting room grate which puffs threads of woodsmoke back into the room. She prepares sirloin steak and mushrooms for dinner. The wine is poured, and later whisky when the guest settles himself in front of the fire in *virasana*, a yogic kneeling pose. Amy surmises that this is the cause of those thick callouses on his knees and ankles. Not that she would presume to ask. Such things belong to the aura of her guru, things she would never speak about, fearing to diminish the *mysterium* of his presence. Instead she watches him through half-closed eyes, with sidelong glances, sometimes looking quite openly into his face. Then, such intimacy takes her breath away. It fills her with a sensual warmth which, these days, she has no trouble keeping free from desire, let alone lust, which seems to have deserted her altogether.

Wolf goes to bed after dinner, the other two sit up by the fire, with sleeping dogs and cats sprawled around them. It is here in the firelight that Alfred firsts hints that he may be going away. The Community has a new mission for him, he says, although it is very much under wraps at the moment. Amy is jolted out of a blissful reverie; her heart gripped by an iron fist. She feels devastated. But Alfred is asking her if she will write down her ideas for the fraternity, and pray for him from now on until the end of the year when his future will be decided. She conceals her shock, saying of course she will pray for him. She will actually practice fasting, to make her prayers more effective. And she would love to write down her ideas about the fraternity.

Alfred indicates with a noisy yawn that it is time for bed. She has placed a hot water bottle under his duvet, and smiles as she imagines his pleasure when he finds it there.

§

6th August 1978

Dear Alfred,

Bless you for your phone call yesterday. You spoke about the Lord's grace in taking time to build a firm foundation for my future ministry, and you reminded me that the Community expects a novice to be in training for three years. You also gave me a chance to explain that you cannot demolish me with a careless word any more. I am no longer that fragile.

Thank you also for answering me honestly about my letters. You can't remember what I wrote? Nor can I exactly. But I have learned to mistrust neat descriptors and perfected theories in the realm of the spirit. God is only possible whole. So all truth is bound to be imperfect; doesn't quite fit; loose ends.

On another subject, I am a bit concerned about the work of prayer in Nazareth House chapel, which you ran past me some time ago. I have the feeling that nothing has been done about it. An idea came to me which you may like to consider.

You told me, and I treasure the confidence, that your morning prayer time was not blending gracefully into your daily routine. I am sure that it is wrong to deprive yourself of sleep. In other words, if you can't get to bed by nine-thirty there won't be time for prayer before mass without missing out on sleep. The time between breakfast and leaving for work is too short and fraught with anxieties. It seems to me that if you arrive at Nazareth House, have a cup of coffee and then let it be known that no-one may disturb your hour's prayer time in the chapel, a number of good things will ensue.

Firstly, the poor deserted little chapel will be inhabited. Secondly, the many people who look to you as an example will get the idea that personal prayer is vital to daily life. Thirdly, you will be infusing your work place with the source of your strength – prayer.

When I survey that morning prayer gathering at Nazareth House, where all present tacitly agree to the mystery of sitting, sprawling, lying down together before God (whoever he is) for an hour or so – I am reminded of the first prayer meeting I sat in on at Nazareth House. Bare boards, dim light, traffic noise, one old lady, four young adults from the street, myself and you. Your prayers haven't changed, but the house certainly has.

10th August 1978

Dear Alfred,
It is true that God heals and protects a person, as new areas of life come to light. But I can't cope with this intensity of life in too big chunks. It blows all my fuses. God is so superabundant. It is like transporting a desert animal (me) into an Amazonian rainforest. But I am still a desert animal and I can't sustain this abundance, the wealth of God's kingdom, the scrappy, leached out person I am. I am pinned down by it – paralysed. I can't live, I can't die – I am just one hollow, mind-blowing ache.

I need you to write to. You are so kind to read my letters. I am sometimes tempted to think that the Lord could console me and clear my mind just as well through these letters if I kept them. But then I remember the enormous cost to you, and me, for me to learn to trust again – and I know God wants you to continue ministering to me in this strange, but very powerful way.

I hope these lines will explain my own private purgatory a little better. I am a cripple who yearns to run.

Belonging to the fraternity makes me glad – tenuous threads of intercession seem to have woven me into the fabric of the Community. Nevertheless, I discern some gigantic resistance to the fraternity within myself – and to the Community.

I have never been able to speak of it before – but being at the priory makes me feel degraded and valueless. Probably because the 'recollectedness' of the brethren tends to throw into sharp relief how unspiritual I am. This is painful. Unfortunately, my practice is woefully behind my aspiration. The more I get to know the Community, the more sinful I seem to become.

It is difficult to know when to stop bleating about one's own shortcomings. Even so, I don't think real love has much to do with being nice all the time.

21st August 1978

Dear Alfred,
The garden Petunia gave me has added a new dimension to life. Gardening was, after all, the first work God gave to humankind, and I am continually amazed how much I learn through this garden. It is the place where the world and the Spirit meet – the one permeated with the other.

I remember surfacing after reading *The Spiritual Man* to find myself in a strange and lovely world where nothing was changed but everything was different. The only way to remain sane within such dissonance was to cling to faith in God – that whatever was happening I would survive it. It was a fleeting time – like a glimpse of faery land.

But now that realm is back. It is infinitely more real than the monochrome two-dimensional world of my everyday life. I am wearing rose-coloured glasses. The warmth of the Holy Spirit is like the evening sun on a dusky rose.

I struggle sometimes with this new 'vision'. It demands intensive participation in the teeming creativity all around me, whilst at the same time requiring *nada* – detachment. It is not easy, 'seeing' like this. I lose focus, very often. There is only a hair's breadth between bliss and the black dog. By 6pm I have usually hit the bottle. It is a quick and painless escape – which I cannot escape. By 4am I am up again, extracting a promise from the Lord to release me from alcohol. This weekend I have behaved like a fishwife towards Wolf.

Self-destructiveness is quite common in my generation. An alienated person can experiment with himself as coldly as a researcher experiments with a fruit fly. I remember deliberately choosing alcohol as the answer to a number of problems. I needed to disinfect my environment from the harmful effects of myself, to absent myself without upsetting anyone, to anaesthetise the exquisite pain of living – for life is just an illusion, after all. In spite of all this I had to go on living because of a powerful instinct for survival. Wine worked!

I weep inwardly when the drunks at Nazareth House pray for release from the bottle, and I shudder when the volunteers do their "pull yourself together" stunt on them. Everyone is so busy doing battle with the booze, although God loves wine and beer, the gentle generosity of spirits – used properly. People don't perceive the real problem of the alienated soul.

23th August 1978

Dear Alfred,
The reason I first concerned myself with your private life (I think a lot of busy-bodying is passed off as intercession), was your flight to Thornybush. When we talked on the night after you got back, it seemed clear to me that the Lord was pulling up your tent pegs, albeit painfully. In short, it was time to move on from Nazareth House.

I believe the reason you may have to move on is because your work there is finished – completed but not ended. Enough organic growth has occurred during your time there for Nazareth House to become well established. The 'body' has been put on, so to speak, and the institution now has a life of its own.

31st August 1978

Sometimes I find it useful to cast off and throw maps, compass and radio overboard. My rule of life at the moment is that I eat only one meal a day, go to Communion once a week, and spend as much time as I like in prayer. I don't bother with all the rest of the paraphernalia.

But after a fortnight I have begun to suffer from what Seraphim called *acidie*.[7] At least I presume that is what it is.

Of course, fasting makes one's blood sugar drop – which in turn heightens one's perceptions. One is bound to end up sick to death with everything. Which includes oneself, and religious communities, and all the books anyone has ever written about God.

It riles me that none of your brethren take the fraternity seriously. Warwick has a wry grin about it; Cuthbert gaily declares, "Well, do what you like as long as you do it regularly". You say, flippantly, that you have never heard of anyone being turned down for the fraternity.

What it boils down to is that the fraternity is just a lot of old aunties playing Brownies to your Girl Guides. I have endured three breakdowns in the last year or so. It is simply not enough, after that sort of effort, just to sign a form, receive a badge, and get a pat on the head for Jesus.

The Community is supposed to be a foundation supported by the prayers of the fraternity; that's explicit in the literature. But the Community is so heavily defended against the world, particularly women, that the prayers of the fraternity probably just add more cotton wool wadding.

I think the Community must reverse the status quo. Monasticism is no longer preserving the seeds of the kingdom in purity and grace, waiting for the barbarians to move on. Instead you are under siege by a whole generation desperately needing what you keep locked up in your sanctuaries and libraries. No wonder religious communities have lost their direction!

In the Middle Ages the monasteries were places of growth and creativity. God hasn't changed – but the world has. Now, instead of withdrawing to protect the doctrines of the church, the monasteries must venture into the world and give them away.

So, whom do you send? What is the fraternity for? We are people in the world, who are at home in the world. Send us out with the solid foundation of your prayer empowering us.

7. Seraphim was a Russian staretz, or mystic.

42

The first weekend in Spring finds Amy in retreat at St Bede's, while Wolf is in the Drakensberg with his gang of mountaineers. The lemon tree at the bottom of the garden is in blossom, a little taller than it was this time last year. It sweetly perfumes Amy's refuge, perched in the tree overhanging the compost heap. Spring foliage conceals her from the eyes of fellow retreatants, who stroll silently in the garden below.

This retreat is altogether different from last year's. A pall has descended upon her; an angst-ridden gloom which no amount of prayer will shift. Inchoate feelings of rage against her companions rise in her throat, shocking her with their intensity. She has met none of these women before – except for Petunia who is making her maiden voyage as a retreatant.

Petunia makes herself almost invisible, as is her custom, spending hours on her knees in a dim corner of the chapel; slipping like a shadow along garden paths; perched on a log, meditating, behind the iceberg roses. In the dining room she withdraws behind the wings of her hair. Jealousy consumes Amy as she catches glimpses of her friend's saintly image drifting about, accompanied by the odour of cigarette smoke. Amy herself feels unkempt, unholy.

At lunchtime on Sunday in the refectory, a vast loneliness consumes her, as the gramophone needle hops monotonously over the scratch in the Brandenburg concerto. Tension cranks up in her core, until she can bear it no longer. She wants to scream. Unwilling to upset the elderly matrons who chew on their lunch with calm contentment, she runs off to hide in her room. There she curls up in a foetal position on the bed, and prays to die.

She must have slept. A soft touch on her shoulder causes her to wake and blink into the light. Alfred and Petunia are gazing down at her supine form, gently enquiring how she is? Amy gulps her surprise, her shock. The relief is unbearable. "Why have you come?" she whispers. "Nobody ever comes". Then she weeps.

They lay hands on her and pray for her, calling sweetly on the Lord to bless this daughter of God, asking for peace in her heart, giving thanks for Amy's ministry in the church of God. She folds her limbs like a lamb, and sleeps.

§

4th September 1978, On the train going home

Dear Alfred,
There is no point in being foolish about going home. Every retreat brings a new submission to God's will – to remain in the place I am, with the man I am married to, plodding along for days and weeks and years.

Since discovering the life of prayer, I find marriage mostly intolerable – although I greatly respect Wolf as a person. It is probably better to learn obedience this way. Having found the One I have been looking for all my life, if my foot were not nailed to the floor by this marriage, I might be tempted to walk barefoot to China, or become a nun – or some such ascetic foolishness.

I feel overwhelmed. Prophecy and vision – insight – are made from the stuff of experience. Like poetry, it is both painful and a rewarding process. No wonder so many poets, and probably prophets, die young. You once described the life of the Spirit as 'wildfire'.

I have spent most of my life resisting any attempt to make me conform. Now, thanks to you and God's faithfulness to your prayers, I find myself in an integrated, powerful state of being. I am still 'becoming', yet – as even God seeks recognition in the human heart – I find I need to be accepted. I need a nest; a frame; I need my own patch of ground to stand upon.

This is very different from clinging to false security. I am still happiest when I am on the road without a cent in my pocket. My possessions are a burden to me; I hate the responsibility of them. But now I need a place in the church where I have publicly committed myself to God, with the earnestness of a religious vow, and the church has publicly accepted me as I am.

Have you ever considered, in the disintegrated life we live today, how schizoid the spiritual life can make one? Partial commitment is no good at all. In fact it is worse than useless, because the Holy Spirit demands the whole person. Partial commitment leads to a schizoid state of being. Ordained clergy, monks and nuns are professional disciples, yet there is no provision for total, deep, passionate commitment by lay people. The parish churches certainly don't seem to be much good at accommodating such people.

Women in the church are treated like the great harlot Babylon. Unless a woman looks like a hag or is ancient, it is taken for granted that she is planning in her black and sinful heart to seduce the (male) saints. I think this attitude has produced two dreadful female stereotypes – the empty-headed drip who is always fawning on the vicar; and the bossy tyrant who enjoys cutting everyone down to size.

I could actually go on all night, darling Alfred. The highlight of my life would be a whole day or two shared with you. As usual something intervenes – my pencil is getting blunt and Pretoria station is approaching.

14th September 1978

Dear Alfred,

I wish the fraternity could become more effective. But then, people who arrive new in an organisation always want to change everything! I have probably just not seen enough of the fraternity and what it gets up to.

On the day I was so dreadfully unhappy in retreat two things happened which have led me into a new way of prayer. Whereas before prayer was like a sparrow flying into the sun, like self-immolation, now it appears as if all things are flowing through prayer into a flame in the centre of my being. *The Pilgrim*, Brother Bertie, and Patanjali have all helped me discover this place of the heart. Previously my life, my soul and body were a sort of sacrifice to prayer. But now my life – my soul and body – stands guard over and pays attention to the spirit within.

This prayer is not imposed by me on myself, or upon me. It is a more like a flow of life through me; from created things in praise and joy and love to God, and from the Spirit in compassion and healing and authority to creation.

I am awestruck when I consider how Jesus in his perfect sensitivity to the Spirit and the creation must have walked on earth, feeling each blade of grass beneath his feet; how he must have known intimately every breeze against his skin.

This is *nada* — having everything, possessing nothing — being entirely vulnerable. Allowing the Spirit and the world to find whatever consummation the Lord has decreed, in one's own being.

As for tongues, when the Lord is present a lot of chatter seems uncalled for. So for me, so far, my God talk comforts me only when I am in the dark. I will continue in the joy I am in, as you asked me to do. But I will draw you into it, to share a little of the melancholy you are bearing at present.

15th September 1978

Dear Alfred,
So you are about to "enlarge the place of your tent". I am very happy for you. I hope Nazareth House will remain your child in your heart, although it has grown up now, and you must leave it behind.

I had not realised what a struggle I would have with the prospect of you going away. Although I am no longer dependent on you for the air I breathe, I do love you very dearly, and it will be as painful as losing an arm to let you go to Rhodesia. I never knew there was so much sadness in the whole world.

I have enclosed letters from Anna and Ruth because I feel my whole family belongs to you. There is such an intricate thread linking us all. When you were a pilot in the war you ended up in the same German PoW camp as my father and my South African cousin here. The year I was born Dad was called to the ordained ministry, probably about the time you decided to become a monk, while you were a lumberjack in Canada. Twenty years later you met my mother in England; returned to South Africa; and when Anna came here, I met you. It's like a labyrinth!

43

TWO German-born missionaries, Father Gregor Richert (48) and Brother Bernhard Lisson (68), who between them had served in Rhodesia for nearly 60 years, were shot in cold blood by a small group of terrorists near their quarters at St Rupert's Mission, 60 km north-west of Hartley, on the afternoon of June 27, 1978.

The murders were confirmed late yesterday afternoon by Combined Operations Headquarters, Iana reports. The regional supervisor of the German Jesuits in the Sinoia area, Father Ulbrich, said in Sinoia that there was no apparent reason for the killings.

"Was there a reason for the Vumba massacre?" he asked, referring to the murders last week of eight British missionaries and four of their children who were hacked and battered to death in the Eastern Highlands, reports Iana.

Father Ulbrich travelled to Sinoia from Salisbury yesterday to inquire into the deaths of his two colleagues. He said the two men were "extremely dedicated" to their work in the small, isolated mission and hospital complex not far from Sanyati, where they had made their homes for more than five years.

Father Ulbrich said he believed three terrorists had committed the murders. He understood the small group of armed men had taken the two missionaries from the central mission complex to their quarters before shooting them.

He said although terrorists were known to have an active presence in the area, he could think of no reason why St Rupert's Mission had been singled out. "It's like so many other cases," he said. "It just seems to be indiscriminate."

The Director of all Catholics in the Sinoia area, Monsignor Helmut Reckter, said his Jesuit organization had no plans to withdraw the 16 missions left in operation.

Asked why the murderers should have chosen helpless and dedicated missionaries as their target, Monsignor Reckter said: "It's extremely difficult to give an answer to this. I don't understand it. It is, of course, a very hateful business. There is no reason that makes sense to me."

He said the 40-bed mission hospital, which catered for local tribesmen over a wide area, had already been closed.

Reporting the murders in more detail, a communique from Combined Operations Headquarters said last night a sum of money was taken by the terrorists when they left in the late afternoon, and shots were fired into a mission vehicle.

Three armed ZIPRA terrorists entered the mission and demanded to see the priest in charge. Father Richert was seen by them and went with the terrorists to Brother Lisson's quarters, the communique said.

Both the victims were then forced to return to Father Richert's house, which they entered together with the terrorists. Their servant was told to leave.

Shortly afterwards a single shot was heard, then three shots followed by a burst of automatic fire.

Source: Rhodesian Information Agency

§

6th October 1978

Dear Alfred,

Sammy is trying to sit on my lap and I am shooing her away. Shooing away life, and loving, has been my habit for so many years. Learning to love you has been wonderful, because you love me too, and God will never separate me from you, ever. I wasn't certain of that until I heard that you are going to Rhodesia.

Now I have let the dust settle a little, I see how adventurous it will be for you! You have the spirit of the frontiersman of any age. You would have been an intrepid gravedigger in the Renaissance,[8] or fighting the Turk at Gallipoli, or packing a Colt in the Wild West.

Should you ever need loving companionship up there, you are to call on my love for you (this is from the Lord who is the Spirit). He in his mercy allows us to be there for one another far beyond the

8. Cemetery robbers in the time of Leonardo da Vinci, one of Amy's heroes, dug up dead bodies for his anatomical studies.

boundaries of physical presence. I am saying this to reassure you that I know that it is in God that we love one another.

So there it is. A fairly calm acceptance of your departure. I am used to the people I love going away. I think all the ones who went away before have been training me for this one. I shall enjoy writing to you and praying for you – and growing into a new awareness of this dreadful war.

13th October 1978

I got up just after half-past five and was going out to water the garden, when I felt this gentle restraint, calling me to prayer. It is milder than the inertia of being "slain in the Spirit" – what a violent description for such a sublime experience! I haven't been able to praise God for the past week. Well I can now, and I've forgiven him for taking you away.

When I went out into the garden I found it had rained.

2nd November 1978

Dear Alfred,
I am just a little fish in a big pond. But as a gesture I could make my life and possessions available to the Community to use according to the brethren's discretion. This with Wolf's permission of course. This would provide the Community with material possessions, hospitality, money and labour for mission – without the difficulties of administration, or indeed legal possessions. If such a practical commitment became fashionable, Community and fraternity might just begin taking each other seriously.

44

Summer in South Africa and Amy's sister Ruth has come to visit. A five year gap between the sisters made them more or less strangers in childhood, Ruth was only sixteen when Amy left England. Now, in the breathing space between university and her new career in the Royal Air Force, Ruth is spending two months with Amy in South Africa.

Petunia has somehow obtained a cottage on the Natal coast, where they will all go, together with Alfred, for a holiday before he leaves for Rhodesia. By some adroit sleight of hand Alfred has gained permission from the Prior to spend a week at the coast for this farewell party with his friends.

It is an overcast morning on the Highveld when they set out. Wolf, Amy and Ruth have Alfred with them in their car. Petunia will travel with another vehicle from Nazareth House. At first Amy takes the wheel. By the time they descend the winding road from Harrismith into Natal it is raining. After Pietermaritzburg, Wolf drives.

Squalls on the coast road make for patchy visibility, but Wolf takes no heed of the poor conditions and drives fast, as usual, for there are no speed limits on these roads. Amy urges caution from the back seat, which she shares with Ruth. But Wolf is not in a mood to listen. For best part of an hour Amy travels with her heart in her mouth, whilst an oppressive silence descends on the passengers. She is not the only one who is nervous. Finally Amy commands, in a voice that cannot be ignored, that Wolf must stop the car.

They skid to a halt in a layby and Amy immediately disembarks. She politely asks if anyone would care to hitch-hike with her to their destination? Alfred sheepishly murmurs that someone had better look after Amy, and gets out too. Ruth vacates the back seat and silently installs herself beside Wolf in the front. Then, with a whiff of burning rubber, the two of them zoom off into the mist.

Very soon a Mercedes stops at the side of the road to offer Alfred and Amy a lift. Alfred has donned his cassock, which is always irresistible to passing traffic. "What religion are you?" is the usual question as he climbs aboard. Conversation is lively with the couple in the Mercedes, who are on their way south and drop the hitch hikers at their destination in Southbroom, so that Amy and Alfred arrive not long after the others. Wolf is sulking. Ruth reports that he grumbled all the way down about that monk going off with his wife.

§

The holiday cottage is set on a hillside with a view of the Indian Ocean. Before sunset Alfred gathers his flock for evening prayer. Wolf has gone down to investigate the beach, not being inclined to prayer. The others sit in a circle on the front lawn, a patch of coarse kikuyu grass which is surrounded by banana and pawpaw trees. A zephyr of ocean breeze fans them. It feels like paradise after the long journey.

Obediently they fold their hands and close their eyes. Alfred gives thanks for safe travel, and makes petitions for a happy and blessed holiday. When at length they open their eyes again they discover that they are encircled by a tribe of grey vervet monkeys, squatting at a safe distance, solemnly observing their devotions. Visitors and natives alike regard each other for a long moment. Then someone giggles. Screaming, the monkeys scarper into the surrounding bush.

§

Amy volunteers to cook dinner for the company. People can make their own breakfast – however, Amy makes Alfred his favourite b&e most mornings. Wolf and Ruth are conscripted to collect driftwood for the braai. The others will do shopping and domestic chores. Everyone will help with the washing up.

Halcyon days, together with Alfred, pass like a dream for Amy. Usually, after breakfast he goes out alone for a walk on the beach. She respects his desire for solitude, but one morning she follows him, catching up when he sits on a rocky outcrop to gaze with melancholy eyes at the far horizon.

"Are you sad?" enquires Amy, anxiously. He regards her for a long moment. She bathes in his regard while the ocean sighs upon the sand.

"Sometimes," replies Alfred at last, "there is a sort of miasma which descends. Not much one can do, except wait for it to go away."

Amy is shocked at the pain in his voice. But at the same time she is encouraged. If holy Alfred suffers such sinister moods, perhaps her own bouts of depression are not so disgraceful after all.

Morning and evening offices are routinely said out on the lawn, frequently attended by the band of monkeys, who watch with intelligent eyes, black faces solemn. Nothing edible may be left on the verandah, or near open windows, or the monkeys will pilfer it.

One night Amy is awakened by caterwauling outside her window. It sounds like a stand off between tomcats. The dreadful sound continues into the dawn, while she tosses and turns and tries to block her ears. At daybreak she ventures out into the damp garden to investigate.

She finds the remains of a kitten which has been mauled by the monkeys. The poor creature's eyes have been gouged, there are savage wounds on its body, which lies, legs akimbo, like an abandoned toy on the grass. Amy gathers up this scrap of fur – causing renewed piteous yowling. She settles the wounded creature in a cardboard box which she finds in the kitchen, and goes to alert Petunia and Alfred.

Petunia locates a vet in the telephone book and the three of them set out in the car with the injured kitten, now merely whimpering in its box. The vet, who fortunately lives on site for it is still early morning, shakes his head. He says the best he can do is to put the creature out of its misery, which he quietly does; and refuses to take any payment.

They drive back to the cottage in silence. Amy is worn out from the anguish of the past few hours. How could she have lain in bed, trying to sleep, instead of going to find out what was wrong? The needle has brought peace to the kitten, but her pain continues as she flogs herself with shame and guilt.

When Wolf appears at the front door to find out what has been going on while he was sleeping, she curtly tells him to ask the others. It is this incident which Amy will remember from her first holiday with Alfred, before he left for Rhodesia.

§

Dear Alfred,

It is Ruth's birthday and she is up a mountain with Wolf. How she relaxed and blossomed in those days by the sea. Wolf, with a new-found freedom embraces her at every opportunity, and holds hands with her when they walk together. He rejoices to have a sister, and she is happy to find a man who loves her without wanting to gobble her up. I hope he doesn't fall in love with her; that would be rather inconvenient.

So, the muse is upon me, as you once phrased it. If you will put up with me I will shew you some of the things I see happening – rather as one walks at night in a garden, and points out stars and constellations, and gives them little names. God has made us creative in his own image. I name that unimaginable splendour overhead, 'the Milky Way', and with those three little words create a gesture of understanding between us.

Now, for a time at least, there is nothing I desire, not even God. I could lie forever in the great deep of *nada*, as I lie on the cool floor in my oratory. There was a time when I tried not to wonder where I was on the inward journey; it was sufficient to hope you knew. But I am no longer a child. I have a sovereign will and various faculties at my disposal. I am confident that, whichever of the circles of prayer I happen to be in, I am quite definitely over the threshold of this vast new world. How difficult it is to talk about such things. God is only known to me in lostness, the formlessness of the great deep within me. But it is impossible to talk about prayer without creating forms.

It would be pointless for me to tell you what I think God is or isn't, because although your Lord and my Lord is One, his relationship with each of us is unique. There is some wisdom in the traditional view that prayer should not be freely discussed, like cabbage, or the price of eggs. But you are my companion on this journey. I need to share these things with you. What purpose that sharing has I don't know. But I am bound to do it, and that's enough. It is rather extraordinary, isn't it, that this should happen to a rather mundane housewife with countless bad habits, and only eighteen months old in the Spirit!

I have just spoken to Joe, who had been made temporary warden at Nazareth House. I gather that he has been made mincemeat of by the committee. He lit a fire up in the toolshed one night and it got a bit out of hand. He is apparently on 'holiday' while they make up their mind what to do with him. He is back in Jo'burg now but off again tonight. He's obviously had a dreadful mauling.

He sends his love and says I must tell you he is fine and you mustn't worry! That is classic Joe. But I do think he is well enough, although living under such a cloud is a strain on anyone. The chief cause for concern is that he might head for the hills, instead of staying put and weathering the storm. That would be a pity because Nazareth House is so important to him, and the house needs his sort of stability. He is due to report back when the new director arrives – second week in January.

Probably everyone will forget about Joe's bonfire over Christmas, and in the inevitable excitement over the new director everything will return to 'normal'. Joe will come back braced for a fight and there won't be one! Poor Joe is too straightforward to be subjected to all this gunboat diplomacy.

Enjoyed a brief glance at *The Elements of the Common Life* this afternoon. Am now beginning *The Rock and the River* by Martin Thornton. Also looks good. The author sounds quixotic, as if amused at himself for discussing such matters at all.

I am smiling quietly at the thought of your rollick through Rhodesia; hitch-hiking to your new home; cracking the champers on arrival. Blessed are the peacemakers!

Yes, it is just like you to walk into the lion's mouth waving a bottle of bubbly… and the lion lay down with the lamb, besotted with joy: "What were we fighting about?" he growls softly.
"You were just hungry," murmurs the lamb, maternally.
"I'll never be hungry again… *hic!*" replies the lion.

Isn't it odd that I never asked you about your own prayer? It only occurred to me today, then I remembered: "And they asked him no more questions because they were afraid." Being afraid to ask is not exactly fear of asking, but a lack of any firm ground to ask from. In the presence of mysteries it doesn't seem possible to ask questions. The question is as yet unformulated. I could not ask you because I did not know what I wanted to know. I had to wait, keeping my soul in patience, for that which you knew and I did not.

I sometimes wonder if you have suffered rather from the messy business of caring for a soul like me? Spiritual direction is "ascetical guidance…to give practical instruction in the right method of prayer…" as *The Rock and the River* puts it. But I wanted acceptance. Someone to see the torment behind my glazed eyes and stupid conversation. You accepted me. That acceptance was sufficient for me to want to live again.

The rain is falling sullenly on my parched garden. The wind is worrying at the house as if it doesn't know what to do with itself. I love God dimly and inadequately; I love you with a parched brightness. So, with love, good night.

Wednesday

What is that school of yours like up there? Is religion taught as a subject? Does geography, literature, history, fine arts and reading present your students with an integrated world view? I suppose European text books would largely frustrate that purpose? The text books of the world will have to be rewritten when God's Spirit is restored.

And what about you – teaching children in the crucible of this new renaissance? It must seem good to you to be working with the young generation of black leadership, albeit at great risk to your own safety? I imagine you have felt more keenly than your British-born brethren, the injustices of South Africa. Especially as you probably unwittingly took part in them when you were young?

I wonder how many future African leaders are amongst your boys – two or three maybe – and what memories of the brethren they will carry with them into the new world? Unnerving, isn't it?

I am remembering the smile you bestowed on me at the priory, two years ago now – and all that has grown from it. That little spark of life you gave me has kindled hearts across two continents. How far will your smile travel with those boys in their lives?

I suppose you can't walk about much? Must be a bit like PoW camp, but more grown-up; no guards, and beautiful hills instead of the fence and the pine trees. You have been there a week. Are you still very much on the *qui vive*? Or have you already acquired that special wavelength that cowboys, hunters and soldiers tune in to, in order to sleep peacefully in the most precarious of places?

I hope my copious letters don't embarrass you there. It does look rather like undying, and probably unseemly, devotion. I will parcel them up and send them about once a week from now on, together with some newspapers to keep you up-to-date.

Thursday

Dear Alfred,

Baron Von Hügel also wrote a lot of letters. In his *Letters to a Niece* I notice that Gwendoline got one at least every ten days. So I am excused such a profusion of 'em, aren't I?

We have only had two good rains this season here, and my garden is giving up hope. I am going to lose a lot of it unless the rains come this week.

I discovered on my rounds that masses of ground cover had been scratched up, and concluded that it must be those two chickens of mine. They keep flying out of the pen. I've been meaning to have their wings clipped for a while. No rain, and now this! I grabbed the kitchen scissors and, although I have never clipped wings before, took off after the marauding poultry.

First the rooster who thought it was a great joke – until I caught him. The snip was quite easy. No squawks, and they both seemed happy to sit in my lap after the operation. But I was covered with muck, having fallen into the compost heap during the chase. I suppose that is why they felt quite at home?

Yes! One of them grew up as a rooster. So much for my hopes for a steady supply of new-laid eggs. I've got two pretty white ducks; two useless geese who don't bark;[9] a rooster, and one hen.

One can see wonders in a garden. I was watering deep under the trees and noticed one of those bright orange hornet-type insects with the droopy black fuselage, dragging its prey out of a pool of water. It had its sting deeply embedded in a baboon spider many times its size. The spider's body was as big as a marble with great thick legs flung back, paralysed or dead. Quite unnerving, although I realise that neither of these creatures would harm me.

9. Purchased for their reputation as excellent guard dogs.

I am so privileged to have found someone, in you, to whom I can write. The human mind has a habit of becoming what it pursues, and having no one dear enough to 'write upon', I lost my foundation in reality by pursuing the imaginary Judge all those years.

Friday

Action, even a word or a thought, seems to be more of a hindrance than a requirement when grace is moving with indomitable power in one's foundations (not the right word 'indomitable' – I don't mean 'stubborn' or 'unyielding,' as the dictionary says it means). *Puissance*, perhaps is the word?

Prayer yields all too easily to the slightest move I make. I wish I had the tenacity and strength to hold still, and be continually filled with this prayer. Then all action would take place on the surface of it (the prayer), without disturbance, and God would have a space to work in the world through me.

I can't see an inch in front of my face – so profound is the darkness. I am not afraid of it now, but it is so difficult just to hold still and wait, impervious to the world teeming around me, and to my own frenetic life.

18th December 1978

On Saturday night Wolf took us to supper at an Italian restaurant – full of families, good bread and straightforward pasta, plus an excellent two-man band – one of whom turned out to be a football buddy of Wolf's. They played Spanish songs and Wolf's eyes got all misty. We talked of you, and missed you, and right on cue the boys on stage sang The Waters of Babylon – the rock version.

Ruth asked me to send you her love, and I know Wolf would, if he could get the words over his lips. Anna will be arriving on Friday to spend Christmas with us. Greetings from Elsa. She keeps me more or less on the rails.

Late Monday

Wolf and Ruth are planning something for Christmas Eve. They want to know how long I will be out for midnight mass. Now they are off on a secret mission. I haven't the foggiest idea what they are up to. But it is belting down with rain at last, and I am listening to Missa Solemnis, and I have peace to write to you. So it is easy to defy

Wolf's attempts to provoke my curiosity about what they are up to, and concentrate instead on this letter.

Wolf took me to task on Saturday afternoon when I tried to introduce my idea of a feudal-style commitment to the Community – making all our goods and time available etc. It is funny how someone close to you can hit you so hard below the belt, just with a comment about how this nonsense with the church is going too far. Quietly weathered that remark (except for smashing a cup), and pointed out that Wolf's chief criticism of church people was that they were only Christian on Sundays.

He accused me of only ever talking about the church. His tone was full of contempt. It made me feel like a short-sighted, dull, hypocritical, old maid. I replied, somewhat defensively, that I almost never inaugurate a conversations about the church, but people notice something different about me that makes them curious, and they ask. Anyway, all Wolf himself rambles on about now is his resentment of the church.

Thank you for giving me *The Rock and the River*. It has cleared up so many question marks for me. It has made connections between the reading you have given me on the spiritual life, my biblical studies at Unisa, and the structure of the church. Most important, it's explained my experience of 'aridity' as a normal condition on the path of prayer.

You know I have always preferred to be alone. Weeks and years alone with a pen and some imaginary pen friend satisfied me. But now, having implicitly agreed to take part in the Whole, of which I am only an infinitesimal part, I find I can't survive alone any more. I now find I need to be loved. This is such a humiliation.

22nd December 1978

Good to get your round robin – more than good to have a description of 'the scene' – and to know that the mail takes only four days. Almost as good as Albion to Jo'burg.

My mother arrived today, to spend Christmas and New Year. I haven't had a chance to read your letter to the household yet, except to say you are safely there and happily in the midst of a 'recce', to use Ruth's term. Anna was of course sad to miss you, but is immersed in maternal hyperactivity. She is so anxious about my emotional state because of your departure, she is in fact incubating one! I have just put her firmly to bed, or she will suffer tomorrow after the flight and all the excitement. The others have followed suit.

Good, in your letter to read Fr Frank's phrase – "watch God working". You fail to add that God only reveals himself to those who are looking. Today in the city I passed a beggar, a man sitting on the pavement with his crutches. All I had to give him was a note, rather more than I could 'spare'. It must have given him a bit of a shock, because he looked up at me. I saw a man who had nothing to give his children for Christmas, and I wept for us Christians who celebrate Jesus's birthday in comfort, while people in the streets cry out in hunger.

I feel rather bashful about my letters, after reading yours – yours is so full of joy and life and warmth. Mine seem a trifle gloomy and too full of solemn things. But I think I will continue writing – loving you the only way I know how – in the more or less sure hope that I will one day know joy like yours.

Tonight I was trying to keep order in this new dynamic of the family at home. Wolf had lost his nerve with all the visitors and was doing his yobbo act; Anna's mood was manic; Ruth was manfully trying to maintain her equilibrium.

Spatz played scapegoat and saved the day. That black dog of mine is hypersensitive to any disturbance in the atmosphere. She tore around the sitting room, flinging herself *seriatim* at each person's feet, sprawled with her legs in the air, flagrantly promiscuous, generally insufferable. She finished up, panting and trembling, on my lap. Anna declared, "That dog's neurotic". I jokingly explained that Spatz seems to express all the neuroses I have recently been released from, and by rights she should rush into the sea like the Gadarene swine and, (lovingly to the dog), "be drowned".

Wolf grunted approval. When we got her as a pup it was to make up for his dog who had been run over, and he derided her. A '*bitzer*', mostly dachshund, was rather a poor substitute for a pedigree Cairn.

Ruth said, "She's sort of obsequious, isn't she?"

Spatz gazed at me with embarrassing adoration, winking an eye occasionally, then went quietly about her business. Everything settled down after that.

Much later – nearly tomorrow

Anna brought with her all my letters and diaries etc which have been in the attic for years. I am stunned by what that person – whoever she was – wrote all those years ago.

I know that these artefacts would be nowhere near as fascinating to you as they are to me. However there are two items I will share with you. One, a note left for me by Wolf in his cabin when I was ship's steward, before we became friends. It stuck in my memory, was the source of my trust in his inner life. It was written in splendid high German and translates thus:

> "One would like to think; that one should 'sustain' another as oneself would wish to be sustained. But this is precisely the devil of man; that seldom anyone believes that the other has anything to endure in him."

It is doubtless a quote. He must have memorised it, this boy who was punished at school for expounding to the classroom Schiller's *Der Taucher* (The Diver) as "Glug! Glug!"

> The other bit is part of a diary entry I wrote at about the same time.
> "I want to write. This protesting, squawking, trembling shell of my life is breaking up. It's time to put out a tentacle, grey with fear, and take hold of something, anything! You? Beware of me. I have been sleeping, dreaming for so long. I am ravenous.'Wool-gathering' they called it… what I do. It is packed down tight inside me, suffocating here."

That "tentacle grey with fear" found you, five years later.

25th December, 2am Christmas Morning

Anna and I have just got home from midnight mass. So we are sitting here – Anna, Wolf and I – listening to Jonathan Livingstone Seagull. Ruth has gone out with a friend of ours, and Anna is already planning the wedding.

A four-hundred-litre tropical fish tank illuminates the gloom – my Christmas present from Wolf. Miraculously installed while we were at church. He is sitting on a bar stool, his nose pressed against the glass, observing piscine society. I am so glad he didn't buy a television.

I've been trying to put my finger on my feelings – following about six hours talking with Anna. It's like the feeling I had after reading *The Spiritual Man*. It was as if I was walking along a city pavement and suddenly heard a deafening roar behind me. Turning around I viewed with horror a pile of smoking rubble on the pavement where I had been standing a moment before.

Christmas Day

Sunlight filters through the jacaranda upon this page. There is a gentle breeze. Anna is nearby in a deckchair, sucking on a mango. The turkey is basking gently in the oven for dinner.

Last night, before midnight mass, we had a cold buffet with a whole troupe of friends as guests. Ruth sang grace (Anna had never heard her sing before). We also opened our presents, respecting the German custom of doing this on Christmas Eve. Now we find ourselves with a day of real leisure.

The breeze ruffles the syringa trees. Birds and bees are pursuing their appointed business. I am grateful for the peace, dumb with praise. (Wolf now approaching across the lawn bent on destroying the peace.)

Note in Wolf's handwriting: *Und nun sage ich, Du müßt mehr schreiben damit ich mehr Breifmarken kriege. Mamf.* (And now I tell you, you must write more so that I get more stamps. Yum!)

26th December 1978: St Stephen's Day, Boxing Day 11pm

I'm lying on the floor, so 'scuse the writing, listening to Debussy's La Mer and watching Angel fish fighting in my fish tank. Odd world isn't it!

Everyone's finally gone to bed. I've been dying to write all evening but now I can't think what it was I was wanting to talk about. It was a sort of dream of deep ravines filled with forest, and the smell of evening dew on pine needles. I would much rather be walking in that forest, holding your hand, than writing about it.

Mohican is about to settle down for the night on my back; I must look pretty relaxed. A satellite passed this way tonight, due east, bright and low and unwinking. I talked about St Stephen at breakfast this morning, because it is his day, and how St Paul killed him. Then Ruth told us how they kill wrens on the Isle of Man on Boxing Day because of some bizarre superstition. Such an odd world.

Roger visited to show us his holiday slides: "That's Fisherman's Paradise – bloody 'orrible dump". He kept complaining about how this or that fish in my aquarium was going to die, because it was

swimming squew, or too close to the surface; putting his great hoof
in it about where the tank came from – he sold it to Wolf. It is a
stunning tank. You'll love it. I will just need to plant some water
weed. With Wolf's usual efficiency he's installed five aerators. It
looks a bit like an operating theatre at present.

~45~

12th January 1979

Cher ami,

I visited your brethren on Wednesday. I was in Jo'burg on business and went over to the priory for tea. "Oh Amy, ha! ha! Didn't think we'd ever see you again now Alfred's gone," said one tactful fellow, who shall remain nameless. Your yellow Golf was sitting demurely in its garage as I trudged up the drive. There is a sign saying 'Laundry' on your door – but the furniture's still in there. I looked through the window.

Thank you for keeping my letters. BB returned them to me. He's doing some of that knotted embroidery stuff – forgotten its name – very clever. They have a clergy conference on at present – led by what BB describes as a rather violent Canadian. Boisterous clergy routinely shatter Greater Silence.[10] BB says he's going to hobble out in his nightie and tell them to shut up.

Cuthbert is planning lots of conferences this year with titles like 'The Charismatic Church' and 'Women Priests: Yes or No?' I thought I would get a chance to chat some more with BB but he disappeared, terrapin-like, during the beano at teatime.

Lester, the new postulant, is at the priory for a couple of months. I spent much of the afternoon talking to him – which was not very profitable for either of us I think, although maybe I just feel guilty about airing my views too openly. That young man will make an excellent monk – caught between seeing me off at the front door, and a summons to the refectory for supper, he chose the latter, and I let myself out.

I get the feeling that the brethren hit the turf (metaphorically speaking) when I appear. I suppose they imagine I am looking for a substitute for Alfred, to whom I can fasten myself – barnacle-like. Poor fellows – I understand their anxiety.

My household is very well organised at the moment. I don't have to do a thing except get my two house guests up with a cup of tea in the morning, and cook everyone dinner at night. I've even

---

10. The hours from 9pm after Compline until after breakfast the next morning, during which the Community keeps silence.

persuaded Anna to say Mattins for us both, so we have time to chat before I go to work. "Contemplation is everything you do," BB says – and – "It's s'posed to be fun, Amy". Tra la! It is, rather.

Ruth and Anna and I are going down the Simmer and Jack Gold Mine[11] on Tuesday, so we'll go and cast an eye over the joint at Nazareth House, and hopefully see Petunia, afterwards. Christopher Carpenter has started work as the new director.

17th January 1979

Petunia is not back at Nazareth House, which seems to bode ill for her future there, even if she wanted to stay. Joe is looking marvellous – tremendous savoir faire, cool, panâche, you name it. I said, "What shall I tell Alfred?" and he said, "Don't worry. I'll tell Alfred". So he will be writing to you *d.v.*

Ruth, Anna and I had a sandwich at the Wemmer Pan, and a snooze under the willows there, before visiting the priory for tea. I have very little more news from the last week. I suppose interesting things have been happening. Like, Ruth has fallen in love. But these things fade into the background, because life is dominated – like one ginormous toothache – by my mother. It's like living with a boa constrictor. If you are kind and loving it threatens to throttle you with affection; if you are not kind and loving, it collapses in a heap and looks dejected. Really Alfred! The whole household is shell-shocked by her moods. The divorce has deeply wounded her.

Ruth has disappeared completely into herself, as she does in times like these, spending as much time as she can out with Drew. Wolf goes out drinking every night. Everything I suggest to make things better, Mother denounces as either hopeless or impossibly idealistic. I am sure she is on the way to being healed of her sorrows, but all I can do to help is to try and control my temper. I feel like a mother-batterer.

Drew has a farm at Hartbeespoort Dam where we spent the day on Sunday, together with his mother, and my Afrikaans friend Nikki. It was a good day. We rode his horse, and shot tins with his bow and arrows, and waved at a puffing billy which passes his front gate (it waved back), and braiied. Got back in time for mass in the

11. A tourist gold mine.

evening. Nikki came too – which was splendid because now she wants to join St Wilfs.

Pru and Dick came to dinner with us on Monday. And I did a dreadful thing, in contravention of submissive wifely behaviour. Wolf didn't come home for dinner because he said he was doing overtime – only by chance I found out he was actually in the pub. I completely lost my rag and drove down there. Leaned on the car horn until a row of spectators assembled on the pub steps.[12] Men with beers in their fists yelled at me to stop the noise. Which I did, having extracted a promise from one with a red nose that he would inform Wolf that his wife was waiting for him outside.

He didn't come out (nor would I, actually, under those circumstances). So I leaned on the horn again. Red-nose came out to preach at me about how to behave towards my husband (he had to shout above the din). I sent a message back, that Wolf had three minutes, or else. When three minutes were up, with no sign of him, I revved the car and rammed the front fender, into the nearest tree, which made a splendid crunch. And drove off.

In spite of my rage, I had to smirk at the image in my rear-view mirror. Scandalised chaps, disturbed from their beer, concertinaed down the pub steps, aghast at the wilful demolition of a red Toyota.

Wolf was very cross, but I think he got the message – he mustn't tell me lies. And it is better to beat up the car than beat up your husband isn't it? I suppose it is better not to beat up anything, though?

Anna and Ruth return to the UK on Friday. Wolf says he has overtime until the end of April – so it looks like a spell of solitary for me. Very nice. I will try and get the bulk of my Unisa studies done early this year.

I am very sorry I have coped so badly with Anna, but I think she is impressed, in spite of herself, by the way I don't rise to her bait or her barbs. I have lost interest in gossip, and critically assessing other people, and though she gets cross with me, I think she can see the virtue in it. With our matrilinear gift of insight it is dangerous not to respect other people's privacy. O dammit! It is probably wicked to talk like this about her, but it helps me to tell you.

I spoke to Christopher Carpenter today when I dropped in to Nazareth House with Elsa from work, because we had a printing

12. Women were not allowed in public bars at this time in South Africa.

assignment in Jo'burg. He wants a reprint of the brochure as it is. He said he liked it very much, which is encouraging. I said I thought he'd better delay that decision pending a review by the committee. I am sure it must need some revision.

There was a lot going on at the house in an orderly, relaxed manner; a very good atmosphere. A Brother Ted (Roman Catholic), whom I haven't met before, was there in a helpful sort of way. Elsa was shown the chapel – next thing she is on her knees turning over that old carpet and oohing and aahing over it. Apparently it's a collector's item – Turkish or Persian or something. 'Mazing house that!

Dear Alfred, I must post this now, although there seems to be little in it that is edifying for the saints in Pedregoso. Your promised letter hasn't arrived yet, which makes me think sadly that you have scrunched it up. It does take a lot of effort and courage to write one's thoughts down – and it usually only comes off if one posts it all in a rush.

Love to you and all the brethren up there. You are very often in our thoughts.

20th January 1979

Dear Alfred,
Good to hear your voice yesterday evening. So sorry to get you out so late. Had I known you were so far from the phone I would not have caused you – and the brother who answered the phone – to risk life and limb just to yak to a bunch of casual callers.

But it was very good that Anna had the chance to speak with you. She needed that conversation to renew your friendship. Ruth read your letter, which we finally got a couple of days ago, and Anna read the pertinent bits – both visibly impressed by your prayer for us at the end. I have yet to translate it to Wolf.

I took Ruth and Anna to the airport this morning at 5am. They should be well on their way to that disaster area of the UK by now.[13] I wish I could have kept them here for a bit longer – but it's good to know they are together. Ruth spent last night attempting to tear herself away from Drew, who drove sadly home as we left for the airport.

13. UK's Winter of Discontent

Anna got over what she called her 'rebellion' on Thursday. I think the friends she made at St Wilfs helped her immeasurably. I hope she finds substantial support at the other end. It also emerged in the last few days that Ruth was afraid to commit her life to God because all the people she had met who had been baptised in the Spirit suffered upheavals in their lives afterwards, and she didn't want to upset her future career.

It would be lovely to have some photos from Pedregoso. How about drawing a ground plan? I would like to know where you are in the mornings – what does the chapel look like, and where is the refectory? This is an authentic catholic desire to know the incarnate life one shares in spirit. I often used to join you all in spirit at the priory during my prayers, because I could picture you there. As Fr Warwick pointed out – relationship is vital to prayer.

How good of you to get into *The Rock and the River*, so that we can discuss it further. Don't forget that I was ignorant of church doctrine when I read it. It was valuable to me to get a glimpse of fundamental differences between the protestant and Roman Catholic churches. I took to his description of the world and the church coming of age like a thirsty duck to water: reactionary (rather than revolutionary) protestant individualism; the sacramental nature of creation; the 'framework' of the liturgy. Many of my own unformulated intuitions found expression in the pages of this book.

I think, I hope, it is proper to be subjective in devotional reading? The conscious mind is like the tip of an iceberg. When studying, I read critically, selecting what I need for specific purposes. In devotional reading, I give myself to it, and allow it to form me. That is why I need guidance

I will get *The Divine Milieu*,[14] and the de Caussade book in due course, and will very much enjoy "passing a bit on" to you as I read them. I do appreciate your caution in giving me assignments. I will try not to over-react by writing you a forty-thousand-word review.

As for visiting you at Pedregoso, I have seriously considered it. I thought about visiting at Easter. However, it is irresponsible to burden you with house-guests at this fractious time on the border. It would be downright foolish to come up there just for a joy ride. Or would it? I will ask you nearer the time.

14. By Teilhard de Chardin

Do you take much notice of dreams? I have lately. I am sometimes faced with painful or important decisions in dreams. It makes me realise how deep the unconscious is. Circles within circles. Only the tiny circle of my consciousness is given to me in trust to recollect and maintain. When there is equilibrium between the conscious and the unconscious mind it feels like perfect synchronicity – like the way a man with a pulley can lift a hundredweight with one hand.

Oh it is so good to hear from you! I so easily forget what you are really like. Do you remember finding me so despondent at Nazareth House because I didn't have anything to do? You told me that in the Community novices are not trusted with anything to do 'outside' for three years? Tremendous comfort that. My three years of novitiate will be complete in July.

Sunday

I'm sending you a newspaper advertisement about the South African Christian Leadership Assembly, which was on SATV this evening. Nikki and I searched the neighbourhood for a television, and eventually rushed into our landlady's house just in time to watch it. Good coverage, although the interviewer couldn't quite grasp the notion of a conference of ten thousand people without an agenda. I would like go to SACLA in July, especially if you can come too.

23rd January 1979

Thought I would take a break from Teilhard de Chardin. Finding him a bit heavy going. I like his prayers and excerpts from letters, but the bits in between are very heavy. Perhaps I am at fault; even getting up in the morning is heavy going at present.

Some gems from *The Divine Milieu*:

- "In each one of us, through matter, the whole history of the world is in part reflected."
- "Owing to the interrelation between matter, soul and Christ, we bring part of the being which he desires back to God in whatever we do." (re: "Contemplation is everything we do." BB.)
- "The soul does not pause to relish this communion for it is wedded to a creative effort."

- "(W)hen men, having been awakened to a sense of the close bond linking all the movements of this world in the single, all-embracing work of the Incarnation…there will be little to separate life in the cloister from the life of the world." (You knew I would like that one didn't you?)
- "It is only the fine point of ourselves that comes up into the light of self-conscious freedom." (re: My consciousness is only the tip of the iceberg.)

When I was younger I used to throw a tantrum every time I found one of my ideas in a book. I thought it was intolerable plagiarism. These days, with my sanity in doubt, I am heartily relieved to find I share my bizarre thoughts with others of the human race.

It worried me when I read about extraordinary visions and abysmal trials in the lives of the mystics, and recognised shadows of them in my own experience. I feared I was turning into one of those delusional instant saints, who are so devilishly trying. Fr Teilhard has put my mind at ease thus: "That final 'excess', glimpsed and accepted *from the first steps* (my italics), inevitably puts everything we do in a special light and gives it a particular significance."

"Teach me to treat my death as an act of communion." Found his teaching on death very helpful. I've been in the habit of thinking about death quite often. Not in a general way, just my death. But I only got as far as thinking of it as an ordeal, or a crisis of faith. Not as "an act of communion".

I had packed the idea of the resurrection of the body away in a forgotten cupboard, but Fr Teilhard has got it out for me. I will consider the matter, in a circumspect sort of way, when I am less scared of it. Of such timid stuff are your witnesses to the resurrection made.

Wednesday

A very overweight gentleman by the name of Colin might visit you. I saw him yesterday in town when he came down from Rhodesia. He is a Selous Scout. I got to know him in a pub one lunchtime a couple of years ago. When I gave him your address today he said you would not even give him a glass of water! I told him you had been a pilot in the war, have been to sea, you like a beer, and are in Rhodesia under orders – like him. I think he is worth (even his) weight in gold.

Am ploughing on slowly with Fr Teilhard. Slowly, because I have found the last chapters very difficult. He talks about something which drove me into isolation so many years ago – my fear that all one's words and actions continue to echo and re-echo through time and space. The appalling potential consequences of them! But, it seems, this is the act of creation and redemption in each individual Christian.

I will let the last chapters ferment for a while and read them again.

Don't much enjoy returning from the dizzy heights of mysticism to the mundane drudge of housework. Still. Having been brought up to believe that everything that is good for one is bound to be nasty, I will persevere.

Thursday

They are beginning a course called The Edge of Adventure at St Wilfs. I've joined it very much against my inclination. It would make Petunia wake up screaming in the night. About seventy people with expensive watches and lipstick meet in the hall and yak nineteen to the dozen until someone raps the table and we all get 'Jesus orientated'. Then we clump into little groups – knees almost touching, giggle giggle, for a time of sharing. We are doomed to spend Wednesday evenings for the next twelve weeks together. We've got to pray for each member of our little group and see what happens. Yuk! It's supposed to make us 'open up' to each other.

On two occasions I glanced at my Lord for courage (he looked humorously back), then I 'opened up' a little. Everyone looked faintly offended, and changed the subject. I've been labelled a bohemian at St Wilfs. They have all decided they don't know what I'm talking about, even before I open my mouth. Aren't I charitable?

27th January 1979, Saturday

We went for a swim in a neighbour's pool today. Wolf threw his sandal up the nut tree – scored twenty nuts and a lump on his head. It is snowing in Germany, and there is a public outcry about the latest American anti-Nazi film.

I had a reply by return of post from a lady I stayed with in Paris during school holidays, to learn French. She was critical of my presence in apartheid South Africa, which somehow seemed less personal than the press clips she included, with an added insult about being married to a German. I have answered her gently, but feel clumsy at this task of reconciliation. She was one of the activists deported from Algeria for waving the flag for the oppressed. She has brought my position as a world citizen painfully near.

It is important to notice sequences of events: "Watch God working," as Fr Frank says. God rarely brings great revelations to ordinary people, but he does expect us to add two and two together.

Sunday

The 'conservatory' I made with plastic sheeting didn't work, so I am building a shade house with trellis instead, hopefully with creeper growing all over it eventually. Did some work on the roses. I didn't spray them and consequently they are being eaten alive. I hate insecticides but the time has come to be brutal.

I practised being brutal yesterday by doing some pruning. It really hurts me to cut things I have planted and watched grow. But I guess this is all part of growing up? The garden is at its last gasp with the drought. It was a national day of prayer for rain on Friday, and for peace in southern Africa. Wolf takes a great deal of pleasure in the fact that it doesn't look like rain.

Yesterday he deposited a large rock in the feral nesting place of our broody hen, while she was out foraging. It seems to have worked. She's back in the farmyard today. I suppose even hens don't see the point in trying to hatch rocks. Maybe I could take a lesson from that?

So many people these days seem to be obsessed with 'rejection'. We all suffer from it: Elsa, Wolf, Petunia, you, Anna, me, Ruth. Anna had a shocking flashback while she was here, of beating me off while she was breast-feeding my brother; although only a toddler myself, I was ferociously attacking them. But I'm sure I was none the worse for it. A horse with a foal will kick away her yearling filly; a crow tips her young out of the nest (although sometimes they do make errors); a cat shuns her young when she's pregnant again. Rejection is a vital part of growth.

Monday

The first frog has moved into my new conservatory. She has beautiful burnt orange eye-liner. She is not at all thrilled about the advent of the pigeons who bathe in her pond, so I will have to get a net for the roof.

I've just read this very drawn out and muddled letter through. I am not very happy about sending it – even having censored the worst bits. It does, however, express my state of mind quite well – muddled. Probably just what you don't need up there at the moment.

Is the rainy season upon you yet… or don't you get such a thing in your parts? I understand the Superior is in Rhodesia already. It will be nice for you to have him there, and good for you to know that he has seen first hand what is going on in your neck of the woods.

I am due to spend the day at Holyrood with Petunia next Sunday. I gather she has written to you, but maybe she didn't post it again. Quite a problem, this business of getting letters off the ground. I must confess I am having difficulty with this one – but once one begins tearing up letters there's no an end to it.

I appreciate your reservations re the arrival of kids coming back to school. But hordes of little faces do in time settle down into a few special little faces in the crowd – with or without the Shona.[15]

15. Alfred was learning Shona, the language of the region, spoken by most of the students at Pedregoso.

46

Holyrood is not far from Pretoria and is home to a small community of Anglican nuns, whose mother house is in England. Bishop Timothy has recommended that Amy make a visit, and perhaps find a new place of sanctuary there, now that Alfred is no longer at the priory.

The train stops at the village close by Holyrood, which was founded nearly a hundred years ago. The tranquil estate is bordered by meadows, where black-and-white Friesians graze alongside a river fringed with willow trees. Blue gums line the drive to the main house, which is set in wide lawns surrounded by herbaceous borders full of late summer flowers. A retreat house and several whitewashed rondavels are just visible behind dense shrubberies. A modern chapel with panoramic views of the gardens is linked to the main house by a glazed cloister.

Amy ascends the red-brick steps to the front entrance, ducking as a pair of swallows flash past her like blades. Chalky accretions on the top step indicate that the birds are nesting in the porch.

An elderly nun answers the doorbell. "You're just in time for tea," Sister Clare exclaims, as if Amy is a member of the family. Tiny but forceful, she tucks the girl under her arm and transports her to the common room. A hum of conversation between a dozen nuns and several visitors, blessedly, does not abate as Amy sidles into an armchair. A low table with an embroidered linen cloth is loaded with cakes, biscuits, and a victoria sponge. Petunia is already here, slender, pale, graciously eschewing cake, sipping tea. Amy finds herself in possession of a cup of strong tea, a fine china plate and a napkin. No, she will not take cake. But her host is adamant, cake will help build her up. Amy has a sudden sense of herself as frail. She shrinks in the company of these vigorous women, who tuck into their tea and cake with such gusto.

Later, flushed with conversation, of which she cannot remember a single detail, she happily agrees to walk with Sister Clare in the gardens. Petunia has already gathered herself up, her long garments and her swaying hair, to go to the chapel to pray.

Amy strolls out along the avenue of blue gums, her arm captive in the octogenarian's grasp. She finds herself telling her story — watching the skein of events over the past couple of years unwind before her eyes without any effort on her part – as she held out her wrists as a child for the skeins of wool which her mother wound into balls. She tells Sister Clare about meeting Brother Alfred – whom the nun appears to know. She tells her, obliquely, haltingly, about reading *The Spiritual Man*, about how her life was changed after that. She tells her about Wolf, how he resents her new life in the church.

Sister Clare listens, and murmurs, and pats Amy's hand, as they stroll in the warm fragrance of the eucalypts. At length the nun embarks upon an ode to marriage. Her face, which still bears the memory of the old-fashioned wimple, a seam where her skin was for decades protected from the sun, is beaming with joy. She sings a song of praise for the sacrament of marriage; the coupling of men and women; the blessing of children. At which point Amy revolts. She stops in the dappled shade of the avenue and yells in the face of this frail person, that she, Sister Clare, hasn't the foggiest idea of what marriage is really like. That she, Amy, has never in real life come across such a thing as a happy marriage. That marriage is hell on earth for her.

Sister Clare remains calm in the face of this frontal assault. A hint of a smile, of admiration even, crosses her wrinkled features. Amy is nonplussed. People usually tremble, or flee, or strike back, when she loses her temper. But the little nun merely pats her hand and smiles meekly. "Well dear, I have no experience of these things," she says, reclaiming Amy's arm, and they continue their stroll as if nothing has happened.

§

5th February 1979

Dear Alfred

I was going to sulk this week – not write, in the hope you would notice, even possibly worry. Reason? Envy! I had a squiz at the screeds of fascinating information, compiled and edited by Petunia, to you from the folk at Nazareth House. She's reading *The Shape of the Liturgy*, and goes around singing St Patrick's Breastplate all day, like a lonely angel.

223

But here lieth your letter upon my desk – arrived Friday. I wasn't in the office to receive it. Now here I am, seduced into doing that which I would not, after the joy of reading it.

Now you are thinking to yourself, "She's having me on! How can she be joyful about old Alfred's letter? I just made a few comments on her letters, and nattered on about life up here," etc etc, murmur, murmur.

A letter from you feels like a country ramble on a summer's afternoon. You don't tie ideas up in neat packages of words. You just stroll around and share glimpses of your day, and the way you feel. That way you pack pages of 'dope' into just one-and-a-half sides of writing. I hope the 'major blast' from the Superior wasn't about you asking to come to SACLA in July?

I hope you are right about my current 'heavy time' being the Lord's preparation for my future ministry. Deep down I know you are right, and it's good to hear it said. I have certainly dropped out of the race. It occurs to me that our generation probably misunderstands St Paul's 'spiritual race'. We compete to win – acclaim, money, celebrity etc. But the generation Paul was writing to worshipped human prowess for its own sake. So the spiritual 'race', for them, meant striving for God's sake, not for rewards. Since I have given up that latter race, I have realised that it was 'goodness' I was so futilely pursuing. God's goodness is a gift and cannot be won.

The parish course is doing me good. I didn't want to go, but it has helped me to find myself in the maze of the contemporary church. When one is confronted with the question: "What is more important to you in your life than God?" and one can fearlessly reply, "Nothing," one wakes up to the reality of being a child of God!

I have spent a year and a half giving up everything I have and am, with the ungracious attitude of, "Take my life, it's no use to me!" But I haven't let God in to change me – to love me.

Trouble is, I have been locked in my own little fortress ever since I can remember. A few have been allowed into the foyer, but you are the only person who has ever had the freedom of the house. Now I have the feeling that the landlord is considering extensive changes.

They say one's spiritual aspirations are followed at a sedate pace, and usually after a long time, by their fruition. I am at the bit where Jesus says, "Only one thing remains for you now. Sell everything you have and follow me". Some of this became clear at Holyrood at the weekend.

It's amazing to discover how delighted people are to find out what a bad person I am! I am not sure if I have been a holy terror or if I am just standoffish – though I think my solitary times were necessary. I'm relaxing in the acceptance I have found, particularly at Holyrood.

Why were you sitting in your room writing me a letter on a Sunday? Nowhere to sunbathe, or is it the rainy season now? Tell me more. Where's my ground plan? How many kids? What ages? All boys? Where's the swimming pool? Is it just three of you at weekday mass? Who cooks? What do you do all day? Do any of the boys speak English? Are you drawing yet? How about portraits? They'd love that! It's my birthday next week, St Valentine's Day, whoever he is. Sounds a bit wimpish.

I am so glad you had a tiff with your prior. It makes it sound much more like family life; to have the liberty to quarrel, instead of padding around being humble all the time. Anyway, you'd never have the opportunity to forgive each other, and your dear selves, if you never had fallings out.

It's so good to hear words of encouragement from you. I'm not sure if loving endurance is the right attitude towards one's mother, but I can see now that I have been keeping her, along with everyone else, at arm's length all my life. With her own need for acceptance, she has felt this as rejection. Love is a tough game and everyone who plays it gets a bloody nose sometime or other. I should have let her into my private places, together with all her insensitivity and bitterness, and taken the risk of losing my temper.

Wolf's just phoned. I gave him your greetings and the substance of your letter. He rang off hurriedly. Talk about love being a rough game – that big, tough blacksmith flees at the very mention of the word. Woe is me! He must have felt fairly safe from it whilst living with me for the last seven years.

One of the Sisters spotted Wolf waiting in the car park when he came to fetch me home from Holyrood yesterday. I found him thoroughly enjoying himself in the common room, with half a dozen women plying him with tea and cake. We came home with a woolly squirrel from the convent craft shop. He felt obliged to behave like a moron all evening, to pretend he had hated every minute of it.

I am looking forward to meeting the Superior on the 17th, although I will find open day at the priory very intimidating: church authority in the person of the Superior; brethren's patronising attitude to women; the complacency of the fraternity; and my aversion to publicly speaking my mind. If strength is perfected in weakness, I should be unassailable, because I feel as weak as a kitten at the thought of it.

I hope you like the book I've sent. The bit about the Spirit brooding over the waters, *vis à vis* the gift of tongues, is very valuable to me. I took control of that charism, instead of just letting the words flow as they will. I begin to understand Paul's description of tongues: "It is the Spirit herself…with sighs too deep for words". No wonder I got bored with tongues, when I thought I just had to put in a certain amount of time talking nonsense – like an exam. Now, I think I understand that I give the Holy Spirit my faculties, so that God in some extraordinary way, talks to me. It is much more companionable that way round. I think that within the Trinity the Spirit is the most vulnerable person. Imagine what it must be like to live in the mire of people's souls, and even when people become aware of her holy presence, to be pushed around like a serf, and bickered over.

Dearest Alfred. That's all for now. I would love to go for a real walk with you. One doesn't stop loving people just because they are not here. My stiff upper lip wobbles a bit at times, when the going gets rough and there is no-one to phone up. But there are no more separations in the kingdom of God, are there?

Thanks for your letter. I hope God blesses you with a loving, rewarding ministry to those boys, and plenty of courageous patience with their teachers. I should think that teachers and freedom fighters are an awfully volatile combination?

Monday: On receiving the news that Alfred is to visit Jo'burg for Chapter.

Well! How about that![16] Petunia read the first sentence and read the rest of your news while she was dialling my number. When are we going to be able to meet you and fall all over you and weep for joy, without embarrassing anyone? Petunia will have to be tethered with a ball and chain to restrain her from actually boarding the plane at Jan Smuts Airport when you arrive. I am naturally totally level-

16. Alfred's argot for amazement.

headed about the prospect, and will await your pleasure. Don't count on it though.

Wolf made appreciative grunts about your visit, with accompanying demands for stamps, then said, "You see. I told you he'd be back," as if he personally had arranged it. He is demanding that you should bring him a devil. I have pointed out that it is not quite the thing for a monk to transport devils – but what he means is a certain sort of carving in ebony. I've forgotten the Swahili name for them – family trees and all that. I don't know if it is possible for you to find something suitable, or if you have enough liquid capital? He would naturally reimburse you (English euphemism for 'pay you back').

Wednesday

Your friend Petunia is writing your itinerary. It's a symphony involving umpteen persons, with multiple duets, and the odd solo. She has to convince the brethren that you are not merely socialising, so many of the appointments are billed as 'counselling'. She has decided that I should meet you on Sunday at our house.

But I hope I can get to say hallo before that. You can't really expect me to wait for six days in Pretoria with you in Jo'burg can you? Perhaps I will appear at midnight on Monday, in a false beard and bowler hat, at the door of the 'laundry'.

Oh yes. That brings to mind a recent sermon from Fr Albert on 'loving one another'. The message was that one must be prepared to be loved by another on their terms. These are our terms, beloved brother, so it might be as well to enjoy the peace and quiet up there, while the going's good.

12th February 1979

It's my writing to Alfred time and I can't think of anything to tell you. Probably your momentous news has taken the wind out of my tattered sail. Instead of feeding 'our man on the border' morsels of news from the city, we are awaiting a homecoming hero, who is not likely to be interested in anecdotes of what Mathilde, the hen, has been up to.

13th February 1979

Dear Alfred,

I had a letter from the Superior today, in reply to one you encouraged me to write to him about my ideas for the fraternity. His straight message is that the fraternity should not be a watered-down religious life – or mini monks and nuns; that a tangible commitment on my part by making my goods available to the Community for mission would be tantamount to being unfaithful to Wolf. But that a deeper commitment is necessary within the fraternity – sometime in the future, different from the brethrens' of course. Also, that one cannot ask people to describe what the resurrection means to them in written words.

There is a great deal of truth in all he says, but the way he puts it, he clearly thinks I am a harum scarum, who knows nothing of fear and weakness, and never felt the bleak wind aft. Having spoken to your sunshine voice last night, I can probably cope with meeting him on Saturday. Though I have the suspicion you are gaily encouraging a catastrophe.

§

Amy goes to the priory on open day, as Alfred has encouraged her to do, although she spends most of the morning skirting around the Superior instead of introducing herself. He is the main attraction, all the way from England, and constantly surrounded by people wanting to meet him. At midday, during the celebration of the eucharist, she notices that his hands shake slightly as he administers the chalice, and her heart warms to him. She imagines he knows who she is, but of course he has no idea that this wisp of a girl is the harridan who wrote to him. Eventually, when Lester introduces her, he stares, amazed. At last he expostulates, "I never imagined you to be like *this!*"

"Oh," replies Amy, unmoved. "Did you expect a harpy?"

"Well, yes!" he says, before he can stop himself, and she smiles at him.

There is a small silence. He thanks her for her letter, apologises that he is a little weary after today's events, and might she be available to discuss these important matters further with him tomorrow? Calmly, as if in a fog, as if she has had a heart transplant, she says she would. They agree to meet at 10am tomorrow in the garden at St Bede's.

§

He arrives punctually, unlatching the gate, walking up the garden path with that particular English briskness which is so at odds with the chirruping of cicadas and the fierce African sun. She is waiting for him, and he follows her to a bench shaded by the mulberry tree. He is very tall and she has to crane her neck to look up at him as she invites him to sit down. She perches on a tree stump close by, so that she can look straight up into his face. She enjoys this slightly subordinate position. She wants to reassure him that she means him no harm.

He is a talented listener. She tells him far more than she intends to; many things about herself which are private. She begins by describing the anomie which haunts her, which haunts her generation. Their wanderings eastward in search of the meaning of life; the pharmacopoeia of substances which help to combat the ennui of living in an aridly materialistic world; the suicides. She tells him of her joy, but also of her dismay, to find here in Africa, of all places, the treasures of mystical Christendom hidden away in the priory library. Why, her generation is dying for want of this food, starving for lack of it. How could the fathers of the church sleep on such a priceless hoard, not share it?

He explains that such esoteric books have only been of interest to people in the religious life. That they are certainly not squirrelled away on purpose. But she is not a monk, she wails; not everybody is a monk; what about us? He mildly observes that there are religious communities for women as well. But that is not the point, Amy objects; what about all the people who can't be monks or nuns?

"What do you think we should do?" he enquires.

Confronted by such breathtaking candour, she is speechless.

It is warm in the speckled sunlight. He asks if she would consider writing down some of her ideas in an article for the Community journal? Entirely overcome, she whispers that she might consider it. He says he cannot promise anything because he is not the editor, but he may be able to bring some influence to bear.

§

19th February 1979

Dear Alfred,

I feel as if I have been in a war. Everything is small and strange and terrifyingly different, like a dream where everything is normal except one's self. I feel as if I haven't seen you for a thousand years – and you too may not be the person I remember.

Maybe it's the effect of contemplating the article which I have to write for the Community journal. Yes! The Superior asked me to write it! He wants to see it first and rather dryly said he might be able to influence its publication, as long as he didn't think it would actually destroy the Community.

It will be heavy-going though. It is exhausting trying to assimilate such vast matters as the way the world is rocketing t'ward oblivion, and how the religious life is well placed to discern what God is saying to humanity at this time. It is doing me good to slip out of my trite, bland little daily round and, under sealed orders, to try to put the case of a whole generation into a coherent message.

I am actually experiencing what I want to write about – the painful growth that comes from discipline and commitment, when demands are made upon one. Don't expect much of the article though. It is already proving to be very difficult, and is cutting me down to size p.d.q.

I had a wonderful weekend at the priory. Wolf was working overtime, and then playing Bridge on Saturday night, so I stayed over with the Sisters. You know how afraid I was of going to the open day, and bearding the Superior in his den? Actually I behaved with unusual decorum, so I knew God was with me. About two hundred and fifty people came, including Bishop Desmond Tutu from Lesotho. Fr Superior preached what seemed, to my fevered brain, a direct put-down of all I had written to him. Then we had this wonderful meeting. I feel as if I have swum a moat full of sharks, and, instead of encountering boiling oil and pikes, have been met by the commander of the garrison with something like respect.

So, you will be here in three weeks. Maybe we will seem small and different to you? Life is more highly strung up there. I was on a bus on my way home from the priory on Sunday, and I saw my friend Colin, the Selous Scout, walking down Bree Street – on leave from the army for exams, as it turned out. I inadvertently cried his name. He looked up, his eyes searching across several lanes of traffic for whatever had disturbed his reverie. He couldn't see me of course, but he knew someone had focused on him. I suppose his life depends on that sort of extra-sensory perception up north?

Fr Warwick and the Superior both addressed the company on Saturday. Warwick was good, and very funny. He seems to flower in Fr Superior's company. They told everyone about your new job, and asked for our continuing prayers for you all at Pedregoso.

Petunia has the 'flu'. I saw her yesterday. She is working for her brother in the landscaping business, and getting to grips more positively with 'the middle class'. She seems to have been accepted by the upper echelons at Nazareth House, which has done her morale the world of good.

BB has had another operation and is hobbling around in plaster again. I'm very sorry about that, especially as he hates attracting attention on account of it. Giles has got a whole collection of skull caps. Did he have them before you left? They have finally persuaded him to take the black one off at communion, with the argument that even the bishop takes his mitre off then.

Warwick said on Saturday afternoon that they had enough food left over to invite the Sisters to supper and breakfast. So Sisters took him up on the supper, and we all had coffee in the quad afterwards. Very nice. Giles had a good dig at me about being there so often I ought to join the Sisters; Sister Elizabeth flew to my defence. Things got so fast and loose after all the wine that someone even allowed themselves the remark, "Are you staying for breakfast? Oh I suppose you can't sleep with the Fathers!" Giggles all round. I got the distinct and happy feeling that I may now be becoming accepted as part of the furniture.

Integrating Wolf into this growing fellowship is more difficult. Talk about an irresistible force meeting an immoveable object. We clash pretty often now. But heavy, good, solid fights which leave us each eyeing the other with respect. Not the rancorous bickering that happens in so many unhappy marriages. Nor the silent non-relationship we ourselves have lived in for so long. Wolf's doing a countdown on your arrival, by the way. Maybe he thinks you will improve my temper?

Anyway, my letters to you have got serious competition for the next little while. The Community journal calls!

47

At the end of February Amy runs away from home. It has been a particularly arduous few days with Wolf. The last straw is when she begs him for money to buy cigarettes, having spent all hers. He is fiddling under the bonnet of the car at the time. He pushes his glasses up his nose, leaving a smear of grease on his cheek.

"Go and look in the fuse box," he says, nastily. "You'll find some fags in there."

Amy takes serious umbrage at this. It sounds threatening. As if he would like her to electrocute herself. She packs a small bag and takes a bus to the motorway where she proceeds to hitch-hike south.

She gets several good lifts on the N3 to beyond Harrismith. It is late in the afternoon when a lorry drops her off at the turning into the mountains. Cheerfully the driver waves her goodbye as she trudges off onto a minor road, into encroaching night. Soon she is walking in pitch darkness, stumbling on tussocks of grass alongside the bitumen. She sets her jaw like flint, puts her trust in God, and forges on.

At last a small black sedan approaches, headlights searing the night. The car passes her by, does a u-turn and, alarmingly, slows to a crawl beside her. The passenger window is wound down, but it is the driver who hails her from behind the wheel. "Get in!" he yells, a note of panic in his voice. Beside him is an Indian lady dressed in bright silk. She smiles reassuringly at Amy, and leans back to open the rear passenger door. With a prayer of thanks the girl leaps in.

For the first ten minutes Amy endures a tirade from the driver, a courtly Indian gentleman. He expounds a litany of fates which could befall a lone white woman on this road at night, which includes black men, robbers, and porcupines.

"Where do you want to go?" he demands at last, having exhausted his own angst on her behalf.

"I'm going to Montville," she replies, naming the nearest town to the small community which Alfred has told her about, which is her goal.

"We are going there," says the lady quietly.

"But you were going in the opposite direction," objects Amy.

"We were just going for a drive. We often do that in the evenings," replies the driver. "Now we are going home."

He has a fine, hawkish profile, she notices, and wears a golden silk shirt.

It is 11pm by the time they reach Montville, after puttering along at 30mph. They will not let her go without knowing for sure she is safe. So she asks them to leave her at the Anglican rectory, which they find at length. Then they wait in the car while she rings the door bell. Eventually, when a sleepy clergyman opens the door, she waves enthusiastically to her benefactors and they drive off.

Explaining her situation to the parish priest is rather more complicated, but, hearing of her destination, he gives her a bed for the night.

"The sisters are only ten minutes down the road," he tells her, before returning to his own bed.

She leaves the rectory early, before anyone else is awake, and finds after an hour or so that the priest's information is for drivers of vehicles, not for people on foot. She is very hot and sweaty by the time she reaches the tiny hamlet where the sisters have made their home. There is a sign on the main road pointing up a dirt track to a cluster of wattle and daub huts. A corrugated zozo house[17] is off to one side. In the yard is a hand driven water pump.

The three sisters are all fit and tanned. One of them is Indian. They are wholly accepting of Amy's request for asylum, particularly when she names Brother Alfred as the one who has recommended her visit. Without question they show her to a cool hut with a thatched roof, and ask her to make herself at home.

Later in the afternoon she finds the Indian sister in the garden harvesting chillies. Hundreds of them raise their fiery fingers out of the khaki weed. It is very peaceful, sitting there, picking chillies to be packed in jars for the winter. In the evening Amy joins the sisters in the corrugated iron hut for a meal of goat meat, mealiepap and stewed vegetables. They tell her that they have a meeting after dinner called the chapter of errors, when they tell each other about anything disturbing that has happened to them during the day. Amy finds this intriguing, but chooses to go to bed early instead.

17. Shed.

§

Dear Alfred,

Nice here isn't it? Sitting at a pinewood desk looking up through the rain to that little hill with a flat head on it. Forgot my toothbrush. Yuk! Never mind. Everything else is in good order. Except my feet. "Just down the road" the vicar said, Ha! Ha! I got the priest at Montville out of bed at 11pm on Saturday night, kipped at the rectory, and had to walk ten miles in the morning to the mission. Blisters!

Only five lifts to Montville though. The last one was a nice Indian couple who turned their car round especially to drive me into the mountains, and spent an hour regaling me with all the things I could be killed by at this time of night: "porcupines, black people, snakes, exposure…" I could have added, "my husband".

I haven't really got anything to tell you, except that I'm here, and so are the Sisters who remember you well. They are very nice. They didn't give me a lecture on the dangers of hitch-hiking, or make imbecile noises about leaving my husband. We worked in the garden this afternoon, harvested potatoes and chillies by the hundredweight. The little cat is about to produce kittens.

Sister Cheryl has just arrived with tea, and sends her regards. There is a money spider parcelling up an ant on my window sill.

Elsa phoned the mission this morning. I haven't the foggiest idea how she found out that I was here. I shall wend my way homewards tomorrow, and try to make a submissive beginning to Lent.

I finished the draft for the journal on Friday. Went much quicker than I thought. Maybe most of it was already formed in my mind and just needed to get out. But I don't know how much of it the Superior will want rewritten. He is on his way to Lesotho today – hopefully with the draft – so I won't hear the verdict until next week. He did ask me if I was coming over to visit you during chapter – so presumably I may? Please don't expect much of the article even if Superior does accept it. There is nothing new in it and it is very conservative — it's just a gentle nudge for the brethren that the rest of the world actually exists.

I've been reading de Caussade's book[18] which is plunging me further into the weariness which is apparently going to go on "for ever and ever until you're dead," as the sinister voice in my head intones.

It's as much as I can do to get up in the morning at home, let alone get to the breakfast table, without sinning violently. Living moment by moment is the secret — you virtually have to, when the memory of yesterday or the prospect of tomorrow makes you go cold with horror.

That God can, and eventually does use one for good purpose, if one has submitted entirely to him, is very good news. But Père de Caussade does not elaborate on enduring the interim — in my case the forty-two years between age twenty-eight and seventy, when one presumably reaches maturity. I am very glad to read him though. Thank you.

It's about 5pm and prayer time. Things will go quickly now. Prayer, evening office, supper, sew my trousers, finish book, morning prayer, breakfast, hit the road and hope to be back in time for confession and mass. And then home. "Is not this the fast that I choose…?"

Home crouches like a glowering heap of all that is negative — rejection, destruction. Everything clamours for my attention and nothing is satisfied by it. The sort of cold hell which takes joy in nothing. I suppose everyone feels the same when things get on top of them? I can't imagine how you retain that infectious joy of yours, even in Pedregoso.

9pm

Sorry about that outburst of retreat blues. Feel a lot better now. The place is full of mellow lamplight. Sisters and I had a good talk at supper. And I forgot to collect the needle and cotton, so I can't sew my trousers. I hate sewing anyway.

18. *Abandonment to Divine Providence*

Got back yesterday in time to miss confession and mass. Met some good people on the road. Wolf was glad to see me. The chickens have wrecked what's left of the garden and the vegetables have died for lack of water. The dogs ate as if they had been starved for a week, so I guess the Lord requires me home. Wolf broke his foot yesterday, so he was a sorry sight.

I dropped into Nazareth House where Petunia is in an agony of indecision about staying or leaving. Christopher is a lovely person – very young and gentle looking. They want a monthly newsletter, so I can help with editing that.

Not much else to say. The de Caussade book will help me a lot in the next few weeks as I absorb it during Lent.

I am looking forward to seeing you. We must pray that the Lord will protect the mission while you are away from it. Everything is so uncertain in Africa, and I think the Lord will ask strange things of his people here. The Sisters said some things which are making me rethink the whole question of witnessing to God in the world.

1st March 1979

Dear Alfred,

I want to give you screeds of feedback on Père de Caussade. Everyone reads a book like that differently, so my reflections shouldn't trespass on your own appreciation of him. I'm using your pen, by the way. I'll get a refill for mine today (payday yesterday). I wrote the Superior's article with this one. Hope there will be something left in it by the time I give it back to you.

I am in a peculiar place at the moment. I can't pray alone; but if I pray with others – the brethren, sisters – their presence keeps me centred, so to speak. I don't count praying at St Wilfs, because that is for the church – it's liturgical. It seems very wrong not to have a personal prayer time, but I know I am growing in the love of God because, sometimes in the evenings, when I am reading or whatever, I find myself caught up in such joy, for no reason at all. I used to deliberately psych myself up to a prayerful state of mind to get anywhere near that sense of presence. Now God shares *ipso facto* in everything I do, it seems a bit rude to make a special compartment for prayer.

At the same time it's so easy to go off the rails, thinking you can do anything you like, now you are a member of the royal household. Père de Caussade said that if you've once abandoned yourself to God you mustn't worry about anything else that happens to you. Well I did do that. Remember? That time with *The Spiritual Man*? All I took through that lacuna with me were grog, cigarettes and you. Everything else was left behind. There was no connection at all between my life before and after that eye of the needle.

So presumably I mustn't worry about exploring this strange and apparently uncharted territory of having no rules at all?

Père de Caussade has given me confidence to try it anyway. If it goes wrong God isn't going to annihilate me. I am the sort of person who can easily take pride in spiritual feats like praying in the middle of the night, fasting for days on end, and having out of the body experiences. Maybe God just wants me to be an ordinary person this Lent?

There is a certain 'rightness' about what I am doing, or rather 'not doing' now. But this is a time when I really need you. The ego is very subtle and all this may be just an excuse to escape discipline, which is no friend of mine in the normal way, although I immensely admire people who have real self-discipline. It is a gift of the Spirit after all.

I won't lay upon you the burden of advising me one way or the other, but it is important that you know what is going on. I suppose the real issue is God — the only signpost around here. It is true that I delight in God's presence more and more. I am gradually 'living into' those years of pathetic longing for something or other — that Presence who visited, and left, in childhood. The One who was here all the time, but I did not know where to look.

I'll read de Caussade again in a week or two. Just one thing — about lighting people up — about auras. It must have happened pretty often in the Middle Ages. You can see it from the halos people have in medieval paintings — before the Renaissance discovered that humans don't have electric circuits. You need special eyes to see auras. I've seen you lit up a few times. I don't think it necessarily means a person is holy, and one mustn't get too serious about it. It happened to me when Fr Superior was celebrating mass. He was consecrating the elements and he looked up and forgot the words. I'm almost sure he must have seen me lit up, because he's not the sort of person to muddle his words.

I said to Sister Elizabeth that there was method in Alfred's madness, getting me to meet the Superior. She looked quite bustled. I can't make out if she adores you or disapproves of you, or both.

6th March 1979

Welcome! Welcome dearest friend, the earth was bare without thee and the valleys chilled with shadows.

Wolf wants to see you too, although he will doubtless do his best to make you feel you're the last person he wants in his house. He certainly makes his loved ones work hard for it.

No, I haven't 'hit hard' in my article. Mainly because if you hit hard at clever, elderly gentlemen they beat a hasty retreat with their worst fears about upstart young women confirmed. If anyone takes time to think about my message they will find it rather iconoclastic. I do myself. It places the church (including me of course) in the position of someone who has mothered a child and left it on the streets to die of cold and starvation; or to be picked up like Oliver Twist by some passing malevolence.

But you are back in the land. So never mind all that now. Just give me a call when you can, with one thing clear in your mind to tell me – namely when I can make a midnight visit to the priory and say 'hallo' to you, or I will be a nervous wreck by Friday.

Your description of Disaster Sunday at Pedregoso was utterly delightful. You really do have a gift for gathering up a whole situation in a couple of sentences – a sort of prose caricature. A sketch of a St Bernard who got in amongst greyhounds – all looking down their aristocratic noses at this extraordinary creature who thinks it is one of them. But the moral of the story isn't in the St Bernard's performance at all – it's in his totally charming St Bernardness, which could never in a million years be greyhound.

I would like to read Frank Lake's book[19] – but I too had better come clean about something. You remember how unsure I was about allowing Hilda the freedom to lay hands on me that time for the healing of memories? She took serious liberties with that freedom, as I knew would happen. So now I am lumbered with a mistrust of Hilda from that evening, together with the very idea of the healing of memories.

19. *Clinical Theology*

We are the sum total of all our experience, and only the finest, most humble craftsman should tinker with that. Now – this moment – already has three or four dimensions. If one begins to travel in time – unless one is without form or substance like the Holy Spirit – one is dealing with multiple dimensions, refracting millions of influences. Too many people try to work from the outside in – the Holy Spirit begins from the centre, and draws all things to herself.

Petunia has just phoned. I hope she will get a good session with you – it will be like popcorn on a hot stove! S'cuse the liberty, but she needs love – in the same way most of us do.

I will take Monday off, and sit like patience on a monument, hoping to catch a glimpse of you. I can see it will be a very full few days for you. I would rather not be part of the triumphal procession, because you have never been absent for me.

48

On the evening before Alfred must return to Rhodesia after his flying visit to the priory for chapter, he summons a few friends to a surprise meeting with him in a Johannesburg mansion, procured for the occasion by Petunia. The gardens are in twilight as they arrive. Velvet lawns slope down beneath a canopy of trembling silver birch leaves towards a reedy pond where frogs sing their evening chorus. Banks of daisies tumble like white water around the silvery boles of the trees. The owners are away, but have left ample supplies of wine and whisky.

Alfred and Petunia are joined by Amy and several of the usual suspects from Nazareth House, who come and go during the evening, smoking, jawing, hugging each other, following Alfred's example. Quadrophonic speakers provides wraparound baroque music. Petunia has brought pizzas, which Alfred groans over with orgiastic pleasure.

Replete now, and with a glass of whisky beside him, it seems that Alfred has more serious business on his mind.

Since he has been away, he says, he has been pondering ideas for an alternative Christian community. He seems grave, almost diffident, stripped of the cloak of bonhomie which usually envelopes him at social gatherings. He wants to hear what folk think about forming an ecumenical household. A Christian family living together in an ordinary house.

He listens quietly, intently, frowning in concentration as people variously sketch their notions of such a community. Petunia wants a house of prayer – with no arrangements for catering, as Amy crossly notes. Joe thinks a shed would be a good idea, where guys can meet up and make things – instead of drinking, he adds, virtuously. Amy muffs her go, with a mumbled few sentences about creating a bridge between God and the world – which causes puzzlement, and a lull in the conversation.

Eventually, when the topic is exhausted, Petunia goes off upstairs to pray. Gradually the folk from Nazareth House go in search of entertainment elsewhere. Amy is left alone with Alfred, who is reclining on a mohair rug beside the log fire, which occupies an alcove big enough to accommodate a board meeting. Sleepy warmth envelopes them from the flames, the smell of burning timber melds with the fug of cigarette smoke.

"You are not thinking of giving up?" asks Amy at last, anxiously. His enquiries have caused her both terror and hope. She is thrilled beyond measure that he should trust them, his friends, with his doubts and fears, possibly with tentative hopes for a future? At the same time a taboo has been broken. Men's secret business, worse! monks' secret business has been aired in the market place. His vocation, her own anchorhold, may be at risk.

"How about another whisky?" asks Alfred. She adds three fingers of chivas regal to their glasses. He talks about personal things. He tells her about a horrible thing that happened to him when he was a little boy at primary school, not far from here as it happens. The class was learning to sing a chorus in rounds: 'Roses are red, dilly dilly, violets are blue…' Alfred's mother was called Violet. Six-year-old Alfred was carried away with the song, closed his eyes and warbled on and on until all had fallen ominously silent around him. His eyes opened upon the scenario of his classmates pointing, giggling, jeering, as the final notes of his solo rendition fell to pieces around him. 'Roses are red, dilly dilly'.

Amy reclines beside him on the rug. They regard the little flames licking at logs in the fireplace, sipping their drinks. "What did you do in the war?" asks Amy at last, snuggling into the intimacy of the moment.

Alfred flew Spitfires in the war. But one early morning over north Africa, he ran out of fuel. At least he thought he had. There had been a party the night before, with the inevitable hangover. So many aircrew never came back from raids, partying helped to numb the pain. Three hundred feet above the desert Alfred at last remembered the correct procedure. He needed to turn the fuel tanks over, but by then it was too late.

A platoon of Germans soon appeared over the crest of a dune near the crash site. Alfred offered the commandant a cigarette, but he took the whole packet, remarking with a certain schadenfreude that the war was now over for Alfred.

After a miserable journey up through Italy in a cage, on display like wild animals for the amusement of the population, Alfred and his fellow prisoners-of-war ended up in Germany, in Stalag Luft III. In the same camp as Amy's father, as it happens. But Alfred has further humiliations to narrate.

"For months I could not speak about what had happened. I skulked around the compound talking to no-one, thinking incessantly about what an ass I had been. What a waste! What a complete *nincompoop!*" Alfred sprays the word. "In the end the padre noticed that something was eating at me. He ferreted the story out, and then he laughed! He pointed to a chap on the other side of the compound, and told me what happened to him. Then to another fellow with a worse story. Everyone had a horrible story to tell. I felt I could join social life in camp after that."

Amy wraps herself in the memory of this evening with Alfred beside the aromatic wood fire in the beautiful house. It keeps her warm throughout the coming winter.

§

20th March 1979

Dear Alfred,
Thank you for sharing your feelings with us last evening — in that lovely house with good music, the goodness of the Lord so much with us all. Sharing is in itself such a generous thing; it implies trust and calls forth trust.

I sat for a while in our garden, with the dogs and the moon for company, after I got home last night. I had hoped to hear that chapter ended in rejoicing, embraces and singing in tongues! Clearly no luck on that score.

Now you have braved the monkish reticence and told us your mind. I see that what is required of us is not a day of prayer, but weeks and months learning how to pray, shaping us to sustain God's purpose.

Meanwhile I know what you mean about the loneliness of not being able to share the life of the Spirit with your brethren. You and Petunia are really the only ones I can do that with, and I don't see either of you very often. I think St Paul suffered from that sort of loneliness. He lashes out at the Jerusalem apostles, saying they have companions, why shouldn't he?

I suppose all one can do, being driven to it, is to work day and night to make companions in Jesus with the company available?

But I cannot warm to the idea of the household you mooted – one of like-minded people. One has to just start with what's already here. It is one thing to bring people to Christ through a desire to serve God. It is quite another to birth Christians through a passionate desire for the divine life in others.

When Jesus asked Peter "Who do you think I am?" I believe he was crying out in dismay, unable to bear the weight of his own identity, needing his friends to affirm him. Everybody needs someone to tell them who they are.

After I had given up trying to 'convert' Wolf, I stopped telling him about the wonders and hilarities and sadnesses of my spiritual life. But, unshared, that life began to turn sour. So now I chatter on to him anyway, as if Anna singing in tongues, and instant healing of slipped discs are the most normal things in the world. I don't know what he thinks, I don't ask. But I see him whiffing the breeze, like a wild horse smelling oats for the first time.

I haven't accepted your absence yet. I note, rather crushingly, how quickly I abandon the Lord's mercy if something doesn't go my way. Then after I have complained bitterly, he gives us that lovely evening together and persuades you to leave us a way of serving you – you who have spent so long praying for us.

I went through the concordance on 'obedience' today – hoping to write you something helpful. It must be dreadful to agonise with one's conscience when one is constrained by rules. If rules and conscience demand different things I suppose the only resolution of the impasse is a new understanding of the word 'obedience'. I haven't yet thought or prayed or read enough to find the comforting word I would love to give you. But I want you to know that we have taken you seriously.

I suppose Jesus didn't break any rules or promises.[20] He grew up in Jewish society, and was obedient to the law and the prophets. He gave his gospel to the son of a Pharisee to take to the gentiles. He obeyed the Father. I pray that you will be given the knowledge of the will of God, without having to break anything at all. Especially not your own heart – because a man can never go back on a vow without breaking integrity with himself.

20. Except rather a lot of the religious, political and social mores of his day.

I can't see that it is bad — this time of rest and loneliness and uncertainty and prayer — should it end with you finding your vocation elsewhere. By the way, during his speech at open day, Warwick twinkled all over and spoke of "our apostolic delegate Brother Alfred".

Forgive me for putting my foot in it like a bull in a china shop — I shouldn't write with so little discretion. You will doubtless be anxious about the wisdom of having shared such 'dynamite' with us last night.

In his letter, the Superior ruefully wrote to me that the Community has been called "God's bloody Gestapo". It will be difficult, up there, not to tremble at the thought of having even whispered your doubts about the Community's future. But in doing this, you have amply responded to what my article for the journal was trying to say.

God cherish you in the loneliness and the silence, and bless your difficult, slow work of peace in the heart of war.

21st March 1979

Yesterday I was filled with joy because it did not matter if Alfred was in Timbuktu or next door. For somehow, the beloved in Jesus are united in hope, waiting for the day when every tear will be wiped away and grief will be no more! The all-embracing heart of the Father; the tenderness of the motherhood of God; the pervading Spirit who can burst one's heart with love; and the memory of Jesus himself, in the breath of the Spirit — all promise that day will come.

But today I have to pay the bill for loving you. Because you have gone and are going…. in spite of God's promises.

I don't wish for anything to be other than it is; that you should stay or leave Pedregoso — or go anywhere else, so why am I in pain? I don't understand. Why should one weep and one's heart overflow for no reason?

I have poor circulation and my feet go to sleep when I sit in prayer for a long time. They hurt when they wake up again. I feel the pain but it doesn't seem to affect me. Maybe love is like that? When the Holy Spirit is in a person's heart, that person gets bruised and wounded by everything that grieves the Spirit, by every blindness, and injustice, and parting, but is nevertheless at peace.

But the more a person feels and cares, the deeper the pain. If I loved you with the feeble, possessive little affection of my own heart I would be in pain because you have gone. But not pain like this. I hear a voice which says, again and again, "My heart overflows for Alfred, and I weep for him until he is with Me. Tell him!"

There are no words, nor enough tenderness to express this adequately. But I am afraid of grieving God by not passing it on. You are so shy of being loved, and I suppose it is because you think you are wicked, or unworthy, or something. You might be, for all I know. But God can't see sin.

I think I carry burdens like this without knowing it at the time. Like the donkey. I am sure the donkey that day in Jerusalem seemed glossy and drowsy-eyed, carrying his burden through the exultant crowds. But he had to go back to his stable, to spend the rest of his life in drudgery.

Roger has just arrived with his brown, lost eyes. Marie next door has informed me that she will go to church with me tomorrow, and has given me a house-plant, an aspidistra. I am looking at the lovely bearing of the ebony madonna you brought us from Rhodesia. Wolf is right about her strength. Her proud, earthbound stance, and the child, precious and protected in her arms. Thank you for that gift. It will come to mean a lot to us. I have just told Roger that you brought it for Wolf from Rhodesia. Wolf glows visibly.

22nd March 1979

Dear Alfred,
You see how you bring me to life? I have written every day since you left. This, my favourite pastime, had dwindled to writing once or twice a week before your visit.

You mentioned that many of your brethren are hot on the nasty disciplines, such as washing up! Like many of your passing remarks this one has lingered in my mind, and begun to enlighten me.

I also have felt it is virtuous to do nasty things dutifully; proper to deny myself things I love doing. But then the Lord said to me, "Who made your heart?" So I said "You did, Lord". Then he asked me if I loved him most of all. So I said I probably didn't, but I wanted to. Now, after this exchange, I know who my heart belongs to, so I can pray for and do whatever my heart desires. Unfortunately, this doesn't let me off the washing up, but at least I won't suffer the delusion that there is virtue in doing something I don't enjoy.

Please would you send me the names of the brethren most concerned about the current direction of the Community? You mentioned some in England. If you could tell me something about them – old, middle-aged, young; their gifts; their personality, sensitive, energetic, shy etc. It is not enough to just pray vaguely. The Lord doesn't like me making airy generalisations about the Community – he says that's prefab and he wants one built with bricks!

Did I tell you that my brother is playing Bunthorne – the lead in Gilbert and Sullivan's Patience? We are very proud of him. Ruth seems to be growing into spiritual seven-league boots.

Wolf, last night, launched into an unsolicited narrative of the frustrations of his youth, and ended up asking me to visit a Bridge friend of his who is in hospital. I sat transfixed throughout, and tried not to breathe in case I blew this miracle away. There didn't seem to be anything more to say after that, so I wandered off to the oratory. When he asked me where I was going, I said I thought we had better find out what was the matter with his friend from the inside. He nodded wisely and went to bed.

You thanked God for my ministry, and I suppose I do have one. People notice. I can't tell you what it was like to hear Wolf asking, almost humbly, if I thought he was justified in the bad things he did in his youth; and asking me to visit his friend. It wasn't me he was asking. He was asking my Friend.

Petunia is with Fr Frank, that young eighty-year-old with the healing hands, at the priory. She says she is going to "force the Lord to heal her". It seems to have been crucial that you laid hands on her while you were here. For a long time she was strangely hesitant about asking for healing in that particular way.

I am trying to be good about prayer time, since you said I should. Only, after I've said all I have to say I feel so peaceful that I fall asleep.

Saturday afternoon

This is usually a nice house – but it is especially lovely in the afternoon when it pours with rain. It gets snug corners, and the trees leaning in the windows are wet and happy.

I've spent most of the day ambling from room to room – lying on the beds, looking at the trees and trying to get pure in heart, as a sort of secret present for the Lord. I'm in our room now, the purple colours of the leaves make it dim in here.

Do you remember nursing me through that traumatic time when I broke my heart over 'not being useful'? You said I should enjoy this time as I will be far too busy in future. I've gone too far the other way now. I'm quite happy doing nothing at all.

I was looking at the velvet curtains in the guest room today, and thinking about the robes French cavaliers wore – and remembering that photo of Queen Elizabeth in a simple black cloak. If there is something of honour, or something regal in a person, even their clothes reflect it. Petunia displays that austere elegance.

The Superior made a wry comment to me about monks running around barefoot – disparaging the romantic image of St Francis, I suppose. But these things (clothes) are important. I sometimes get a glimpse of the fellowship of heaven – which is continually "taking on flesh" for me. I suppose, being an artist by inclination, though not in fact, I visualise the resurrection of the body as the essence of personality; heavenly citizenship as a sort of 'transparent flesh'. Classical diaphanous Hellenistic garb is suitable for such beings. Proper clothing would be much too chi-chi, too middle-class.

I begin to perceive the portentousness of the drape of a cloak, the fall of a linen garment, of swaddling clothes. I see the ebony clothing of the woman wrought in wood. The way we carry creation on our backs – back to the Lord.

That outrageous hat you brought us from Zimbabwe is hanging on the guest room wall. It makes me smile. All the plastic and kitsch that went into the making of it is so delicious, so sheepish, so clownish.

When I went to visit Wolf's friend in hospital, all I did was sit and listen to her talking to her other visitors. But the Lord's healing shows – a sort of warm, girlish joy to be alive that I've never seen in that exceptionally beautiful woman before. So I praise God and hope she does – she and her husband are NGK.[21] Mostly, people are just happy in the world of going to work and sundowners in their nice houses.

I will never be pure in heart. I am much too fond of doing things, like writing all this nonsense. But isn't it just like our God, to take a person like me, dying from an inability to articulate herself, and make writing her job? I know why the Old Testament bangs on and on about a God of justice – the irony of it leaves me gasping.

21. Dutch Reformed Church.

~49~

28th March 1979

Dear Alfred,

How tremendous it is that the attempted impeachment of a South African president should throw the parliaments of Britain, USA and Scandanavia into uproar! I return to an interest in politics for the first time in years.

So we are sitting here listening to The Gypsy Baron – who has just demanded in a bloody tenor, "So! Here am I! And what am I doing here?" I have accused Wolf of the same dilemma – not knowing what he is doing here. He loves The Gypsy Baron, and is peeling onions, tears streaming down his beard.

The garden is full of bats and frogs and moonlight at this time. I was thinking out there tonight about your ideas for a house of like-minded people. I think self-sufficiency is not a good direction. Plants and trees show me how dependent they are upon the seasons and rain, and the care I can give them. But it is not enough for my garden to need me; I must need it also, otherwise it would never have come to life in the first place.

Unless that desire – "that empty well" as Ruth so beautifully put it – is there, we just trog along with 'forms' of service as if they were the reason for living. Unless the Lord teaches me my famished need for everyone around me, I would merely chuck them the odd fifty cents in passing – I would not plead with my life for them (I don't, but I should).

I think Christians need to be lonely with God – to make them hungry, so to speak, so they will passionately desire companions for the perfect fellowship of heaven.

I met Petunia at Holyrood yesterday. When he fetched me, Wolf insisted on abducting her as well, buying us all cigarettes, driving us home to supper, scrounging beer from goodness knows where, and personally driving Petunia back to Holyrood at 11 o'clock at night.

I was very ill yesterday, and woke up this morning with that 'cleansed' feeling which comes after pain and weakness. These mornings when I open my eyes I can see the first flush of the sun through the verandah windows.

I had a charming letter from the Superior on Tuesday, saying thank you for the article etc. He gave me one of the greatest compliments of my life by asking me to write it.

You know, I think one rather negative factor in community life – any community, whether monks or sailors – is that it diminishes the faculty of responsible decision. I say 'faculty' because decisions are a direct consequence of the exercise of the will. Free will is a God-given gift by which we strengthen our own authority, over ourselves and our world, in the ever changing pattern of decisions in everyday life. This gift is the key link by which we make or break our spiritual lives.

I suppose this is what is asked of you in the Community – to maintain your own free will within the material restrictions you have chosen. Then obedience becomes a sacrament, without violating your sovereign free will. That's the theory but I guess it's not that easy in practice?

If the Lord should choose to test me again, I think I would be wrecked within the hour. I am so much weaker than I was. It's all very well for me to talk about the power of decision, but I am about as decisive as a jellyfish.

I would be one who sublimates my free will into a corruption of obedience – i.e. leaving all decisions up to others. It is much easier to be gentle, meek and kind, to keep out of trouble, when leaving the responsibilities of life up to others. Anna used to passionately denounce those who "never did anybody any harm" as society's parasites. I see her point.

I would much rather be ambling around the mission with you than stuck in a cold, empty office. It seems years since you left and took your special brand of sunshine with you. Tell the birds of paradise in Pedregoso that I have heard their call, and I will meet them in person one day.

I don't miss you as I did before. By asking us to pray for you and the Community, you have somehow established that "threefold cord which is not easily broken". I am beginning to come to terms with grief, and living more and more in the moment – which is really quite enough to cope with.

Wednesday night

This happens every time there's Bridge at our house. I feel like a cat whose people are moving out. I'm scrunched up in our bedroom – as far away as I can get from the bloody British Embassy, the diplomatic corps, and the Potato Board. They are delightful individuals – but *en masse* they are insufferable – especially when playing Bridge. Oh! And the Argentinian Embassy is here; she is moving to Nice this month – "to a nice little *pied à terre.*"

I've had a penchant towards Petunia's obsessive loathing of the 'middle-class' ever since I was born. They can all go to hell! Except, when you get to grips with them, you find there is no such person as the middle class!

I am bitter and twisted. There's poetry shaking up in my mind, and I can't get it down on paper. This happens roughly twice a year, and mostly not much good comes of it. I'm working on a ballad; unless I sublimate like mad it will take me over. It's like laying eggs – there's not much you can do about it.

'Sublimating' for me, by the way, means drinking. But I don't enjoy that as much lately. There is nothing I like doing much, except praying and writing to you. And praying is like eating, you can't do it all the time. And if I write all day to you, you might have me certified.

My father is a worry to me. I fear he is sweating blood, trying to break out of his mental prison, and nobody over there even knows. They all say, "Oh he's quite happy in his own way," as if he's a tortoise or something. I don't think there are wicked people – we won't be accused of wickedness – just criminal negligence, and culpable ignorance.

I've fed the Bridge party now, so I feel better. I made lamentable sandwiches, which everyone mumbled on, trying to grin compliments through the crumbs.

British Embassy (male) is from Manchester, and actually extremely nice. *Pied à terre* and diplomatic corps speak Spanish together, which Wolf listens in on like a Cheshire cat, pretending he understand *nuzink!* Peta held the company entranced (or were they glassy-eyed?) with anecdotes from the office, and the rather charming Potato

Board wafted around demanding wrought-iron gates. Wolf, with a suspiciously straight face, suggested he wait 'til after Beckett, because the theatre needs dog-proof gates for that show, and after the show…
"Who knows?"

"Who knows?" echoed Potato Board, and made plans to knock down his garden wall to accommodate Wolf's wrought-iron gates.

I've just marched back into the cards room to pour myself an enormous whisky. How about that! I even got an awestruck, "Gee!" out of *pied à terre*.

30th March 1979

I ought to be outside with the sickle moon and the beginning of winter. It's drawing me so strongly I shall have to go out later, but I can't see to write out there. I have an unexpected evening alone with tropical fish, Mozart, and Uncle Alfred for company. Though lately I fear I will have to save a good portion of my news for the kingdom of heaven, because there doesn't seem to be any means of describing it here.

Spatz is spoiling the atmosphere of peace, having a violent battle with her fleas on the carpet. I went to gym tonight, had a good sauna and ambled home in the dusk to find a penitent Wolf just on his way out to soccer: "Hadn't I remembered?"

Two bunches of flowers made me suddenly remember – so here we are, blessedly alone again.

Wolf is taking Sue, the English volunteer from Holyrood, to the mountains at Easter, and I shall be going to St Bede's. Sue is beside herself with joy that the Sisters gave her leave, bless them. Wolf's mountain gang will have kittens! Yet another lovely young damsel sharing his tent.

Yesterday, out of the blue, someone at the cathedral phoned to invite me to a SACLA action committee. I haven't the foggiest idea how they came up with my name, or what I was to do there – but I went because John Tooke came up from Pietermaritzburg for the event, and I think he's rather smashing. I still don't know what I was there for – except putting the odd back up for criticising the proofreading in the publicity brochures.

Oh enough talking for one night. Here we are – "and what are we doing here?" The dogs snooze, and there is a space of about a thousand miles between me and thee, and the Lord's smile is there, and here.

3rd April 1979

Wolf is thirty-five today – he is relaxing, winding down, shedding layer after layer of crustacean shell. Getting hurt. Trying to respond, instead of hiding. That dreadful watchfulness in his eyes is fading. I dare hope that he is deciding it is safe to come out.

He helps me understand the LORD's love for Israel. "You are a coward and a liar; you are lukewarm and unfaithful and I spit you out. But nevertheless you are mine and I love you." What a strange marriage – it certainly wouldn't do for Hollywood.

Petunia has just phoned and I'm to give you her love, and tell you she won't write for a while because she has nothing to say. Her telephone bill would throw that testimony out of court! I hope to see her at Holyrood on Sunday. Wolf seems rather keen on the place. Last time he was there he allowed himself three cups of tea and four bits of cake, while Mother chatted with him about tennis. He had stiff knees the next day, because half-a-dozen nuns and several female guests came in to the common room *seriatim*, and he politely stood up for each of them.

Thank you for your letter. I don't know if it is because you are getting into the swing of letter writing, or if you respond extra speedily to those who are poor in spirit and who mourn – but your written word is as healing and comforting as if you yourself were here, which of course you are, insofar as the kingdom of heaven is.

Later

I know that the Lord is with everyone on earth, and knew each one of us before the world was made. But that cannot excuse the corporate responsibility of the church for the real-life experiences of her own children. When the Holy Spirit moves within the mystical Body of Christ – the church – which must by definition include all baptised Christians, each member must be affected, consciously or unconsciously. Insofar as the church is commissioned to bring people to the knowledge of Christ, she is responsible for their spiritual welfare.

It is as if she tramples through the world, basting whole populations with the sign of the cross, then abandons them to their fate in an alien secular dimension. How many Christians actually get a chance to grow up in a spiritual environment? The mortality rate must be incredible. Please think of some reason why this is not true. I find it profoundly depressing.

I'm broke this month so I've got to write on both sides of the paper. You do anyway, so I'm sure it is good manners in heaven. I wish I didn't have to write so much. You put into ten words what I can't encompass in ten pages. But these letters are the only means I have for dealing with what's going on with me. Moan. Weep. Yak, yak! Pity all the deluded people who think I am the strong, silent type.

Wednesday morning early

I see you offering yourself and everything around you to the Lord – in stillness, like crystal. It is as if the divine light is strobing a black velvet cloth for something to reflect upon. The black velvet is all the lives where the divine is not allowed to reflect, to make light. But where you are it finds its mirror, and sparkles. That sounds a bit highfalutin, but it is how it seemed to me, and it might edify the saints to say so?

There is a place for silence in all conversation (as the Superior says), but I have spent too long remaining *stumm*. Petunia's gift to me is that she is very ready to talk about God. In fact, nothing can stop her.

If it is so that the world was created through the Word – "God said, Let there be light" – then there is a creative relationship between words and action. Prayer without words brings life because it is prayer beyond words – not just dumbness.

~50~

Alfred dear... tomorrow I go to St Bede's. I haven't kept Lent very well. Once again I approach retreat as if it heralds the end of my life. I'm tying up loose ends. Wondering how this or that person, or the dogs, will get along without me.

Everything contrives to prevent me going to confession, although I don't ponder excessively about what I need to confess, following Baron Von Hügel's advice to his over-sensitive niece. I don't want to go out at all. When I have an important appointment, I watch from a great height as a demon takes over my body and I drink myself into a daze, and either don't go, or go and make an exhibition of myself. It's terrible to be helpless like this.

Now, hopelessness descends...klunk! I don't stop knowing that God is almighty and loves me... I just don't particularly care. Don't want to live or die... fed up with the plod of it. Fed up and disgusted with my own warped, sick, leached out little life. Can't sleep or stay awake. The whole shebang is too much effort. *Selah.*

Wolf is heavy work too. At present going home is like going into battle. Not with him, but with the things that molest him. One minute he is proud and strong, next minute he's drowning in sorrows, dragging me down with him. I have to protect myself from the one persona, and respond lovingly to the other. It's hard work and I often make mistakes. It is not easy to discern between good and evil.

Petunia confronts institutional evil head on, while I can't even see it. I refuse to see it! You can't submerge individuals into categories. If we just throw up our hands at the National Party, or the terrorists, or the holy catholic church, we are being no damn use to anyone. But Petunia would think I'm wrong – and you probably do as well.

I think we propagate institutional evil ourselves, by giving it an identity, by objectifying it, by moving away from our corporate responsibility for it. I do deplore complacency in the Community, but it's no use me yelling at the brethren, because they would just circle the wagons and we would all be excluded.

The sadness and weariness I'm talking about is visible in that Holman Hunt painting, The Light of the World. Such weariness and loneliness in the eyes of the Ancient of Days. "See, I stand at the door and knock."

Wolf is off to the mountains on Thursday with Sue and Drew and Roger. I hope they have a good time, and good weather, and good fellowship. It will be good for Sue to have some rough and tumble companionship, and I can't think of better company for that.

On Saturday I would like to be free from everything and everyone, and maybe the Lord will resurrect me? Holy Saturday is the centre and focus of history – the end of the beginning and the beginning of the end. I can't see that it makes any difference whether it is now or 1,950-odd years ago. If the nuns hear an almighty bang in the night, and Amy is ne'er again seen in the flesh, you'll know all is well – I've been taken up!

Meanwhile I've got to go to confession. But I daren't confess anything about Wolf, except generally, so that my confessor doesn't know what I am talking about, otherwise he will suggest we have children, which seems to be a general antidote for anything short of marital bliss.

Wednesday

I was rebellious in confession, and did not accept what the priest at the city church said. I even called him a fool in my heart. So the Lord dropped a maggot on my head halfway through the mass. Really! It was a healthy job, about one and a half inches long, very muscular and white. It fell out of an apparently unblemished plaster ceiling. As it had the whole church to fall upon and chose my head, I take it that it was from the Lord.

Having a dim recollection of how it rained maggots in the Wilderness of Sin, I checked out that Old Testament story this morning – and behold! It was the Israelites grumbling at the Lord again; disobeying as usual; stashing their manna away against the day when the Lord stopped providing. So what's new?

I've never been so rebellious in confession before. My confessor explained the difference between remorse and repentance, while I grumbled in my heart that this priest was not on my wavelength. Then the maggot! "Whither shall I flee from thy presence?"

§

S t Bede's keeps the *triduum* in catholic simplicity. On Wednesday
evening the relentless psalmody of the office of Tenebrae is sung
in chapel. A litany of psalms chanted on the in and out of the
breath, antiphonal, swaying like a cradle back and forth, immersing
Amy in quietude, calming her panic to get here on time.

Following the celebration of the Last Supper on Maundy Thursday
the altar is stripped. The Sacrament is left to rest by candlelight in a
side chapel, where nuns keep vigil overnight. Amy insouciantly puts
her initials to the two to three a.m. watch. To her shame, she falls
asleep in the candlelight

Good Friday is an altogether more austere affair. A breakfast of
bread and milk is available "for the weaker sisters," such as Amy.
Ante-communion is said before the reserved sacrament. Then they
all troop off to the cathedral for the three-hour devotions.

The cathedral is bare, no flowers, no candles, the nave whispering
with hushed voices and slow footfalls. The high altar is stripped of its
finery, a bare stone monolith, its cross shrouded in purple damask.
Unannounced, a priest appears in the pulpit, wearing a black cassock.
So begins the solemn remembrance of the three hours when Jesus
hung dying on the cross. Every half hour the priest gives a homily,
which is interspersed with long silences and triste hymnody.

Amy notices that there are a number of black and coloured people
in the congregation. Outside, queues of non-whites encircle the
cathedral, waiting for taxis to take them home for the long weekend.
Amy gets bored with the sound of the priest's voice, but she loves the
silences in between. Then they go home and eat sardine sandwiches.

Holy Saturday marks Jesus resting in the tomb, when, it is said,
he visited hell to free tormented souls from captivity. Sisters keep
silence all day, gravely going about their business, keeping custody
of the eyes. They dust and clean and burnish their bailiwick until
the air is redolent with the scents of beeswax, lavender and bleach.
Amy's task is in the chapel, where she takes each hymnal and missal,
every prayer book and bible from the shelves and the pews, wiping
each one with a damp cloth. She is so absorbed in the rhythm of this
activity that it becomes no activity at all, more like breathing.

Meals are simple. Bread and cheese, broth. An apple for anyone
who needs something extra to see them through the day.

At eleven on Saturday night they all pile into two cars, still in
silence, and go back to the cathedral for midnight mass. This time

the cathedral is packed to the gunwales, and pitch dark. Amy finds it spooky to wade blindly into such a sea of humanity, whispering, shuffling, whiffling of sweat and the aromas of late dinners, of stale wine. Sisters are recognised by the profile of their veils and space is made for them to wriggle into pews near the front. Amy is given a small white candle with a paper collar. This will be lit from the new fire when the liturgy begins.

Soon there is a commotion at the west end of the nave. A mitre is silhouetted against light flashing from a tinder box as new fire is kindled. The pascal candle, a tower of beeswax scored with five nails, is lit, and the procession begins.

"The Light of Christ!" heralds the cantor, a black deacon with a soaring tenor voice. *"The Light of Christ!"* hails the congregation, bowing the knee as the procession unfurls into the nave.

Gradually light pervades the cathedral as hundreds of candles are lit from the paschal fire, little flames flickering one by one along the pews, passing from hand to hand, row upon row. Three times the cantor sings out as the burgeoning light advances. *"The Light of Christ!"* responds the congregation with solemn joy. Banks of candles flare into life in the chancel, in the sanctuary, until the whole cathedral is ablaze. Everyone can see everyone else. For some this is a profound relief. Amy is sorry that the darkness has passed.

There are baptisms. There are confirmations. Scripture readings trace the course of salvation history from Genesis to Revelation, on and on. Finally the first communion of the new year passes her lips, and her heart is at peace. They go home in the early hours of the morning and eat hot-cross-buns, chattering amiably, with newly loosened tongues, about the great day. "He is risen!" "He is risen indeed!"

§

Easter Day feels like Christmas. Amy's breakfast place is wreathed with handmade cards from the Sisters. A clutch of little chocolate eggs rests on her plate. Boiled eggs are coloured with cochineal. After the silence and austerity of the past few days this feast is almost too much to bear.

The brethren come over for morning tea, bringing with them anecdotes of Easter Day further afield, from Soweto, with gossip from the inner rings of the diocese. Amy feels drowsy. She feels perfectly at home, as if wrapped in parental warmth. But this is not her home. Tomorrow she will go home.

§

17th April 1979

Dear Alfred,

Well here I am – yet not I! Tremendous four days at St Bede's – about six hours altogether in the cathedral on Friday and Saturday night. Finally got around to having a chat with Fr Frank on Sunday afternoon. I've never really spoken to him before. He gave me a thin book by Baron Von Hügel – and there I found for the first time an allusion to the 'neural cost' of prayer.

No wonder I get so fagged out doing nothing. I have suspected that prayer, contrary to appearances, costs me physically, but it is good to have it confirmed. I've had a lot of nonsense shaken out of me. For the first time I am content not to itemise it all. Sigh, from Alfred.

Fr Frank is at Holyrood for a week's retreat and I was able to introduce Sue to him. She did well in the mountains, though she sprained an ankle. She is a lovely girl. Wolf has taken her under his rather muscular wing, and it may become a four-way friendship between Sue, Wolf, Petunia and myself. Friendship is more than just being together; just as love is not only being loving.

I read *The Book of Margery Kempe* up to about chapter twenty-nine – chapter fourteen especially. I pored over 14a about the unfriendly monks. Next day I discovered the appendix with chapter 14. Finding it hidden away like that made it like Treasure Island – a whole new dimension, and timely too. The editor meant the book for scholars of Middle English, not aspirant saints, so he relegated the 'mystical' chapters to addenda.

I also began Père de Caussade on letter-writing, and am looking forward to reading more tonight.

I got an invitation to tea with the brethren on Easter Monday. Giles and Fr Frank and Cuthbert and BB and Lester were there. James drifted by and strongly resisted Cuthbert's attempts to introduce him to me – again. It was altogether hilarious; Cuthbert discussing the spelling of 'kudu' at the top of his voice, as BB murmured "there's nothing else you kudu". Lester swapping rather risqué jokes with Warwick. Giles got on his high horse about liturgy, before being drowned out in a ribald account of how the roof got blown off in Orlando; how the congregation had to leap about to escape the leaks. Fr Frank chuckled and said wise things, which went largely unnoticed.

BB came and chatted to me until Midday Office, about politics and history and ships and the Lake District. I am happy about that. I feel he has viewed me somewhat askance until now.

I gave my article to Sister Elizabeth to read and she was pleased with it, which is encouraging. I just hope the editor won't chuck it in his waste-paper basket.

I have offered accommodation for two people here at home during SACLA, but if you can come too, and would like to stay with us, you will have the study – which is more comfortable than the guest room anyway. It might be a bit of a snarl-up in the bathroom, but that's half the fun and will ensure that no-one stands on ceremony.

Dearest Alfred, the cloud has lifted a little, and I feel sure that the Lord does not require me to attach myself to any specific fellowship, cause, or even congregation. It seems, by force of circumstance, and by the voice of the Spirit, that my task must remain as broad and 'unanchored' as possible, which means I have no label at all except 'Christian'. I am relieved now it's come to that. I can see a wholeness and an at-one-ness of all things in God. Any special attachment is, by nature, more or less exclusive.

I have always been solitary, and it would be unnatural to suddenly change the essence of my character. With no special fellowship I am free to share all fellowships, which is much better than belonging to just one. That leaves me with one task, which is prayer and intercession. Now that I appreciate better the cost of it, at all levels of experience, I don't mind so much that I have no clear ministry that everyone can see… for the time being, anyway. I am not afraid any more of putting a foot wrong, or of falling headlong into a bottomless pit. Is this the freedom of the children of God?

Does this sound alright to you? I suppose it means going back into silence. But I am quite looking forward to it; I am so weary of everything else except prayer. Trouble is, I don't really know how to pray. Anyway, all is well here and we hope you will weather the elections without too much drama.

Thursday

The gladioli are blooming – flaming orange. Did you know that they are indigenous South African wild flowers? The chrysanthemums are in bloom too – yellow, white, mauve and gold. They came from various friends as pot plants. I harvested green peppers from the garden today, and I think there is another egg. The tomatoes will be ready soon. Early this morning a neighbour brought three more house plants, and this evening Marie next door sent us a home-made loaf of bread.

Today a curious thing happened. A black youth followed me around a shopping centre, and told me he loved me while we were going up in the lift together. I warned him he must be careful of saying such things, because people will tell the police. But I called him 'boy', and I think I might have hurt him. I would have called him 'boy' if he had been white; I forgot it means something rude to a black man.

This morning I went to Drew's studio. I think he had been up all night. I made coffee in the percolator while he worked. We sat in the oil-paint-smell and muddle of an early morning studio, and said almost nothing for about half-an-hour – which was very companionable. Ruth lies between us like a well-kept and very precious secret. We both secretly hope we might become brother- and sister-in-law, but that is with the gods and may not be spoken about.

This morning I got a filling in the lower right molar and Bokki Pretorius, my dentist, embraced me because he said I was such a good patient and didn't make a fuss. But I think his own affection embarrassed him... so we laughed over-loudly.

Wolf came home, and I told him what you said in your letter, about how one's reactions to being hurt and despised as a child conditions our reactions to life as adults... which started an hour or so of desultory to heated conversation about life; about whether or not the Germanic sacred oak is in the bible; where the Jews came from; and if Peter and Paul are the same person. I think I managed my end of the discussion quite well, although I had to pray now and then to not hurl the vase of flowers Wolf had bought me at him.

Today I got a letter from you. I've read your words lots of times, and some bits more than others. It's a risk to commit oneself to words – more so to written words. If Uncle Alfred pens a four-page letter, he really must mean it.

I know it is pointless trying to circumscribe the work of the Holy Spirit with words. It is where it all went wrong, ever since Babel. The truth is that meanings have words, not the other way round. Words are merely servants of meaning. As the Superior wrote, "Language is the womb in which we are being created and in which we create one another".

Silence is the deep place where we learn that words are not the truth itself, but only reveal, disguise, warp, or interpret truth.

Nothing could touch Jesus until he willed it… as you wrote, "the freely willed necessity of his own life offered unto death." You have given me no new fact, but the fact that you wrote it down just for me makes it live.

Friday night

Tonight feels like a flashback to two years ago. I'm afraid I might wake up to find that the interim was all a dream, and that my nightmare existence before that is real life.

Wolf is being very kind to me lately, which, funnily enough, I can't cope with. He bought me cigarettes yesterday, arrived home with a bottle of wine tonight – and mumbled something about paying for a flight home for me to see my father. I feel like asking, "Why are you being so kind to me? I can't stand it. Why don't you be horrible, I can cope with that?"

Later

I am learning how to bear my burdens more lightly. I thought at one time that my intercessions depended on my own brute strength. Now that I know it is not so, I am not ashamed to ask you to pray for my father. I wish Dad had been able to talk with me, and share his vision of life when I was young – but I have a suspicion that PoW damaged him rather badly. He was only nineteen.

Now I'm on a slow, deep current of thought pursuing the creativity of words. When God said, "Let us create man," he was not making polite conversation. The Word became incarnate. One learns from the mystics about the creative tension between words and silence. The liturgy mirrors the play of words and silence – the yin and yang of life.

I could never understand why Almighty God wants me to pray for people he understands and loves much better than I ever could. Maybe this was because I believed, being a rationalist, that understanding was better than faith? But now I see that faith and understanding are not opposed, but that the latter is born of the former. So, I do God's will for me by allowing myself to be created in the divine image.

I could not believe, expect or hope for this, unless I believed in the creative power of the word – *logos*. My quixotic ups and downs of mood would just be diagnosed as manic-depression and I'd be packed off to a mental asylum.

23rd April 1979

Dear Alfred,

I read your lovely letter again and now begin a reply, as my little bird struggles to give up the ghost, beside me here on my desk. It's so tiny it hasn't opened its eyes yet. We found it on the back steps yesterday. We hunted high and low for a nest to return it to, but found nothing. So we kept it warm, gave it a hot water bottle last night. It swallowed its breakfast of bread and milk this morning. But now it is dying. I hope there's room for it in heaven. It has just gone – as I wrote those words.

I'd love to clarify my childhood 'scene', as you request. You might be able to clarify it for me! I had a time of intense experience which makes other childhood memories fade into insignificance. It is something I can only look at obliquely – too dangerous or too precious maybe to look at full-on? I think it was a time when I knew I was loved. I was about nine, but time does not seem to fit into these events. The actual episodes were diverse, but the one I remember best was not exactly 'leaving the body', because my body went with me.

Of course, my mother thought I was dreaming. But I told Ruth apparently, because she could remember me telling her about it, when I mentioned it this Christmas past. She was only four at the time, so my story must have been pretty galvanising.

I used to lie in bed at night and sing at the top of my voice. Strange words and harmonies made themselves up as I sang. Sometimes I would listen to myself in amazement, and wonder why everyone in the household didn't come rushing in to listen. If I tried to force the songs into intelligible words, they went away.

Then there were the Narnia stories by C S Lewis. Even as a child I understood the analogy of Aslan as Jesus. I tried with all the power of my childish will to bring the beauty and honour and justice and love, which found expression for me in those stories, into church. I still remember the cold stone chancel and the far-away crucifix, willing all that flesh and blood life to show itself as present in the sanctuary. Of course it didn't work.

I had a hell of a time in my teens. I believed, and was told, that my 'idealism' was fantasy and had nothing to do with real life. There are a thousand excuses for my parents and teachers, but if only someone had stood with me, and believed that justice and goodness are possible, and honour and valour are to be cherished in real life. Why did they bother to have me baptised and confirmed if that were not so?

No-one even mentioned the 'titanic struggle', which I now believe began in me at confirmation. In confirmation classes, the teacher made a few remarks about not wearing bikinis on Sundays, and mentioned other temptations, which was all rather grubby. We twelve-year-olds shrank and giggled. A breath of the old love wafted over me at the altar rail during my confirmation, and was gone. I was dressed in white, with a silver chain around my neck. I felt like a bride. But that was the end of it. Until I met you.

So here I am, with a badly infected, if not permanently crippled will, and the ghost of a notion that sin is separation from God. There is a possibility that the years of exile, of alienation, were profitable. Now I remember God did promise to restore the years that the locust has eaten. So maybe it will all work out in the end?

I've put this in a confused way. I haven't forgotten the redemption – nor do I think I could have been holier, or better – though I may well have been. I can't actually describe it. Maybe it is God's own sadness for sin that I feel? My father feels this sadness. They killed his Lord stone dead at theological college.

It's rather nice to discuss it. If I've ever been 'out of the body' it was about eighteen months ago, in a concrete place somewhere between earth and heaven, when someone – maybe an archangel – gave me a choice one night. The choice of staying here in this life or leaving it. It's nice to think sometimes that I had the strength to choose hell on earth rather than heaven, for the sake of my friends.

Heavy stuff, heh? You wait 'til I get you alone again. I'll make your hair stand on end with the stories I can tell you. That being said, I am not "withholding information from my director". I'm only just beginning to be able to formulate it all. I have the feeling I shouldn't think about it too much.

Tuesday

Marie from next door wafted in last night and stayed for supper. Apparently half the doctors at Verwoerd Hospital are praising God for her recovery. She's informed Fr Albert that she is going to witness to his congregation about her healing. I shudder! She's like me… she brings profound messages but forgets to explain what she's talking about.

Wolf fetched Sue for the day on Sunday from Holyrood. He had an exchange with Fr Frank who was in retreat there, painting a watercolour on the lawn. Amongst other badinage: "When Alfred come back?" – no doubt accompanied by a pugnacious look.

Sue also had a good chat to Fr Frank. She's not confirmed which is nice because she can do it properly now.

Wolf is suffering terribly with stomach ulcers, and hardly ever gets a good night's sleep. Nor do I, but it is possible to lay hands on one's husband under cover of natural affection. Praying intermittently for about an hour during the night seems to help, but I can't keep it up all night. His stomach writhes around like a snake pit. I wonder if it is part of his battle against the Lord? If so it feels like a life and death struggle.

What a drab letter… ground out on the butt ends of empty days (cheap imitation of T S Eliot). I'm suspended between the world and prayer this week – and have the feeling that total commitment to one will mean total commitment to the other. But at present I'm caught in between, and partake of neither.

30th April 1979

Dear Alfred,

Petunia and Sue came for lunch and supper yesterday. It was very good except that I lost my temper with Petunia. We parted friends but I'm a bit torn up today. I almost never lose my temper, even for a minute, but it's rather catastrophic when I do. Wolf went to fetch the girls from Holyrood without even telling me, which was nice.

We went to a cocktail party at the Argentinian Embassy on Wednesday. Much discussion beforehand on what 'afternoon dress' could possibly mean, and airily confident descriptions from Wolf about procedure. "How do you know?" I ask. Oh he used to go to cocktail parties quite often when he was on Wall Street.

After an evening spent hanging over the bar with *mein* host, speaking Spanish, said host declared his house was Wolf's house. It appears they met years ago in 'matada plata', or something like that, when the attaché was a humble naval captain, and Wolf was in jail. Can't take him anywhere!

I'm probably going to England at the end of the year. I phoned Daddy on 'the system' on Friday. He sounds dreadful. I don't think he can remember much at all. It will be good to see England. If I get a rail pass I might be able to visit the mother house.

I could do with some of your company, Alfred. I'm now very much at home in this waterless wasteland that I seem to be erring around in. Everything seems to be going according to plan – but it's too quiet. Do you know that eerie feeling when you are trotting along and suddenly you notice the birds have stopped singing?

I've got no-one here to check with if I am on the right track. My imagination has woken up at last, and it's a brand new medium. There is a right use for imagination isn't there? But having been a slave to fantasy for so long, I don't know how to manage it properly.

Friday

Busy pottering around the interior life – having climbed through the windows of my mind like a hobbit. It's all rather interesting in here – and I have no intention whatsoever of coming back, naughty child that I am. I would hate to spoil this beautiful playtime, by diving head first into Frank Lake.

You know, I think I am happy. It's all very odd and I can't get used to it. Study is meeting with some success. I am keeping an orderly household. At peace with most people. Managing some intercession most days, which seems to be bearing fruit. I sleep well, and I am not frightened of anything, except Petunia. I'm reading *The Lord of the Rings* in the evenings.

Wild! What a combination – Tolkien and Gerhard von Rad's exegesis of Genesis. All rounded off nicely with a letter or two of Père de Caussade before bedtime.

Parts of the Old Testament would have struck terror into my soul a year or two ago. But now it enchants me. For instance, how David could terrorise the countryside, make a total exhibition of himself in public, sleep with his friend's wife, have her husband knocked off – and still be called "beloved of God".

I'm also loving *The Lord of the Rings.* I understand what happened to Gandalf the Grey – as of course Tolkien did. Gandalf the Grey became Gandalf the White by passing through death to return, for a while, because he laid down his life for his friends – who were dwarf and elf and hobbit and all the peoples of Middle Earth.

Since the age of seven – when I longed to be ten – I have struggled with the anguish of trying to share precious moments. On my first ever visit to a cinema when I was seven we saw The Wizard of Oz and Bambi in one afternoon. I tried, in vain, to share the overwhelming emotions with my mother. But she couldn't hear me. What I was saying was going nowhere – a moment of grief and loss which I did not recover from until I met you. So, a dammed-up lifetime is now breached by your patient enquiry: "about your childhood?"

So since I was a child I never tried to share precious things with anyone, except, maybe, in secret language with horses and dogs. It really is no wonder that when I venture into speech nowadays, most people wonder what I'm talking (Tolkien) about.

Many of my childish notions about creativity and melancholy, love and heroism – all the things that move my heart most – are being restored to me, as the image of God emerges amidst the ruins of sin.

Western Christianity focuses on 'changing' and 'doing' things. But I suspect something important has gone missing in translation. We should be 'becoming' and 'being', as part of the existing universe – as it is. The created order is not perfect; it is not immune from suffering. Otherwise every felled tree, dead fledgling, diseased rose, sick dog, mutilated body, mental wreck, would be beyond grace. We are not called to overcome the world – but to come home to the world as sons and daughters of God. To become what we were born for.

11th May 1979

Dear Alfred,

I hear you have had a week in Salisbury? I guess this is the most important week in Rhodesia's history, with the Lancaster House talks at a watershed.

I've just borrowed Frank Lake's book from Unisa, along with an Iris Murdoch novel, and one by White of *The Sword and the Stone* fame. I am up to my neck in life. Finding it difficult to be involved and detached at the same time.

It was Keats who wrote something about the heights being only for those to whom the world's misery, is misery. In other words you can't scale the heights of life unless you have plumbed the depths. People who do, often end up as nervous wrecks, or impervious to it all. I've been both.

I'm finding it hard to invest in study because I can't see the point of it. Self-improvement seems very self-indulgent. But here I am, studying, and doing things I suppose I like – running in preparation for the mountains; reading; prep for SACLA; keeping house – and trying awful hard not to lose sight of the relative unimportance of it all. How to live in various dimensions at the same time? How to remain detached? You know about all this I suppose?

I tried to chat about it to Fr Albert last week but, with all due respect, he hasn't got the foggiest idea where I am coming from, and he hasn't got time to find out. Our new priest at St Mark's seems bent on getting the congregation to idolise itself, regularly conflating 'the sinful world' and 'the terrorists' in his sermons, compared with us saints here in church. I spent most of the sermon yesterday quashing my impulse to leap up and yell, "The Spirit has departed from this house. Repent!" and march out.

I am so aware of my own isolation in this strange new world of the Spirit. I fear going off the rails. My sanity is fragile, with no solid point of reference — such as you have been for me. It is not enough just to maintain a prayerful life — because I am quite capable of getting lost in what I fondly imagine is prayer, when it isn't. The Spirit doesn't make a rumpus when abused, she just quietly departs.

19th May 1979

Dear Alfred,
Sitting on the grass in the garden, and it is afternoon. I am very satisfactorily melancholy and brattish — drinking beer.

I am finding Frank Lake, as I suspected, a profound strain. But I have learned enough in the past couple of years to give it a rest when it becomes too difficult. As always with your prescribed reading, I find myself vulnerable to Frank Lake's book. I trust you, and trust that any changes which seem to be necessary, can only be for my ultimate good. It would however help to have a man of God handy.

I smile sheepishly, reading *Clinical Theology*, recognising my own stations of the cross during the past couple of years. Realising also the reasons for your discomfiture, interludes of horror, and desperation at my behaviour.

I have had to fight with various demons in these past few days. One of them is doubt about your goodwill towards me. Intolerably unkind. I catch sight of this fear in shadows, out of the corner of my eye, at any hour of the day or night. I also fear that knowledge of God will exclude me from real life — will kill me. Of course, it is not true; but this is how I feel.

One never stops battling. It is time now to stop bemoaning it and get used to it — glory in it almost — the way old-wise soldiers get used to war. The kind of love you gave me, in the name of God, has made me whole, to the point where I can wage my own wars. Where I can look at my own wounds without revulsion. Wounds are the workshop of the Spirit, where strength and endurance is forged. I'm making myself cry!

It is almost a relief to know I will not be healed — because I will not be, in the sense that all scars will be removed. A person acquainted with grief can never become unacquainted with it. I don't believe in exclusive goodness. Until I can see clearly what I now glimpse — that even hell and evil are somehow within God's jurisdiction, I will be a willing servant, but not a daughter of God. I am offended by Christian protestations of exclusive happiness and the milk-sop goodness of life in the Spirit. A bit like Jehovah's Witnesses' bland illustrations of heaven. I can't be expected to lounge around in heaven pretending that hell is not the place where I myself have been forged.

Monday

Your letter arrived this morning. I am beside myself with delight to hear that you are gardening! Why haven't you got any compost? What about your kitchen refuse, and the weeds? Let me tell you what happened to me when I was first launched into Eden. Thus I will prepare you for your first children of the earth.

Initially I felt only terror when Petunia began filling my garden with living things, which were apparently entirely dependent upon me for their well-being. She impressed upon me that their little roots were like raw nerve-endings, and although some had to be pulled apart in the interests of living space, sun and the open air hurt them horribly. They could not just be left lying around. Each corm and cutting, each bulb and seedling must be treated with respect, as individuals.

As for Gandalf – all good literature is part of real experience. So Gandalf's fall is real, in the sense that the mortal combat, the darkness, the horror, his disappearance from the world, really happened. Tolkien must have experienced this, although the narrative is Gandalf's. There is nothing written that has not been, in some sense, known.

It is this same function of imagination which allows Frank Lake to construe the nature of Jesus' experiences as fundamentally human, shared by all humankind, more or less. I plan to study philosophy next year – so hopefully that will help me be more coherent about such things.

28th May 1979

Dear Alfred,
I have committed the cardinal error of leaving Frank Lake at home on the washing machine So, having cleared my desk at the office for the day, I have time to write to you.

I am short of news this last week, but as I told you I was reading *Clinical Theology*, I imagine you understand why? I am absorbed in childish pride, reconstructing the crises in my own interior journey from the gospel according to Frank Lake. I suspected, after reading St John of the Cross, that *The Spiritual Man* experience was a dark night of the soul, although a servile sort of humility prevented me from saying so. However, Frank Lake calls my odyssey of the soul an 'abreaction'.

One positive result of reflecting on my journey over the past two years, is a better understanding of the cross. I don't think I have ever wept so much, or praised God so much. In fact, at the moment, I can only see blessing in that first death; in the surrender required to be brought back as a new creation into the land of the living. Indeed, is it possible to understand the meaning of the cross without first being nailed onto it?

Frank Lake's book underwrites my belief that I belong to a generation of starving people. The decade or so since he published has made it quite clear, even to the dimmest observer, that a schizoid society is flourishing nicely under western capitalism. I have seen with my own eyes for years, that apathy, that ennui, assailing so many of us who search in vain for meaning in life. Where is the meaning in all this leisure and wealth we are supposed to be pursuing?

For the first time, I identify with humankind in our weakness, sinfulness and failure. I must admit it is a lot more bearable than trying to be a saint.

Later

Once, after I read *The Spiritual Man*, I was on my way to Nazareth House, when suddenly, walking up towards Hillbrow from the railway station, I was overwhelmed by a sense of unreality. Everything looked familiar but was at the same time frighteningly alien. I was lost in streets I knew well. I recognised buildings and cityscapes, but did not know where they were. I was getting used to strange phenomena by then, so I just gritted my teeth and abandoned myself to God's mercy. By the time I got to Nazareth House things were back to normal. Or as normal as they ever are.

During this time I was consumed with dread that God would require me to go through what Jesus endured in his last moments, when God abandoned him. I prayed fervently that this would never happen to me. Not knowing the power of the unconscious, it seemed to me when that catastrophe with Auberon occurred, when I thought I had lost you forever, that this was just such a dereliction.

I have never given myself the luxury of blaming you for not holding my hand at prescribed moments. Your greatest triumph as a friend has been to remain undisturbed throughout my cadenzas; just being there, without getting sucked in to my hysteria.

There is a scene in *1984* (George Orwell) in an interrogation chamber, where a man betrays his lover, under threat of rats. The two meet again afterwards and can no longer look each other in the eyes. I praise and thank God that I never did betray you, and that you never ceased giving me to God throughout this journey.

Frank Lake has shown me that my friendships in the past were mostly just attachments. It is possible that the only genuine interpersonal relationship I have ever had, is with you.

Then there is Wolf. I can see now that we colluded to create a façade of marriage. Although neither of us wanted emotional involvement, we did want to care for one another as mates. The equation seemed perfect. Companionship with no emotional commitment. I don't know if we even really spoke to each other in the year before Anna introduced me to you.

Wolf can 'shut down' at will on painful experiences, but I can't. He has been watching my struggles over the past couple of years with something like respect. He has witnessed a battle that he knows is humanly impossible to survive.

Once, when we were driving back from the Eastern Transvaal, I was idly describing some torrid experience of my prayer in the night, never thinking he was listening. But he was. He said, "Be careful or you will lose your mind." I replied that I had no intention of being careful – I would dare and dare until I die.

It comes as a surprise to him that freedom is not a myth. "I must fight every minute for my little bit of life," he once told me. At least I can remember a time of freedom in my childhood; for me the sound of the Golden Horn has perdured. For him there is nothing.

We talk now and again for a few minutes, before the subject becomes dangerous. He told me, years ago, that the one person he would trust in his whole life was his marriage partner. No wonder my defection to the enemy turned him stir crazy.

Tuesday

It has been painful to abandon my 'mystical experiences' as an illusion, in the light of Frank Lake's teaching. Thank you for the stern reading you have given me, and your tactful silence on the extraordinary experiences I have babbled on about.

However I found these illusions very useful as a prop, until I could face the mundane reality of life. Now, a more orthodox approach to my experiences seems proper. Visions now seem rather garish, compared with the daily round, the common task.

Enough for now. I quite understand if you feel inclined to close my file with a sigh of relief, but I hope that will not be the case.

~51~

On the first weekend of winter there is a blizzard in the Drakensberg as Wolf, Amy, Roger and sundry friends begin a thirty mile hike to traverse the mountain from Cathedral Peak to Champagne Castle. As they trudge up Organ Pipes Pass, bellies of cloud pregnant with snow loom from the south. On the flank of Thunder Dome there is an eyrie, high above the plains of Natal, where they halt to consult about finding shelter for the night. Close by, just around the mountain, across the Lesotho border, there is a gulley in the lee of the wind where they could set up camp. BaSotho patrols are unlikely to be out in such severe weather.

As the first snowflakes fall, the party begins a long scramble up a slope cumbered with scree. Amy is overcome by a panic attack and collapses on the stony ground, gasping for breath. Roger's face swims into view above her, making encouraging noises. Wolf's voice barks from afar, "Leave her alone. She will be okay."

Amy is left blessedly alone to cope with hot waves of panic, which gradually abate, leaving her recumbent in a simulation of rest: "As if you are far from home in the snow; so weary that you lie down in its embrace." Shocked awake with a crystal clear perception of the danger she is in, Amy scrambles to her feet and stumbles in pursuit of the others, whose footprints in the new snow lead over a nearby crest.

By the time they reach the gulley it is almost dark under the lowering cloud. Hastily they pitch their tents on level ground between two crags; huddle together in the entrance to Wolf's two-man tent, shielding a guttering gas flame which heats melted snow in preparation for a dinner of rehydrated stew. Elbow room is cramped, dinner is served in tin mugs, which are then swilled with snow melt, ready for coffee and a generous slug of brandy. Amy remembers Jonathan's warning that alcohol increases the risk of exposure by umpteen per cent, but she swallows her dop[22] gratefully.

During the night snow builds up on the windward side of their tent. Amy sleeps well from exhaustion, augmented by her bedtime

---

22. The 'dop' was a measure of alcohol doled out in lieu of monetary payment to black and coloured workers on vinyards in the Cape Colony.

noggin. But at three in the morning there is a whooshing sound of dislodged snow and a savage roar, which awakens both Wolf and Amy. The tent shudders and sways, as if a pterodactyl is attacking their fragile shelter. Wolf emits a curse; unzips the tent flap; leaps yelling like a banshee into the frozen night. Another commotion ensues, followed by the sound of cantering hooves which fade into the distance.

"Cows," reports Wolf nonchalantly, zipping up the entrance and wriggling back into his sleeping bag.

"What sort of cows? Up here?" squeaks Amy, imagining bison.

"Hairy ones. Looking for warm place. Go to sleep now." With that Wolf returns to his slumbers.

Next day they hike the ten thousand foot high watershed, the spine of the dragon, with Amy bringing up the rear of the party, as usual. She likes this position as a camp follower, just keeping up, wrapped in her own thoughts.

She is deep in contemplation when from a crag above their path a BaSotho tribesman appears, as if emerging from the mountainside. He is robed in the traditional blanket, a long staff marking out his easy strides on the precipitous slope. It is a misty grey morning, but the snow has melted. The silhouette of the tribesman, ephemeral like the weather, vanishes as mysteriously and silently as he appeared, melting back into the mountain. Amy glances ahead, but her comrades seem not to have noticed this apparition. She wonders if she has seen anything earthly? The membrane between temporal reality and the vastnesses of unknown worlds seems to be thinner up here.

§

4th June 1979

Dear Alfred,
'Scuse the tatty paper and cramped writing. I'm surrounded by animals, lying before a new-fangled electric fire on the sitting-room floor – with aching muscles, blistered feet and lacerated skin. What a weekend! Thirty miles, between 9,000 and 11,000 feet, in four days.

We had a blizzard on the first day, witnessed the hysterical breakdown of yours truly on the slopes, camped in the snow, shared a night in a cave on a precipice. Various kind young men carried my pack up awe-inspiring regions such as Bugger's Gully and Windy Gap. My self-respect was the only real casualty. It was interesting to notice, from the other side of dignity, how people try to be brave whilst killing themselves in the process.

I seem to have been invited to the SACLA leadership assembly before the main event. I certainly didn't apply. Did you put my name in? I'm very glad to go of course. But I rather wonder how they came up with me? I have difficulties enough relating to myself, without trying to give leadership to others.

Fr Albert has chucked me out of editorship of the parish magazine. The silly man doesn't realise that this is my only material link with the parish. The 'outsider' is not desirable in the inner ring. Never mind. The whole parish makes me sick with their continual jollity and ersatz solutions to the world's problems.

5th June 1979

I don't know if that last sentence is strictly true, but it is what I feel at the moment. It is good to admit my nasty reactions to people. Trouble is, it is getting worse, not better. I think I am capable of murder at times. Those parish poobahs would have kittens if they knew I had been selected to go to the leadership assembly.

Petunia, as I told you on the phone, has been in a bit of a tangle trying to be released from smoking. I cannot believe that her smoking habit is open to healing until she can accept that the physical and material, everything she incessantly calls 'carnal', is God's concern also.

I am sending you *The Mail* today, as it seems to be an historic edition. Don't worry about postage. If I haven't got money I don't send things. Anyway I have saved a bit for your trip to SACLA, in case you can come, so I could send an encyclopaedia if you had need of it.

Wolf is now looking for another job because the Performing Arts Council is getting nasty towards him. He wants to go back to Germany. The prospect horrifies me. If he does go I will stay here for three or four months, to maintain the household until he is sure that's what he wants. I am inclined to think he will find he has grown out of his old haunts there.

In the meantime I am investigating the possibility of a job for him in the Department of Forestry. He is more at home striding over mountains in what he calls his 'church', than anywhere else in the world. He seems to shrink by a couple of inches when he has to return to civilisation.

I have lost touch with my assurance that the Lord is in control of our future. My prayer life has become short periods of just resting in weakness. I am exhausted and have lost my grip on hope. I can't believe that God expects me to force myself into formal prayer at the moment. At the same time I am aware that I am more acclimatised to general aridity, and definitely prefer it to running around in small circles chasing 'experiences'.

This is very different from the trials of depression. I feel lost, and quite often experience what Frank Lake calls 'depersonalisation' – when the world appears alien and one wonders who on earth one is. But it doesn't worry me over much. You have taught me to wait on the Lord, and that is all I can do at present.

Elsa is doing her psychology major this year and I proofread her assignments. It is amazing how illuminating that is since I have been reading Frank Lake. A better understanding of psyche has also made it much easier for me to be gentle with Wolf's inner tangles.

Spatz got mauled by the dog next door, but is recovering nicely. My lettuces are growing well and we got a good crop of tomatoes and onions. I'm also having a bash at peas, sprouts, carrots, cauliflower and cabbages. I will be more than a little peeved if we have to move.

Now I must get down to an assignment, due on Friday – exegesis of Genesis 12:1-2.

12th June 1979

Dear Alfred,
Well, I've done the Frank Lake marathon. Like switching a light on isn't it? I'm very glad I read Watchman Nee, Augustine, St John of the Cross, St Teresa, Mersch, de Caussade, Von Hügel, de Chardin, Merton etc, first. It makes the assimilation of all that material so much easier when one has read about the evolution of the spirit in historical order, so to speak.

I got a letter from my father yesterday. The first since last August. He sent me a lucid criticism of that article for the Community, which thrilled me to bits for two reasons. First, it means he has come out of that intellectual bunker he has been in for so long, and is thinking again. Second, his criticism led to exactly the point I wanted everyone who reads the article to arrive at. That is to say, not a discussion of whether what I have written is true or not, but a sort of desperation about the task implicated. "It is the turning around and joining hands bit which is so difficult," says Daddy, and goes on to say why.

Wolf is being chucked out of his job for undefined reasons – so there is a strong likelihood that we will move after the end of July. He was going to stampede off to Germany, but seems to have dropped that idea. If there is nothing for him in the vicinity we shall probably be off to the mines at Welkom. What a fate! Well, if nothing else, it might give me a little insight into your predicament.

I've had my hair lopped off. I look about twelve, and consistently feel about twelve, with everyone squeaking about how nice I look.

Have you read *I Never Promised You a Rose Garden*? I am almost sure that the psychiatrist who treated the girl with schizophrenia in that book, was the same Frieda Fromm-Reichmann to whom Frank Lake refers. I gave my copy away so I can't check it out. I suppose the reason that title came to mind was the prospect of the mines, together with this beastly haircut. The world could not look bleaker.

13th June 1979

You remember the main reason I wanted to go to England was to see Daddy? Having now had my wish granted, I have realised that I will have to get to know his new wife, and new circumstances, to get anywhere near him at all. Then there are the obstacles Daddy himself puts up when anyone tries to get close to him.

I've got my DP for Biblical Studies II, which means I can write the exam. My minimal studies are all the bible reading I do at present, except listening in church. I have never been able to get down to private bible reading, except in relation to particular questions. I mean, I don't enjoy it for its own sake. Is that a bad thing? It is strange, because worrying out the kernels of meaning in other literature is something I enjoy very much.

We are experiencing bitter cold and gale force winds. The 'boys', about ten of them, went off to camp in the Magaliesberg this weekend. Yours truly ignominiously backed out. Roger, in a stroke of unprecedented and inexplicable generosity, bought Wolf a pair of mountain boots, so Wolf had to try them out at once. He is very well. The ulcers have stopped plaguing him for the time being. We spend most evenings at home together, which is a pleasant change.

Your instruction to buy the newspaper has had far-reaching effects. Wolf now reads it from cover to cover, so his English is improving vastly. I read him most letters in English now, by the way. Since the family's letters – whether discussing faith matters or not – have become common property, his aversion to such topics has noticeably diminished.

Don't laugh. I wrote him a letter myself, in German, about the loss of trust which you so often speak of, and what the gospel has to say about it. It was read in private and vanished into some secret place, and has never been mentioned. Some marital situations really are absurd.

I'm going to a SACLA leadership meeting tonight. I've missed a couple. I am super-aware that these preliminary meetings are designed to produce crises in interpersonal relationships, preparatory to our role as leaders. It's group dynamics. While everyone gets heated about some exegesis of scripture, I am once again on the outside of the fish bowl, looking in, observing the action.

I suppose my reserve is a personal problem – which I was unwise enough to confess to Fr Albert, who immediately tramped all over me with hob-nailed boots, telling me how I should get over it. I wish I could make myself do things which are basically unpleasant. It seems I can't do things against my own will any more. Maybe it is a sort of passive night[23] but it could just as easily be a floppy will.

There is one thing I would like to ask you about, because it has been on my mind for a week. During the *The Spiritual Man* episode, somewhere in the middle I guess, I 'met' something indescribably awful. Up to that point the experience seems to fit into Frank Lake's description of birth trauma. This encounter came about five days after I made a conscious attempt to leap into the unknown – which felt like insanity and/or death – which was pre-empted by some outside force.

There was a lot of willed struggle, casting myself into surrender, tunnel scenes, headaches (as if my brain was moving in the roof

23. One of the spiritual states described by St John of the Cross.

of my skull), light at the end of a tunnel, all of which eventually vanished, leaving me in blind, passive suffering. These days were accompanied by what felt like a gong stretched across the universe, which was struck at irregular intervals. The sound was shattering. But eventually, waiting in the darkness for the strike was even worse. Then the cloud came. I couldn't have spoken about it without choking until recently, and it still makes me weep.

Afterwards, I thought it must have been God. It was blacker than the blackest night which I was already in. It moved towards me in the cosmos like a cloud of ink, formless. It embodied all the power in the universe; and it was without gender.

But it was not threatening. The very sight of it made you know that it would be better if you never had been. The fight was over. Suffering was over. Endurance of suffering was over.

In the days after that, whenever someone spoke to me I was surprised that they thought that I was present here at all.

Writing this, I can see I have answered my own question. What I wanted to ask was, "Will I still have to enter that cloud?" Because its touch would dissolve me as if I had never been. But I suppose, in view of what I have written, the succeeding days of non-experience were the cloud. If it was non-being, its very nature would defy description.

Isn't it wonderful how helpful you are, even so far away. If I had not been able to ask you this, I would have worried about that cloud forever.

4th July 1979

Dear Alfred,
A man called Barney Mtemba is coming to stay here as a house guest during SACLA. Wolf is taking that – and my proposed absence thirteen hours a day for ten days – very quietly. In fact he seems quite pleased. I went to church as usual last evening, got home to find supper well under way, and after supper was peremptorily shooed off while Wolf did the washing up. It's all rather confusing.

We've been sent a tremendous amount of preparatory material for SACLA. My recce of group dynamics has been fascinating. Had my first taste of being deliberately put on the spot last night. Finding it very difficult not to hide behind private superiority though. In my church everyone smiles lovingly at each other through bullet-proof glass. Not having had any practice in accepting criticism gracefully, I am inclined to throw rocks back. I thought it was just me who didn't relate, but now I have observed group dynamics in action, I think it's most people.

I am worried about quite a lot of things actually, since I decided to try and live better, and give up drink and cigarettes. I haven't done it yet, but this time I am armed with some pills from the doctor to help deal with symptoms which pop up like a child's nightmares when I try to give things up.

I've had a postcard from Daddy in Austria today. He sounds very well. Jonathan has written to tell me he is getting married. By all accounts a lovely girl, a teacher, very accomplished, from a farming family. He says there is a grave with his name on it behind the church where they will marry, dated 1649. "Spooky!" he writes. His fiancée's family has been there for generations. He has come to know and love Ruth for the first time, lately. Net result – I am no longer dearest sister, as this would be unfair to our younger sibling, but simply 'dear'. We really are a very odd family.

The sun has come out again. I was walking to the city church last evening, sorrowing over the ruin of my life and health. I was asking myself, "Did you have to go so far down the path…" and the words, "to Calvary?" echoed in my mind. And somehow I saw how sin is in the suffering, and suffering is in the sin. Through it all there is the gold thread of faith, which becomes love as it endures. Everything else is circumstantial. Then I saw a rainbow shining over the city.

Yesterday I visited an old friend of mine in hospital. We have been friends ever since I came to South Africa. Very glamorous and talented, but what unalleviated misery that girl lives in. She said to me, "Oh Amy, where did all the poetry go? It is as if I am in a cage, with all the sunshine outside". I just sat with her for a bit, and felt bankrupt.

Well I've run out of things to tell you for a change. I hope you are well, although the situation doesn't sound too healthy. We don't get much news from the border, although BB reports that they are closing down schools up there.

Wolf has just come in to the office and quietly informed us that he has a job with Siemens as of August 1st. He called in to their head office this morning, the first visit on a list of job hunting, and they wouldn't let him go. It is maintenance engineering, like on board ship, and is his first love. Starting salary same as now and ten per cent rise after three months; seven kilometres from home; better holidays; better bonuses; proper workshop; lots of sports and a canteen. They bought him lunch and lured him into accepting with six beers. They will let him train for diplomas, and he can go anywhere in the world for Siemens after three years. After telling us all this he became very quiet and said he was going into the mountains on his own for a week, after our trip to Umfolozi. So, praise God. The dawn is breaking. It's a new day.

52

The South African Christian Leadership Assembly (SACLA) was the brain child of Michael Cassidy, a South African Anglican layman who had pioneered the Pan African Christian Leadership Assembly in Nairobi three years previously, through his organisation African Enterprise.

It was a bold endeavour, bringing together thousands of Christians from South African churches of all denominations, to meet for a week that winter at the Pretoria showgrounds. The plan was heroic and provocative in equal measure. Ten thousand people from all races were to mix freely on equal terms in the administrative capital of the republic, which had legislated against such fraternising between whites and non-whites. It was against the law.

The formal agenda enshrines this flouting of apartheid law. Plenary sessions include Piet Koornhoff, a cabinet minister, on the same platform as Gatsha Buthelezi of the Zulu nation, and Bishop Desmond Tutu, who has not yet reached his future status as the apartheid regime's public enemy number one, but is head of the left-wing South African Council of Churches. The exhibition hall is jammed full to witness this extraordinary debate. Amy notices a handsome, broad bosomed white woman in twin-set and pearls, with a gentleman in a suit beside her, looking gaudily out of place amidst the scrum.

Halls and malls in the showgrounds are thronged with people flocking about the business of the assembly. Amy finds it invigorating as well as intimidating to be part of such an august insurrection. Refectories and alleys are pocked with purple shirts, and once she spots Bishop Timothy, strolling in deep conversation with a huge black priest dressed in a brown habit.

Many of the delegates are housed with Pretoria residents, also against apartheid law. Amy has a man from the Transkei staying with her in Albion, although she barely sees him, as he comes and goes by night. He is very timid. Perhaps he is afraid of being in a white area after curfew? Even Amy has to quell anxieties about attracting the interest of the security police. Wolf takes it all in his stride. He works with all races and is equally racist to everyone. After her guest has gone back to the homeland she finds the waste paper bin in his room full of urine. Clearly using their bathroom was beyond the pale.

No uniforms are in evidence at the show grounds, although there are stewards with red armbands everywhere, who are ready to help with directions and information.

Music plays an important role in keeping things on an even keel. When discussion in plenary sessions gets too heated, the choir and orchestra take over. Musical interludes take place under the baton of a conductor who has an authority disproportionate to his stature. As he rises to his feet he instantly becomes the focus of musicians and delegates alike. Hymnody unites the conference as African voices extemporise in exquisite harmonies. After about twenty minutes of devotion and praise the assembly gets back down to more temporal business.

Alfred has not been given permission to come to SACLA, which has deeply disappointed Amy. But he has asked her to pass on his greetings to some friends of his, delegates from a Durban parish. There is a poste restante at the assembly where one can leave messages, and this is how Amy first makes contact with Bob and Fran Pickwick.

The Pickwicks take Amy under their wing. Until now she has slipped in and out of sessions, mostly unnoticed. Now the Pickwicks have an eye on her she feels obliged to take part, for they will surely report on her behaviour to Brother Alfred. Over tea in the refectory one morning they extract, oh so gently, from Amy the story of her marriage to Wolf. Later she is astonished that she has divulged such intimate information to complete strangers. And yet they are not strangers, they are friends of Alfred.

Afterwards Bob and Fran Pickwick want to pray with her, and she willingly accepts their offer, sitting herself down upon a low brick wall in the sunshine, where they lay hands on her and ask the Lord to set her free from all oppression. Clearly they want her to pray out loud in response, but extempore prayer, indeed, spoken words of any kind, do not come easily to Amy. She ransacks her mind for the right words, but all that comes, on a outward breath, is the whisper, "I thirst." Bob Pickwick frowns a little. There is no Christian reason, they explain to her, with serious expressions, why she should stay with Wolf, if he chooses to live in hell.

§

Dear Alfred,

I am rejoicing exceedingly in your letter, which arrived on Tuesday, together with a long letter from my sister describing her withdrawal from her training course and her consequent witnessing in high places. From her eloquence I am sure that she is guided by the Holy Spirit – even before hearing that, between nerve-racking interviews with her superior officers, she received the gift of tongues.

Her long-term plan is to come back here, but she is waiting to see me in England first. In the meantime she is coming down to earth and testing her mettle as an auxiliary nurse. "After all, a hernia is a hernia, whether you're the Air Chief Marshal or the caretaker," she writes.

Your letter is also a revelation. I don't think I have ever heard you so forthright, so transparent, so beautifully human. I hope the monastic throat is not still sore after all the Shona teaching practice. I think you will get nowhere trying to learn Shona just for the prior's sake. The only way is to fall in love with somebody Shona. It is the way of love to wish to be like the beloved. Perhaps you could find a delightful Shona speaking child, who reminds you of yourself when you were young, to practice on?

I don't often get physically sick, but I have the dreadful lurgy today. I am in good company. Michael Cassidy got it on Tuesday. He told us that the Holy Spirit persuaded him to throw away his paper on the Holy Spirit, after two-and-a-half days of suffering this 'flu, and to speak from his heart. That went down very well. But the rest of the assembly all seemed to be coughing and sneezing by the time we went home. There were many spirits abroad at SACLA, and one was the flying 'enza'.

The conference has begun to consolidate God's work in my life, by turning me inside-out. In all seriousness. I think the time has come to leave the internal 'watch-making' to the delicate hands of the Spirit, and to become useful to the world by learning to tell the time.

I was two years old in the Spirit yesterday, and an old Zulu lady (Pentecostal) prayed with me, for a birthday present. I need the well-being, the abundant life, which God has promised us.

Today I called in at the office to do some urgent work and found the Community magazine had been airmailed to me. I find my own article a bit tiresome; maybe I have read it too often. But am I dreaming? Is that old rag really transformed? It seems there is warmth previously lacking – a human interest. Maybe I am just full of pride because my byline is in it?

Monday

There is something about such a rich feast of opinions of church leadership which helps give me a purchase on reality. I am floundering within myself, as always, but my perspective on the world is taking on substance. I am finding that little patch of solid earth which someone begged for me in prayer at SACLA. God becomes daily more unknown, but I expand into the reality of the world as I respond to people around me.

I am surprised and delighted that you will be coming down to lead the fraternity retreat, together with Fr Frank, later this year. Naturally there are several ladies who require three days of peace, and being well-fed, and one must take account of them. But could you conceive of a retreat at two levels where the usual talks, silence, offices, were interspersed with discussion (optional) – possibly even a walk round the Wemmer Pan? I sincerely hope you will not condemn me to silence. It was necessary, no doubt, before. But I have had enough of silence for the time being.

As for a holiday after the retreat, Wolf is delighted that you are coming but he cannot take leave again this year. Bob and Fran Pickwick are equally delighted about your visit and say please visit them anytime. But short of resigning my job I cannot take more leave because I am going to England in November. I don't know quite what to suggest. I know Petunia has written to you about going to the coast – she blithely declares my job null and void and insists that I should come too. It seems to be as I always feared – my precious friendship with you will have to await the kingdom of heaven for proper time together.

I spoke to Sister Elizabeth on Wednesday and she told me that Sister Angela is now prioress. I seem to have very exalted fathers and mothers.

There is only a little time before getting packed for our trip to Zululand, so I cannot share all I would like to at present. I'm very sorry you couldn't come to the assembly, especially as it means you can't come with us to Umfolozi.

If there really is a new wind blowing in the Community, Bob and Fran Pickwick are the sort of people the fraternity would attract. What a foundation the Community could provide, if only they could open the doors and windows a little, and let the breeze in.

I hope and pray that the breeze stirring in my spirit will grow. How often is one born again? I couldn't endure any more suffering of that sort. But then, how not to become hard-hearted and proud and independent? Bob and Fran gave me a message from the Lord: "My grace is sufficient unto thee." I wish I could respond to that. I wish I could believe that. For everyone else, yes. For me, it is too hard to believe.

Everywhere I turn is vanity. I have not yet learned how to rest in God. I resist God at every turn on the central issue. How dare I? I don't know. There is something more terrible than dying, or living in pain, and that is being loved by the living God. When I laid hands on you in the garden, the night before you went away, I saw the eyes of the Son of God, blazing like fire – but they were looking through me at you; not at me. You, in your gentleness and humility, can endure that love. I don't feel as if I can.

53

Umfolozi Game Reserve is in the hills of sub-tropical Zululand. For five mild winter days Wolf and Amy, Roger and two other men from the mountain club walk through the bushveld and river beds of this undulating game reserve. They walk in single file, accompanied by two rangers with rifles, one at the head and one at the foot of the crocodile. "It's tempting fate to say crocodile," joke the mountain boys amongst themselves. "Can you see those two little eyes staring at you? There! There!" Such silly levity continues throughout the five days of the hike. It drives Amy to drink.

In the evenings she is happy to take herself off and relax on her own, away from the boisterous group. They camp each night in a different kraal, hedged with thorny acacia to keep out predators. She breathes in the aromatic smoke of mthombothi burning, a hardwood so dense that even termites cannot chew it. Rhinoceros rub their hides on trunks of mthombothi until it shines like mahogany, bizarre stumps of french-polished furniture in the midst of the veld. The wood is unsuitable for cooking as the fumes are toxic, but it smells wonderfully aromatic smouldering on the camp fire. Amy sups her beer and listens to the muted conversation of servants preparing dinner over a cooking fire at the far end of the compound.

Roomy green tents with banana matting and canvas stretchers provide accommodation for the night. Latrines and showers are set discreetly apart. Packs and provisions are transported between overnight sites by donkeys, which are led along a different route from the hikers, so as not to put the tourists in harm's way. Lion and leopard are partial to donkey meat. Pack animals are corralled for the night at the far end of the kraal. One night the donkeys break out with much heehawing, and gallop through the site in panic. "Hyena," diagnoses the Zulu ranger, sniffing the air. Amy sleeps through this incident.

Days are dry and sunny here in mid-winter. The river is shrunken to stagnant greenish pools encircled by wide, sandy beaches. Crossing the river bed one morning Amy notices a sinuous imprint in the sand, about seven feet long. A wisp of steam rises from a green puddle in the middle of this shallow impression. Amy is mesmerised by the image of absence — which translates itself instantaneously in her mind as crocodile. She scans the shallows for the leviathan, which only seconds before has defecated in the sand and slipped away into the water. But she sees only a lazy ripple on a stagnant pool.

The bush is secretive like this. It keeps itself to its self. Amy is the intruder, the guest, the passer by. Wildlife here is not in captivity, not on display for the benefit of her curiosity, as in a zoo. Sighting a crocodile, a water buffalo, a rhinoceros, even wildebeest or zebra, is a privilege here.

The rangers have briefed the party on what to do should they attract unwelcome attention from a predator, or other potentially dangerous wild animal. How to seek shelter. Behind a clump of grass will do in the case of the gentle and short-sighted white rhinoceros, should one take it into its head to charge.

Most of the talking is done by the Afrikaner ranger, who carries his rifle breeched over his arm while they walk in open veld, but at the ready when in acacia bush or rocky gorges. The white rhino is the same colour as the black rhino, he tells them, but it is vital to know the difference. 'White' derives from the German word *weit*, or wide. White rhino have a broad lip, and are bigger than their black cousins. They graze on grass. Black rhino by contrast browse on low hanging acacia and other shrubs. The important difference is that black rhino are quick, bad-tempered and not at all short-sighted. It is a good idea to climb a stout tree when a black rhino is after you.

On the morning they encounter water buffalo in a clump of dense bush near the river, the Zulu ranger is first to sense the danger. He hisses a word from the rear of the party. His partner cocks his rifle and freezes to the spot. Nothing can be seen or heard in the thicket but the occasional crack of a twig. The ranger has told them how these creatures employ the deadly tactic of quietly encircling unwary intruders, then they close in. The only safe place is up a very stout tree indeed, as half a ton of water buffalo will knock down a tree when aroused. Amy gloomily inspects the thorn studded trunks of the surrounding acacia. But after several minutes of petrified silence, the group withdraws slowly, carefully, and safely out of the thicket.

§

"Midden," declares the ranger, prodding at a mound of dried rhinoceros dung with his boot. White rhinos are territorial creatures, he tells them. "This fellow is in the prime of life. His territory is on the river. If another rhino wants a drink he must come to this midden, because it marks the border, and wait with his neck bowed until the big chap comes and lets him in."

On their last evening in the bush the ranger takes Wolf and Roger out to look for lion. On the way to camp the donkey wranglers have passed a lion kill – a wildebeest. Amy pours herself a cold beer and retires to a deckchair beside the camp fire. She breathes in the familiar aromatic smoke, admires the watermelon hue of the western sky as the sun dips towards the horizon.

All at once the earth shakes with a sound Amy has never heard before, but knows instinctively, without a shadow of doubt, that this is a lion's roar. She hears two shots, one after another. Then there is silence.

Amy, beer bottle frozen halfway to her lips, once again contemplates widowhood. The men who stayed behind run back and forth yelling at the cooking staff to do something! The Zulus smile and make soothing gestures.

Twenty minutes later, as night falls, the safari party returns bright-eyed to tell their story. Wolf, the ranger says, behaved immaculately. "When the lioness charged us Wolf stood perfectly still, as I have instructed you to do in this case," he crowed. Wolf basks in the compliment but looks a trifle sheepish. Amy suspects that her husband was rooted to the spot, and could not have moved a muscle, even if he had tried.

No harm has come to the lioness. "It was our fault," confesses the ranger. "When she heard us coming she hid herself, and then we got between her and her dinner. This made her brave enough to attack us. I fired two shots over her head and she ran away."

§

Dear Alfred,

Thank you for your letter and helpful comments on my parochial situation. SACLA is only just beginning to take shape in my mind, but I hope I will be clearer about it by the time you come, if you have time to listen. It was such a life-changing experience I find it hard to explain at the moment.

We've had some rain here, although it is still bitterly cold compared with Zululand. Wolf will be starting his new job next Wednesday. He's got a dose of 'flu' at present. Otherwise all is well. The geese and the hen are laying merrily, and there are some lettuces in the garden. Am feebly warding off chronic depression, probably the result of so much excitement in the past few weeks.

Am painfully entering a relationship with the bible, following the Pickwick's ministry to me. The feelings and impulses which arise in me are disturbing. I find nothing which is kind, just or true within myself at all. Sad isn't it?

Wolf is naturally apprehensive about the job. His dose of 'flu' is getting him down. I feel inadequate to help him. Everything positive in my life is incomprehensible to him. He suspects he is missing out, and it's all my fault: why can't we be miserable together like we used to be? I must admit the prolific "*Scheiß* church" comments are beginning to sound less convincing.

26th July 1979

This, poste haste, to ask you to ignore my bad-tempered little note amidst the last batch of newspapers. I wasn't myself, and it's actually quite exciting why I wasn't myself. Let me tell you about it.

Pickwicks gave me a book on the inspirational gifts, which made it abundantly clear that gifts of the Holy Spirit are not bestowed according to a person's goodness. That rid me of one delusion. Then I learned that I have been like the servant with the one talent, complaining that my master reaps where he has not sown, because I don't believe that God can bring healing through an unclean, unhealed sinner like me.

I was puzzled and muddled by all this at first. The previous week in Umfolozi had left me with a bitter residue of discontent, which came out in my nasty note to you. Then everything fell into place, and I got on the phone to Bob to confirm my suspicions.

I'm not sure if this is right, but I must tell you anyway and you can decide for yourself.

Between SACLA and going to the bush, on the Monday, I laid hands on someone for healing following a breakup with her boyfriend. The anointing of the Spirit was very strong. During this time a wave of the most racking pain passed through me, although it didn't actually hurt me. It was like a soundless cry. The woman felt much better after that, and I went home on cloud nine.

But I was terribly tired, which I accredited to my 'flu', and I went to bed for a few hours. Those hours were filled with weird hallucinations. I had been in a very elevated mood, and they seemed quite pleasant at the time. I thought perhaps I was having visions. How naive! For seven days after that I was harassed, and harassed people around me, with a spirit of malcontent.

On Tuesday evening I remembered the cry that went through me, and realised that probably the woman was delivered of some beastly spirit, and I had been too naive to realise it and clean myself up properly afterwards. We had prayed for an indwelling of the Holy Spirit for her − but not for me.

Bob confirmed that this is probably what happened, by describing what often happened to him after deliverance ministry − before I even mentioned the hallucinations!

I was about to write how exciting this is, but then I remembered that bit about not rejoicing that the spirits are subject to you; but rejoice that your names are written in heaven. I didn't even have to search for it − there was a bookmark in that page.

So. That's my news. I'm in the process of writing a short story about Umfolozi, which I will send you in due course.

I am going into battle in earnest with myself over my abuse of alcohol, and smoking. I am reliably informed that if the intention is sincere God will take care of the results. Well, we'll see! I've spent too long jibbing at this problem. Bondage of the will is a frightful thing; there is no release except by God's mercy.

Keep well, dear Alfred. May the Lord provide us all with some of the hidden manna, and give us all faith to overcome everything that stands between us and the kingdom.

Give my best regards to the fathers, and my apologies for the magazine article. I think I was so afraid of treading on their toes that I ended up being more than usually obtuse.

If you don't want to keep the tape of David Bosch's[24] speech from SACLA please could you forward it to the Superior with my compliments.

2nd August 1979

Dear Alfred,

We have just moved into a new office – a bigger one. I am sitting in the sunlight, looking up now and again from my work at our new view of the Union Buildings from the east-facing windows. It is so quiet here. We are well away from everyone else in the production unit because we need quiet to concentrate on our proof-reading. The air-conditioning hums like the inner walls of a ship.

I have been surrounded by rice-paper screens this past week. That is to say in a poetic sort of way that I have remained within myself. I haven't contacted anyone, not Petunia, nor Sue, or anyone. I feel that the Lord is moving in at last – I must have signed the final contract lately. I am delighting in being led, childlike, into Life. I have even found it necessary to apologise to myself for treating my life so badly. Poor life. It couldn't help it. It got lost when it was little, and fell into bad company.

I am delighted you have leave following the fraternity retreat, and I will do anything I possibly can to make it a beautiful holiday. I would like to go to Turfloop with you and visit Fr Esau – the chaplain. Do you know him? He trained with the Community. I met him at SACLA. Did you know that black priests only get about half the stipend that white priests get? I hope Wolf will come with us. Maybe we could take in Thornybush for tea?

I would also love to go to Durban with you but I think Wolf would frown on that. Petunia would go gladly. Of course, I hope you will spare us a weekend. I want to show you the new office, and we can have tea with Elsa, and visit Drew's studio on Saturday

24. David Bosch was a missiologist, an Afrikaner theologian who espoused the anti-apartheid cause and was tragically killed before he saw the new South Africa. He spoke at SACLA.

morning, where we might get a beer. Maybe we could all go to his farm on Sunday for a braai. And I will take you shopping. We can stroll around the teeming metropolis of Pretoria and buy something to take back to Pedregoso.

Our house is a pigsty at the moment. I am about to do the spring cleaning. I usually let it get really run down first, so that I can see the difference when I've finished. Wolf has bought some second-hand carpets, and we were given another one, so we shall be padding around like the filthy rich by the time you arrive. Wolf has also got into playing darts, so you will doubtless be expected to chance your arm at that. If you've forgotten how, never mind. Have a beer first and blame it on inebriation.

54

Alfred leads the fraternity retreat at St Bede's, together with Fr Frank. They are a wonderful foil for one another. Alfred is lanky. Fr Frank is short, broad in the beam and bent with age. The younger man is spontaneous in his speech, careless even; the elder monk is unhurried, deliberating over every word. Alfred defers to his brother, but misses no opportunity to extol the joys of life in the Spirit. This exuberance is a trait other brethren prefer to take with a pinch of salt, or a cold shower.

Amy has now stayed at St Bede's several times and feels a touch of proprietorial pride because she is so familiar with the routines of the retreat house. In recent letters to Alfred she has freely bestowed advice about the retreat, which, as the weekend progresses, she notices has been ignored. Pride and chagrin rub against each other, making her irritable. This discomfort is exacerbated by the nearness of the beloved Alfred, who is however taken up with other people. Conflicting emotions pitch Amy back into the halls of gloom. Trapped in the silence with all this turmoil in her breast, she slips into despondency and fails to turn up for lunch on the second day.

Amy hides in her room submerged in shame, wishing she could die, wishing above all that she had brought a bottle of whisky with her. Buoyed by her recent elevated mood she had decided not to pack any alcohol. Now she trembles and whimpers in the alternating frigidity and furnace of unmediated emotion. Her soul is first rinsed then scorched by this process. Helpless to help herself, she gives up hope; then goes to look for Alfred who takes one look at her ruined face and invites her out for a walk.

They have not spoken since exchanging a few words at dinner on Friday. Silence commenced, as usual, after compline. Now Alfred smiles a secret, naughty smile as he leads the way out through the garden gate, through the Sunday afternoon siesta of suburban streets. They walk in silence to a well-trodden track around a tailings pan – the dregs of an abandoned gold mine. Scrub has grown over old slag heaps which are now populated by small birds busily collecting threads of this and that for building nests. A tumbleweed skips past, sailing on a sudden breeze, as the two of them walk silently beside the quiet water. Several pairs of mallard float upon the lake, but otherwise all is still in the afternoon sun.

They come to a fork in the dirt track. "Which way now?" murmurs Alfred. Amy chews her lip. She does not want to speak, to make decisions. The silence between them is pregnant with unspoken things — unfathomable feelings, mysterious yearning for she knows not what. She wants to stay wrapped in this deep, perturbing intimacy, this enigmatic silence. She feels as if she is smelling warm earth for the first time, the touch of the breeze like a caress on her cheek, welcoming sunlight on her skin as if she were a new creation.

Alfred picks up a stick and tosses it to where the path bifurcates. It lands with the pointed end lying to the right, then lifts itself up, turns over and rests pointing to the left. Alfred and Amy look into each other's eyes and laugh gently, reverently, then they take the path to the left.

§

On the weekend after the retreat Alfred visits Albion for a party to which Amy invites all and sundry. Wolf's friends Gail and Marius come, as does Marie from next door, and several people from the house group. Frederick comes from Eersterus.

It is dark and cold outdoors, so most of the company make themselves at home in the spacious sitting room of the old farmhouse, where Wolf has made a fire. He has swept the flue especially for the occasion, dislodging a bird's nest from the chimney pot. This distressed him as there were two little eggs in the nest which got broken during the operation. Wolf has recently taken up bird watching. Marie occupies the big armchair, resting her leg on a pouffe. She has a glass of water beside her. The other guests make inroads into carafes of red and white wine, and bottles of whisky and gin.

Wolf and Marius are outside feeding the braai with piles of lamb chops, steak, and marinated chicken. Spatz and Pauli sit hopefully nearby. Amy, Gail and sundry other women occupy themselves with mixing bowls of salad, while bread rolls warm in the oven. A pot of tomato and onion sauce simmers on the stove.

Alfred is lounging in his usual position on the sofa, still clothed in cassock and scapular, which counts as evening dress. His legs are stretched out towards the fire, a glass of whisky in his hand. It is hard to say whether the fire in the grate or Alfred himself is radiating more warmth, as he bestows his avuncular smile on his flock, lazily waves his glass, appreciating the colour, the aroma, sipping now and then. People who have not met him before at first keep a respectful distance, but those who know him better gather round, some perched on the arms of the sofa, some sprawled on the floor. So far only Petunia has ventured to sit beside him.

"Oh aye, this is nice," sighs Mr Plod, warming his goblet of Tassenheimer in gnarled old hands. People gossip, watching the fire, sipping their drinks, the odour of grilled meat floats indoors, whetting appetites.

Mr and Mrs Sherlock, newcomers to the house group, have each accepted a small glass of white wine which they sip cautiously, surreptitiously watching Alfred enjoy his drink with characteristic gusto.

"A monk, you say?" asks Mr Sherlock in an undertone, when Amy comes in to announce dinner. "I didn't think they drank."

"Oh yes," replies Amy fondly. "He's quite a normal person most of the time."

"D'you mean like a man?" Mr Sherlock is bent on pursuing the matter.

"Well yes, he's a man. He's just chosen to be a monk. But I suppose he hasn't stopped being a man."

"Well young Amy," concludes Mr Sherlock with a coy smirk, "I wish you would look at me like you look at 'im."

Blushing, Amy bolts back into the kitchen to supervise serving up.

After dinner Amy is stacking plates when she catches sight of Alfred and Marius walking together in the dark garden. They stop to light cigarettes and Marius's lighter flares briefly, illuminating their faces. Alfred's demeanour is grave, Marius is agitated. The tip of Alfred's cigarette describes animated circles as they resume their stroll.

When they come back indoors Marius discreetly calls Gail aside and all three withdraw into Amy's oratory. Amy is agog, but assumes the role of protector, of guardian angel, making sure no other guest strays in that direction. In due course the threesome emerge and rejoin the party. There are traces of tears on Gail's face, which is radiant. She seems spaced out, dreamily evading conversation for the rest of the evening.

§

Dear Alfred,

I feel I must write to you now, although you will not read this until you get back to Pedregoso. Our talk on the phone last night has left me with a burden on my heart.

You frightened me by advising more regular prayer time "to see me though the dark times up ahead". I don't want any more dark times. I've had enough of dark times.

One night I was praying for Wolf with my arms around him, and the Spirit left me. I can't begin to describe the blank desolation of those moments. I didn't know what I had done, and I pleaded for the Spirit's return to fill this aching void. The next morning I realised that, for a few minutes, I had experienced what Wolf lives with all the time.

I do sin daily, and often, and I don't want to. Yet if I fear sin the love of God cannot remove it; while I am bound by that fear I reject salvation. "If anyone says he does not sin he is a liar," also, "Sin has no dominion over us." It is very perplexing.

At the moment, I prefer to believe Baron Von Hügel, that internal aridity is a sign that I must look outwards for a while. I give up the Lord within, whom I have come to know and cling to, in favour of the Lord manifested in creation. When I return within, I come with new eyes that see more clearly. I go in and out and find pasture. Of course, any familiar image I had of God is erased in this process.

When I am grown up in prayer my entire being will be a constant inward and outward turning – like the wings of a butterfly – showing creation to God, and God to creation. Or maybe it won't. Maybe it will be something quite different.

The desolation that has settled on my heart comes from your words about preparing for the time of trial. You see, I hoped the Lord has already done what the Holy Spirit had to do in me in terms of trial. Maybe I will have to undergo some sort of physical suffering? I have no physical courage. I still persist in despoiling my health. But the Lord knows I cannot endure even a few moments of dereliction. Surely he is not, at any time, ever going to leave me?

Prayer is a relationship, so it is proper that there are times of absence. But because, tangibly, God seems absent, I do not cease to live and move and have my being in him. Just as I don't love you one iota less when you are in Pedregoso.

Why should God try me further – except in the healthy sort of discipline that athletes have to undergo? They must increase their own limits of endurance, but without damaging themselves. I have been through the fire and I live in the age of the resurrection. Why should God desire to send me back there?

If I get proud, God will give me someone like you to put me right. If I go lusting after the things of the flesh, like drinking too much, the bottom will drop out of my world eventually. Nothing compares with knowing God's loving kindness. If I cannot believe in God's constant vigilance over me in love, then I might as well lie down and die now.

I don't know what the future holds but if God is there, and he must be, it can only be glorious. As long as there is logic (God's logic) in it, even suffering and dying for someone you love has been glorious, ever since Calvary.

Many of us in the world see your monastic life as one of voluntary material deprivation. We sometimes forget the exigencies of sensory and emotional deprivation. That sort of life demands a different calibre of spirit than my own way of life.

I have the privilege of living in the world. You have the privilege of living the religious life. The circumstances of the lives which the Lord has given us are different. Is it possible that the rules which govern religious are not suited to my way?

I hope and pray that I have not upset you, but I am glad that I am beginning to be able give you other points of view to mull over, if you think they are worth it.

Tomorrow evening I will begin to keep an hour's prayer as you suggest, between 5.15 and 6.15pm. I will try to keep an hour for the rest of my life, because of course you are right in principle. It is not the fact of the prayer time that I take issue with. It is the motive.

My life must spring from that hour – the hour is not a protection fee, an insurance, for my life. Neither will I fear going astray, because God rejoices to see his love being worked out in us through falling and going astray. As you rescue me from my shortcomings, maybe some day I will rescue you.

22nd August 1979

Our little post-SACLA prayer group met yesterday – four of us all from different backgrounds; two were absent. We drift in and exchange a real African greeting – which takes about fifteen minutes. Frederick from Eersterus led our prayer in Afrikaans. Then we sat in silence enjoying the Lord's peace for about twenty-five minutes. We were too shy to look at each other after that. Our conversation was profound – and we forgot all about the comparative bible study.

So. To the retreat. How the retreat was conducted is none of my business. But what I do miss is the opportunity to share our growth and experience. A problem with retreats is that we all disappear into our monastic cells, and only get to know each other when it is time to go home. For me, silence in retreat used to be a way of ensuring that I was safe from my fellow retreatants. This is a malaise which could be cured by at least one hour of shared prayer a day. I don't think this should be an optional extra but an intrinsic part of the programme. Of course, one can't insist that everyone takes part, but neither can one insist that everyone eats breakfast.

I've heard from Anna, who is at present camping with Ruth and dog in Tintagel, Cornwall.

Thursday

Last night I had a talk with David Bosch – yes me! There was a cheese and wine party after the post-SACLA seminar, crammed with professors and doctors. All in Afrikaans, which was very good for me, although largely incomprehensible. I told Professor Bosch about how gratefully the audio-cassette of his lecture was received in England, and he kindly sent a personal message for the prayer group at Anna's place in Bristol. Frederick was altogether joyful about it. "That's evangelism!" he yodelled. Dad did once prophecy that missionaries would one day be sent from Africa to the UK.

We may go to lunch with Frederick and his wife in Eersterus when you come for the weekend. Maybe we won't go to Turfloop. It is about 300km, and we would spend eight hours of our weekend driving. We will see how we feel when the time comes.

Friday

I want to begin writing again. It's sort of welling up inside. You've spent two years murmuring about this honeymoon that I am supposed to be having with the Lord, and I think this must be it. LIFE is sprawled in large letters across the universe. The downcast

Amy has disappeared completely for the time being – which is very satisfactory, because her inner turmoils really are rather boring – and rather hard work.

Maybe it is like the book of Revelation – once you actually meet the Lord they are all talking about, spooks and demons just vanish?

12th September 1979

Dear Alfred,

Are you now plodding along an empty road in the dust and heat of the day, gazing towards a shimmering horizon? Or are you draped over the leather upholstery of an air-conditioned BMW?

What a joy it was – is – to have seen you. To refresh a companionship which will surely last forever. How wonderful to see a person in glorious technicolor, in sunshine, in prayer. All the letters and phone calls in the world cannot compare with meeting you, meeting in the flesh someone whom one has learnt to love in this way.

The first darling seed sown at the party, at the braai at our house, appeared above ground last night. I was washing up and Wolf was watching me. I told him that you prayed with Gail and Marius that night. He then told me about how he helped Gail, a while ago, when she had a serious attack of hysteria.

"I lost two hours working time between lunch and tea," Wolf complained. "I made her do things like making coffee, so that she would have a few minutes alone now and again, to take it all in. I had to make her understand that the God of the bible couldn't possibly want her to suffer like this."

I tried to concentrate on the washing up, and cautiously remarked, "Yes there is such a lot of wrong teaching."

Wolf continued briskly, as if that were a facile remark. "I know what is in the bible. I studied it for long enough. I have studied three religions, and if you look for the truth you find they are all saying the same thing anyway. What's important with people in mental pain, is to make them look at life outside their head, then they forget the pain. Marius couldn't believe it when he got back. He wanted to know what I'd done. Huh! Lost two working hours. That's what I'd done."

I am sure I didn't move a muscle during that conversation, and that extraordinary husband of mine smirked as he walked off.

I am practising the fundamentals of the Alexander Technique, as you explained it. If Watchman Nee is right, the Holy Spirit begins work in the centre of a person, in their spirit, and continues the renewing work outwards, completing it in the body. I have felt for some weeks a sense of the Holy Spirit claiming me bodily, as it were. Although when I talk about sensations and feelings I don't mean physical sensations and feelings.

I test 'feelings', on the basis of whether they have a physical location or not. I find physical sensations gross in comparison with the subtle movements of the spirit. Eastern mystics understand the spiritual body much better than our church does. For instance, there is no doubt in my mind that chastity is related to powers of healing. That creative energy is so potent when tamed.

However, concerning the Alexander Technique, for about ten months I have been feeling discomfort in the base of my skull. I feared I had a brain tumour at SACLA, the pain was so bad. Now, any time I become aware of it I sort of attend to it with a loving awareness, and the discomfort goes.

The point of all this is that I am becoming physically aware of relationships, and where feelings are located in my body. I am conscious of the balance of my spine, the poise of my head.

This essential, growing awareness makes me conscious of people's troubles in their bodies. When I walk to the swimming pool at lunchtime I see people on the street carrying burdens of despair, and loneliness. I can see a dis-ease by the way a person moves. Only hope can carry one through seeing all that, just walking around. I am aware that this insight could be a gift, and I pray that God will (gently) keep me – make me – humble in it. People's lives are sacred ground, and must not be gawked at out of mere curiosity. What bliss it is to swim and lie in the sun for this hour at the pool at lunchtime.

Last night, at our little house-group, I confessed to the three women who were there the pain I felt after your departure. I needed some comfort. One of them responded with disarming honesty that she, and many others, should be forgiven for thinking I am weird and immoral! Well, there it is! Out in the open at last. I know people at both St Wilfs and St Mark's gossip about me, my peculiar background and lifestyle, the fact that I drink and smoke, that I am friends with a monk.

Anyway it was comforting to share my sorrow. June had a glimpse of the well of loneliness that the Lord himself must have known when parting from his friends. She said it felt like she was completely empty inside. Our novice member casually remarked, "Oh, I get that on Good Friday."

I hope it doesn't embarrass you that I asked for prayer. I am tired of maintaining a stiff upper lip.

We also prayed for the Lancaster House talks in London. For our government here. And for forgiveness for our public, and clandestine, criticism of our priest.

Forgive me for my alternating tactlessness and hypersensitivity. I'll get it right one day. Thank you for our walk at Wemmer Pan.

Friday

I have had Marius here for a while and we talked about cooking. He was once an aspiring chef, like me. I ordered the whole Cordon Bleu cookery course from England when I got married.

The washing is squeaking around in the machine and the cats are watching it through the porthole, like a mouse on a treadmill. I told Marius I miss you, and he said oh-so-gently that other people need you too. It is nice to be reassured that you haven't been taken away as a punishment.

Saturday

Wolf whisked me off to dinner at The Caponero last night, because his boss called him in yesterday, said all his jobs had been classed A1 up to now, how much pay rise would he like, and would he prefer beer or whisky? So casting pecuniary caution to the wind (and I think a little worse for beer) he bought me dinner, and gave me his share of the housekeeping. I think he is also more than a little fed up with the endless curries I have prepared from all the leftover meat from your farewell party.

Am sitting in the garden, blinded by a sea of white daisies, trying to ignore my text books. I feel as if I have gained the freedom of the children of God. It is a strangely wonderful experience. Transparency within and graceful, potent stability all around in the world. Before, I worshipped God from afar; now I worship God in my own shrine, which is me.

Before, was a time of passive (is that the word?) endurance — having things done to me. All I could do for myself, insofar as I was capable of it, was to resist everything deemed to be 'bad'. Now it is as if the Lord has handed me a bunch of keys — to act, to work with the divine will, responsibly, and to resist evil. I know I am God's. But I cannot yet say, "He is mine," with confidence.

Alfred, dearest, we really do live in a new realm, where mourning and crying and pain have passed away. It is not just a honeymoon, or some transitory, ecstatic experience. The labour is in continually paying attention to it. It is like a wave on the ocean. No-one can tell it to be careful about the momentum of its great ride into the shore. "I will take the shore with me, and begin all over again. These are my boundaries, which God has set for me. Why should I be careful about meeting them?" Even pain is part of the joy, and the pain is a new beginning.

Does God laugh with his waves? Or does he wish they would keep their heads down, tug their forelocks, and creep unnoticed up his beaches? How marvellous it is to accept pain as a new means of affirming the ultimate power and love and goodness of God.

There is a speckled hoopoe on the lawn, taking advantage of the cats' siesta to peck around for insects.

Monday

Still battling a little with studying… tend to hit the bottle whenever the "you must get down to it" feelings arise. But instead of long periods of heavy slog, I've been letting my studies leak in to my day here and there. Now I rather look forward to it.

Contrary to all our expectations — mine, yours and Fr Frank's — the Lord does not expect me to get up at sparrow's twit to pray. The fact is that Wolf is desolate if he wakes up alone. It might read a little oddly in the spiritual handbooks, but the Lord is infinitely concerned with the reality that Wolf is a betrayed personality. God foregoes his rightful time with me for Wolf's sake. So there!

All your alarm bells may be ringing, but there's not much I can do about it. I do have a short period of prayer after Wolf has gone to work, in which I consecrate the day and myself; brief interludes of thanksgiving or intercession during the day; and an examination of conscience at night. A daily meditation too of course.

It is good for the Community to collect a fraternity around itself. but the rule has to be formulated differently. I am really coming up against the discrepancy between the religious life and mine. I can't even begin to copy your rule of life, even in miniature. Not because I am weak (although I am); not because I am not able to pray for hours at a time; but because my life imposes different demands upon me.

I have had conversations with twelve people today. They are, potentially, my prayers. If that could become, by some sovereign grace, a reality, mine would be a life of prayer in the world, just as authentic as any monk's life in the cloister.

There are degrees of prayer, I think. The first is very specific, and prays for grazed knees, and cut fingers. The next prays for loved ones, and healing, and happiness. The next prays for nations, and for peace, and for animals. The highest prays for the glory of God. Here Community and fraternity are united in this family of the church.

What an obtuse letter. It has more or less complained from beginning to end. Sort of maudlin. I think I will send it, but after this I will write about the weather and "who-said-what-when" sort of stuff.

Wednesday

I should be studying, but the prospect is too horrible. You did encourage me when you said it is good to study if I can. The grim-browed authoritarian father looms in that area of my life. My Dad suffered from him too, and somehow communicated to me the Victorian grandfather who needed the intellectual blood of his son to keep him alive.[25] So in defiance of my fears I am listening to music, with Spatz at my feet. I am engaged in a mental fencing match, which is threatening anathema unless I buckle down and put my nose to the grindstone. Grisly contortion that!

Only grace could have got me through English Lit last year. All the right questions came up in the exam. I hadn't even read some of those books since A Level. Maybe it will happen again? In the meantime I refuse to be bullied into abject toil when it should be a joy to study. My generation believes that we are damned already. We

25. This is a reference to the culture and does not refer to Amy's paternal grandfather.

are the untouchables, as far as the god of our parents is concerned. We need a gospel of acceptance and forgiveness, not of morality.

More and more I am led into the bible narrative as my own life story – the big picture. "And God created…" as the experiential human knowledge of evolution. My existence begins with the crushing turmoil of the earth in her formation; her blessing as she is clothed with vegetation; the teeming animate forms of life she bears; her emerging consciousness; all this is mirrored in my own little life. How could anything be left out of a story as grand as that? Sin, failure, weakness, wilfulness are all part of the narrative. Now I understand a little of what free will means. How could I ever begin to love my Lord if I had never had any choice?

Be there for all your students, just as you are. It is doubtless true what your prior says, that the most impressionable and intelligent youngsters will disappear over the border.[26] But it is also the case that the best propaganda wins, and your presence will be attractive as a safe harbour in the midst of conflict. If we cannot free ourselves entirely from oppression, which we probably can't in this life, how can we free our children? We must teach them how to live gracefully with it.

1st October 1979

Dear Alfred,

The war in your area has been very much in my thoughts since Saturday morning, when I heard about the latest atrocities. However, I think the chapel at Pedregoso is a more effective nerve-centre for the operational area than Salisbury is. I become more convinced of our effective power as we gather the government and the London talks, to say nothing of events in Uganda and Cambodia, into our prayers.

Now let me tell you about Wolf's latest disaster. Nikki arrived proudly with her new scooter on Saturday, which Wolf decided to try out. To cut a short story shorter, the machine took a huge leap, spraying gravel, then crashed in a crumpled heap on the drive. Nikki, to her eternal credit, ran first to help Wolf. Only after we had

---

26. To join Robert Mugabe's guerrilla force in Mozambique.

got the sand out of his mouth, and established that he hadn't broken his neck, did she straighten out her bike and ride off, muttering, "No stoppa da Vespa".

Wolf had concussion, a vast black eye from his right shoulder to his hairline, and what I diagnosed as a couple of cracked ribs. Siemens' X-ray reveals just a bruised lung. That man is amazing. He's thirty-five. Ribs aren't supposed to bend at that age. Of course, what really distressed Hamburg's most dreaded Rocker is that he fell off a scooter!

Doing two to three hours study in the early morning has transformed my day. Academic work is beginning to make sense of theology. Biblical studies is giving me an understanding of the bible as a whole library, edited by a cast of thousands, over millennia.

So to your most important news. You have been called to the priesthood. Not as a youthful vocation, but with full knowledge of the pitfalls that humankind, and the world, to say nothing of the church, can put in your way. Christ chooses his priests as he chose his disciples. Priests are not made by the arbitrary wisdom of men in the church, but by God, insofar as his people have an ear. I hope chapter will have a listening ear. I also pray that you will be given the necessary patience. You are still young, as popes go.

Sunday night

Wolf has gone to my aunt Pru's house to collect a hundred ivy cuttings for our garden. I was planning to do a load of washing, wash-up, and get myself groomed for the week. However, I throw all aside to write to you. How good it is to relax. Although, even now anxiety knocks at the door. "What about cutting your toenails? Look at the state of the kitchen! It's getting late!"

I spent a couple of hours today reading about the two hundred years of controversy over the Pentateuch. This has left me in no doubt about the futility of "the best laid plans of mice and men".

Tuesday

Am enclosing the Anglican rag with your newspapers. I don't have much news. Days follow the same pattern at present, hopefully until 12th November, the day of my last exam. After that I may continue the early morning routine in my study, and get down to some creative writing.

The garden is turning a delightful shade of green, mostly weeds. We have prepared that big square bed in the front for hollyhocks and several hundred marigold seedlings. Wolf bought me three fruit trees. I've also planted more coreopsis daisies all over the steps in front of my conservatory, which is a rather ramshackle affair over the front door, which we never use anyway.

It is very good to wake up and hear my heart praying. To remain safe, even through nightmares, which still happen sometimes. I think that is how the Christian life should be. If one maintains a constant attitude of attention one remains recollected. But I think prayer in the spirit, or tongues, may be better. Recollection depends on attention; it can be subject to 'closing down' in the same way that a marriage partner can close down on a relationship, it becomes just a routine and not a living, growing thing.

But the prayer in the spirit – manifestly pure gift, like the Pilgrim's Prayer[27] – is constant whatever crisis is going on around it. I know the Lord will eventually grant me this sort of prayer, because he wouldn't give me a desire for it if it wasn't for me, and I'm no good to anyone until I can cope with my errant self.

I'm so looking forward to seeing you again. Though sometimes I think I am freer with you in writing than face to face. Your gladsome presence (how on earth does one describe it?) makes me feel like an alley cat who has been visited by a Persian.

Lunch time, yippee – off swimming. Bye bye. The Lord be with you.

Thursday

Just got home. I am contemplating my garden, which is soaking up water from the illegal[28] sprinkler. This business of study is having some odd side-effects, and I'm not sure if I like it. It fires up my imagination. When I was a kid I used to lie in bed awake for hours planning the house I would build for my parents – right down to the paper knife in the desk drawer. Now I find myself doing it all over again, but with this place, as if it were mine. Maybe it is part of 'the book', which is gradually forming itself in the back of my mind.

27. An ancient Christian mantra.
28. Water restrictions were in place.

How I fear fantasy – its voracious appetite. I discovered to my shock lately that I could not remember a single detail about my life between my marriage to Wolf and my first meeting with you – a period of about one-and-a-half-years, immersed in a fantasy world. Elsa has since reminded me that I wrote a book during that time – and I vaguely remember it. The title was 'Shells' and it was about my life at sea.

I feel close to a precipice when trying to recall those times; remembering those days grasping for my lost humanity, then trying to build a pen friendship with you. Our God doesn't allow one to vegetate. Even as I am digesting these latest insights, whilst riding the steeplechase of theology, God backs me odds–on favourite for the next race. I'm more than a bit shaky about the pace.

Although I have fallen *de profundis* into God's providence before, then it was a case of suffering and endurance. For some obscure reason this was easier to accept than all this excitement, and LIFE. Maybe our religion has suffered from an over-emphasis on Calvary, and not enough teaching on the resurrection?

Friday morning

If all of us are to become one in the Body of Christ, we are going to have to get used to all sorts of people, and things and ideas, which get up our noses. Charismatic renewal of the church is wonderful but I cringe when someone is called 'a charismatic'. Probably my linguistic prejudice. Words are one of our great means of communication, and if they are used badly they make things bad. Why do we say 'alcoholic' but we don't name someone with cancer a 'cancerite'? It reduces a person to the sum of their disease.

More directly, on the scene of prejudice (mine, that is) I have recently revised my views on women as priests – which I formerly took a dim view of. The Roman Catholic nuns' protest in Washington made me realise that my view is based entirely on prejudice – a stereotype of some doll at the altar. I remembered my own strife with the Community – the pain of its pigeon-holing me as something distasteful because I am female. I don't know if you are conscious of it, but in times past when I referred to nuns as 'women' and the brethren as 'men' your hair almost visibly stood on end, as if gender should not be mentioned in the same sentence as monks and nuns.

I have noticed that truly holy men and women seem to be both masculine and feminine, without being either emasculated or whatever the equivalent is for women. Sister Angela, for instance, is already a priestly woman.

The article on the poor and the oppressed in the Anglican newspaper is, of course, first-class. We had a lot of that sort of teaching at SACLA. God clearly loves the poor and the oppressed. However, such a doctrine can get skew-whiff. Firstly, it tends to be overlooked that you can't give to the poor and needy if you haven't got anything yourself. There have to be wells and springs of material wealth to which the poor can come, and Jesus did not say that the rich must be abolished. One can over-emphasise the blessedness of poverty. As one who has sincerely tried to surrender my wealth to the service of God, I am convinced that when Jesus sends the rich empty away he is sending them on a journey into selfhood, not banishing them.

As far as oppression is concerned, a good look at any street full of people in the city here shows me that the worst oppressed are white people themselves. Black people are deprived of their human rights, political and educational rights, freedom of movement, but they have somehow retained their humanity. *Ubuntu*[29] has made them more human. They look each other in the eyes, they touch each other, they care about life, about mealipap, about children – their own and ours.

Whites, by comparison, drift along the pavements in their silent, monochrome world, worrying about whether they have enough of this or that, whether people are taking advantage of them, how they could enjoy themselves more. White people think they are invisible on the street. They are embarrassed if you meet their eyes. Not everyone of course, but most.

I'm not sure if I should mention this, because I have never really broached the subject with you before. But I'll risk it! I believe I am understanding something of the ghastly machinery of oppression through my relationship with Wolf. Nobody who has known us for any length of time can fail to see that Wolf has highly developed

---

29. The African principle, variously interpreted, that a person is not a person without people.

powers of manipulation, mostly unconscious, but sometimes deliberate.

Oppression, which feeds on him like a horrible parasite, almost finished me off through the symbiosis of our marriage. Those deadly threads have been severed recently, but only after I had been given grace to understand, admit, and accept that I had been mortally oppressed. Forgiveness takes on a vast new dimension. I am poignantly aware of how mean and bitter my own heart is, compared with that heart on Calvary. I seem to cry a lot lately.

15th October 1979

Dear Alfred,
Oh Joy! It is raining. Big drops, as if it is in earnest. I planted (me and Wilson[30]) five hundred seedlings on Saturday and I'm so tired of watering them.

What a life-saver to get your letter today. Who is hurdle number seven in your bid for the priesthood? I meant to ask in my last letter but I forgot. I couldn't help a twinge of schadenfreude at the thought of you chewing your fingernails for a whole week – the prior forgot to tell you that chapter had agreed, did he? *Ag* shame!

I wrote to the Pickwicks today and sent your love. I'm also getting ideas at warp velocity about a prophetic ministry to the church itself. I am sure the Lord will arrange the proper time for this – probably not soon enough for me! You might bear this in mind.

Compost is very interesting. That Eastern Orthodox bishop, Anthony Bloom, wrote a soliloquy on compost. My gloss on this is that cast-off life feeds new life, that nothing is wasted. How I abhor suburban South Africans' oft-repeated comment about trees, particularly jacarandas – "They make such a mess!"

Tuesday

A little time to breathe amidst the orderly chaos. My boss, Jack Hillman, has taken up prayer. He actually wept when he told Elsa and me about it.

Sometimes I can visualise the infant Wolf give up crying – the glaze that films a child's eyes when fixated in hopelessness, until

---

30. Amy's gardener.

someone comes along to set us free and we can weep again. I used to slam the trapdoor on my feelings of despair – with a drink, or overwork, or even writing. So many of us have been captive to hopelessness. But I am not afraid of pain any more. Now we can give ourselves up as vessels for sifting out the pain of the world. It is true isn't it?

Wednesday night

It's Bridge night and I have the house to myself – catching up on the laundry.

Bonds inevitably weaken with absence; with me it takes about a year. Most separations heal within two years, unless the trauma was unbearably severe at the time. Now I observe myself seeking new means of support since you have been gone for so long. The church fathers were wise in assigning only one director to a person. I was tempted to write to +Timothy instead. Until I remembered what the fathers taught about having one director only.

Language changes, rapidly in our time. The words 'sin' and 'grace' in bible language are analogous to 'badness' and 'goodness' in modern terminology. Both 'sin' and 'grace' have acquired the worldly accretions of morality. If the church was listening to the world, instead of throwing up earthworks against it, church leadership would be abreast of contemporary language and could adjust the message so that it made sense to people today. These days one can't go around pronouncing, "Repent, the kingdom of heaven is nigh!" without sounding silly. The vernacular says, "Oh shit! How dreadful! Thank God he's still around".

I am very tempted to go and see +Timothy before I travel to England. He said I could. A year ago I would have leapt at the opportunity, but now I have a sneaking feeling it might just be self-indulgence. I have however arranged to be at a prayer meeting at his house, between his visit to the border and dashing off to Middelburg. I revere him as a true man of God, as you are too of course. +Timothy recognised me in the divine grace of friendship, as you did, when we first met. But there's a worm in all this. I don't believe I should have him as a friend. There are hard things I need to say to him about the church. At the same time I fear it is ridiculous that such a holy man should need any sort of ministry, whether encouragement, prophecy or anything else, except prayer, from anyone like me.

Friday 18th October 1979

It is pouring with steady, soaking rain. Has been all day, so I've just had a kip on the sofa here in the office, instead of my usual swim. A rainy day and an afternoon snooze under a blanket arouses childhood memories.

I remember my father riding his bicycle on his day off, following Trigger and the milk float down our road, bucket slung over the handlebars to scoop up horse manure for our vegetable garden. It was such a posh neighbourhood that no-one recognised him in his overalls.

I leave for the UK on 26th November and hope to visit the mother house sometime between 10th and 21st December.

Tuesday 22nd October 1979

We had three days rain. The garden is vibrantly green, humming to itself and fat with moisture. My first exam is next Friday week. It's a strange feeling to approach an exam quietly, just getting on with the reading, as calmly as getting supper. I think I must be quite bright, because I don't seem to have much trouble with studying now. Maybe everybody is bright if they find out what they are supposed to be doing, and just do it.

Things look hopeful for Zimbabwe/Rhodesia don't they?

18th October 1979, St Luke's Day

Just had a bit of a shaking up. I was searching for a piece of prose I wrote years ago and entrusted to you. Naturally I looked back through those letters which you returned to me, and through my own file marked 'letters not sent to Alfred'. I wonder why I didn't send the latter? Maybe I thought they were too inflammatory? They are, some of them. But the more disturbing matter is, who wrote those letters? Not I, surely? I know I did, but they were definitely penned by a different person from the one I am now. Some hymn is gaily rendered in church about "those in thrall". I think I was in thrall, and it is not good to look back, although I may have to when I begin writing again.

On Tuesday I reclaimed my office book from mothballs. The booklet I have been using for daily bible readings will run out in about three weeks. I feel I am now ready to begin saying the daily offices again. I just couldn't cope with it before. Of course I rediscovered your Christmas card of '77, which I had used as a bookmark. When I first received it I read it often. I think it was the first mail you sent to me. I was a bit disappointed at the time because it didn't say 'to Amy' or 'from Alfred'. But the message was nice – *Love was his meaning*; you'd bought it from the Sisters of the Precious Blood in Lesotho. It puzzled me at the time that someone had coloured the Babe's face black. About a year later I found where the message came from, and copied the holy mother's words on the back in felt-tip pen:

> *Who shewed it thee?*
> *Love.*
> *What shewed he thee?*
> *Love.*
> *Wherefore shewed it he?*
> *For love.*[31]

The card then became even more precious, because my friend had sent me a hidden message. Of course you knew exactly where the words came from. You were just waiting for me to find out.

Monday 29th October 1979, Simon & Jude

I can't remember the last time I sat quietly and listened to Missa Solemnis. I have been revising my notes on the origin of Genesis and the mass. But I'm now idling towards bedtime, and want to share a few moments with you.

I haven't thought much about England yet – not wise to indulge in that before exams are over. However I think the trip will be very good for me. I am already reflecting on the last seven years in South Africa as a chapter in my life, rather than a permanent state of affairs.

Wolf meekly listened to a long sermon from me this evening about people who can't take responsibility for their own lives, but blame all their sorrows on the world, or their parents. They make futile comments such as, "I never asked to be born anyway". He embarked on a counter-attack over my sentimental and pointless complaints about the plight of the poor. It all ended in a hopeless tangle, until I said, "I meant you! You blame everyone else for your misery". He has gone off to visit Nikki, and think about it. He

31. Julian of Norwich.

always listens to what I say, although he spends a lot of energy trying to stop me saying anything worthwhile.

I got the latest Community journal today, and glanced through it. You know I find it a very intimidating publication? Maybe it's like the Old Testament, you have to study it in depth, and know about its origins before you can like it? I noticed a few heavy hints about subscription dues. I'm still a bit peeved that they've never included me in the new companions column, and they still get my address wrong. If you have survived in that bleak sort of atmosphere since you were thirty, you must be a saint. It sounds more like the Atlantic whaling industry than fishing with St Peter. 'Scuse. I'm sniffing fascism round every corner these days. People are astonished. The slightest hint of emotional blackmail or surreptitious tinkering and I explode in a shower of sparks.

I am also reminded somewhat sharply by the journal that if my quarterly report to my warden hasn't yet been received it is overdue. There's a cricket in the fireplace singing along with Beethoven. Isn't that nice?

31st October 1979

Dear Alfred,
Wednesday evening, and my work for the Old Testament exam on Friday is done. How amazing! I have the day off tomorrow for revision. Exams have never been so pacific. My mind, long atrophied, is flexing its little grey cells.

Our landlady called in today, and left three flowering barberton daisies on the back steps. I came home from work to find them here. She is a lady of Scottish descent. She has grown about four hundred of these plants from seed, which is apparently very difficult, and offered them for sale. But no-one would give her the asking price. Such a generous gift is proportionate to three sapling oaks from Petunia. Our landlady has been poorly lately.

My garden gives me such pleasure. It is transformed since you were last here. Velvet lawns dip to the fragrant syringa trees. Platoons of irises march beneath the jacaranda. Star jasmine perfumes the verandah.

Johanna, our maid, got into hot water on Saturday because she ripped up a vine growing beside the back steps, "…because it was in the road," as she explained. I had a Petunia-style conniption: "This is not a ★★★★★★ road! It's a garden!"

I made her replant it and water it all morning. We pray together, Johanna and I, which makes such contretemps possible. I once celebrated communion with her in the oratory, because I missed church. She is Apostolic Faith so she trembles and yells a lot when she prays.

We are celebrating our patronal festival at St Mark's tomorrow. The new dean is preaching. I look forward to getting to know him better. He looked on, open-mouthed, as I read the riot act to someone at the bishop's bible study when we were having tea and should have been making polite conversation. I noticed +Timothy in the background, with that composed cheshire cat look that you get sometimes when someone else says something you would like to say, but can't.

Saturday 3rd November 1979, 16h30

My exam went well yesterday. I enjoyed it. Wolf didn't think to wish me well, and that triggered nasty memories. Now I've fallen into post-exam hyperactivity, which will inevitably end in collapse. As I've got another exam on the 12th I had better try to calm myself down. I could do a doctorate in behavioural science without opening a book – my psyche has been so thoroughly ploughed over these past couple of years. Now I can observe myself without indulging that morbid flea-picking obsession which must constantly analyse its own motives. Undeniable fact is, I don't know why I do things. It's all a mystery.

My drinking is the real enigma. Every now and again I get some new insight, but only when it is over will I understand. It has taught me so much about powerlessness, fear, and helplessness – this must be why it is written that the children of God can eat poison and be bitten by snakes and not be harmed. I fight a constant rearguard action against the judgement, condemnation and contempt I feel from the church – even if it's not real. Out of this maelstrom I plead for healing and forgiveness.

I think a lot of so-called sensitive people just have a very low pain threshold, and either split off, or break down, especially in response to events which recall former distress. The truly sensitive person is one who can process all situations into the creativity of life – either into intercession, or ministry, or in the case of destructive distress, into "completing the sufferings of Christ in the body". I am so easily tempted into self-condemnation, or feelings of having let God down, because I sin all the time. I want to be a hero of the faith, and ride a white horse, and hear the Lord say, "Well done".

The garden is going wild. It really is a garden this year. It looks as if it's been here for decades. The way things have multiplied amazes me. Next week, Wilson and I have got about a ton of compost to dig in. Wait 'til it gets its teeth into that! The veggie garden is also offering up good things faster than I can cook. I think I've got the trick of it now. You just keep planting all year, and piling on compost, and the garden manages itself. It seeds itself, feeds us, and the chickens – and friends if they're lucky, and provides compost for the next season. The garden is making me reconsider the mass production/consumption process which focusses only on product and price.

In point of fact you cannot treat a garden as purely functional. Witness the people who chop down trees because they soak up all the water, forgetting how much water their shade saves. Nor can you be effective in avoiding waste if your life principle is not almost irresponsibly 'wasteful' from a utilitarian point of view.

I mean, if I didn't have 'Phina and Simon living in the servants' quarters, and if I didn't have all sorts of domestic animals, and poultry, and a garden teeming with insects and bees, and trees and flowering plants – all from the economic point of view useless to me – I would in fact waste far more than I do. Even the washing machine waters the creeper.

Nor can I abide using poisons in the garden. If you have enough, planted in the right place, there is enough for everyone, even the aphids. The ants milk the aphids, and the hoopoe eats the ants. What a joy to have hoopoes – what a joy for Sam unfortunately, but it's all in the game. When my community is established we will also keep bees.

It is a sin to treat a garden purely functionally – as bad as using a person for what you can get out of them. A garden has its own way of life, operating under the same fundamental laws, but by different principles. If one doesn't humbly respect them, and be willingly taught by the garden itself, one ends up with an exercise in aridity.

For instance, last year, when the garden was new, I hovered over every plant in an excess of maternalism. Consequently I lost quite a few good shrubs because I couldn't bear to cut them down when they transplanted badly, or got sick. I freaked out when that toxic parasite, dodder, struck. In panic I rooted out plants which I could have just pruned.

I do want to feel that this place is my permanent home. Really it shouldn't make any difference, should it? You taught me that, by renovating Nazareth House although it was only a rented property. One cares for every place as if it is one's own — as everything is, for a time.

Wolf wishes me to politely ask you "Where's his stamps? His patience is almost at an end."

I suppose I had better go to bed. Thank you for being there — yes even there. I am happy about you being at Pedregoso now. Especially as you are wielding a pick-axe, swimming, having enough time for prayer, gardening, together with children, even in the middle of a war. I'm sorry to hear about the deaths on the border and the Umtali district. Yes, thanks for being there because you are the only person who could help wind me down after this over-active day.

I'm very happy about your call to the priesthood. It has sort of harmonised a discord. You are, and have been, a priest after the order of Melchizedech all along. I am sure that if you are called to the priesthood all you have undertaken in the past is in that context.

Wednesday

This will probably turn out to be an old-style 'let's-sob-on-Uncle-A's-shoulder' type letter. But do not despair, it's only a temporary crack in the fabric. My world caved in today… just too much pressure. It's amazing how the wolves know to move in when one's exhausted. In the normal way one has a bit of reserve to deal with them, but they sense it when nothing is left. Maybe I owe this breakdown partly to the creative buzz I am in. I was up in the night composing an audio drama which involves five people and is called 'The Generation Gap'.

During the retreat I was turning somersaults to avoid the prospect of 'opening up' those parts of my life which I had so completely repressed. Catching a glimpse of the pain, even out of the corner of my eye, made me burrow out of sight like a crab into sand. Now a brave new world beams upon this ghost crab who pans the unknown with the antennae of faith. Its faculties of discernment are not tuned in yet, which means quite a few collapses, like today. Thank God there is no pain − at least not the tearing, demonic pain I used to feel. It is good pain and there is no despair in it. Do you know what I mean?

Your lack of confidence, which you write about, is very enlightening. I thought that the painful times of silence you sometimes subjected me to came from God, but now it seems to have been a result of your extreme delicacy and reticence. As it happens, those misunderstandings taught me things which had never crossed my horizon before − such as patience and forbearance. So the misunderstandings turn out to be one gorgeous romp of human error, with God calling the tune. God gets forgiven, because it wasn't him after all. You get loved even more, and shamelessly, because you are human after all. And I get mightily blessed because of the whole drama.

I spoke to Mum, and Dad on the phone today − illegally, on the system. Daddy sounds blooming and Anna's on top form, preparing for her eldest's visit to England. I suppose I'd better start getting my rags together. It's going to be so cold, *brrr*. Wolf is suddenly waking up to the stark horror of having to fend for himself for five weeks. The awfulness of it came home to him on Saturday when he was persuaded to do the laundry, as a trial run.

I could do with an hour of Alfred's company now. My leonine confidence about going to England has evaporated, and I'm not sure if I want to go after all. Still, if I write it down I seem to grow out of it quicker. The exam went well yesterday − not well enough to make me swell-headed, but okay. Wolf took me out for a Chinese meal to celebrate. He is still bleating about the stamps you promised him. We have decided to take you out for a Chinese meal when you visit again − "yoo vill eat wiz chopstix, ja?"

Saturday before D-Day

There's a whopper of a thunderstorm going on outside, and I've got Pauli on my lap. She's having a nervous breakdown − going into spasms and yawning. I never realised how terrified she is during storms. Reminds me of the nights when my mother sent me back to my room when I appeared quaking at her bedside, back on the long, dark, terrifying journey to my own bed − back to the Cyclops, to giants, to the morphing nightmares I had fled from. According to Frank Lake, there is no way any human (or animal) can escape trauma in their life. The variable factor is how much love and care is available to survive it.

Spatz is in a jealous heap under my foot, pretending to sleep through the storm. Mohican is on the armrest, anxiously petting his beloved Pauli, who is too beside herself to care. Sam is snoozing in the reflection of the lightning – Ms Cool herself. We were supposed to go to a braai tonight but it is, fortunately, impossible in this weather. I would rather… oh dear! Apparently it's not impossible. Wolf has just arrived to say that the incorrigible little dears are defying the storm and braaing in their garage. Goodbye.

Thursday evening

I've been contemplating the startling notion that creation is in humankind's stewardship and offers itself for our well-being. So I don't just yank out a lettuce and cuss because it has been nibbled around the edges by slugs. Its root goes to the compost, outer leaves to the chickens, the rest I prepare for our table and we are grateful for lettuces. Early this morning I was thinking about an omelette for breakfast. When I looked outside the lawn was spread with mushrooms. Ah! Mushroom omelette!

I like Huxley's ideas on self-sufficient communities. But I prefer to think of them as a refuge, a place of shade, a rock for the neighbourhood – not as a special or exclusive enclave. For me it would be proper to have no identity apart from 'Christian'. Just a normal household of three or four families; a street number; a steel and carpentry shop; a study and library; a brewery under the water tower; a dam to swim in; and a little nursery, vegetable garden, and orchard.

Ruth could teach kindergarten, and give guitar lessons. Simon and 'Phina could be caretakers. I would write stories to earn money. We would have to build a second house of course, so that everyone has their own place to be alone in. We could look after children in the mornings, and they could instruct their parents at night.

~54~

19th November 1979

Dear Alfred,

I'm awfully sorry about the state of my letters lately. I've just re-read the last scruffy epistle. Yuk! I will try and make this one tidy – at least on the first page, before my writing deteriorates.

Stains on the other letters are not tears. I cart all my stuff around in a bag together with a little bottle of milk for tea at the office, which gets condensation on the outside (I've never understood how that works), which drips all over my papers.

I didn't go to visit +Timothy after all. I'm very glad I didn't. It was unnecessary. It really would be stupid to imagine that the Lord ministers through personalities, rather than through the church. Okay, a year ago I might have believed I had a message to give him. But it would be going backwards if I believed that now.

Vast areas of the world, and the church, suffer because of the reticence of spiritual people. I suppose I must learn to discern the difference between my need for companionship, and the need of the world around me for the gifts I am custodian of. Not that easy, is it? These matters are so subtle. I have a desire to talk, be in companionship with people who know the Lord – who doesn't want that? But it is not possible. Under the circumstances it looks as if I should retire into splendid isolation – but that is not allowed either. I am, after all, married.

Anna and Ruth are taking me to Lee Abbey for a week from 3rd December. Also, I am strongly urged to tear myself away from Daddy's household to join Anna's prayer group on 28th November. It looks as if I will have a good spiritual springclean keeping up with those two.

I was at Holyrood yesterday for mass. Petunia wasn't there. But she's left her mark on the garden – your favourite 'round hovel' (rondavel) is buried in coreopsis daisies. I stayed for breakfast after mass, and had a chat with Sister Clare. She was talking with serene common sense about how a person is tried (like Abraham) in the moment when no-one, not even God, needs them. She also says she observes an improvement in our mutual friend Wolf – softer, not so angry.

I must try to see Frederick before I go to England. I've had enough of preparations now – I just want to be gone. I also want to get down to writing – to forget about endless meals, and cats and dogs, and other people's stupid brochures, and shadow-boxing with Wolf's neuroses. I will return on New Year's Day to enjoy my life here again. But it will be good to get away. I have sort of begun writing – only a couple of sides, but I am hopeful. Trouble is, a book takes over one's life while it is in the making, and there are too many other claims on my time at the moment.

I talk in such riddles. I think it will be a good thing if I get down to my book and clothe it all in a story. Then if anyone bothers to read it to the end they will understand, and I can stop trying to explain myself.

Tuesday

The Grapes of Wrath have moved in next door. A family, with 250 tumbler pigeons, and umpteen children. Wolf has given up trying to count them as they go in and out. The husband has got long grey hair and anxious, honest eyes, like a gun dog. He lets the family drama roll over him unnoticed while he tends his beloved pigeons in the back yard. The family seem to have been shipwrecked often, and lost a few lives in the process. Yesterday I found a gift shyly dumped beside our veggie patch – three-and-a-half sacks of pigeon poo.

Marie has moved into a veritable palace over the road. She is quite slim now. She walks and talks almost normally – goes to the hairdresser regularly too. I wish her church would thank God for the healing in her. I suppose most of us make a habit of grabbing God's gifts and running off without so much as a thank you. But Marie knows who to thank.

24th November 1979

Dear Alfred,

An hour or so of absolute calm in the midst of winding up my affairs. What a cleansing process it is – clearing the office desk, making arrangements for the house and garden, making everything independent of me.

Your generous gift of stamps was a Wow! Wolf was quite shaken. It took him all of ten minutes to recover himself and say, "Write to him. Say… say he can send more". He was truly overwhelmed, and kept pouncing on ones he had already been looking out for – thrilled with the Rhodesian set and quite awestruck with the old New Zealand ones. Several of the British stamps were ones he needed to complete a collection.

His lordship was also most impressed by your zeal in actually going to the post office to buy stamps, and would give his eye-teeth (not that I suppose you would want them) for first-day covers. I can research the possibilities of sending Rhodesian dollars to you when I get back, but if anything is issued in the meantime, and you have the available capital – pleez.

Tonight we are off to the SATA Christmas party, at the President Hotel, no less. I have hacked off my 1972 evening dress to the required cocktail length, and will appear wrapped in furs (it's cold now) and a Mark Anthony hairstyle. I've always contrived to be ahead of fashion with my second-hand clothes. Did I ever tell you about the grey maxi-coat that got me followed by the Stasi in East Berlin?

Last night Wolf took me out to supper and to a film. If you ever get the chance to see The Deerhunter, please do. It is a revolution. Such intense human dilemma expressed on celluloid. I didn't know it was possible to portray interior struggle so visually.

Thank you for your letter. The postmistress always has a big, secretive smile when there's a letter from Zimbabwe/Rhodesia. She makes a point of handing me the bills first. When that whopper letter arrived she looked like Father Christmas. Thank you. There were many good things in it, which have made me happier about going to England.

Your advice had the effect of re-orientating me to the Lord's ministry through me. It is easy to get carried away with one's own ideas about how to relieve suffering, forgetting God's wisdom on the matter. To rush out and 'save' people in one's own way. People who experience the pain of compassion are tempted to do this, I think.

As for my 'pin-up', the Superior, who has just slapped me down as soundly, if not as violently, as he did you; he loves the brethren to bits and feels intensely protective towards the older ones, who fear the winds of change may blow away their life's work. I wrote to him the same evening as I spoke to you, and laid my continued existence in the fraternity on the line – a sort of throwing down of the gauntlet. He must acknowledge me, friend or foe, with my ideas about the fraternity. I had a vision of myself camped once again before the castle gates. Last time the drawbridge came down and I was welcomed in. This time round, I am not at all sure whether I will be welcome at the mother house.

You ask about my ideas about community. Community life is normal for Christians. If one hungers and thirsts for fellowship, to share what one has at every level of life, it is the only way. Formal communities are the vestigial remains of what was once the norm, when the Spirit reigned.

Because our society is hostile to such a lifestyle, disciplinary measures became necessary to maintain it. However, with the free outpouring of the Spirit in the world today, such communities are spontaneously emerging. They must guard against factionalism, as did the early church. Soon, hopefully, they will exist in every neighbourhood – for the sake of the neighbourhood.

You have, in a very real sense, given birth to me, and other people like me, who will continue where you leave off. A common *snafu* between parents and children is that a parent wants a child to have everything he/she didn't have – but the child wants something else. So the parent accuses the child of arrogance, selfishness etc. The over-protective parent is then rejected by the self-determining spirit of the growing child. Times change. The next generation will dare, where the last one couldn't. So it is with the growth of communities.

Only if we take proper account of time and history, and our place in them, as powerful determining forces, can we relax and watch our children grow as they will, with the wisdom of liberated people. We know we are loved. Not for what we could have done or been; just loved. And it doesn't really matter what history will record. We are at the right time in the right place, adding the odd detail to the umpteen million-year-old painting. This gives strength to hope, and watch God working in the history of salvation. It makes it possible to be satisfied with one's own place in that history, because one can only act one part on that great stage.

This screed is really saying be comforted, even if you are stuck in the Community, as it is, for the rest of your life. Because your training and third-degree within the Community has paved the way for the next episode, which could be something very like what you visualise as authentic Christian community life. Building foundations can be gruelling work, especially when one may never see the completed structure. But it is the foundation that gets the honour. You have the prophetic insight to see how things could be. This probably causes you a lot of pain, because things are not already so. But I believe your pain is part of the creative effort which is building the renewal of community life.

All this illustrates the mechanics of growth *à la* St John of the Cross, doesn't it? Being prepared to ditch one's coveted plans, visions, even spiritual growth, for the unknown God, for the darkness of faith, for the joyful humiliation of being poor and helpless but sustained by God. You have that freedom, and you have given it to me. To be honest I am not even saddened, although I feel for you that you are in travail over the prevailing conditions in the Community, because I know that the kingdom is built out of such yearning and pain.

I am holding forth aren't I? It's lucky I'm not a novice. I'd probably be clapped in irons and thrown in the dungeon on bread and water, for spiritual pride

My community is difficult to describe because it doesn't exist yet. Basically what I visualise is a natural growth of what is already here. I don't like being pigeon-holed – it constricts growth. People have pre-conceived ideas (prejudice) about every one of their precious stereotypes, which makes it impossible for them to really get to know anyone.

I think the kingdom doesn't have to be built or created, it just has to be uncovered. For instance, the Grapes of Wrath next door have just been over – nearly all of them I think, in the rain, and have carted off armfuls of plants. They want to make a garden. "*Oaw*, I loves flowers!" So really what is happening is that the garden given to me by God, through his little saint Petunia, is now spilling into next door. God's grace is at work over the road in Marie's house, and creeping into the respectable hell of this neighbourhood.

Our care for the Grapes of Wrath and for Marie has been noticed by our churchwarden, who in an extraordinarily out-of-respectable-character outburst denounced his back-biting fellow parishioners as heathen and said he wished he could be more like Mary, June and me, and be friends with God.

The community is already here in essence. Practical details are slowly coming into being as we obey the nudges of grace. It is entirely organic – it has no walls, boundaries, rules or titles. As soon as something like this is named, given a constitution or rule, it withers. As soon as God was named, he was appropriated, and church law brought death. God is one. There is nothing apart from God because anything alienated from the divine and its revelation in creation doesn't exist — it is lies, hell, death, limbo. Therefore the community you wanted to know about is merely a Christian neighbourhood, functioning normally under grace.

Bless you for your letter. Pray that I might move the odd molehill in England. Also for Wolf's continuing awakening. That he may not suffer bad things through being left alone again. May you all rest in the protection of Almighty God — who is somehow powerfully present with you in that gruesome war.

~55~

Friday, In My Father's House, UK

Dear Alfred,
Just got back from Bath, and have a quiet hour or so to share some of the events since I arrived last Monday. Bath hasn't changed – still the same old town clothed in prehistoric, Roman, and Edwardian remains. One forgets how old things are in England. It was drizzling and cold, but by the time I came out of the abbey the sun was shining again, as it has done every day so far. Looked round the abbey and the baths for old times sake. Tasted some of that dreadful spa water.

Yesterday I walked the whole of old Bristol from Broadmead to the top of Park Street, climbed the Thirty Nine Steps as winter sunlight shone on the cobbles, ghosts materialising as I reached each familiar district. There is a liminal place in the old city walls, near the Nails on Corn Street, a stark Norman chapel, like a fox-hole under the ramparts. Something about the way the light falls on ancient flagstones, a stone altar, the stillness of this little bunker amidst the bustle of the city, caught my breath. It is a 'thin' place – where the membrane is flimsy between our world and other dimensions.

Spent a little time in the cathedral. Then wound up at my school-friend Peta's flat, for tea. She's lived in France, delicious food. Same old scene – dog-eared books, second-hand furniture, Dylan, guitars and flutes strewn all over the place, pot plants. Then I went out to Whitchurch by bus, where Ruth is teaching Taizé music to a church orchestra of motley musicians.

Wednesday was my day for mooching around here, where Dad lives. Narrow, steeply pitched lanes. Dry stone walls patched with ferns and moss. A river with ducks on it. The old village armoured with iron crosses to keep the walls up. It's not changed. There are ammonites built into the walls, traces of the cretaceous extinction when sea covered this part of Somerset.

People seem very at ease here, and they talk back. It feels strange to be able to strike up a conversation with anyone – about anything at all. To see feisty old women waving their brollies at bus-conductors without fear or favour. It made me realise how fearful life has become in South Africa.

On Wednesday evening Anna and Ruth took me to their Life in the Spirit seminar. I couldn't hear much because my ears were blocked after the flight (this has since been remedied). I felt helpless in this strange, but familiar, environment. One of the ministries I was invited to share in was deliverance. But this time I went straight to the priest afterwards and he prayed and anointed me with oil, and I felt fine. We prayed for a young Nigerian doctor who was going back home, which was especially significant because he knew I was from apartheid South Africa.

On Tuesday, my first day, Peta dropped everything and flew over to see me – red hair flying in the wind, and armfuls of flowers. She's been in contact daily. Dad and Eirene have a delightful little nest here, and so obviously adore each other one cannot help being happy for the happiness they have found with each other. With a bit of luck we will investigate the local church together on Sunday.

Ruth is plodding on regardless, as usual, and has been adopted, together with her dog, by the local vicar and his family. There is a huge crucifix behind the altar at Ruth's church. Only, it is not the crucified Jesus on the cross but the ascending Lord – arms spread like wings, head flung back in triumph, and in greeting. The church is shared with Methodists – perhaps they cannot cope with a traditional crucifix?

Anna is not happy. She is my only source of worry amongst all these reunions. We leave for Lee Abbey on Monday, and I hope something will happen there to relieve whatever it is that is bugging her.

Wednesday

Lee Abbey is a nineteenth century country house built about three hundred feet above a Devon cove and surrounded by its own estate. It is run by a community of about a hundred, many of whom are young people from other countries. We arrived here on Monday after a memory-lane drive down in Ruth's car. Catching our first glimpse of the sea was like going on holidays when we were little.

When we had settled into our rooms, our hosts asked if we wanted to join the conference. "I don't know. What is it about?" Anna replied doubtfully. "Michael Harper's leading it," they said. "Oh yes!" cried Ruth. "Oh no!" cried Mummy – which was rather confusing. But of course we decided to join in, so once again I am trying to be holy on my holiday.

Ruth and I went riding today up over the moor, trotting along bridle paths through the heather. So warm on horseback in spite of the wind off the Atlantic. Yesterday we went on a cliff walk and nearly got blown off by gale-force winds. But it's not really that cold.

Anna's got her teeth into a few Anglican clergymen and has clearly worked off some of her frustration. She seems much better. The clergymen look a bit worse for wear though. Bit embarrassing, parachuting into a conference like this accompanied by a priest-baiting ex-Anglican.

I'm not feeling very holy at the moment. It's too much. These charismatic conferences have the effect of dismantling me and playing scrabble with the pieces. And my heart is so hard against Anna I could howl. Maybe you have suffered from my pestering as I am suffering from Anna's right now?

Dad is not as well as I thought at first. We had a good relationship going by Sunday, and we did get to the local parish church, which was something of a triumph. But it's a bit distressing how, metaphorically speaking, his bones show through. I think the visit to the church was a bit harrowing for him. They are taking me to London to visit my grandma the weekend after next. I might stay an extra day or so in the Big Smoke and visit your friend Gonville.

Next week I hope I am going to the mother house – if your friends in the village, Jane and Peter Buckingham, will have me to stay for a couple of days. I'm going by train on an army warrant so that'll cost me nix (unless I get arrested). I really must write to the Buckinghams to introduce myself, before I phone and invite myself to stay. I'm not altogether happy about going to the mother house. Only your phone call made me reconsider it after I received the Superior's chastising letter. It will be rather like paddling up the White Nile before Blashford-Snell discovered it.

Jonathan, my brother, seems in imminent danger of becoming the classic British prig. His wife brought him over to see me last Sunday, briefly, so we didn't really have time to get to know each other again. Perhaps it was the shock, because I've never seen him in a three-piece suit, standing up for ladies, flashing a silver cigar case, stalwartly holding forth about the coolies in the rest of the empire. That's what Sandhurst does for you, I suppose. I'm used to him all rumpled, six foot of jeans and tangled hair, roaring out pot-holing songs over tankards of cider – and funny. Ruth and Anna and I are spending Christmas with them. I hope we won't have to spend the day sipping sherry, and avoiding religion and politics.

It's late now, getting on for 11pm. It's dark outside of course, but you can hear the sea, and a tap-tapping from a branch on the window pane. I am curled up on a sofa in front of a log fire in the octagonal lounge. I'm smoking cigarettes, and I've got a flask of coffee beside me. I could go on like this for hours – *yak, yak, yak.* Everyone else has gone to bed. Maybe I'll potter up to the chapel soon. It is on the second floor – low rafters, royal blue velvet curtain hanging at the east end behind the altar – an antique table with a silver cross on it. It is odd that in a conference like this there never seems to be time to pray.

Saturday, Anna's house at Whitchurch

Anna received the laying on of hands for healing at Lee Abbey, from the Harpers, which did her so much good I feel my anxiety was rather shameful – plain lack of faith. Ruth is seriously considering joining that community for a year or so.

I'm sitting on the floor by the gas stove listening to a guitar concerto on one of Ruth's cassettes. The night I wrote to you last, I did go up to the chapel, until just after midnight. Then, on the way to my room, I heard the most exquisite guitar music wafting up the stairwell.

Downstairs, in the octagonal lounge, in semi-darkness, sat a waif from the stockbroker belt. I listened to his playing for one-and-a-half hours – no score, he plays from memory, can't read music. What a gift. This young man said he felt trapped in his prosperous middle-class life, like Petunia was, before she broke out. Maybe he will come to South Africa?

The days at Lee Abbey stoked up my confidence for the mother house. It was such a diverse mixture of churchmanship, but mostly Anglicans, a melange of charismatics and clergy who found it difficult to cope with the very idea of renewal. The sensitive way the community dealt with this potentially flammable mix was a great inspiration to me.

The papers report the warmest fortnight for this time of year for over a century. How I was dreading the cold. This music is bliss. England is beautiful. The Lord God reigns. I am at last looking forward to the coming days.

Leaving tomorrow for the mother house. Super welcome message from the Buckinghams.

With love, and joy on hearing news of Zimbabwe's imminent birth as a free nation.

Amy's train journey to the mother house is uneventful. Walking up the lane past limestone houses with front gardens clad in heather and miniature conifers she sees nobody. Only the village pond displays signs of life, with mallard and moorhen paddling about, rummaging in the water, quarrelling.

Amy raps at the door of a limestone cottage fronted by crazy paving and delicate alpine plantings. There is a goldfish pond and a sundial. Amy feels at home already. Jane answers the door and makes her welcome. Soon the children come home from school and Peter arrives from his office in town. They are a knockabout, friendly crew. Amy settles into a room which one of the children has vacated for her use. At the dinner table it soon becomes clear that Alfred is the hot topic of conversation.

Amy feels both embarrassed and proud to find herself as chief witness. They want to know how Alfred is, what he looks like now, what he's doing in Rhodesia, how he is *really*. She feels embarrassingly coupled with her guru. She would prefer to maintain a more discreet reserve on the subject of Alfred. But clearly his parsimonious habits with letter-writing extend to his friends also, for they are starved of news. Uncomfortable, but yearning to talk of the beloved monk she embarks on a lengthy story of the adventures of Alfred. She basks in their shining eyes, the laughter of her audience, the unaccustomed fluency of her narrative.

The next morning, when the family has departed for the day, she lets herself out of the house with a spare key and follows the pencil map Peter has given her of the route to the mother house.

§

Once a stately home, now with the addition of a large church, Alfred's community headquarters is imposing indeed. Amy consciously squares her shoulders as she tramps up the drive past gnarled mossy trees which seem as old as Methuselah.

Lester, now a novice clad in black cassock and scapular, has been appointed to host her visit. She is glad to see a familiar face. Awestruck by the sheer size of the place, she does her best to maintain custody of the eyes, to not gawk as she is led through a vast foyer with a broad staircase leading upward to hallowed realms. Somewhere behind these panelled walls the Superior is at his desk.

The church too is huge, austere. She treads reverently through its dim spaces. Many small chapels nestle alongside the nave, where priests used to say their own mass in the old days, as Lester informs her. Several priceless icons are displayed in the church, which he includes in his comprehensive tour. One of them came from Russia before the revolution.

Later he takes her outdoors into the grounds where a wintry sun conjures diamanté droplets on webs of bare boughs, where mists gather over lawns and arbours. Red squirrels still survive here. An amphitheatre is quarried out of a small hill – for concerts in summer, explains Lester.

§

The following day when Amy returns to the mother house she is permitted to meet Fr Oswald, Alfred's brother in the Community and close friend, who has also been touched by the charismatic renewal. Oswald is as keen as the Buckinghams to hear news of Alfred, enquiring of her, with disarming affect, how his old friend is. She cannot help disclosing something of Alfred's anxiety about the Community. Oswald listens with owlish eyes, and nods. He takes her hand in his, patting it, and asks if she would like to come to a seminar with him at the local parish church that evening. She is of course delighted to accept, charmed by this disarming priest.

§

Friday, on a train

Dear Alfred,
So I did get to the mother house after all. I arrived late afternoon Tuesday and am now on my way back. The experience is still too fresh for me to decide about it one way or the other. The very evening I arrived, Peter phoned the main house and organised a meeting for me with Oswald. I know already that the trip was valuable – not

least because Oswald has asked me to write him a more definitive account of what direction I think the Community should be moving in – re my article. Oh dear. Let me try and get some organisation into this letter.

First of all, the Buckingham family. How warm and welcoming they are – how they all adore you. Loving greetings all round. Young Sarah curled up and giggled when I told her you would probably be desolate if she didn't send you her fondest and best love. The family have acquired a golden retriever – or rather the retriever has acquired the family. It digs up the garden and chews the household with joyful impunity. Name, Rufus – it is that sort of colour. Jane is of course bliss, as you described her. I love Johanna most, and Sarah is a bundle of fun – exhausting actually. I had a basinful of Peter's rather heavy-going humour, gave up laughing at it, and came to like him a lot. The train is moving off now so I'd better pack this up, or it will be illegible.

Later

No, I'll continue writing – you'll just have to decipher.

Oswald gave me a thorough interrogation, after I told him you had asked me to spill the beans about the Community. He was thereafter very open, and disarmingly free with his opinions. Dominic joined us for a while, and so did Fr Frank, who is here on furlough, as you know. He walked three-and-a-half miles this week and looks very fit. He misses the sun and South Africa and the children, but he feels he is more useful to that part of the world he loves most now he is here. Dominic, of course, is so holy he practically floats. It is no use, is it, trying to explain an encounter like that? Suffice it to say that Oswald trusted me, and that means more to me than I can possibly explain. Clearly, he loves you dearly, and misses you still, and, I think, longs for a source of warmth and affection in that rather dour place. He phoned Peter and asked if I could stay an extra night, to hear a rather remarkable doctor speak at the parish church, about his new book, *Healing the Family Tree*. Unfortunately, after the book launch, Oswald got rather carried away and asked me to address the congregation.

In spite of the embarrassment to the audience, this turned out to be very useful for me, because I suddenly realised why I am so afraid of addressing gatherings of church people. My last memory of church life, before I left England, is of my father being rudely assaulted by an irate parishioner, after a sermon which the man took umbrage at.

I asked during my three-minute, rather garbled address, how many people knew Brother Alfred, and about a third of the congregation put its hands up. Ivy sends her regards (tearful, I might add); so do Kathleen and Joyce. I flashed a few snaps of you and Seraphim around, and one of you on holiday – and I'm afraid they've nicked 'em.

21.30pm, back at Dad's house

They've gone out and left me with the run of the fridge, which I've just munched my way through. I seem to have been travelling during meal-times over the last few days. I've also helped myself to a fat whisky from Dad's special bottle to round off supper. Marvellous.

The Buckingham family did me good. I was afraid to even sneeze in my own father's house, 'til I saw how that rumbustious lot behave. Lester nearly passed out when I went to say hallo to him at teatime on the second day. He and a mob of other novices had been sitting behind me in the refectory discussing who the 'harpy' was. He spent two-and-a-half hours on my first day showing me round the grounds and the various establishments of the mother house. I think he is happier than he used to be. I didn't attempt to see the Superior. It would have been bad taste to clamour for his attention. He would of course have known that I was there, and I think not bothering him was an eloquent gesture of friendship.

I've just phoned Peter to confess that I've walked off with his back-door key. I dunno. I think I've made a friend, and suddenly I find I'm talking to a granite cliff. Peter seems to have a built-in filter for "that sort of thing". English people seem so much more reserved than South Africans.

Oswald was interested to know if your departure to Rhodesia was a trial for me. I said it was timely, also that you are settled now, in Pedregoso. Most people wanted to know if you are happy, and I told them you are. Writing this sounds as if I introduced myself as Brother Alfred's protégée – but actually I didn't, not on purpose anyway. Peter began it with that telephone call to Oswald, saying Alfred's girl was here, and the ball never stopped rolling from there.

Lester gave me Harry Williams' *The Best is Yet to Be*, and *The True Wilderness*, which I've been looking through on the train. The former is something of a bombshell, isn't it? I feel like a cactus transplanted into leaf mould after encountering your Community in the flesh. I can understand how people can feel glutted on the sheer richness of living community life.

Oswald took me into the church, to the high altar, for a few minutes quiet prayer. This was after the book launch, and just before compline. If you get the chance, thank him for that, will you? I never really expected to be invited in. I had the feeling I might be hidden behind sofas. But to be taken to the heart of things, to the high altar of the mother house! I am still just a cactus – this soil is too rich for me.

By the way, the reason The Airedale[32] is out of bounds for the brethren is because somebody in the village made snide remarks about the monks' Sunday binge – about two years ago now. So all the brethren are suffering a ban on having a pint at the local on Sundays because of a couple of mean-spirited gossips. The villagers really miss them, Peter says.

Sunday, Winchmore Hill, London

Gonville has got an ordination retreat on – he seems to think that is more important than seeing me! I'm at my grandmother's house now. We drove up yesterday. I'll be off to St Kit's[33] tomorrow.

Went to church here in London this morning with grandma, aunt, Dad and Eirene. Laid to rest a stillborn child of our family who never had a funeral. I learned how to do that from the book launch of *Healing the Family Tree*. This child was lost circa twenty years before I was born. I am waiting to see what effect this healing prayer will have on the various ailments which plague our family.

Interesting man, Dr Kenneth McCall, who wrote the book. Apparently, after +Anselm, your brother bishop in the Caribbean, held a mass of the resurrrection for the souls of the slaves who were thrown overboard during the slave trade, mysterious shipping disappearances in the Bermuda Triangle stopped altogether for a while.

These past three weeks have carried me along on a wave of prayer. Peace within, and around me – as palpable as the rock of salvation.

32. The local pub near the mother house.
33. The Community's London house.

I have never been as aware of, and secure in, the prayers of other people as I am now. It's like those effortless flying dreams.

Tuesday, back at Mum's place

Whew! A moment to breathe before Jonathan arrives. I keep meaning to send this, but more news comes up all the time, and I want to include it. I went to St Kit's in London yesterday – short pause for effect – and met David. I thought people like that died out with the angels. I was not expected there so only got a couple of minutes with him and should have been on my way. But the Holy Spirit had other things up her sleeve.

I went to pray in the chapel there – I want to tell you this like it was – because I was disappointed that I didn't have more time with David. I was resting in the peace of the spirit, which I'm getting used to now – it's like mother's milk – when a gentle voice spoke my name. I thought it was an angel. Eventually I dared to look up and there was Gabriel himself inviting me to lunch because some guest hadn't turned up and there was room. What's more, the charming old gentleman who had booked David's time until 3pm bowed out, as a Christmas present to me. So after lunch I got an hour with him.

We went upstairs to the prior's pad, the *sanctum sanctorum*, which was very comfortable, and talked about you and the Community and the mother house. I heard from David that your friend Ronnie is beside himself with grief because you haven't written. Everyone has assured him that your inimitable ways of communicating with people are just not cut out for letters – and that you pray for everyone anyway. But he is not comforted.

This morning should have been restful. But Elsa phoned at 6.30am (I didn't get home until 1.15am) to tell me I passed biblical studies, only just, with fifty-eight per cent. I was so sleepy I thought I dreamt it.

Chat to Anna – long chat to Ruth. Then the next-door neighbour arrived for coffee. She's an epileptic whom Ruth had to drive to hospital on Sunday. Delivered some books to Ruth's pensioner friend, Terry. Phone calls – now Jonathan is about to pounce – and three dates to choose from this evening. Never knew life could be so busy.

I got your letter this morning. I knew, somehow, that you would be going back to the mother house, and am happy to know that

Oswald will see you. He needs your company – and so does David. If it is their idea to have a house for the renewed brethren, I can understand that.

Thursday

Right! I am about to finish this letter, or it will never get posted. I spent the day with my brother yesterday. I feel as if I've been done over with a blowtorch… scorched earth! But I was getting too big for my boots. I was beginning to think I was a big deal with all these marvellous things happening, and a patch of sunshine following me around Britain like a trusty dog – truly, marvellous weather wherever I go.

Friday

Ruth and I are off Christmas shopping in Bristol. Going to St Mary Redcliffe with Anna on Sunday – hope to lay a few ghosts. And make a space for the divine in that den which should be God's house.[34]

I think of you often and sincerely hope you have a peaceful Christmas and New Year (and birthday). There is a present in the pipeline, but it may take some time to reach you. The family has been alerted and is ready to receive you whenever you choose to appear in England. Don't hesitate to contact Anna and Ruth. I am sure they will move mountains for a chance to meet with you.

There is an extraordinary wellspring of love for you in the Community. I hope it won't go into hiding when the beautiful brother himself appears.

34. John Betjeman made some pungent remarks about St Mary Redcliffe.

~57~

Christmas in the UK is a mixed blessing for Amy. Pain accompanies the celebrations because she can only be at any one time with one parent and not with the other. Christmastime had been idyllic at the vicarage. She remembers the sheer magic of a bough of the old yew tree transformed overnight into a Christmas tree, glistening with tinsel and coloured glass balls, gaily-wrapped parcels beneath it. Once there was even a bicycle under there with her name on it. She recalls a midnight mass full of people in party clothes, the drunk who came in and wandered down the nave during her father's sermon, smoking a cigarette. How her father gracefully shook hands with him.

This season is so different now the family is divided, now her life is in another hemisphere. But the wintry cold and the bustle in Broadmead make her smile for Christmases past. A Salvation Army busker looks her in the eye and says, "You look 'appy; 'ave yer finished yer Christmas shopping?"

On Christmas day Ruth, Anna and Amy go to Chepstow, to Jonathan and Liz. The sun at midday is heavily masked in cloud, ephemeral as a full moon. Liz stays in the kitchen rebuffing all assistance with her first Christmas dinner as a married woman. Anna keeps up a commentary on the wrinkles of successful entertaining. Amy tucks into the sherry.

§

3rd January 1980, Albion

Dear Alfred,
Things really moved into top gear after the last epistle. Ten days of family gatherings, reunions, turkey and Christmas pudding. Jonathan and Liz gave us the nine Beethoven symphonies for a Christmas present.

The flight back on New Year's Eve was magnificent. I was swathed in nostalgia, glued to the porthole watching the great lighted cities of Europe and the Med slip by. Athens exploded into fireworks at midnight their time. In fact we had three midnights, all with drinks compliments of the captain.

Then home to a summer garden – house spick-and-span with Johanna slaving over the ironing. Presents – Wolf has bought me four of Mozart's violin concertos. Somewhat overshadowed by Jonathan's *grande geste.*

I'm not into letter writing yet. Too sad to have left the beautiful people, and too aware of my inadequacy in being a loving wife to Wolf, who was most impressed with your card. He got lots of letters over Christmas. More than he's ever had in his life.

There is a lot of nonsense talked about wives and husbands being unable to save each other, but I think this is unscriptural. I think the modern talk has made an extraordinarily difficult work into an impossible work. The truth is that a man or woman is vulnerable before their spouse and therefore faith and love must be exceptionally strong to weather the storms. Oppressive vibes in this household are so clear to me now because I have been away. I am not going to pussyfoot around Wolf, or be afraid of him any more because he is oppressed. We are one flesh in the eyes of the Lord and I see no reason why the Lord cannot deliver him through my presence. Of course we tremble. The devil would throw us off the Himalayas if he could, but Jesus is Lord and his Spirit maintains even the breath of our bodies, so all dominion and power is his.

8th January 1980

Dear Alfred,
Good to hear your voice on the phone. I forgot to ask how long you will be in England but I will alert the family. They are all half-expecting you anyway. I hope you will have time to spend a day or two with them. I'd love you to meet Dad if possible.

As for a stopover in Greece, the man to ask is Lester. He stayed with some very hospitable people whom he hadn't even met before. Also at other places in Europe. I think he got about five stopovers. Then there are the Little Sisters in Mombasa – but I suppose you don't want Africa? I could do some research for places to stay if you let me know when and where.

It would be lovely to see you. Somewhat unlikely though isn't it? Of course you know that our house is yours any time you can make it down.

My trip to England was a breakthrough for me in many ways – one of them is a recovered identity, which I hope to maintain. It is very good to be able to speak freely and relatively coherently to most people. Naturally, I would love you to see how I've grown. It is difficult to comprehend the dimensions of the mental breakdown I've been immersed in during the past ten years or so – without anyone really noticing, except you.

On my last evening in England, whilst praying together with Anna and the couple who drove me to the airport, I saw the light of Christ – or as much of it as I could bear. Purity, or sanity, is somewhere out there for me, and now I have an idea of how it looks I am encouraged to keep up the battle against uncleanness.

Dad, shyly, and at the last minute, so there would be no time for embarrassing thank you scenes, pressed upon me his own crucifix as a gift. It is pewter with a stoup for holy water. "Even more meaningful in a country where water is so precious," he said. It now hangs in the oratory.

We have been showered with gifts for Christmas. I must try to appreciate material things more. It is very ungrateful to be inundated with good things whilst being unhappy about having so much property.

Everything has changed since I got back, and I don't feel able to probe the reasons why. The abiding peace of the Holy Spirit is with me although outwardly depression is lurking in many areas. I seem to be able to endure suicidal despondency, panic, love and grief, without losing the inner knowledge of peace. It is marvellous. One can take risks – even knowing that the price of love is grief. It is the victory of the cross, isn't it?

I will pray for your acceptance into the priesthood. I hope the prospect of presenting yourself at the mother house doesn't intimidate you. It is a very intimidating place, but there was so much joy there from hearing news of Brother Alfred. I think you might seem changed to people who may have opposed you before.

Wednesday

Feeling very well today. Went to confession and mass last night. With very surprising discretion my confessor didn't offer any counsel at all. Wolf fetched me and we walked in the park and watched tadpoles. He is suffering badly with his ulcers at present. I don't know what to do. The doctor says it is nerves. He eats properly and sleeps far too much. He looks very fit and drinks and smokes very little. He has just spent a week running up and down mountains. I am afraid that the constant irritation of these damn ulcers and the tablets he takes will start some growth or other. It is a bit worrying. Will you pray for him to stop resisting the divine will? I have been in the wrong place with Wolf, and have probably done a lot of damage. He is a leader not a follower, and anyway the Lord will reveal himself very differently to Wolf.

This Saturday is garden day. I have about a ton of compost to dig in. I hope his lordship will help me. We've had three inches of rain this week, but today it is fine. Time to start swimming again. Life is brand new and good.

Oh well, I have a vast list of letters which I really must begin. Please let me know more of your movements as of March. I was amazed, impressed, and finally most honoured to receive your marathon letter before I went to England.

9th ~~October~~ January 1980

I can't think why I keep writing October instead of January. It has happened with monotonous regularity all day. I am so sure it is the ninth of October. If I were superstitious I would mark it on the calendar.

I have spent the day writing letters on those useful airmail jobs which limit one to so-and-so much space. It has bridged the painful gap between here and England, without being a burden.

I am sorry for my harsh comments on your friend Peter. Oddly enough it is Harry Williams who has taught me the humility to accept that people are led in various ways to God. If I hadn't learned that I would be desperate about my father, and still be battling with Wolf.

Something came out of that three-minute catastrophe of mine at Oswald's gathering. I remember saying it, if no-one else does – "We are very, very lucky to know God (in the personal way we do). It is a gift." We know so many who serve God in sorrow, and straining, and how can we say they are caught up in works without faith, or insist they must be filled with the Holy Spirit? If there is truth in the doctrine that the sufferings of Christ must be worked out in the Body, then these suffering ones may in fact be in holy dereliction – in dark faith for the sake of the whole world.

How much better would it be if those of us blessed with the holy indwelling Spirit, and the knowledge of her, should be supportive (if agonised) observers of those brothers and sisters who depart this life without her intimate acquaintance? Maybe we should be more humble in our rejoicing, and more particular in our care for them?

As a good catholic, thanks to your guidance, I believe in praying for those who have died. Why therefore should I believe my prayers ineffectual, or my prayers unanswered, for those who die – or those who continue to live – without the knowledge of God? The charismatic movement is marvellous, and I love people in the Spirit, but it is still a gift, and a mandate for alerting the Church in the coming decades of chaos.

I see less and less a sort of martial bringing of people to the Lord, and more and more a permission from God to bring the divine will to humankind. This flows partly from your retreat – also, very much, from my own growing weakness and helplessness regarding God's will in the lives of others.

15th January 1980

Dear Alfred,
Isn't it exciting about Zimbabwe? All the borders being opened and everyone talking about peace! *The Sunday Times* article on Russia by Ginzberg is also very good. We must pray all the time for all southern Africa.

I've taken to baking bread, so you can look forward to that if you come down. I'm also planting vegetables again so we'll have a regular home industry going by then. Wolf has weeded in the garden three times since my return, and done the washing up four times. Though I must admit the latter was partly under duress.

16th January 1980

I can't write any more now. I've already put the newspapers off for a day because I can't find it in me to write. That incredible sadness

I told you about, which used to strike in retreat, is growing day by day. It is like the "all is vanity" passage in Ecclesiastes. It goes on and on, and there seems to be no point in writing, but I must at least explain why my letter to you is so thin on the ground. It is not because I have forgotten you.

21st January 1980

Dear Alfred,

What a lovely letter you wrote. All full of good news and the prospect of England – and very sobering comment on the "holy mysterious" things the Lord is doing in my life. How ungrateful I am. I am still enjoying Harry Williams' *True Wilderness*. I think it is that which has finally precipitated a pretty drastic decision.

I only began thinking seriously about it this morning but everything is falling into place. It looks as if I will resign from SATA on the first of April (I know, April Fools' Day!). I have almost two thousand rand in my pension fund. I will stay at home for ten months living off that money. If I haven't made a go of a novel in that time, I will have made a mistake and will just have to look for another job.

Apart from that, I am going for my major in biblical studies this year. That, together with philosophy should account for three hours study a day. I have a house and garden which are already badly neglected and could do with some attention. Also Wolf is opening up and responding in a totally new way and I feel I ought to spend evenings and weekends with him.

What d'you think? I forgot to add that this job which keeps me away from home for ten hours a day has become very debilitating. Maybe because I ought to be writing and have spent so long trying to squash that obligation? I will ask +Timothy on Friday, and I'll also see Professor Burton who is head of the English Department at Unisa. If anyone can, he can give me an idea of my chances of writing well enough to publish.

It will mean a fairly lean way of life for a while, but I could do with that. Life is to be lived, not eked out with coffee spoons. Tell me what you think. I am full of joy already as if life is beginning all over again.

Of course, one bonus is that I will be home in May when you visit on your way back to Pedregoso after your trip to England. I will need reliable people to talk it over with if I am writing – one gets too introspective if one just writes. So if you don't mind being a guinea pig?

Do you really want to go to the mountains? We can probably just go for a weekend, because Wolf has only got the odd day's leave until August. If you are prepared to go up a mountain on Ascension Day (which seems apt) we could go for four days.

You can stay with us for as long as you like. We will make ourselves comfortable with Beethoven. On Saturday Wolf arrived home with a high-fidelity outfit which will blow your mind. He's sold our other one. This is the best I've ever heard, and I shudder to think what it cost. We listened to the ninth yesterday evening. Wolf read with pleasure Schiller's Ode to Joy, as the great choir sang. I think we will spend a lot of time listening to music now.

What a lot of people you have to visit in England! I am sure that Anna and Ruth will make every effort to see you. There is also a lady in High Wycombe who has been praying for you, who would visit you if I passed the word. But maybe you have enough people to see?

It will be a wonderful trip for you. Four years is long enough to forget – and it is all such a surprise – the friends, the land, the humour, the freedom. I wept over England the day before I left, rather melodramatically shouting "Bless this England!" from the top of a grassy knoll near my mother's house. I have good friends there. I have been so lonely there.

The Lord is bringing so much to my attention. So much anxiety and fear, which I never knew I had in me. My prayer time is mostly resting in a helpless sort of way in God's peace. I am resisting the demands of intercession a lot of the time because it is no good if prayer make one anxious – as if the well-being of the world depended on me. Maybe things would be better if all the world gave up the mad rush and rested a little in the Spirit. I don't know if this is so, but I think so.

Tuesday

I risked phoning Ruth on 'the system' this morning – pity it doesn't work to Pedregoso. She has a week's leave in March and would love to meet you somewhere in UK. I told her about my plans. She was so enthusiastic and even asked me what the book was about – and was pleased.

All I have here is militant opposition on all sides, and the general intimation that I'm a naughty girl not to want to work from eight to four and spend the rest of my waking hours housekeeping.

I did ask Wolf how he would feel if my book was published – proud maybe? His enlightening comment was that they print all sorts of rubbish these days. He rather plaintively asked why I didn't want to do knitting, or crocheting?

Anna has a lovely response to these ghastly setbacks. "Life is full of a number of things," she murmurs, peering with wondering eyes into the middle distance.

24th January 1980

I posted your newspapers today, without a letter, and I can imagine you looking for one, and not finding it. I could at least have written 'Hallo'. I get totally obsessed when I am writing my book; I must try not to abandon everyone.

Did I tell you that I intend writing two chapters for Professor Burton's perusal? Two days have passed, and I have just under four pages written. I must have spent about five profoundly taxing hours on them. I am amazed at how hard it is to write well.

I am also amazed at the demands this book is already making on me. I am subjected to it, already it requires me to remember things I would rather forget, and be honest in ways I never thought about. It makes me insecure, and then deeply satisfied with my life. At bottom, writing again makes me blood-red real! The prospect of giving up my job for it gives me the self-assurance I had in England – when I knew I was here for a reason.

The story is a mystery to me, but that is always so, and it is anchored in the assurance of God's blessing. He gave me the first paragraph at church on Tuesday. It will be the thing that binds everything else together, provided I handle it well; that is to say, that I restrict it to three hours a day, and don't allow the world to revolve around it.

Good that I write this to you. I had forgotten what happened last time I wrote a novel. The fantasy sucked me in until I couldn't tell the difference between fiction and reality. Maybe that is what is happening now? I hope not.

Books are immensely influential because people have a naive faith in the written word. But it is also wide open to misunderstanding (the written word, that is). I think I must be more responsible on the

whole issue, and pray always, before I write. You see, dear Alfred…
your loving kindness to me may have just saved a whole generation
from the unholy influence of a half-baked book.

28th January 1980

Now I'm in a right fix. I've just told everyone I am going to write a book
– and I've got cold feet. The beginnings of all three parts are established,
but I would die if anyone read them – let alone Professor Burton.

I talked with Frederick (Eersterus) yesterday, and I had him on
the edge of his chair whilst telling him the story – but that's very
different from writing it down. If I write two pages a day it is a
lot. And I have all sorts of nightmares about ending up writing a
romance. Oh God. The frightful possibilities are endless.

I saw +Timothy who will be attending a conference in
Grahamstown to discuss the implications of the informal deliverance
ministry which has arisen in the Anglican Church. He will write to
me about it, as he feels unable to give direct guidance now.

Also told +Timothy that you have offered yourself for the
priesthood – I gather that is common knowledge in Johannesburg
now. I hope it wasn't wrong to divulge that?

It was a strange encounter. As usual I took him some eggs and
greens from the garden. He accepted the gift wryly saying, "Do
not muzzle the ox…" for it seems he is now my spiritual director.
To my shame I wept when I told him that I appear to have lost my
connection with you. He replied that it is possible to lose a director
to friendship.

We said evening prayer together in his chapel – including the
Albion siege in our intercessions.[35] The siege was going on as we
prayed together. Those three men who held up the bank would have
suffered hell in custody so perhaps it's as well they got shot. First
blood of the martyrs – *uMkhonto we Siswe*[36] has arrived in South
Africa. When I got home the ambulances were humming on a
conveyor belt down our road. I hate sirens.

35. At the time of Amy's meeting with +Timothy, a suicide mission of the armed
wing of the ANC was taking place at Amy's local bank. There were five deaths
in the operation – all three ANC activists died, and two bystanders.

36. Zulu for Spear of the Nation, the armed wing of the ANC.

A new dimension is opening up for me; being committed to life on the basis of all of it being transitory. There is a wedge in the middle of a man or woman, which insists on permanence. It is probably the image of God telling us that something is forever. Maybe everything is, in a way. This is a paradox.

I've been reading some of those letters I wrote you in the beginning. They may well be useful for the book. I find them enormously unsettling. I spend more time being frightened and lost and lonely than anything else, like last year, when waves of anxiety came over me whenever I tried to study. Most new undertakings seem to bring this sort of distress into my life.

Can you imagine sitting in front of a book which has to be written and you can only see about two inches in front of your face? That's about three sentences – and you don't know where the story is leading, or whether it's leading you anywhere at all, and you wonder what sort of nightmares it will bring, or if you are dreaming, and what on earth is real and what is not?

I read the first couple of pages to Wolf last night, which helped a bit. He is so flint-faced and unresponsive about it, so that through this lens I can clearly spot the sentimental junk as I go along, and mark it for a rewrite. Bless him! The secret life of Amy scares the pants off him. You chuckled with sympathy there, didn't you?

I spoke to Petunia this morning – that carmelite nun behind the raw linen grill. I gather she has written to you, so you will soon know how she is better than I do. Maybe I'll go to Holyrood on Sunday. Though I think we've got to go to a shooting festival at some Swiss friends' farm. The Swiss make anything into a festival.

I got army worm in the lawn, but we sprayed it and it's going green again. Frederick gave me enough chicken manure for the whole garden so it might be flourishing by the time you get here – unless it has expired from the smell.

Wolf wants you to get ten first-day covers when the new stamps come out. But I've told him he must send money first. He sends his regards. Let us know how things are with you.

1st February 1980

Dear Alfred,

I feel like getting drunk, which I probably will be by the time this letter is finished… and the terrine is out of the oven.

Had a lovely surprise last Wednesday, when a letter arrived from an American friend we met in Kenya seven years ago while we were still at sea – postmarked Nelspruit. He's arriving tomorrow to spend the weekend. He is one of those guys who tinker with the weather for the plantations up there;[37] so I've probably got him to thank for all the lovely rain we've been having.

I discover that I am not really such a reprehensible character when I dress myself up as the child, or the brother, or anyone else in my book. I can feel compassion for bits of myself when I write about the degenerate Beth, or the anxious Mary. In short, I think I'm doing what I was born to do, expressing myself in the only way I know how – first person once removed. I sent the first two chapters to Professor Burton today and await his verdict with resignation.

Naturally, this concrete statement of personhood is having its repercussions in 'real' life. I have just held forth for nearly an hour to Wolf about his illness, his inability to perceive anything but bitter battle, mistrust, and misery in life. How this infects me, and how his suspicious mistrust of me has no rational grounds – according to our experience together. Such boldness – taking the bull by the horns – would have been out of the question a couple of weeks ago.

I've come across this before. Admit a lack of forgiveness, and you suddenly find genuine cause for resentment. I've never before admitted how bitterly unhappy I am, or faced squarely Wolf's emotional poverty. Now I can do both these things it is possible to cope with them in a grown-up fashion, and do something about them, instead of pretending they don't exist; or hoping that someone will wave a magic wand.

I am too much myself at the moment to be heartbroken if Wolf doesn't understand what I am talking about. It appears he is trying to, because he expressed concern that I will only get six hours sleep tonight. Unprecedented concern. One thing which provided a suitable context for our evening discussion, was that Pauli (the fluffy

37. Cloud seeding.

dog), was mauled last night and we didn't see until this evening. She is in hospital now. Poor little toad. I hope she will live through it.

Life is gradually filling itself with Beethoven, flowers, and friends, and the smell of baking bread. Life is to be lived, not suffered.

5th February 1980

Dear Alfred,

Good to talk to you on the phone. Sorry to burden you with extra worries at this time, but I was almost out of my mind. No-one else knows about the scene with Wolf, and there's no solution to it. Elsa finally brought herself to advise me that I'm getting seriously neurotic again, and there is no way out of it except getting away from Wolf.

But you can't give up a seven-year battle with a sigh and leave a note on the door saying you just weren't up to it. Nor is it sensible to stay until you are so punch-drunk that there's no chance of recovery.

At present, I haven't even got the strength to wash up at night, let alone pray with any conviction. I feel like a rat in a trap, with a malevolent eye peering in occasionally – promising further drawn-out misery.

6th February 1980

So this was the day of the crunch. I phoned Bob Pickwick, who was very helpful also, though in a different way from you. I tried to get the bishop on the phone but he was in a meeting. Went to mass in a sort of dream – and left Wolf after that.

I will housekeep for him, and cook an evening meal if he wants to stay here. But he must amuse himself in the evenings and look after his own room. I just quietly told him that I was going to have to leave him because I couldn't live in hell any longer. And because he chooses to live in hell, I would have to leave him for my own sanity.

He asked me to describe hell, and I did, and he listened intently. After that he said he must have a devil in his own body. He said it, I didn't. He said he didn't need help, so I told him he could try and gain his freedom on his own, but if he couldn't, there are enough people who love him who would help.

I asked him, as an experiment, to say "the Lord Jesus Christ". He insisted he wouldn't, and couldn't, because that is the beginning of belief, and, "If you give him your little finger, *dat* bugger takes your whole arm." He lost his temper after that, and I refused to listen to more. But it is clear that he is not to be abandoned, although I can do nothing more except stay away from him, and pray for his protection. It is going to be hard, and the worst enemy is pity.

He is very sad, and so am I. Had a dreadful night but this morning I am at peace again, as I was in England.

12th February 1980

Dear Alfred,

I will phone you tomorrow to assure you that all is well in the eye of the storm. I thought I would not be capable of writing about what's happened here at home, but old habits die hard. I've just spent a quarter of an hour with my guitar, and although I hardly got one satisfactory sound out of it, I am encouraged by my progress. I am no longer afraid of making mistakes. I am taking an interest in my old hobbies of music, painting, and crying my eyes out.

Wolf seems to have gone to bed, although it is still very early. By the frightened glances I got from his friend Marius this evening, I gather that there is a new wave of calumny against me. I have written to Bob and Fran, to assure them that I didn't, in the end, undertake the deliverance of Wolf alone and unarmed. I have also written to the bishop to tell him I have effectively left my husband, and asked him to believe it was the right thing to do – but he probably won't.

The rest of this missive will be devoted to filling you in on this matter. I hope you will be patient with me. My welfare and Wolf's cannot easily be separated. Today's epistle is 2 Corinthians 6.12-18, which I do not use to justify what I have done, but as a comforting word for what has happened. I have experienced in microcosm some classic symptoms of divorce in the past week – despair, resentment, hatred, murderous wrath, and withdrawal. None of them harm me because I seem to be in an inner fortress which protects me.

It seems that I have done the right thing, although I am frightened by the consequences. The precipitating events were that I was on the brink of mental breakdown and two trustworthy friends, separately and on the same day, suggested I should leave Wolf for my own good. Each day since Tuesday, when it happened, I have felt more confident that it is right to leave that unhappy man crouched in his miserable cell. I have been through the pilgrim's progress of conversion, been alienated from human and worldly relationships, broken in to myself as human and worldly, finally pledging myself to the world and humanity. God now sees fit to take me away from the fellowship of darkness. No-one will believe me of course. How would you feel if the Lord asked you to leave the Community? It is a rhetorical question, and there is no suggestion in my mind that this might happen.

I hope you meet Dad in England. Don't be put off by his polar bear act, should he put it on for you. He is even better at hiding his feelings than I am. Depend entirely on the Holy Spirit for what you say to him. I enclose a photo of him to give you confidence (I'd like it back sometime). Dad will see at a glance that he could frighten the daylights out of you with his Cambridge education and his Chichester diploma. He would use that to keep at a distance that wounding, amputating presence, the church – which you may represent to him. Or perhaps he will see you as someone who is a threat to the secret church he holds in his heart – which could well be nearer to the Body of Christ than the other one.

15th February 1980

Professor Burton wrote today, and told me to carry on writing. His comments on the two chapters I sent him were very helpful after I'd got over the shock. Philosophy studies are helping me to welcome constructive criticism and be a bit more rational about things – things of the world anyway.

Wolf is in bed with 'flu' and I'm feeling pretty grotty myself. Do you remember *All Hallows Eve*,[38] how the baddies surrounded that house with fog? That's how it feels here at the moment. It's awful. I won't even ask you to stay here if it's still like this in May. Probably won't be here myself.

Sunday

Actually, things are settling down in an odd sort of way. I never cease to wonder at the quirkiness of human beings. Wolf is being most considerate. Brings me coffee in the mornings, primly locks the bathroom in case I surprise him in his ablutions. Very odd. Maybe

38. By Charles Williams

the marital regime was rather bothersome to him also? Wouldn't that be bizarre, after we had bowed to social pressure and got married against our inclinations, to find ourselves mutually despising each other for doing so?

The fog has gone. Someone at St Wilfs said this morning that he had been 'convicted' for months over Wolf, so I asked him why he hadn't done anything about it? He seemed surprised. Anyway, people at church are praying for us. I think I am expected to collapse in a tearful heap over the apparent wreckage of my life, but it is not wrecked really.

It is raining softly outside, my cats and dogs are gathered around in peaceful sleep. Wolf speaks to me as if I am a human being. A whole new dimension is opening up with my writing.

I ask the Lord God, Yahweh Sabaoth, to anoint you every morning and surround you with his legions of angels, to mark you with the sign of the priesthood, and I look forward to the prospect of watching you celebrate mass.

Monday

We both stayed home today – pretending to have 'flu'. But I suspect the truth is that both of us are finding the present crisis far more interesting than going to work. The cats sleep on my desk while I study, and dogs snore around the place. It's been raining all day again. I'm still in my dressing gown.

I got a bit of chapter three written and cleared up the house. Wolf visits the study now and then, taking respite from the appalling book he's reading about the destruction of Europe in the third world war. He ventured out and bought the most exotic range of goodies we've seen for a long time, with his own money too – smoked ham, camembert, coffee beans, apple cake. I think I should leave him more often.

58

Amy is farewelled from SATA with the gift of a rug kit, to knot herself, and two dozen HB pencils to write her book with. Afterwards she spends Easter at St Bede's, while Wolf makes his customary pilgrimage to the Drakensberg. Alfred is still in the UK pursuing his vocation to the priesthood through sundry meetings and dialogues with his brethren.

7th April 1980 (in pencil)

Dear Alfred,

It is 11.15pm the Monday after Easter. I confront, once again, the debilitating effects of Wolf's malignant spirit, following a few days away at St Bede's. I am almost inclined to let go, to let him go. Why on earth should anyone be bothered with this bitter malevolence, year in year out? Let him go to hell where he wants to be anyway. Let him take his sticks of furniture and move on to the next squatter camp, snare himself another sucker who feels sorry for him, turn her into mincemeat, on and on until he shoots himself, as his grandfather did – with a complaint on his lips that the world was not good enough for him.

Such are the heroes of this bloody-minded generation. I don't admire Wolf. I detest him. At the same time I know we are all detestable – and why we are like that. We have no place, we have no identity. We weren't wanted. We arrived by accident, and by God, we will make our mark on this careless world. Even if we have to destroy everything in sight. The omnipotent infant wants to kill, murder, destroy, rape.

How does Christianity respond to this? Where does it put its meek and mild face? Where is its vaunted humility but in the acceptance (as in a mirror) of a hideously deformed, carnivorous and self-willed beast, designed to be the receptacle of the Spirit of God?

I mentioned a battle in the heavenly places which I could not describe. Maybe this is the end of it for the time being. An awareness of one's own ugliness, the immense relief of at last knowing how hideously disfigured one is. There is no need to pretend one is ugly any more. No false humility. No need even to try to be good. At the same time one knows through that lovely storyteller Victor Hugo, that even the hunchback of Nôtre Dame was infinitely lovable.

Before the Easter midnight mass I was feeling absurdly guilty that only about a hundred people had turned up at the cathedral, when there was a commotion at the south door. Trying not to be a busybody, but too restless to concentrate on prayer, I went to investigate. A black man had ventured in, but a sidesman with a medal round his neck told this man to sign his name on a communicant's slip. The man barked like a dog, and fled. For the rest of the night there we were huddled over our candles while this man roamed the city in the rain. The church is not God, to decide who comes in and who does not, and what they must do to qualify. The church must serve God in all those who come, or woe betide her.

Well. There we are. I held forth to Sisters on the Community's arrogant attitude towards 'the world' – which opened up a few surprising avenues of discussion. Apparently the 'whore of Babylon' treatment meted out by clergy to wanton lay women like myself extends also to the holy Sisters. For some reason I find that immensely comforting.

I look forward to speaking with you – even seeing you – on your return.

Friday 9pm

Wonderful to speak to you at the priory. It was like peering back into another world. Your own self nearby is a blessing – like iodine. It hurts but heals.

My letter to you in England was prompted by the spirit, for I know not what reason. I am not in the habit of airing my relationship with Wolf to that extent. Once or twice I have seen him transfigured… briefly, a muted light. He was cursing about his feet this evening – three open sores, one of them more than a year old. But for the prayers I think he would be crippled by now. They heal and open and heal and open continually like the ulcers in his stomach. It is a constant battle.

I once tried to explain to you my intuition that one should not try to get too close to God because, like the sun, the sheer power would destroy one. I found this very idea described in Harry Williams' writing. It was so encouraging. As was Baron Von Hügel's allusion to the neural cost of prayer. This encouraged me enormously because I do feel exhausted and desolate at times for no apparent reason. In such times one should maybe turn one's attention outward? Perhaps God takes away the inner life that one may return to the world order?

I am sure that God will not ever again abandon me to the pleasure of demons. I am sure that he wants to give me life in abundance – whether here or in the next life makes no difference. And if I suffer any kind of despair, loneliness or disappointment I do not believe it is from God. It is either because I have unwittingly stepped outside the divine will, or because God wishes to bring some new benefit from my travails. What is more, I know that every day I must endure is like a thousand years to God.

So. You may find me changed. I hope you do. It would be sad after six months, and a trip to England, if I were the same mousey, inarticulate Amy. I am happy you liked my father. I hope you really did. People tend to love him, or hate him – few like him. I feel like a bull in a china shop with him – too clumsy, too aggressive.

Wolf appreciated your greeting and advises against going to the Magaliesberg, especially if you intend to fast during your retreat. If the Holy Spirit wants you to ascend to the snowline and live with her in a tent for ten days then please do. But remember Jesus was inured to fasting when he went into the wilderness. He was also a fit young man in his late twenties. The Little Sisters are probably your best bet for making a retreat; or Masite. You would be in the mountains there, and need not sacrifice your future priesthood by freezing in a tent in the snow.

I'm thinking of going to bed now. Come to visit when you can, and stay for as long as you like. Try to make it at least overnight. I get a bit frenetic about seeing you for just as long as I need to relax, and then you're gone. It is extremely rare, you see, that I meet someone I can talk to like this. The experience is both rejuvenating and enervating. It took me a month to build up the confidence to hug my father, and even then he wasn't ready... thereby hangs a tale!

28th April 1980

I will phone on Thursday evening when you get back to the priory. If Wolf doesn't want to fetch you an alternative might be to load as many brethren into a car as possible and make it a Community outing? Come for lunch, or tea, or supper. Stephen[39] said he would like to visit us here and I guess he couldn't come without the novice master, or some sort of chaperone? The house is a little more organised than in days of yore because I'm home now and have time for proper housekeeping.

§

At the end of April their landlady turns up on Amy and Wolf's doorstep with the devastating news that she must sell the house. She needs the money to go into an old age home. Her relatives no longer want to look after her. Amy regards the septuagenarian, who is in fine fettle for her age, although somewhat stooped. She has walked here without a stick, and has climbed the back steps without difficulty. Amy offers to take her landlady in as a lodger.

The thought of having to uproot the household and move somewhere else, just when she has left her job in order to write a book, is too dreadful to contemplate. She has put all her eggs in one basket here in this house in Albion. This is her anchorhold, this house with its neighbourhood which has become her still point in the turning world. Moving house would gobble up the precious space she has created here in order to follow her vocation. Wolf is bemused by this bilateral initiative of taking the landlady as a lodger. But he is no longer surprised by Amy's odd choices.

Fortunately Aunt Kath, as they call her out of respect, will not move in until late May. Alfred wants to spend a day or two in Albion when he gets back from England. Kath will move into the guest room after that. Amy will buy a put-u-up for future guests.

When Alfred finally arrives to stay he is unusually pale after his weeks in England. Gaunt even, his face more deeply lined, visibly aged since she last saw him. Amy notices for the first time that he has false teeth, although his smile is as infectious as ever. "What colour was your hair?" she asks, as she shows him to his room. Alfred throws up his arms, looks heavenward and cries, "Alfred old chap!

39. A novice

You've made it!" But he doesn't answer her question. His hair is now snow white, and somewhat wispy. Amy is aware of a tectonic shift in her friendship with Alfred. She is no longer needy. She no longer drinks in his occasional glance as if her life depended on him.

They do not talk a great deal. It seems as if their friendship has found a place of silence, an intimate place where words are no longer necessary. Aunt Kath visits while he is in Albion and submits with pleasure to the laying on of hands and prayer from Alfred. She is a Presbyterian with Quaker connections.

§

17th May 1980

Dear Alfred,

I should be studying, but the icy blast from the window continually reminds me of you. There must be snow on the berg – pretty serious judging by the sudden drop in temperature here. I hope you will be persuaded to retreat with the Little Sisters, and not camp out on your own.

God blessed me with a time of prayer this morning that fled by, and I don't remember much of it, except reverence.

I think you found it a little difficult to orientate yourself with me, until the end of our days together, and I with you. It is because, as I have prayed and you have always prayed, the Lord is ascended and above every other name in my life. It is a great blessing on his part and one is at last at peace, in spite of the turmoil and brutality in the world.

I would have been glad of the opportunity to explain more fully, but it did not arise. I love you, as I have told you, but you may have forgotten. You are the first and last person I loved 'unto death', so to speak, and it was hard to leave you even for a little while in order to get to know God – whose arms, and eyes, and comfort are not seen or heard, or known in the human sense.

Reverence. It was not entirely correct to say, "I used to revere you; now I just love you." There is a certain reverence, always, in love. God's own reverence for his creatures is a lovely, gentle, tender thing. I think I should have said, "I used to worship you," which I did, as you know. I don't think it was bad, although it would be very bad if I did it any longer. You revealed the Lord to me, as a father should reveal God to his children, therefore the honour I gave you was right, until I grew up a little. Now I give God the honour and glory, thanking him for you.

This sort of realignment causes all sorts of bumps and fissures in a friendship, and I thank you for your sensitivity last weekend. I was astonished to hear your confession about taking kindness for granted. I have never felt more at home with you, and I was particularly grateful to you for pursuing my comment about your 'unquietness'. It is terrible to try to build a friendship when attempts at understanding the other's mind are swallowed up and disappear without trace. One never knows when one is angering, or hurting, or what gives pleasure. We are asked to share all good things with our teachers and I would never knowingly hurt you.

Wolf. I rarely talk about him, although I did a bit to Petunia, and quite a lot this year with Elsa because of her wisdom in his particular area of suffering. I'm sorry I mentioned that label to you, because I think maybe you are aware of the 'psychopathic' state only in its criminal or certifiable manifestation – as I was until recently. In fact it is a major and very widespread socio-psychological problem, which can be treated on a very broad basis – that is, not only by psychiatry but also through the sufferer's whole environment. Stability and loving kindness, and understanding being the prerequisites for any hope of a life free from mental pain.

Elsa says there are many statistics, but one thesis shows that illegitimacy, a broken home, and hatred of the mother towards the child are three causal factors, any one of which in a sample of children gives about fifty per cent chance of psychopathic states.

As Wolf's parents had to marry because he was on the way; as he did not see his father until he was seven; as his mother abandoned him when he was a nursling; and as his earliest memory of her (whether true or not) is of her trying to kill him with a rock – in view of these things he would have been extraordinarily lucky to have escaped this affliction.

This, plus my own inadequacy as a person, is why Wolf and I cannot begin to conduct a marriage in the generally accepted sense. We only married because of social pressures here in South Africa.

My desire was to save him from endless misery and loneliness at sea. I did not know it would be a lifelong job.

He has also played an important role in knocking some of the selfishness and obstinacy out of me. The fact that he nearly killed me in the process is irrelevant; I believe we are all constantly killing and destroying, until the Lord sees fit to call us into the work of re-creation. It is possible now to tell you all this because I feel in right relationship with you as my brother in Christ since last weekend.

Another priceless blessing on Sunday was the intimation of the glory of the wounds of Christ Jesus. As so often happens, it was like a 'truth in apposition to an untruth' – "Love is not... does not..." etc.

Wolf's identity, and mine, and yours, and Petunia's, are all marked with wounds – pre-natal wounds even. I desired total healing but flinched – as from one of those Jehovah Witness caricatures of heaven, of perfect beings in a perfect garden – fearing I must forego my wounds. I saw the glory of those wounds which we all bear made beautiful by Christ's bleeding hands, and I began to understand why in the great ages of faith – whether pagan or Christian – scars are considered to be marks of honour.

I realised why Hellenistic art expired close to perfection, and why pride of life is the arch-destroyer. I caught a glimpse of the utter magnificence of Calvary and began to understand the import of that hymn with the line "O happy fault..."

I began to realise the significance of that crown of thorns, and I see before my eyes now, as I gaze at our pepper tree, the man-god wrestling (as my father once wrote in a poem) naked with the tree – cast-iron, broad-shouldered, one foot racked from the nails as if to ascend, bent like Atlas beneath the uprooting of the world, arms flung wide in total embrace, hands and head studded with bronze, all clothed in a steely sweat, and absolutely alone... "Deliver my darling from the power of the dog."

Saturday morning

Dear Alfred,
There is a great peace here. It is frightfully cold at night, but joy comes with the morning and the verandah is filling with sunlight. At last the pictures are hung, and the house begins to look cared

for. It responds so well to care. Today I will give the garden my undivided attention.

This week I learned from Aunt Kath that not only did her father quarry the stone for this house from the hill but he made the bricks for it as well. Did you note today's reading – "unless a man build on rock…"? Maybe you've noticed that this house is built on bedrock?

Kath is flowering – maybe because I repented of my fear of her. I told her about how it frightened me that she communed with invisible spirits, and I apologised. Yesterday she was striding around in an old gaberdine jacket that any student would give their eye-teeth for. She's a remarkable person, with flashes of such beauty and fun at times.

She was a bit hair-raising when explaining about her 'prayers'.[40] She says it happens when she's cross, or wants something. She was surprised I had noticed, and said she wanted her spirit books back. I had packed them away. She said you also read such books, so now I don't know what to do? Some of her books do look quite harmless, but it's not the books so much as the spirit behind them.

St Paul says faith leads to understanding, and understanding to love. I can't extricate obedience from faith. Therefore I think all 'other gods' must be eschewed until the age of understanding when they can be dealt with for what they really are – namely not gods at all but rather the manifestations of human curiosity and desire.

I have told Kath that I am praying for the medium who lived here, her friend and house-mate who died suddenly of emphysema twelve years ago. I will go to mass for her tomorrow. I am sure this is a prayer in the Spirit, because I have been given a little awareness of the power of love over hate. In place of the dreadful paranoia and bitter attacks of the past weeks when I have been alone here, I am now aware of the love of God filling me for this woman. And also, in an obscure way, of her yielding to a Lord who can love through such bitterness and hate.

Of course, one keeps in mind the possibility that I suffer from an errant imagination. These things are so subtle, perceived not with the mind. But Watchman Nee taught me the fundamental yardstick of judging actions by their fruits – and there is so much harmony

40. Kath would talk to the ether with great intensity at times.

here now. Possibly because I've repented of treating Aunt Kath like a leper.

Her back continues to give her problems, and I think there's a block there which only some form of deliverance ministry will shift. During the laying on of hands when you were here she should at least have been faintly aware of healing I think. But she says there was nothing.

I'm sorry to stampede all over your finer feelings. I note my own arrogance, and self-righteousness, and all the other nastier vices of Christians who begin to come into their inheritance. But it is part of growing up and I can't pretend to be meek and mild and humble, and speak only when spoken to, when the lion within is indeed awakening and stretching his limbs.

This is not a time for pretending lions don't exist, or for caging them, or taming them. I need your anger, your criticism, your disgust even. I need response – to see myself reflected in the face of the saints – so that I know where my human life is in need of adjustment, correction etc. I think this is where the authority of God, by the Holy Spirit in prayer, meets the authority Christ gave to his Church.

Possibly this nexus of Christ in God and the Church is the cause of most of the strife in the church militant. Obedience revolves around it, and each age has put the matrix in a different place. Where exactly does one cease to take direction from the church, and receive it from God? Is it in the remote places of personal devotions? In intercession, in fasting, in church attendance, in moral behaviour? Most of us are lucky these days. Joan of Arc was burned at the stake for saying God actually spoke to her.

Enough now. I must go and buy milk for breakfast, and begin to attend to the garden.

Tuesday

I'm listening to The Gypsy Baron. Aunt Kath is reading the newspaper, she sends her love, and I'm hoping I might see you again – but that is very unlikely. I hope above all that you saw Bob and Fran Pickwick. Probably they alone can convince you that I am not just horsing around with my strange relationship with Wolf.

He is at present accusing me of giving his mountain socks to you, because they are missing. It is a strain, you know, to discover you have built for yourself a dwelling place in hell for the most virtuous of human motives. The church has no teaching on the subject of what one does in this situation with Wolf. If I were still forced to share a bed with him I would be drunk by now. As it is I can sit quietly and supervise his packing for the mountains, as his insults fall a little short of the mark. I spent one hour in prayer for him this morning and that helped to blunt the pain.

I was aware of a certain subdued disapproval from you re my separation from Wolf. Please be patient. I am not playing monks and nuns. I want you to understand that beyond endurance is righteousness and the goodness of God. That persons, long enough and badly enough used, are released from the law. I want you to know that God's hand is stretched out still, and there is a limit to endurance.

Above all – for your prayers – I want you to know that your idea of marital bliss is mistaken, and I hope you will revise your declaration that "all breakdown of marriage is of the devil". Besides this – which is enough to offend you if you are human, but I hope you are not just human – I want to tell you that I am lonely.

I had a word for the 'great congregation' at St Wilf's on Sunday, which was not designed to make me popular. But at least I know, in the gasping aftermath of speaking the word of God (*"Put me down; please put me down!"*), at least I know I am in the right place at the right time. Even if I'm slung out on my ear; even if I never hear again from Brother Alfred; even if the house burns down. At least I know, when God takes me that seriously I'm going his way.

So, *Shalom*.

P.S. There is intransigence, harshness, and unkind criticism in this letter. I hope you'll forgive me. It would be falling into a trap if, after three years of speaking to you in sincerity and truth, I hid from you the realisation that I am irreparably hurt, and there is no-one in the world, not even you, who can help.

This damage is fundamental and I praise God for it because it is so debilitating that I could not hope to live on except by divine grace. Therefore, while I get used to this new knowledge of my own ugliness, weakness and utter uselessness, I cannot be bothered with any insincerity or false kindness.

Life is raw, I am raw, and although my new knowledge of it gives me more compassion and patience with the weak and deprived and suffering, I have considerably less patience with our leaders in the church. And because I really love you, not the wishy-washy sort of sweet adoring love of the adolescent, but the sort that has the courage to care that friendship/love is built on rock – because of this, I insist that you know and, "insofar as lies within you," love me as a whole person and not just the nice bits. It is the way the bits of raw, rough stone, which are ourselves, are thrown against each other in the tides of life, and broken, and ground down, and smoothed, and purified, until we find ourselves on the white beach – part of a multitude more numerous than the sands of the seashore.

18th May 1980

Bishop Timothy dropped in at our house on Wednesday afternoon. I had written him a prim note apologising for asking him to drop in for tea, because afterwards I remembered that St John of the Cross said one should not fraternise with one's director. He made it quite plain that my note was one of the reasons for his visit. The other reason was a phone call he had from Bob Pickwick. As you know our phone is out of order. That lovely pair of Durban saints have offered me the use of their house for two weeks, and if necessary my airfare down there. I do wish I could go. Circumstances here make it impossible, but it gives me such a boost to think they would do that for me. And then holy +Timothy arrives in my kitchen to tell me the good news.

Our parish priest tells me he was praying this week for our situation here at Albion, and that we (the divine 'we') will take action. That gives me such joy. Not so much the 'action' as the assurance that the church will help us. The worst of these past weeks has been the see-sawing between clarity in prayer and inertia, as life-force ebbs into confusion, doubt, paranoia, hatred, fear, loneliness, self-pity.

19th May 1980

Wolf is taking the name of Jesus Christ in his mouth – albeit blasphemously. It is an improvement, as he would not speak that name before. Anyone who uses the name of Jesus cannot resist for long – therefore I ignore the context.

I will now describe a little family scene. This evening I asked Wolf for the fourth time if he would help me to remove the roof of the fish tank, as I wanted to clean it. He said he did not feel like it. As the tank has been an eyesore for weeks, I contrived to remove the lid myself while he and Kath had dinner. I tore my jeans and fused all the lights while I was at it. I had spent five minutes up to my armpits in water, scraping slime off the glass, before something made me investigate a stray wire – on the end of which was an adapter with two live plugs. It was steaming as I fished it out of the tank. I am quite glad to be alive, as are the fish.

Do you think that this sort of behaviour is to be met with patience and endurance? Maybe. But not the sweet smiling sort of *unterwürfigkeit* which says to cruelty, "Oh, I deserve you". That is masochism, and plain stupid, in my opinion. Wolf needs a strong arm, and quite frankly, a good thrashing, before he will come to his senses. I saw in his face tonight his astonishment that I survived to tell the tale. He subsequently got a few volts himself while trying to fix the fuse. Pray that he will say Jesus Christ! more often. In the meantime, I will pray that he gets his thrashing fairly soon. I repent of the milk of human kindness I've been feeding him for too long.

I would like to cut myself off from everyone, and write. That would be very nice, to be a hermit, which I have wanted to be since I was a child. I could still be available for the needs of the household and neighbourhood. I know what true companionship is, and I won't settle for less. The parish can keep their bible studies, their cheerful choruses, their central heating. I despise the placebos of peace and love which the vanguard of the renewal offers to people who gave up on peace and love a long time ago. Okay, it was pleasant for a while. But they fail to add that Christ died. That is the core of the fellowship.

Sorry – I am a bit drunk and my writing hand won't work properly, but I don't recant. I want to stop the booze now – I have run out of money anyway. There's enough food in the larder and the garden for us to limp along to the end of the week, but the soup gets thinner and the cake gets smaller and everyone has to wash their hands with a sliver of soap. I wonder when they will notice? Yes. I want to stop the booze now. It was a buffer between myself and Wolf – a way of softening the blow of coming home in the evening. And more recently a way of deadening the impact of his hateful behaviour.

I think it was a sin to try and carry Wolf. It is surely a sin to make oneself responsible for someone else's life unless under the guidance of the Holy Spirit. It is playing God, and we know the awful consequences of that. So I won't carry Wolf any more – that symbiosis ended last night in the fish tank. Not drinking will set a lot of pain loose, but there will be an end to it. God was, before the pain began, and will be when it is over. One can give up the prophylaxis, the wine, and hope the demons will come out one at a time so that one is not overcome, and has the strength to send them to the place prepared for them.

22nd May 1980

Dear Alfred,
I think my anger is subsiding now. Each new discipline brings its harvest of rebellion, and it is usually the people I love most who cop it. I've been too frightened of offending you to bring forth my 'ooh nasties' in your presence, but that is slavish devotion and goes sour in the end. The Lord in his grace is delivering me from the bottle, and it doesn't hurt much.

Little Cecilia from next door watched her cat die in my study last night. A child's grief is a most terrible and beautiful thing. She finally asked if we could pray for it. So we prayed in the oratory for *Streepi's* everlasting life with Jesus.

Aunt Kath is talking to her familiars again. I wish she wouldn't. It makes me so uncomfortable. It is strange how I feel as if I am forbidden to touch her. It is maybe this which makes me feel helpless and afraid of her at times like these. I have no inkling of what is being said.

I have become so profoundly aware of the prayers of others these last five months. It is like yeast. Yeast grows in milk and sugar, or honey, but once the bread enters the oven its work is done and the heat kills it. Yeast is a powerful symbol in the New Testament – or in unleavened bread where God's grace alone works without supplications. I find the daily round of creating order out of chaos in this household is so full and enriching that I have barely enough energy to eke out three hundred words a day – which means the book would take about three years to write.

I have premonitions of disaster. The book will appeal to a fairly small section of our society and be mocked by the rest – notably the theologians and the literary critics. It will walk out on its own, with nothing to commend it, and anyone who reads it will know me inside-out, and won't like me very much.

On the other hand, if I don't face up to it before long it will never get written. So, if the Spirit so leads, please pray for it as a vehicle of the gospel.

27th May 1980

Dear Alfred,

I'm getting worried about my writing. The thing that bothers me most is the contempt of the brethren – but that's always been so. On one side it is a naive little story, but on the other it is flinging wide the gates on all sorts of sacrosanct subjects such as prayer life, mental disease, and monks.

The contempt of people one respects is awfully hard to bear. I had a foretaste of that in a letter I wrote to *The Mail*. People don't realise that what you say is limited, and they make judgements whether the advice is meant for them or not. What I wrote in the paper was a message to Calvinists who are locked in combat with the bugbear of black supremacy; what they fear does not exist. Naturally, such a message would be misunderstood by people who do not suffer from these delusions. My father was always doing this – describing the situation from the sick person's point of view and coming under the world's judgement for being sick himself.

I have learnt a lot from living with Aunt Kath. There were really forces at work trying to make me fear and hate her. But now I've shared some of my own weird experiences in the world of imagination, I am able to explore that world with her, and hopefully win her trust in me, because I have been there too.

28th May 1980

What do you think of them throwing the bishops in jail?[41] My heart leapeth for joy! I have hardly stopped dancing since Aunt Kath

41. Johannesburg's diocesan bishop, and other church leaders including Bishop Desmond Tutu, were arrested during a peaceful anti-apartheid protest and spent the night in jail.

interrupted my studies to share the glad news. Fancy +Jo'burg in clink! Praise God. Practically the whole church leadership locked up in John Vorster Square. Can you imagine the Queen ordering the arrest of the Archbishop of Canterbury? Or the Pope being thrown into the dungeons of the Vatican? Do they realise what they've done?

From henceforth it will be fashionable in the elite suburbs to get jailed. I feel sorry for this government. What's the state going to do with about a million Progs,[42] all fighting to get jailed and buying the best legal advice to sue for damages etc? What did Jesus say about the gates of hell not prevailing against his church? "Cross over this Jordan," God said to the priesthood – and by God they've done it!

29th May 1980

I phoned Fran Pickwick yesterday (they're in Jo'burg on their way to Europe), and they feel the same way about the bishops.

The trouble with dishonest people is they don't know they are doing it – like Wolf, and sometimes Kath (who sends her love), and probably me too. I seem to be blessed with a sort of super sensitivity about what people are thinking, and although I don't rely on it too much, it is bloody painful to see some people making nice sounds with their mouths and detesting me with their hearts. I would be so happy if they could just say, "I hate you". It's the deceit that hurts.

For instance, Wolf is at present charming Aunt Kath into the belief that I am mad (this may be true), as he convinced Pru and Dick and all our former friends. Probably I was – only a couple of the former friends are still in touch. Some remain disgusted and some are too ashamed of their betrayal to renew our friendship.

The thing is, I knew about it all the time, somehow, and I don't blame them. Wolf can be so utterly convincing in his deceit. Indeed, he believes it all himself. One reason why he hates the church – and all those in the Spirit – is because he is sensitive enough to know that he can't get away with lies, and feels naked, vulnerable and poverty-stricken. This is why he must become acquainted with love in spite of all his dreams of himself as a big deal. And frankly, I feel as if I've run out of love for him.

I've been cut off from you for a long time, fell out of the nest, so to speak, and return somewhat hesitantly as a sister instead of a

42. Progressive Liberal Party members.

fledgling. I haven't heard from you yet, so I don't know what your response to my recent letters is – and expect, by force of habit, to be despised.

My mind knows that my brother in charity will do no such thing, but my heart would be exceeding surprised if he didn't. Why? Because no-one has ever made it, except very briefly, into the netherlands of real love and acceptance with me.

The Lord gives visions to little children. Many of us have glimpsed heaven, and then it was taken away from us, but we never forgot. Love, we particularly remembered. People in the world and even in the church mocked us for our idealism, and so we did our best to close that immortal wound in the flesh called 'heaven' with all sorts of distractions, grog, dope, sex, and often ended up dead, or wanting to die.

It is only when this wound is opened up and cleaned with strong potions, that one begins to stop being afraid of it. That wound is, I suppose, a deep down awareness of what one has lost?

I know you are painfully aware of the sadness of lost opportunities. Some call that sin. I imagine, from where I am that this will be the dread of judgement for us – "If only... oh if only!" And yet, in that Light one also knows that God's omnipotence turns all things to good for those that love truly. So one trogs along and prays for grace to love. That, in itself, makes the uncertainty and slog and mistakes quite bearable – opportunities for God to ride in as the Lord of Thunder and make it all right again.

I was wailing to Fran on the phone about the amount I drink at present. She was very comforting about why I do it and I musn't worry and "a little comfort," and so on. I'm grateful to her, enormously grateful for her prayers, but she knows and I know that there is only one Comforter. I want no sea anchor whatsoever. I am apparently destined to live a solitary life as many people in the world are – the Lord's *Résistance* maybe – but it is fatal to depend in any way on worldly comfort.

It is quite a blessing to live in a country where the holy catholic and apostolic church is becoming something of a dirty word. I begin to see how respectability in a state church can become a cancer. Maybe I'll write a thesis on that in a few years time. That would warm the cockles of Daddy's heart.

In the meantime – may God bless you, and may his face shine upon you, and give you peace.

Saturday

Something of a surprise to discover it is Republic Day, and all the shops are shut, so couldn't send your newspapers. Awfully sorry.

Yesterday a man arrived on a red bicycle with an express letter from Fr Esau at Turfloop. He intends visiting tomorrow, which is very nice. I haven't seen him since SACLA. If my lift doesn't pitch up to take me to church I'll wait till Esau comes and we'll break bread together here.

Aunt Kath is in the bosom of her family in Krugersdorp, but she did rather hesitantly inform me that some Indian friends of hers might visit from Laudium[43] – so I said I was wondering how to break the news gently to her that my coloured friends from Eersterus might visit – then Esau's letter comes, and we are looking forward to seeing him too. Silly isn't it, how we chafe at apartheid, and when we talk about it sensibly it is gone like a soap bubble?

I am rejoicing in my household, slowly and meditatively getting it up to par – looking after long-neglected corners. It is becoming a joy to walk through. I know it is responding to my care by the way people fall quiet and look in upon themselves when they visit. There is peace, and order here. I would like to spend three days working in the garden before it goes into its winter doze.

Next week there is a school of philosophy at Unisa for three days – a very heavy programme and as usual I am well behind with the curriculum. I also have an assignment due, an exegesis of I John, which I haven't started on.

I'm about ten thousand words into my book, which is miserable considering that I must aim for 60,000 to 80,000 by the end of the year. I will submit what I have to Professor Burton this coming week, and hope that his comment won't have the same effect on me as last time – namely to tear it up. I want to write well. Of course it will be unpolished – all first novels are unpolished diamonds – but I don't want unpolished plastic!

The temptation is to violate South Africa. One must somehow walk between the extreme emotions aroused on one side and the

43. A 'non-white' township.

other and give the characters a human face; somehow ignoring the false faces of ideology.

Monday morning

Had a lovely day with Esau, priest and king, who snoozes still in your room, and I must get this off now, so I'll write more next week.

27th June 1980

Dear Alfred,

Your very welcome letter arrived today, together with one from Anna which I'll tell you about later. I am overwhelmed by the mass of correspondence from you, and yes I did note '8.30am'. I suggest more letter writing at that hour – it seems to be a fertile time and I can also be sure that nice things you say are not the fruit of the vine.

I saw +Timothy on the day you wrote. He spent two hours with me for which I am eternally grateful. We went out for a walk in the local streets with his dachshund, who seems to have a penchant for suicide. I suppose it is the dog's lofty office which persuades him to look down his nose at Mercedes, but one wishes he were a bit taller so they could see to drive around him. His name is Fransie.

I'm sorry, I didn't understand. I've known for ages that you were not comfortable being my director – chiefly expressed by an unwillingness to direct me at all. But I thought this meant that you'd rather be shot of me altogether. Tenacity is my long suit and one of us would have to die before I'd let you go. Shouldn't think that would help much either!

"So there we are," as we say in times of mild euphoria. I think I probably know you well enough now to say that I love the real Alfred much more than the simulacrum I've been yelling at in the last series of letters. +Timothy, no doubt observing your dilemma from afar, remarked that it is difficult for a friend to give direction. He suggested he could be my arch-director, with the Sisters at Holyrood as more regular companions. Sister Clare flung her arms round me last time I saw her and asked me to come and stay overnight sometime. So that does look like a possibility.

+Timothy pointed out that intercession is important. I am attracted to that sort of prayer but since it has been confirmed by the bishop all sorts of creative things are emerging, not least a profound sense of relationship with my Lord because I feel useful at last.

Anna's letter is the second in a week. She seems to have got wind of something amiss here. She has put £2,000 at my disposal and urges me to leave Wolf, with various intimations that my continuing here with him is misplaced heroics and dangerous etc, etc. As reinforcement she quotes Isaiah 29.15 to the end.

She has every right to be worried. Since I stopped drinking after I saw +Timothy, I can see how Wolf continually wears me down. You need quite a cool head to be objective about that, remembering he is a victim of circumstance. Mum's letter, together with the Pickwicks' conviction that it is only a matter of time before I actually leave home, is a bit disturbing. At present I do not have the slightest intention of leaving home, but in the centre of my life, as solid as a rock, is the conviction that I will not go back to Wolf's bed. Whenever such a thought arises, my flesh cringes, life begin to crumble. At this moment in time I say with confidence before God, "I'd rather go to hell".

The book is showing signs of life. It may be a longer process than I thought, but if it looks good by the time my money runs out in November, I'll take Anna up on that offer.

Aunt Kath seems to have stopped communing with her familiars. She now spends her time watching the fish and reading her bible. She hasn't been well, which is a good excuse to have a fire burning all day. She sends her love. She always hangs around waiting for snippets of news when there is a letter from you.

I've heard from Ruth, who sounds a bit down, but she's only been at Lee Abbey a week and it always takes a while to settle down in a brand new environment. I gather from various quarters that she handled the move with her usual frightening aplomb. She should laugh more – said the pot to the kettle!

The family next door is moving, to my sorrow. I am watching the pigeons tumbling over their house. I've moved my desk to the sitting room on account of the fire. About 8.30pm, when the others go to bed, I settle down here and listen to Missa Solemnis right through every night. This is part of getting down to intercession. I am sure only whole people, who are at peace with God and themselves, can intercede for the world. I was becoming a household drudge, feeling guilty every time I sat down and did nothing for a moment. Your letter is the cherry on the top of a very difficult but now glorious week.

Later

I'm discovering the mellow loveliness of Mozart. I thought I didn't like him… never had time for him I suppose. Where did that expression 'I've got no time for him' come from? There's a lot of healing going on here. I really did believe that if I let my director go that would be the last I ever saw of him. He'd shake the dust from his sandals, sigh with relief, commend me to my Lord and be gone for good.

Your letter to Wolf disappeared into his cavernous handbag. I don't quite know how he's going to read it. He still has problems reading the newspaper. I am naturally dying of curiosity. I even went to look in the handbag which was hidden under his bed, but restrained myself when I saw his leather mouse purse and cigarettes carefully laid out on top of the letter. Instead I went to pray. Ten minutes later he passed the oratory at a rate of knots with a muffled curse to the effect of "He knew it!" – flying into his room to catch me in the act of snooping. I'm very glad I wasn't there.

As for the trick of writing to the depth of one page only with a ballpoint – I should think transcendental meditation might help, or a tranquillizer. I've often admired your ferocity with a biro. I've been tempted to do a pencil rubbing to find out what you wrote to other people on the previous page. I haven't though. I promise I won't. I'd better embark on some writing for 'the book'. Goodnight, and thank you for your epistle and celebration of friendship.

Saturday

Got a letter from Peta, who was confirmed two weeks ago. Also from my brother, who plans to stay in the army. He's going up for captain's major – says the army suits his Heath Robinson talents.

Wolf went off this afternoon in his usual oafish fashion, without a 'goodbye' or 'how's y' father'. Came back at 5.30pm, did the washing up, and cooked supper! I can only assume someone read your letter to him while he was out – Marius probably.

There's a full moon shining in on my desk. A cosmic Gestapo is whispering in my head, "vee have vays of making you behave…" This is probably due to withdrawal symptoms. I'm used to drinking quite a lot of wine.

Sunday

Roger is here with the Berlioz Requiem for me to borrow. Nice. I wish you were here too. I haven't wished that for a long time because I thought your aloof, detached role was permanent and final. Still reeling a bit from the impact of your letter.

2nd July 1980

Dear Alfred,

I wish I could find as much enthusiasm for writing my book as I have for writing letters to you. And I've woken up to the appalling realisation that exams are only three months off. I've done practically nothing as usual, although I have all day to study. Anna's offer of financial help does give me more psychological space. Maybe I should concentrate on the studies and get down to the book after exams? Winter is always a low time for me – pale and spotty and feeling tired.

Boy! Am I enjoying listening to music since I've been sober enough to hear it properly. That permanent gnawing ache in my gut gets filled up with music. It's just me listening to the composer. Conductor and orchestra are intermediaries – like the prophets. If they get the interpretation wrong you can feel it.

I've dropped my morning prayer routine for an hour drinking tea and smoking. I want to make this playtime into a doorway for my Lord. I have realised how frantically busy my prayer time had become – weighed down with duties and responsibilities, never bringing even one real prayer to birth.

I agreed with +Timothy that I should stop drinking alcohol, and so far it's worked. When I get too frustrated I go out and smash beer bottles against the dam wall; and scream. It seems to help.

All flushed with the miracle of escaping the bottle I tried to give up smoking as well on Monday morning. We were all set. Nine o'clock stopped smoking – prostrate by eleven, paralysed by seven p.m. – slept fully dressed on the sofa with all the lights on. Seven a.m. next morning the only hope of getting up to prepare Aunt Kath's breakfast lay in lighting a cigarette. Amen. So be it.

It's my third birthday in the Spirit on Saturday 12th. No-one knows that except you, so you have an exclusive invitation to celebrate with me. The third birthday is very special and I expect a whopping present. The Lord knows what I want most.

Thursday

I saw the professor who has been perusing my manuscript today. He started by saying that writing is a disease; only insane people do it; that writing is the most agonising, lonely and unrewarding profession. If I am sure that is what I want to do, I am not to ask other people's opinion about it.

Having made sure I was in earnest, he said that my intro is already a novel if only I would write it properly. I have gathered from all this that he does take me seriously, and that my writing is worth starving for. In my mind's eye I am already writing twelve hours a day in a lonely garret, eking out my last crust while creating classics which will be revered in two hundred years but ignored in my lifetime.

Your comment that my continuing presence here is somehow for the good of the whole of creation has been a great help. I don't understand but I hope it is true. Naturally I must quell megalomaniac notions of universal redemption pouring out of Albion. But it is much easier to care that dogs like walks and men like cakes and elderly ladies like hot-water bottles, when someone puts these small things into the context of caring for the world at large. I think that may be what the Superior was saying in his last editorial, when he wrote that the Christian religion stands with the world at its most broken and confused, identifying with, absorbing, and transforming the pain through hope.

I hasten to add that in my own situation this does not mean that Wolf's primal rage must be allowed to crush and destroy me. Sometimes I can weep for him; but the time has come for him to meet something more powerful than his own inner fury. I'm listening to Beethoven's seventh. It sounds like a million springbok dancing across the Karoo – before white men came to Africa and shot 'em.

4th July 1980

Did my three hour stint writing today. I think I'll have to start writing
you daily letters again, or I'll go off my head. This is where we
began about three-and-a-half years ago. Quote from my first letter
to you: "I'm trying to write a story involving terribly complicated
moral and conceptual problems, and it would be lovely to work them
out with you". What delicious irony!

Had a letter from Oswald today in reply to one I wrote. He ought
to have been a doctor with writing like that. I spent ten minutes
trying to decipher the interesting greeting at the end, then gave up.

I want to go to Holyrood for a day at least, tomorrow. Aunt Kath
is so comfortable here she doesn't want to go away for her weekend
with relatives any more. I wish it would occur to them both that
it is not necessarily a privilege to wait on them day and night. I'm
feeling like one of the downtrodden of the earth this evening; even
Beethoven isn't helping much.

I'm trying out a new system with the newspapers – since I no
longer have the resource of SATA's envelopes. Henceforth they will
be rolled up in brown paper with string. Please let me know how
they fare. If they get too battered en route, we'll think again.

July 15th 1980, at Holyrood

Dear Alfred,
All the lights have just gone out. Power failure I suppose. The quiet
is unbelievable. Just the sound of frogs and the peace of a rondavel in
the bush by candlelight. No newspapers, no burping fish tank, no-
one wondering what time dinner will be.

But international dramas press on one's consciousness. Sir Seretse
Khama dying; a whole tribe perishing in Uganda; Menachem Begin
with a heart attack and US wolves at his throat. Counter-revolution
in Iran; some psychotic nurse revealing the Duke of Windsor's death
bed secrets; the government misquoting the bible; and England
headed for civil war.

What did you say to Wolf? He's discovered his manners, which
he usually keeps packed away for special occasions such as Bridge.
I was eyeing his handbag, with your letter in it whilst washing up
last night, when a hairy hand and a suspicious eye grabbed it and
carried it off to his den. You'd think it contained the crown jewels!

He says 'Good morning' and 'Good night', and shows a rather rusty but polite concern for my welfare. He even says the food is good, sometimes.

16th July 1980

Just back from Holyrood after spending the night. Could have cut the atmosphere with a knife when I came home. But now The Pastoral is on the turntable, and peace reigns.

Sister Clare was most helpful. We had two long talks. She gave me some practical advice on prayer and confession, and I told her the whole sad Wolf story. I never liked talking about Wolf. It seemed disloyal. But last February Bob said tell +Timothy, and +Timothy said tell the parish priest, and so several people got to know the bare bones of the matter. But partially breaking silence is not a good idea; the story mutates like Chinese whispers. I ended up floundering around, making excuses for Wolf and myself, helping no-one. Now you and Sister Clare know the full story p'raps I can shut up and let matters take their course?

59

It is St Francis Day. Amy is preparing to go to the priory where two novices will be professed this afternoon. She dresses carefully in a white silk dress with a pattern of blue pomegranates. She is pleased about the pomegranates because they appear in the bible, decorating the priestly garments in Exodus.

She is unaccountably tired. Spring sunshine filters through the budding jacaranda onto the verandah where she stands irresolute, wondering what comes next. She wears no make up or perfume, which is frowned upon at the priory where exotic scents disturb sensitive nostrils; cosmetics simply slide off one's face in the heat of the day.

She is wearing sandals, her legs are already brown from the sun, so stockings are unnecessary. All that is required is that she take up her little bag with her handkerchief and her purse and be on her way to the bus stop, thence to the railway station, another bus and a short walk to the priory. In three hours she will be there.

Wolf has gone to work, although it is Saturday. Aunt Kath is away for the weekend. The dogs are sleeping in the sun, cats lying in wait for mice at the bottom of the garden. All is calm; dreadfully calm.

Amy is so weary she just wants to lie down. She spoke with Alfred on the phone last night about this strange, flat calm that has overcome her. "It is as if," she says to Alfred, "the impala have come down to drink at the waterhole. They know the lion are waiting, and that one of them will die tonight. But they come down to drink anyway." This supernatural calm, this waiting upon the inevitable, this patient acceptance of doom permeates her very bones.

Alfred asks her to give him her burden; to hand it over to him; she need not bear it alone. So she does, sighing deeply, as if released from some intolerable weight. Alfred prays, as he always does, commending her to her Lord's protection, asking for comfort and peaceful sleep for her, this night, and always. The liturgical rhythm of prayer soothes her and she sleeps like a baby.

Now her legs are heavy and she doesn't know if she can stand up much longer. Slowly, as if sleep-walking, she makes her way to the bathroom, opens the cabinet over the washbasin and takes down a brown glass bottle. The pills are pink. She pours them onto her palm and swallows them one by one with sips of water. Then she returns to the verandah and lies down in the sun, next to the telephone.

§

It is by chance that Wolf returns home that morning. He has forgotten to take his chequebook and needs it for paying his subscription for the sports club. She has taken the phone off the hook and cradles it, like a doll, against her breast. A slick of spittle runs down her chin. Her breathing is stentorian. Wolf cannot awaken her, however much he shakes her.

After a while he lifts her tenderly and carries her to the bathroom, where he notes the empty pill bottle lying in the washbasin. He pours a shallow bath, testing the water for temperature, and lifts her into it, fully dressed. The silk pomegranates float around her slight form. She murmurs something, but he cannot catch the words. "Wake up, Owl," he calls gently, using her nickname from shipboard, and gives her cheek a little slap. Her eyes fly open; a shadow of disappointment crosses her face and she closes them again.

Wolf is a resourceful man. He puts some toiletries in a soap bag, collects a duffel bag of clothing and packs them, together with the supine form of Amy who is now breathing normally, into the car, and sets out for Holyrood.

On the way there she surfaces, struggles upright in the passenger seat, bedraggled in her damp dress. Dimly she remembers what happened – the despair, the pills, the telephone. She cannot be certain that she had wanted to kill herself. She just wanted it all to end.

"Where are we going?" she bleats. Wolf keeps his eyes on the road. "*Nach* Holyrood," he replies. A warm glow radiates from her solar plexus through her limbs. But then a pain pierces her like a lance, and she cries out. Wolf frowns, and drives faster. Several times the notional lance pierces her and she writhes in pain, trying not to cry out again for fear of frightening Wolf.

Now they are turning into the high gates of Holyrood, cruising between the blue gum trees, down the long avenue. Wolf leaves her in the car and presently returns with two Sisters who extract her with much murmuring of encouragement, leading her gently down the sloping lawns to the retreat house, where they put her to bed.

379

When Amy awakes it is evening. Sister Clare is in the darkened room, manoeuvring a supper tray to settle it on the counterpane, before switching on the bedside lamp. She then perches her tiny posterior on the edge of the bed. Amy, fearing that she is about to be spoon-fed, sits up cautiously, careful not to upset the tray.

There is beef stew with potatoes and peas, and rice pudding, all kept warm under stainless steel covers. The girl sets to with relish. The nun, satisfied that her charge is recovering, repairs to the kitchenette and boils a kettle for tea. She leaves a steaming mug beside Amy's bed and goes back out into the night, up to the refectory for her own supper.

For the next few days Amy sleeps a lot. Often in the night she wakens, sweating, with half-memories of nightmares. In the afternoons she walks in the gardens which are brimming with flowers. Forgetmenots, pansies and daisies crowd the herbaceous borders, where roses bloom abundantly against a backdrop of delphinium and foxglove, all interspersed with lavender.

A life-size crucifix stands on the lawn on a little hillock, with a cypress each side, standing guard. Here in the shade she sits down on fragrant grass and feels safe at last. She is too tired to remember yesterday, too weary to think about tomorrow. She feels like a husk of herself – light as air. Outside these encircling walls a storm is gathering, but for the time being she lets it be, too weak to engage with what must come next.

On the fourth day she is invited to come up up to Holyrood house for lunch and dinner. Bread and cereals, tea, coffee, and biscuits are in plentiful supply in the retreat house for breakfast. Tea with sugar and milk has become her favourite beverage. "Hourly drinks," sniffs the Sister who renews supplies every morning. She feels convalescent, shucking off her former life as if it were an illness, ignoring escalating demands on her attention. Self-preservation causes her to look the other way. Even Alfred belongs in that other life from which she flinches.

In the evenings after dinner she visits the chapel, before compline when the Sisters sing the final office of the day. Sometimes a Sister is already there kneeling quietly on a prayer stool in the sanctuary, but usually Amy is alone. The air is warm, inhabited by the ancient rhythms of the five-fold daily office. The sanctuary lamp burns calm and steady, a red eye in the dark. A safe place, where she is protected, provided she neither moves a muscle nor breathes too deeply, so fragile is this peace.

§

After ten days there is a phone call. Sister Clare brings a message from home – from Albion. She is gentle, entirely lacking in judgement, which Amy finds astounding.

"Wolf is wondering if they might see you again sometime soon," says Sister Clare, tidying the pillows on Amy's bed.

"Um," says Amy, doubtfully. But there is a faint quickening inside her, like the nose of a small woodland animal, sniffing the breeze from its burrow.

"You might like to go for the weekend, and see how things are. You can always come back again," says Sister Clare, punching a pillow into shape.

Amy remembers Wolf driving her here, giving her up for her own good. She remembers Kath, and wonders what they are eating. She remembers the dogs, and hopes they are not hungry; the cats can fare for themselves. She wonders if anyone has watered the garden. She draws a long, deep breath, and says she will go home at the weekend. It feels like a sentence of life imprisonment.

§

Life in Albion resumes as if she has never been away. Aunt Kath sits in her armchair, smokes, stares into the middle distance muttering to her spirits, reading her books. Wolf goes about his business. He is subdued when they sit down together for meals. The dogs are delighted to see her; the cats look down their noses.

Amy feels chastened, sets about baking biscuits and cakes, cooking rich stews, roasting juicy joints of meat. The rains have come since she was away so the garden is thriving with a harvest of weeds. Wilson doesn't come any more since Amy gave up work and can no longer afford a gardener, so she spends the early morning working in the garden getting the vegetable patch shipshape.

Simon is supposed to maintain the garden in exchange for lodgings for himself and 'Phina in the servants' room next to the garage. But apart from slaughtering the naughty cockerel he has so far shown no interest at all in the garden. Amy was fed up with the cockerel's aggressive behaviour and asked Simon to deal with it. After swiftly wringing the bird's neck, he plucked and boiled it for dinner. Simon and 'Phina are a comforting presence up there in the tiny whitewashed servants' quarters. Amy's conscience is eased by sharing the property with the couple, who go their separate ways each morning, 'Phina to a domestic job in the neighbourhood, Simon to pick up casual gardening work wherever he can find it.

Swotting for exams has displaced Amy's novel for the time being. But she doesn't have much appetite for desk work at all, not even for writing to Alfred. It seems a very long time since she saw him last, but this does not seem to matter very much. Very little seems to matter to her, in fact. Cooking, gardening and housework absorb her energies during the day. These tasks appeal to her senses as she breathes in the smell of freshly turned earth, of biscuits baking in the oven, of lavender and beeswax. New seedlings meet her eyes each morning in the kitchen garden; parsley mounds up emerald green on the chopping board; bed linen wafts on the washing line in the sunshine. During the day she applies herself to domestic chores with gratitude for simple tasks that do not require much thought.

Thinking is no longer the elite sport it once was for Amy. Her mind is tired of puzzles, of conundrums which used to be a challenge to winkle out, of arguments she used to enjoy defending. All that seems pointless now. She just doesn't care about intellectual pursuits any more.

One afternoon she leaves a fruit cake baking in the oven, and goes for a swim at Doug's house down the road. The cake will need another hour before it is done. Several pounds of sultanas, raisins, currants, crystallized fruit and nuts have gone into it. Amy checks the oven temperature before she leaves.

Doug's little swimming pool is sparkling in the sunshine. A kreepy krawly chugs around the tessellated blue walls. She hauls it out onto the poolside to make space for herself in the chill water, and plunges straight in before she loses her nerve. After ten minutes of brisk laps she climbs out and lies down in the sun to dry. A brace of fighter jets scream overhead, scrambling for the Angolan border — such svelte machines bent on death and destruction.

After a while Amy notices that she is having a conversation in her head about how best to drown herself without anyone noticing. Shocked, she sits up and stares at the pool. "But I don't want to drown myself," she says, aloud. The water seems to draw her in, as if the blue depths are tugging at her need for peace. Alarmed, she springs up and backs away from the pool. It occurs to Amy that she is in danger, but she is confused as to the nature of this peril, and whence it came. Her instinct is to pray for protection, but from what?

It comes into her mind to lay out a fleece. The charismatics do this to find out what action to take when perplexed. Gideon in the bible laid out a fleece on his threshing floor to find out if he was to go to war. Amy thinks it is a pagan habit, a bit like throwing the bones, but in such dire circumstances God will certainly forgive her. So she makes a pact. If the cake is baked when she gets back home, all will be well. Those seductive thoughts about killing herself would be mere phantasms, nothing to worry about. If, however, the cake is not ready to take out of the oven she will consider taking herself out of this situation in Albion altogether.

As she returns home there is an edifying smell of baking in the kitchen, but the oven has been turned down. Appalled, Amy stares at the dial as if to will it back up to three hundred and sixty degrees. But it remains set at two hundred. The cake has sunk in the middle. Thoughtfully, Amy goes in search of Aunt Kath who is in her usual spot, smoking in the sitting room. "Did you turn the oven down?" she asks the older woman quietly. "Oh yes," Kath replies. "I saw you had gone out and I didn't want the cake to burn."

Amy feels a preternatural calm settle upon her. During the following days she observes her household from a distance, as if she watches the action unfolding on television. The cake incident seems such a small thing, but Kath has never tampered with the oven before, scarcely ever goes into the kitchen. Laying out a fleece may seem uncomfortably like witchcraft, but she has thrown the bones now. She cannot in good conscience go back on the decree of fate.

Somehow this has opened Amy's eyes to other small aberrations. Neither Kath nor Wolf have given her any housekeeping money since she came back from Holyrood. She doesn't like to ask for money, doesn't want to seem grasping, so dips into her own savings to pay for the shopping. Just out of interest she keeps a record of her daily work in the house – the cooking, laundry, cleaning, shopping, and all the multifarious tasks of caring for a family. She finds she is doing a full day's work, a full-time job, as if she were still going in to the office, but not getting paid. She hesitates to entertain the thought that this is unfair. Did she not want a community, a chance to serve tables, like a good deacon?

On Saturday the day is overcast and Amy cannot get out of bed. Inertia keeps her curled up under the blankets, in the study. There seems to be no point in moving. Threads of anxiety about getting breakfast, preparing lunch, then dinner, snag at her during the course of the day, but still she cannot move. She wonders if Kath and Wolf have made themselves anything to eat. She calls out now and then, a querulous cry, hoping they might hear and come. But only Spatz keeps her company, dozing on the carpet. Night falls and she sleeps, grateful for the end of this day.

In the morning Wolf brings her a cup of tea. He knocks on the study door before coming in. Immediately Spatz leaps up on the bed and lies full length on Amy's torso, raising her lip with a low growl at Wolf. Diffidently Wolf places the cup of tea on the bedside table and withdraws. Amy can't help smiling at her dog, who looks quite shocked by the encounter.

That day she packs a bag, including her study books, and asks Wolf to drive her back to Holyrood. She will stay there until after her exams, she says. The household must get along without her. Wolf looks glum, Aunt Kath looks puzzled. Amy feels an incredible lightness of being.

~60~

Sisters give Amy the rondavel at the bottom of the garden to stay in while she studies for her exams. It is a private place. She goes up to the main house for lunch and dinner. A kettle, a toaster and a small fridge provide for her breakfast needs, and plentiful cups of tea to fuel the days work at her desk.

A grapevine cloaks the rondavel. By day breezes sough amongst the meadow flowers, sunlight dapples the stripped trunks of blue gums, which provide shade and perfume the air with their aromatic oil. By night moonlight casts shadows of new vine leaves upon the whitewashed walls.

Amy feels as if she is hermetically sealed in this capsule of time in this small hut. The walls of Holyrood estate protect her from the outside world. In here she is wrapped in solitude, alone with her studies with only herself to care for. No-one will come upon her unawares. No shock or injury can befall her here in this sacred space. She is aware of herself as fragile.

The household in Albion seems like a dream. Alfred she remembers as if he belongs to the distant past. It does not occur to her to write to him. She would have nothing to say. How could she describe these days which pass so gracefully from dawn to dusk. Seamless hours immersed in old and new testament studies. Silent meals in the company of women who read books at the dining table. Three times a day the angelus sounds from the chapel bell and stillness falls on the estate.

When +Timothy appears, framed in the doorway of her room, coughing discretely to attract her attention, she greets him as if it were the most natural thing in the world for the bishop to drop in. "I heard you were here," he tells her in his gentle voice. "I hope I am not intruding?" He has been visiting the reverend mother on convent business. Tactfully, no doubt, she has acquainted him with Amy's current situation.

They seat themselves on a bench in the garden and enquire after each other's health, as is the custom.

"Does he beat you?" the bishop asks at last, his demeanour serious, solicitous. "Oh no, no, no," Amy demurs, although half wishing she could say that Wolf did indeed beat her, so that she did not feel so dreadfully guilty about leaving him.

385

Gently the bishop probes her domestic circumstances. He is particularly interested that Wolf has lately given up paying his share of the housekeeping. "He doesn't support you?" he asks. "No. Well, I won't have that," exclaims Amy. "I don't want to be dependent on anyone," she explains. Marriage is a contract, the bishop tells her. There are many ways of breaking a contract. She mustn't take the blame entirely on herself.

Later that week Wolf comes to visit and he brings Aunt Kath with him. They sit on the same garden bench where a few days before she had conversed with the bishop. But today's meeting fuels her fear and her sense of shame. Waif-like, Wolf and Kath sit side by side and drink their cups of tea, regarding her reproachfully.

Wolf says something to her. Later she cannot remember what it was that he said, but his words are galvanising. She rushes back to her rondavel where she trots back and forth trying to remember why she came here. Something terrible has happened, but she doesn't know what it is. Panicked, she thinks maybe she should kill herself, then catches sight of her reflection in a mirror on the wall over the washbasin. She focusses on this image which is peculiarly calm, in spite of the frenzy in her head. After a few moments she goes back outside and tells Wolf that she will not be going back home with them.

§

Exams take place at the show grounds, in one of the vast echoing halls which had teemed with life during the SACLA conference more than a year ago. Now writing desks, hundreds of them, are set out in rows as far as the eye can see. The venue is hushed. A huge clock hangs on the wall at the front of the hall. Supervisors patrol the aisles between desks where students sit waiting until all the paperwork has been handed out, then, on the command to begin, with a rustling like a wind in the forest, all turn their question papers over.

She is happy with the examination. One question on the minor prophets could have been written personally for her. What message, it asked, could these fractious polemicists of the Old Testament have for the church today? How she enjoys that! How quickly the time flies until three hours have passed, answer papers are collected up, and the multi-racial horde of students file out, blinking, into bright sunlight.

Amy takes her time going home to Holyrood. The afternoon is warm with late spring sunshine. Jacarandas bloom in gracious avenues through city streets. They were planted long ago, brought here, as she has been, from another far-off continent. The city shimmers lilac with their blooms which drift down onto the streets in rivers of purple.

Few other white pedestrians are to be seen. Whites are in Mercedes Benz and BMW's, which nudge at her impatiently as she walks over a zebra crossing. Blacks throng pavements in Schoeman Street, yodelling to one another, whistling – couriers, messengers, maids. After nightfall these streets will be silent and empty; all this jostling, bawling crowd of pedestrians will be back in the townships.

Central station has a separate entrance for whites, she sits in a whites-only carriage in the little train which stops at every station on its way to Holyrood. Wisteria blooms in the gardens she passes on her walk to the estate, then the gates of Holyrood enfold her like a sigh. She feels her shoulders relax as her pace slows. She wanders down the drive towards her rondavel, shuffling through the fragrant detritus of blue gum leaves.

§

At first she does not notice the letter lying on her bed, where Sister Clare has left it. She makes a cup of tea and changes into her swimming costume. There is a pool near the main house which some of the Sisters use in summer. A plunge into that frigid water is what Amy wants most after the rigours of this day. But then she sees the letter. It is from England. It is from her mother. Inside is a one-way air ticket to London.

Amy has taken to heart the advice of medieval mystics, to live for the day. She has tried to find out how to do it during the past couple of years. She found it very difficult at first to focus on the present moment. Anxiety over what else she should be doing, or what she failed to do yesterday, snagged constantly at her attention. A useful exercise she has gleaned from her reading is to imagine that this day is her last on earth. With practice she has found that this curtails speculation about the future and wonderfully focusses her mind on the task in hand.

Now Amy finds herself at the end of a chapter of her life with no idea of what to do next. It has been easier these past few years to let life happen to her, having neither the energy nor the wit to make any life-changing decisions for herself.

She tucks her mother's letter, together with the air ticket, under her pillow, shrugs into a bath robe and makes her way to the swimming pool.

§

Leaving home is not so much a decision as a *fait accompli*, Amy discovers. She cannot, in her worst nightmares, imagine going back to live at Albion. Meanwhile an escape hatch has opened for her. She has no particular desire to go England, but neither can she stay here. In the end she makes a compromise. She will go to stay with her mother in England for six months, while Wolf makes up his mind whether he wants to go on with the marriage or not.

She is somehow anaesthetised against the pain of leaving all her worldly possessions, her cats and dogs, her garden, and Wolf, for whom at this late hour she feels a deep well of affection. She feels no guilt. The bishop's fiat has dealt with that.

Amy writes to Alfred to break the news. He replies at once, asking if she might make a stopover in Zimbabwe on her way back to England.

§

Leaving turns out to be surprisingly easy. British Airways book Amy's trip to the UK via Rhodesia without demur. Belatedly the parish send a couple of pastoral visitors, who introduce themselves to Aunt Kath and Wolf. Joy and Dave, they are called. Amy serves them tea and they chortle, embarrassed, looking around bemused.

They say how civilised it all seems, as if they expected a state of warfare. The subtext is that Amy's behaviour is true to form, bizarre, conforming to no known rules. She uncharitably puts this sudden pastoral concern from the parish down to prurience. But Joy looks her in the eyes and says God will give her a new name on a white stone. Joy's eyes are pellucid eau de nil, gazing earnestly into her own, with pity.

She leaves home with the red suitcase she bought in Hamburg when she first went to sea all those years ago, and her rucksack. She bids goodbye to Wolf and Aunt Kath, and the dogs and cats, as if she is going on holiday, and departs without a backward glance.

Salisbury in December is hot. Amy has a couple of hours to wait before boarding her coach to Umtali. She follows pedestrian signs to the botanic gardens, a haven of lawns and ancient trees in the midst of the city, where clear streams chuckle over brown pebbles. She leans on the timber balustrade of a little bridge and gazes down into the water. She feels elated, half drunk with the prospect of seeing Alfred.

The coach drives through arid uplands strewn with enormous boulders. She is enchanted with the idea of being in a brand new country, for Zimbabwe has just been born into independence.

Within a couple of hours they reach their destination. Now here is Alfred emerging from the afternoon haze like an angel, a penumbra of white hair swirling around his head, arms held wide in greeting. He hoists her suitcase lightly, allowing her to keep her rucksack, and they drive home, alighting at the top of a hill beside low stone dwellings, sparse lawns, and highland scrub surrounding the priory at Pedregoso.

A vast red brick church with a copper roof is visible from this hill-top campus. Alfred shows her to a cottage set a little apart, with its own garden. This is where the bishop stays, and the superior, when they visit, he tells her. For an instant she feels honoured, then remembers that there would be no place for a woman in the priory itself.

Alfred fusses around, drawing her attention to the mosquito coils, "Mozzies are so big around here they could carry you off". Then he leaves her to settle in, advising that evensong will be at six o'clock.

The first thing that Amy does is rearrange the furniture. It has been her habit for some time to make the best of anywhere she stays, if only for one night. It is a habit that arises out of living for the moment, for one should always seek to live each day to the full. Her bed must face the window, which in this room, fortuitously, faces east. The armchair she positions with a view of the garden, then sits down comfortably in the quiet bungalow to collect herself.

School has broken up for the Christmas holidays so students and teachers have left the campus, which is peaceful, and a little forlorn. Birdsong echoes, plangent, from the wooded slopes below. A panorama of blue hills fills the view to the east, skies turning pink now as evening approaches. Amy realises she is closer to the equator here, that night will fall quickly. She decides to seek out the chapel while it is still daylight and spend some time there before evensong.

The to and fro of psalmody in the priory's little chapel rocks Amy into an unearthly calm. Fr Xavier, the prior, is rather fearsome, but Brother Seraphim is delightful. At table, Alfred tells her that Seraphim still goes out into the badlands beyond the school campus with his donkey, in spite of land mines, or worse. Seraphim and his donkey must float above the ground as no harm has come to them yet, says Alfred. Seraphim makes a face at Alfred, as if he is being naughty.

During the washing up, which Amy insists on helping with, she drops a glass. It is a thick glass for drinking water, which is the only beverage to accompany their evening meal of salt beef and vegetables. Transfixed, she watches as the glass bounces on the stone flags, and miraculously does not break. She scoops it up with a sheepish *'Howzat!'* and carries on with the drying up as if nothing has happened.

The following day Alfred takes her out walking in a dry river bed. This, he says, is the way Seraphim comes, so they should be safe from land mines. Alarmed, she walks scrupulously in her master's footsteps as they proceed in single file through the clamorous rainforest.

Massive boulders, some balanced precariously upon one another, are in evidence here too, carelessly strewn through the landscape by some prehistoric ice age. After about an hour of walking Alfred sits down in the shelter of one of these rocky outcrops, producing a vacuum flask, two mugs and biscuits from his canvas bag. These he lays out hospitably and serves Amy tea, as if this were an altar and this simple repast were a eucharist.

"Listen!" he says, when they have drunk their tea and eaten the biscuits. She listens to the singing silence, which seems to press down upon them from the forest canopy. Continuous sound, like breathing, emanates from a multitude of insects, pierced occasionally by bird calls. But she feels as if there is a deeper note in this cacophonous silence, which is listening. She feels as if the forest, this rock shelter, is bending an ear to them, waiting.

Alfred tells her that these rocks would certainly have been sacred places for the old religions. "You can feel the holiness," he declares, squatting back on his heels, closing his eyes. Amy is mildly shocked. This smacks of the occult to her, having been schooled in the doctrine that anything that is not of the one true God must be of the devil.

Alfred listens courteously to her rebuke. "I feel, as one gets older, one finds that everything belongs to our God," he replies. He wasn't exactly pulling rank, after all he *is* almost thirty years older than she is, but Amy feels chastened.

They don't seem to talk very much during Amy's few days at Pedregoso. One afternoon they are sprawled beside the school swimming pool when Stephen joins them, complaining that the sun has gone in. "Can't you pray for the clouds to clear?" he asks, ribbing Alfred, who ostentatiously prays for everything. Alfred and Amy make no response, but she knows he has risen to the challenge and is praying for sunshine. So she does too. Five minutes later the sky has cleared and Stephen is arranging himself contentedly in a deckchair to sunbathe. Amy suppresses a smug smile.

Not far from the priory there is a private estate which was abandoned during the long-drawn-out guerilla war. Alfred takes her to visit the arboretum there, which is overgrown now with vines. Sunlight rains through the emerald canopy onto a carpet of periwinkle blue flowers. The garden is set on a slope, the remains of serpentine pathways and steps lead upward, threading through the flowers. This place reminds Amy of bluebell woods in her native land. Ivy fingers the tree trunks. Ferns, orchids and other epiphytes droop from the upper boughs in a sumptuous hanging garden.

Alfred has set off up the winding path, ambling slowly, hands clasped behind his back. He wears jeans and a blue short-sleeved shirt. She marvels at how much at home he looks in this verdant paradise, as if in Eden. The thought tugs at her heartstrings. She hears the sound of a golden horn wafting through this woodland, which could almost be Narnia. The place is lit by an unearthly light, as if trees and boughs and flowers and Alfred himself are shining, bowing gracious acknowledgement to another, greater dimension which enfolds them like a benediction. She wants to stay here and worship forever. But the days are passing and soon she will be gone. She places the memory reverently in her heart to comfort her in times to come.

That evening Alfred introduces Amy to a young man who turns up at the priory unexpectedly. Where he came from is a mystery to Amy, as she heard no vehicle arrive. Alfred introduces Thabo to her with some ceremony, as if introducing royalty. He is tall and painfully thin, with the tensile strength of a whippet. He is well dressed and his handshake is gentle. But then she notices his eyes.

She has never seen such naked hatred as that which regards her from Thabo's eyes. It is like an ice-cold shower and she flinches, withdrawing her hand swiftly from his grasp. They are engaged in polite conversation, Alfred, Thabo and Amy, exchanging news of family near and far. Now and again Amy glances at Thabo's eyes, to make sure she is not imagining things. Each time the eviscerating hatred looks calmly back at her.

Later Alfred tells her that Thabo has been over the border with Robert Mugabe's guerilla forces. "Oh so he is a terrorist?" exclaims Amy, feeling relieved. "People don't like being called terrorists," replies Alfred gently, and once again she feels chastised. This is an unfamiliar world. It occurs to her that it is not pleasant to be hated for being white.

§

Alfred somehow wheedles permission from the prior to accompany Amy back to Salisbury to catch her flight to London. Several African Sisters from the neighbouring convent are going to Umtali, so Amy and Alfred hitch a lift into town in their truck. Amy rides in the back with the sisters who sing and laugh all the way down the switchback mountain roads to town. Amy revels in the joy of it, the energy of the women, the light glancing off their white veils as the vehicle twists and turns in the morning sunlight.

By unspoken agreement they hitch-hike to Salisbury rather than taking the coach. Alfred is dressed in his cassock, and outside town they soon get a lift in a red Mercedes. The driver is a florid man who inspects Alfred closely in the rear-view mirror, then offers him a cold beer from a small fridge between the front seats. It is only ten o'clock in the morning but Alfred accepts with copious thanks, producing his own bottle-opener from his key-ring and taking a slug from the bottle with noisy relish. This seems to set the driver at ease.

Amy wishes he would offer her a beer too but he appears fascinated by the passenger in the back seat. "What religion are you?" he asks. "I'm a Christian," replies Alfred airily. "You drink?" the man asks, superfluously. "Oh yes," says Alfred. "Love it!" This appears to be something of a revelation to the driver who thoughtfully removes a beer for himself from the bar fridge, uncapping it on a dashboard bottle-opener. Amy catches his eye and he signals to her to help herself. So all three settle in for a boozy trip to Salisbury.

§

Amy's flight leaves at 9pm. Alfred will stay overnight with friends after he has seen her off. They have time for a leisurely dinner in town before leaving for the airport, and more time for a drink together after she has checked in her suitcase. They buy two beers from the airport bar and scout around for somewhere congenial to sit. Eventually they find a secluded spot, a roof garden overlooking the tarmac where the British Airways 747 is parked. Vehicles bustle about the jumbo jet, delivering supplies and baggage to the aircraft, which is framed in neon lights amidst the tropical night.

There doesn't seem to be much to talk about, but the silence is not uncomfortable. She enjoys resting in Alfred's presence, surveying the busy scene below. Some time later — she is not sure how much time has passed — she notices that all has fallen still around the aeroplane which will soon fly her to London. She checks her watch. It is still only eight o'clock. With a sigh she says to Alfred that maybe they should go downstairs and prepare to say goodbye.

As they appear together on the departure level two uniformed women approach and in urgent tones ask Amy if she is, well, Amy? As soon as she identifies herself she is scooped up and hurried towards the barriers, her feet barely touching the ground. The plane has been ready for half-an-hour and could have taken off early but one passenger was missing. She needn't worry about emigration procedure, the plane is waiting. Alfred canters along beside her and her custodians, out onto the tarmac. No one stops him. She looks him in the eyes and says urgently, "Come with me!" She swears she sees an instant's hesitation in his face, before he demurs, draws back, and wishes her a safe flight.

Amy is on Reading Station, having caught a bus from Heathrow. The December morning is cold but bright, with a winter sun low in a china blue sky. Amy regards her feet, shod incongruously in sandals. She is astonished that she does not feel cold. She has on the khaki cotton skirt and white blouse she wore when she left Zimbabwe, although she has thrown a coat over this light ensemble. Deeply tanned, her hair sun-bleached, the heat of Africa still in her blood, she breathes in the brisk winter air and feels a surge of adrenaline, as if a new adventure is about to begin.

Ruth, who is now a resident member of the Lee Abbey community, has organised a few days holiday in Devon for Amy and for Anna, who is already there. Amy must travel by train via Temple Meads Station in Bristol, to Taunton, where she will be picked up by Ruth.

The dear familiarity of bare trees and hedgerows, little fields with neat sheep and cattle grazing in them, catches at Amy's throat. This country is so diminutive, its pewter skies so low, its colours so muted. It speaks to her from long ago when life was simple, when she was young. On Exmoor, snow drifts across the landscape but does not settle on the ground.

§

Anna is waiting in the busy reception area at Lee Abbey and they all three repair to Ruth's small cottage room behind the main house. There they drink a toast to her safe arrival with a bottle of Jonathan's birch sap wine. Wine-making is their brother's latest hobby, birch sap sourced clandestinely by night from a tree in his commanding officer's garden. The frisson of danger adds to the provenance, Jonathan claims.

After dinner she rests in the octagonal lounge, slipping into a doze on an elegant chaise longue set before the log fire. In her dreaming state she is aware that someone sits down beside her. She struggles towards wakefulness, at the same time unwilling to leave the warm cradle she is dozing in. But lo, here is the warden of the community, perched on the end of the sofa, looking down at her with an expression of kindness that takes her breath away. Amy is suspicious of kindness which has led her down dangerous pathways – like marrying Wolf.

The warden continues to regard her kindly as she shakes the sleep from her eyes, stammers an apology for sleeping on his couch. She feels very young. "We are glad to have you here," the warden tells her, as if she were an important person. Amy attempts to rise to the occasion, holding out her right hand and solemnly shaking his. "I've come from Africa," she says, as if by way of apology. "We know," he replies gravely. "You have been in our prayers for many months." Curiouser and curiouser. Here she is, stripped of home and hearth, of husband, friends and country, washed up on her native shore, brown as a nut in midwinter, on a couch by the fire with a charming man who seems to know her. A log settles in the ash of the hearth, the palm tree tap taps on the window behind brocade curtains, which are drawn against the cold night. She has a visceral sense of having been here before.

"We are very aware of the troubles in South Africa," continues the warden. "Several members of our community come from that unhappy country. And of course your sister keeps us informed of your progress there." Amy ponders this information. She has never thought of South Africa as unhappy, quite the opposite in fact. Of course black people struggle. A shadow insinuates itself into her mind. Perhaps she should feel responsible for South Africa's unhappiness? Dumbly she nods. Quite unexpectedly her eyes brim with tears. The warden pats her hand, brisk now, tells her to rest, to take a holiday from her work, her very important ministry. Feeling more and more like an imposter, Amy smiles weakly and watches him pad away towards the north wing.

§

She decides to set her novel in this very place, at Lee Abbey, and she will call her book *Godwin*. She spends the next few days mapping out the narrative.

Godwin himself is a reclusive landowner who lives an hermetic existence on the top floor of his country house, where there is a gallery of european art featuring French impressionists and German moderns such as Nolde. He is the godfather of the heroine who has escaped from Rhodesia after being injured in the war. Her brother, also called Godwin, who is very short-sighted but too vain to wear spectacles, is employed as estate manager and general factotum. He looks after the paying house guests whom Godwin senior tolerates but never meets, who bolster the fragile finances of the estate.

Nestled into the story is an expedition through the snow to a candlelit midnight mass at the local church. There will be festive food prepared by homespun staff in the old-fashioned kitchens. Plenty of scope for a gothic tale there.

This is the vehicle Amy invents to carry her account of the dawn of a new world into the twilit quotidian. This narrative will tell the story of her inner life, the fall into Moria, the Star Trek of the spirit.

The fact that the G word is taboo in 1980 makes it more than a little complicated to write openly about God. Analogy will have to do. After all, most great literature cloaks the metaphysical in some form of analogy or other. She has no doubt that her book will be in that league.

Back home in Anna's flat Amy kits out the guest room as a study. It is very cramped. The wardrobe takes up the whole of one wall. Over her narrow bed she hangs the Rubrev hospitality icon, the visitation of the blessed virgin Mary hangs close to a small desk which she places under the window with a view of the close.

Peta turns up with a borrowed typewriter and a ream of paper acquired from her office at the university. Amy constructs a cardboard cover to conceal the keyboard and sets about learning to touch type. It is mid-January when she begins the work for which she has given up her job, her home and her marriage.

Daily, after Anna has left for work on the far side of Bristol, Amy spends the mornings tapping away until it is time to make lunch. Slowly, morning by morning, *Godwin* spools off the typewriter.

In the afternoons Amy creates a garden on the patch of turf, bounded by privet hedges, which belongs to Anna's upstairs flat. This is where they hang out their washing on a collapsible line which leans drunkenly out of a hole in the ground.

Over the road from their close several blocks of abandoned allotments await development. Foraging here in the afternoons Amy finds daffodil bulbs, snowdrops, crocuses, rhubarb crowns, lemon verbena, japonica – a wealth of botanical material left by gardeners who cherished the soil here for decades. In addition to plants, Amy finds material for crazy paving to put down under an acacia sapling she buys from a nearby nursery, and wrangles back home on the bus.

She even finds a concrete block with a hole already in it for the washing line. The two of them roll this back home very early one Sunday morning to escape the attention of nosy neighbours. Only the thing weighs a ton and sounds like an earthquake as, like a couple of dung beetles, they trundle it homeward. Digging that into the lawn takes Amy an entire afternoon, but the washing line now stands proud and the sheets no longer droop in the privet.

These months are tranquil, a benedictine cycle of writing and manual labour, hauling loads of topsoil from the allotments, hauling words onto pages which neatly stack up as a measure of her worth.

Half-an-hour's meditation before the desk work is the pact she makes. She pays her dues and God will prosper the work. A nap after lunch, before gardening, supports the wholesome cycle of the day. They eat well, although they have little money between them to live on. Anna has brought up three children on a clergy stipend, which amounts to a degree in hunter gathering. She knows to the minute when Tesco will mark down the fillet steak. They eat like royalty from her skirmishes with the retail sector.

Winter turns to spring. Crocuses bloom, a little field of daffodils appears above ground. Peonies, notoriously difficult to transplant, seem to be feeling at home, raising soft burgundy tendrils from the chilled earth.

§

After five months *Godwin* has reached sixty thousand words, which Amy hopes is enough. The story seems slight compared with the experiences she remembers so vividly. The prose seems banal. Amy has a strong aversion to jargon, but writing about spiritual experience without occasionally employing the jargon of the charismatic movement, or the archaic language of the church, has proved to be impossible. There simply is no language to describe the places she has been in the past few years.

In England the church has never really recovered from the God is dead era, and scarcely merits a hearing amongst Amy's generation.

How then to address others like herself who have been deprived of their spiritual inheritance? How to share with her own kind here, in her native land, what she has been so generously given in Africa? It is painful, this inarticulate yearning to speak the unspeakable. It is like being in prison, in solitary confinement, locked up with a secret that would change the world, if only one had words to broadcast it.

Hers is the dilemma of the gnostic; secret knowledge begging for a language, which can drive you mad if you do not find a way to spell it out. It is such an overwhelming burden to walk around believing you are the only one who knows this stuff, not quite sure if you are sane, but if you are, being duty-bound to tell it.

In the end she has done her best. Later, much later, an editor from Penguin comments that it is hard to make out where reality ends and where dream begins in *Godwin*. Nowadays that would be an accolade, now that postmodernism reigns, but then it merely meant that her narrative lacked clarity.

This makes Amy both sad and happy. She has tried to shift perceptions by mixing up words for the senses, giving colour to smell, taste to sound, provocative words to help her reader perceive the world differently. But in the end her story is so densely encoded that its message will just pass the reader by.

§

At the beginning of June she packs up *Godwin* and takes the manuscript personally to a literary agent in London. Of course, she does not get past the receptionist and must leave her precious parcel at the front desk. Four weeks later it comes back with a rejection slip. Numb with grief, Amy tucks the package under her bed and gives herself up to mourning.

She can no longer speak, feeling only a deep sense of bereavement through which she navigates the empty days. There is nothing left. Everything of value to her has been given away, squandered on this quest to launch *Godwin* onto the world stage. Some terrible error has occurred to leave her abandoned like this, homeless, jobless, penniless. If she has been misled in this quest then, surely, the vessel of her faith must founder.

§

That summer the young prince marries his princess in a fairy-tale wedding celebrated in street parties all over England. Gaudy hot-air balloons sail over the Mendips in the royal couple's honour.

Coming home on the bus from the Old Vic, where Anna has been helping with stage make-up for the cast of Pirates of Penzance, Amy breaks her silence at last to ask what her mother would do if God should turn out to be evil?

~63~

In July a letter arrives from Wolf, the first time she has heard from him since she left more than six months before. It is an aerogramme, closely written in his small, careful hand. He cannot, he writes, go through all that again. True to their agreement he has spent six months considering their marriage and all that has accompanied it, and he must regretfully say that he does not want to go on. She feels a frisson of anger. Surely Wolf has had the better bargain? Surely she has done everything in her power to make his life worth living?

Then, absurdly, Amy feels a sense of relief. Hot upon the heels of this disgraceful emotion she feels profound guilt. Guilt and shock combine as if in a cement mixer, until she does not know what she feels, except that her emotions do not match her expectations. But then, on reflection, she had no expectation of how she would feel should her marriage came to an end. Which it appears to have done.

The local vicar accepts the news without condemnation, although it is still a time when the Church of England will not marry divorcees, and even in some places refuses them the sacrament of Communion. She must mourn, he said. She must spend time reflecting on her marriage and giving thanks for the years she and Wolf had together. Amy has done so much mourning lately this seems an easy penance for the failure of her marriage.

She makes lists of items at her home in Albion which she never expects to see again. The Purbeck owl that Anna gave her; the album of Beethoven's symphonies; the chiming clock she gave to Wolf for his birthday. Long lists, each word encapsulating a memory, a transaction, a loss. Written words which connect her to a former life which is now closed to her. These lists she keeps safe in the back of her journal, so that her worldly possessions are not entirely lost. So that she will remember that chapter of her life.

§

There is no work to be had in England in the summer of 1981. Even voluntary jobs have no vacancies. Amy works every day in the garden, fashioning the privet hedge into an archway with a gate which gives access to the back lane and a short cut to the local bus stop.

In August Anna leaves on a pilgrimage to Lourdes, travelling by coach together with her prayer group, singing renewal songs, drinking red wine out of plastic cups.

Amy had given up up drinking during the months of writing. She wanted to be quite certain that the words she cobbled together each day issued from a heart and mind unclouded by alcohol. There was a time when she thought a glass or two oiled the wheels of creative writing. Writers however, unlike musicians, are in a position to review work they have done under the influence of mind-altering substances. It can be something of a shock to read last night's masterpiece in the withering company of this morning's hangover.

Now Amy finds some cheap wine at the local shop. It is soft and sweet, without the body and pungent undertow of Tassenheimer. She makes do, using this saccharine beverage to soothe her grief, although she feels mostly numb these days. Then the telephone call comes.

§

It is evening and she is watching the television with a glass of fizzy pink wine beside her. There is a news clip of Desmond Tutu, praying in the church at Orlando. He seems to be unaware of the camera. The news is bad, a commission is being set up to investigate the South African Council of Churches. Something about his posture, the way he is lost in his prayer, tells her that he too has given up his life.

When the telephone rings she answers politely with her mother's name and number. But the call is for her, from South Africa. Russell, a former colleague from SATA has been promoted to manager and he wonders if she would like to have her old job back? They miss her, he says. Amy is stunned. It is sixteen months since she last spoke to Russell, another life altogether, so far away from this dreary English summer that it is like another universe. "Why yes," she hears herself saying. "I would love to come back."

§

Sister Clare is in England on furlough, and Amy decides to visit her before she returns to South Africa. The coach delivers her in Oxford just in time to take a bus to her destination, which however makes a detour into every village on the way south, so that when she finally arrives, beside herself with frustration, it is almost time for the return journey. Sister Clare is waiting at the busstop and she falls into the nun's arms with a piteous cry that she must leave with the next bus in barely half-an-hour.

Clare takes her into a cemetery close by where they find a bench and sit down together to talk. There she tells Amy that +Timothy is leaving Pretoria. The news shafts like a spear through the girl and she doubles over with pain. Groggily she regards the little nun, unable to digest the news that yet another guardian of her soul will be leaving after she gets back. Then they say farewell to one another and she catches the bus back to Oxford.

§

By the time Anna returns from Lourdes Amy's plans for going back to South Africa are more or less complete. Anna, calm from her pilgrimage, takes in the news, digests it, and diplomatically does not argue with her daughter's decision, although her heart contracts with fear.

So it is that one early morning at the end of August Amy sets off by coach across England to Heathrow. Skeletal elms shudder into ruin in the foggy landscape, all killed by dutch elm disease. They look like relics of winter, of disease and loss and death, in this green and pleasant land. She has left her manuscript behind, a shameful thing, concealed in the bottom of the wardrobe in her mother's house. But she has acquired a portable olivetti typewriter which she is taking with her. She seems to float through the morning mist, neither here nor there, moving in a shroud of fog towards an unknown destination, although she is sure the place will be known to her when she gets there.

Epilogue

Winter sun slants into my apartment, burnishing the parquet floor. Outdoors my banana palms sway in a breeze from seaward, a pleasant change from the chill sou'westers from the interior which have brought a hint of morning frost lately.

I still depend on sunshine for my wellbeing. After three or four days of clouded skies my mood sinks; the first morning of rain often bringing a faint nostalgia for my home country. I first noticed this phenomenon when I was waiting at a bus-stop in Pretoria, South Africa, newly arrived from the northern hemisphere. A tad melancholic and casting around for the source of this feeling, I noticed that the sky was overcast for the first time since I had arrived a month before. The memory of my native weather patterns had brought on a mild homesickness.

Sunshine is my life-source. Somehow I already knew this when I was a teenager. At lunchtime on warm summer days I would hurry home from school to snatch half-an-hour's sunbathing in the vicarage garden. A pony trek up Crook's Peak on a sunny weekend would leave me basking in the warmth of my own blood, revelling in the afterglow on my skin. Sunlight brought a sheer bodyliness to my being which only sex could match – but unlike relationships the sun did not bring unwanted baggage with it.

I was at sea when the numinous power of sunlight struck me like an epiphany. We were just north of the Canary Islands, sailing south on my first trip to Cape Town. I awoke in my cabin feeling as if I was basking in a warm, primeval sea. The gentle roll of the ship rocked me in my bunk, cradled me in a sleepy languor. At first I dared not open my eyes, so bright was the shifting play of light on my eyelids, as if angels swayed there, ready to carry me off.

Never had I seen such light. It poured into the little cabin with an effulgence, a pure generosity which lifted me out of myself with a silent cry of devotion, a leap of joy which I had not experienced since I was a child. The quiet heartbeat of the ship trembled in the cabin, carrying us onward towards the equator, towards more mornings like this, towards the sun, towards a lightness of being which would eventually persuade me to leave my home country for good.

Light, even sunlight, varies however. Here in the Antipodes the light is as clear as ice, even on a subtropical summer's day when the air is so humid you can scarcely breathe. This pellucid light shows no mercy to the lines on my face. It glares from wide blue skies strewn with broad swathes of cloud sailing undisturbed across this ancient continent.

When I first came here I would complain that the light was different – different from Africa whence I had come. There, I would say, the sunlight glows, the skies are tall, not wide, the mountains young and sprightly, rearing out of the plains with attitude. I desperately missed the glorious technicolor wildness of Africa, before, in time, I learned to enjoy the shy fauna and verdigris botany of Australia.

Homesickness is now a thing of the past. Now the world is a smaller place. You can telephone anywhere for the price of a coffee, skype for even less, and no-one is really further away than twenty-four hours in an aeroplane. The problem now is getting away from it all, something I find I have to do a lot of in order to stay sane.

I am as far from my native land as I can be. I have reached the uttermost ends of the earth. It seems as good a place as any to stop, to try and give a truthful account of myself. There is a certain elliptical satisfaction in peering back through the lens of six decades at my three continents.

§

Truthfulness seems a little quaint in 2015. Everything is so plastic one can construct any sort of world one wants. Reality has become so fluid that no-one seems to have a definitive claim upon it. But I am apprenticed to the truth and that is why I have written the truth here. Mind you, truth being such a rare commodity these days, this story seems stranger than fiction.

Thirty-five years ago I tried packing up the truth in an analogy to make things easier to digest. I tried to hide the pill in a sweetmeat. I gave up my job, my home, my marriage, and my country to write that book, and in the end all my endeavours came to naught. There was no prize, no reward, no thrilling reviews, no cheque. I was not a writer, not yet. For all my pains I ended up homeless and jobless in a foreign land.

Now I sit in my little bayside apartment regarding this typescript which has been gestating for the past four years. It is far too long, like one of those American books which are so thick you cannot read them comfortably in bed. I am embarrassed by its length, by the number of words which have been employed to tell a simple tale about a change of heart, about a love affair in letters, about being born again.

I promised I would tell the truth, but I didn't realise it would take so long. Soon I will qualify for the old-age-pension here in Australia, although there are grumblings – the age of entitlement is over they are saying. But this story is not ended. In fact it has barely begun. The more the words spool out of me, who began with no words to describe where I have been, the more the story grows.

§

ACKNOWLEDGEMENTS

My early readers: Sarah Baker, Marie Thompson,
Dianne d'Alpoim Guedes.
My life support: Eric and Amelia Cooper,
Margaret Henderson, Jim Rodney.